THE
KINCAIDS

Private Mergers

New money. New passions. Old secrets.

Two passionate reads from bestselling authors
Tessa Radley and Day Leclaire

The Kincaids Collection

THE
KINCAIDS
Private Mergers

TESSA
RADLEY

DAY
LECLAIRE

First published in Great Britain 2013
by Mills & Boon, an imprint of Harlequin (UK) Limited, Eton House,
18-24 Paradise Road, Richmond, Surrey TW9 1SR

THE KINCAIDS: PRIVATE MERGERS
© Harlequin Enterprises II B.V./S.à.r.l. 2013

One Dance with the Sheikh © Harlequin Books S.A. 2012
A Very Private Merger © Harlequin Books S.A. 2012

Special thanks and acknowledgement to Tessa Radley and Day Leclaire for their contributions to the Dynasties: The Kincaids series.

ISBN: 978 0 263 90605 9

009-0513

Harlequin (UK) policy is to use papers that are natural, renewable and recyclable products and made from wood grown in sustainable forests. The logging and manufacturing processes conform to the legal environmental regulations of the country of origin.

Printed and bound by
CPI Group (UK) Ltd, Croydon, CR0 4YY

ONE DANCE WITH THE SHEIKH

TESSA RADLEY

Tessa Radley loves travelling, reading and watching the world around her. As a teen Tessa wanted to be an intrepid foreign correspondent. But after completing a bachelor of arts degree and marrying her sweetheart, she became fascinated by law and ended up studying further and practising as a lawyer in a city firm. A six-month break spent travelling through Australia with her family reawakened the yen to write. And life as a writer suits her perfectly—travelling and reading count as research and as for analysing the world...well, she can think 'what if?' all day long. When she's not reading, travelling or thinking about writing, she's spending time with her husband, her two sons or her zany and wonderful friends. You can contact Tessa through her website, www.tessaradley.com.

Dear Reader,

One Dance with the Sheikh will be on the shelves in May, yet I'm writing this letter to you as Christmas fast approaches. Decorations are up in the malls and Christmas trees decked with coloured lights are appearing in homes. It's the season for friends and family.

Dynastic series like The Kincaids are always special. They're about bonds. Family. Friendship. Love. Often sad and bad things happen—in this case a father has been murdered. There are misunderstandings and betrayals— turbulent and troubled times—yet couples still manage to fall in love, the family grows closer and the generations will continue.

There are good times. There are tough times. Just like in real life.

I've just finished re-reading a Christmas story written by my friend Sandra Hyatt, in whose memory this story is dedicated, where she said, 'Whatever your religious persuasion, it never hurts to stop and count your blessings and the gifts in your life.'

That's what I'm determined to do this Christmas—and not only this Christmas… I'm going to spend all of this year counting my blessings and the gifts in my life.

So, even though Christmas will be long past by the time you pick up *One Dance with the Sheikh*, I do hope you will join me in thinking about the blessings and gifts in your life—sometimes amidst turbulent and troubled times. And I'll be right there with you.

Please visit my website at www.tessaradley.com or friend me on Facebook.

With love,

Tessa Radley

In Loving Memory of Sandra Hyatt
Wise Woman, Best Friend and Awesome Writer!

One

Who was she?

Dark red hair hung down her back, and as she shifted, the color changed like tongues of fire. Her tall, slender body was encased in a shimmering silvery grey gown that clung to her like moonlight on a dark night.

Rakin Whitcomb Abdellah had arrived at the giant white gazebo in the garden in front of the house where the guests were gathered in time to see the bride and groom link hands in front of the celebrant. It had surprised him that it had taken the usually responsible Eli only a matter of weeks to set aside the caution of a lifetime and to fall head over heels in love with his bride. But what had astonished Rakin more was the fact that Eli was marrying a Kincaid at all—since, less than a month ago, Kara's own sister had jilted Eli. Yet, once his gaze settled on the wedding group, it was the maid of honor with her glorious hair and eye-catching beauty who captured Rakin's attention as she moved forward to take the bouquet of red roses from the bride.

This could only be Laurel Kincaid, the woman who'd jilted his best friend Eli less than a month before their wedding day.

The woman who Eli had suggested could be the solution to all Rakin's problems.

A child, no more than three or four years old, strutted forward bearing a fat cushion. Rakin squinted and made out the two rings perched on top. Laurel stepped forward and held out a hand to guide him, but he tugged away, clearly reluctant to stand beside two flower girls. Instead he barreled his way between Eli and his bride Kara Kincaid, eliciting both chuckles and sighs as he stole hearts.

The maid of honor was scanning the guests.

Above the bouquet of red roses, her eyes were green. The brightest emerald Rakin had ever seen. Unexpectedly, her gaze landed on him. Time stopped. The murmurs around him, the sound of Kara saying her vows, the heady fragrance of the Southern blooms all faded from Rakin's consciousness. There was only...her.

Then she glanced away.

And the tension that had gripped him slowly eased.

Eli had warned him that his ex-fiancée was a beauty, yet Rakin hadn't been prepared for his body's reaction to her as their eyes had locked. Lust. Becoming romantically entangled with her was not an option. For starters, she was a Charleston Kincaid—not some nymphet with pleasure on her mind. And, if he took Eli's advice, the proposal he intended to put to her had everything to do with business, and nothing to do with pleasure.

Despite the gorgeous green-eyed, auburn-haired wrapping, Laurel Kincaid had *Do Not Touch* written all over her.

Yet even so, Rakin could scarcely wait for the ceremony to end, for the moment when he congratulated the newlyweds— and Eli introduced him to the maid of honor. Then he would decide whether she would fit in with his plans.

The rich scent of jasmine and gardenia announced that summer had arrived in the South.

Her sister's wedding was being held at the Kincaid family home, a two-and-a-half story elaborately embellished federal mansion where Laurel had grown up. The imposing facade flanked by decorative balconies, each with a pagoda roof, had always been home to Laurel and her siblings.

But at the moment she was less concerned with the details of the wedding venue than the identity of one tall dark and handsome stranger. Laurel had a pretty good idea of the identities of all the guests at her sister's wedding; after all, Kara had originally run all the guests' names past her when this was supposed to have been her own wedding.

And the stranger with the dark, exotic good looks hadn't been on it.

So where did Kara know him from? And why had her sister never mentioned him before?

If she didn't quit shooting surreptitious glances at the man her sisters would have her married off to him in an instant. And she wasn't interested in him; she simply wanted to know who he was.

Laurel averted her gaze and watched as Eli took Kara's hands in his, the gold of their newly donned wedding rings glinting in the late afternoon sun. Unexpectedly her throat tightened.

Oh, no. She wasn't going to cry!

She'd never been the type to gush tears at weddings.... She always smiled and said the right thing at the right time. So why was she suddenly feeling like this? This wedding was a joyous occasion, not a time to shed tears.

And heaven knew what interpretation people would put on it if she did start to cry. She scanned the enormous number of guests all dressed up and smiling. Laurel could think of at least one or two who would put the worst possible slant on it. Then the damage would be done, and rumors would be rife around the city that she was heartbroken about Kara marrying Eli—after she had broken off her own engagement to him.

Laurel was utterly delighted for them both. She was relieved she wasn't marrying Eli.

But no one would believe that if she started to weep.

Get a grip.

Her eyes fell onto her mother.

Now there was reason to cry. Elizabeth Kincaid was a legendary Southern beauty. Everyone said she'd have been crowned Miss South Carolina, if she'd ever entered—but soft-spoken, eternally elegant Elizabeth had too much class to enter beauty pageants. Instead, after her family had fallen on hard times, she'd married Reginald Kincaid and become one of the most accomplished hostesses in Charleston and brought cachet to the nouveau riche Kincaid name.

She was smiling as she watched Kara and Eli tie the knot.

Yet the mother of the bride almost hadn't made it to the wedding. She'd been arrested for killing her husband. The police had believed they'd had enough evidence to make a case. In the past months, in the very darkest moments, Laurel had worried that her mother might actually be convicted of her father's murder.

But her mother had been cleared.

And now suspicion for her father's death rested on the brooding half brother Laurel and her siblings had learned about at her father's funeral. Laurel would never forget that day—or the shock that her father had been living a secret double life for decades.

Now Jack Sinclair sat beside his mother, Angela Sinclair. Her father's mistress—and life-long love.

On Angela's other side sat her other son. The Sinclairs had been invited here today because Elizabeth Kincaid believed in always doing the Right Thing—even when it cost her dearly. The contrast between the half brothers was stark. Alan had none of Jack's dark moodiness. Blond and light, he was like the sun bursting through his half brother's dark thunder cloud.

Laurel decided she was becoming fanciful.

"You may kiss the bride," the celebrant was saying.

Eli bent forward, a head taller than his bride, and Laurel found herself looking away to give the couple a moment of privacy. Of course, she looked straight into a pair of dark eyes.

The generously proportioned bedrooms that Laurel, Kara and Lily had once occupied on the second floor of the historic federal mansion had been transformed into an impromptu bridal dressing-room wing for the wedding day. Pausing just inside the doorway of Kara's childhood room, Laurel took in the leftover feminine paraphernalia scattered around the room.

Open shoe boxes spilled tissue paper over the carpet. A posy abandoned by one of the flower girls lay on the bed. The fine lace veil that Kara had worn for the ceremony was already carefully draped over a chair back. On the dresser, between cut-glass perfume bottles, were four sparkling tulip glasses, and a bottle of champagne chilled in an ice bucket beside the dresser. A good way to calm the bride's nerves while she freshened up, Laurel decided.

Amidst the mayhem, Kara stood in front of a cheval mirror examining the hem of her wedding dress critically. "I haven't torn a hole in the hem, have I, Laurel?"

Moving forward, Laurel squinted at the delicately scalloped edge that Kara was holding up. "Not that I can see."

"Thank heavens." Relief filled her younger sister's voice as she let the beautiful white fabric drop. "I thought I might have put a heel through it when I came back down the aisle."

"Relax. It's all fine." Laurel scanned her sister's face. Kara's skin glowed, needing no added artifice. The shimmer of eye shadow accentuated her green eyes, but her lips had lost the gloss they'd worn before the ceremony. Laurel's mouth quirked up. "You make a beautiful bride, Mrs. Houghton—even without touching up the gloss that your groom kissed off."

It was true. Kara's radiance had given her the kind of beauty that came from inner happiness. Taking care not to crush the delicate wedding dress, Laurel gave her sister a tentative hug. But Kara had no such scruples and flung her arms around Laurel.

"Thank you, oh, thank you, for jilting Eli!"

Laurel looked into eyes almost the same green as her own, eyes they'd inherited from their mother. "Believe me, if I'd married your groom it would have been the biggest mistake of both our lives."

It had been one thing to drift into an engagement with Eli, but once the time to plan the wedding had arrived, Laurel had been distressed to discover her heart wasn't in it.

Instead of daydreaming about wedded bliss, she'd found herself dwelling on how static her life had become.

How predictable.

How boring.

And what it would take to get a life. To her discomfort, writing out lists of wedding guests who'd accepted their invitations to the big day had not even featured.

That was when Laurel had created the How to Get a Life List.

Jilt Eli. Item No. 1 on the List, as she'd started thinking of it, had looked so stark, so cruel when she'd stared at the two words topping the otherwise blank piece of paper, that she hadn't known if she was capable of breaking off her engagement to Eli.

His feelings would be hurt. Her family would be devastated. But writing it down had brought such a sense of catharsis that Laurel had known she'd had no other choice.

She and Eli were simply not meant to be.

To spare his feelings, she'd told him she couldn't marry him until the upheaval in her life—her father's murder, the shocking discovery of his other family and the anguish of her mother's arrest—had settled down. But the overwhelming relief in Eli's eyes brought home the knowledge that she wasn't the only one who wanted out.

Almost a month had passed since she'd jilted Eli. Today her ex-fiancé was celebrating the happiness he'd found—with her sister. Eli had gotten himself a life.

However, until putting on Item No. 2—red-lipstick—this morning during the final preparations, she had done nothing more about tackling the rest of the List. Breaking the strictures of a lifetime was proving to be daunting. Despite the List which she carried in her purse as a constant prod to action.

That had to change, she had to start living. Really living.

Like that electric moment during the ceremony when she'd met a pair of dark eyes and she'd been jolted by a surge of energy. That had been living.

Extricating herself from her sister's arms, Laurel lifted the bottle of champagne from the ice bucket and filled two of the flutes, then passed one to Kara.

She raised her glass in a toast. "Be happy."

"Oh, I am. Today is the happiest day of my life."

Her sister sparkled like a fairytale princess.

Laurel couldn't stop a stab of envy. She took a quick gulp of champagne before setting it down.

"Eli and I had always been such good friends, and I think we both hoped that would be enough—I know I did. But it wasn't. We lacked that special connection that you two have." They hadn't even shared the kind of physical attraction that had blasted through her after one lingering look from a stranger.

"It's love. Real love. He's my soul mate. I'm incredibly fortunate." Kara had gone all dreamy-eyed. Then her gaze sharpened. "How funny that you're the one Eli spent the most time with while we were growing up—"

"That's because we were the same age—in the same year at school and invited to the same social functions," Laurel pointed out.

"—But you've never met his other close friend."

"Rakin Abdellah?" Laurel had heard plenty about the grandson of a Middle-Eastern prince with whom Eli had become close friends at Harvard. "Such a pity he didn't make it to the wedding."

"He's here!" Kara put her glass down beside Laurel's, then slid onto the stool in front of the dresser. She picked up a wide-toothed comb. "Eli introduced us when he came up to congratulate us after the ceremony."

Laurel hesitated in the act of taking the comb from her sister. Was it possible…?

"Where was I?"

"It must've been when Flynn swatted the flower girls with the ring cushion and you went after him before he caused more chaos."

Waving the comb in the air, Laurel spread her hands. "How typical! I always miss the man. Every time Eli caught up with him when Rakin visited on business, I had something else going on. Maybe we're just never destined to meet." But she couldn't stop wondering whether the tall, lean man responsible for that shock of awareness during the ceremony could possibly be Eli's best friend.

"What was he wearing?" she asked Kara urgently.

"Who?"

"Rakin!" Laurel shook her head at her sister. "The man you were telling me about."

"I don't know—the only man whose clothes I'm focused on today is Eli."

Laurel laughed at her sister's goofy expression. Dismissing the hunk, she started to smooth Kara's hair where the veil had been fastened earlier. "Speaking of Eli, you'd better re-apply your lipstick," she told her sister.

Kara slanted her a wicked look via the mirror. "What's the point? It will only get kissed off again." Then her gaze narrowed. "Laurel, you're wearing red lipstick!"

Laurel shot her younger sister an indulgent look. "If you've only just noticed it can't be such a big deal."

"You've decided to go ahead with your plan to stop playing it safe!" Kara had stilled. "I know you told me you were going to spread your wings and work on being a bit more uninhibited, but I hadn't seen any more signs of it since I warned you to take care—and not to go too crazy."

"Can you see me, Miss Responsibility, going crazy?" asked Laurel with a light laugh.

"Okay, I shouldn't have told you to be careful—I've been wishing I never said anything. You should have some fun. What about getting Eli to introduce you to Rakin?"

"Don't you dare!" To stop her too observant sister from interfering, Laurel said, "Did you notice how protective Cutter's been of Mom today?"

"I think everyone did. He didn't leave her side."

"I think Cutter will be good for her—he seems to genuinely love her." Laurel patted the final wayward strands in place and stood back to admire Kara's hair. To make sure it held, she added the lightest spritz of hair spray. "And he risked a storm of scandal by coming forward to tell the police that Mom had spent the night of Dad's murder with him. That's what got her out on bail."

"I offered to plan a small wedding for Mom—elegant and discreet. But Mom was dead against it. She doesn't think they can get married until a decent time of mourning Dad has passed—"

"That's ridiculous." Just the idea that her mother was letting what people thought rule her life caused Laurel to see red. "Mom must do what makes her happy."

"I agree Mom deserves a little happiness after discovering the sordid details of Dad's secret life, and if marrying Cutter gives her that, I'll be his biggest fan." Kara swiveled around on the stool and examined Laurel. "And I didn't notice your lip color because I was too busy getting married." She clearly wasn't about to let Laurel off the hook. "But now I've noticed. I'm interested—I want to know what you're planning to do next."

Laurel could feel herself coloring. She wasn't even sure what she was going to do next herself. Confessing to the existence of the List, and worse, to imagining living out some mind-boggling fantasies—even to her sister—was way too much to bear.

"It's hardly world changing," she said off-handedly, thinking about her frivolous desire to eat ice cream in bed.

But that still left more....

Item No. 5, *Gamble all night.*

Item No. 6, *Travel to exotic lands.*

Okay, maybe they were a little world changing....

Tilting her head to one side, Kara said, "Hmm, you've never worn red lipstick—you always say it's too obvious—so that's already a pretty big change."

Red lips clashed with her auburn hair. It was trashy. And trashy was a sin. Leaning past Kara to avoid her sister's gaze, Laurel pretended to inspect her lips in the dresser mirror. There were no smudges—nor likely to be, unless she found someone to kiss.

Which brought her back to How to Get a Life.

Item No. 3 on the list was *Flirt with a stranger.* Her cheeks grew hot. Unlike most Southern women Laurel was a rookie in the art of flirting. Since entering her teens, she'd only had to look at a male to have him cross the room to meet her. Sometimes she'd hated the kind of attention her features brought. To deal with it, she'd cultivated a polite manner with no hint of flirtatiousness. The facade had served her equally well in her dealings as public relations director of the Kincaid Group. So why on earth was she adding an item like *Flirt with a stranger*?

Maybe she should've made that *Kiss a stranger*. The renegade thought startled her.

"You're blushing. Is it a man? Is that the reason for the red lips?" Kara's voice broke into Laurel's musings. "Is that the reason you won't let me ask Eli to introduce you to Rakin?"

"No man," Laurel denied, wishing that her complexion didn't color quite so dramatically. "The red lips are for me alone."

For one mad moment she was tempted to tell Kara all about the List. Then she cringed and the impulse passed.

Telling Kara would be insane. And Kara would start fretting again about Laurel exposing herself to danger—and the last thing Laurel wanted was to cause her sister to worry on her wedding day.

She drained the last of the champagne, then set her glass back down on the dresser. She caught another glimpse of her lips in the mirror above the dresser.

What would it be like to kiss the gorgeous dark-haired man from the church?

The shocking visual of crushed red lips sent a frisson of heat coursing through her.

Laurel came to her senses. What if he turned out to be Eli's friend? How trashy would that be? She'd always been the good eldest sister...the one to do as she was told. To study hard for excellent grades. To obey her curfew. She'd always set an example for her sisters to follow. No mini skirts. No ear studs and torn jeans. No shameless behavior with boys. No wild flings.

No trashy makeup...

She turned away from the mirror, intending to say something light and funny to her sister.

Only to find Kara had risen to her feet and was still watching her.

"I have to admit red suits you, Laurel. Makes you look like a movie star. Glamorous. Sexy. You always wear beiges and creams. I take back all my cautions, you should break out more often."

Laurel's heart lightened as she followed her sister to the door. "Careful! I might take that as permission to do something reckless."

Kara halted in the doorway, looked over her shoulder and smiled. "Why not? Start today. No time like the present."

Now? Tonight? Laurel's hands turned cold and clammy as Kara vanished out of sight with a whisper of French fabric.

It was one thing to talk about loosening up a little; it was another thing altogether to actually do it and let go. The sense of being poised on the edge of a precipice swept Laurel.

Should she take that first step into the unknown and walk on the wild side? Or should she stay in her safe world and risk never feeling quite satisfied?

The answer came quickly, so quickly it took her aback. She was tired of missing out. She wanted to feel more of that pulsing energy that she'd experienced earlier. That flutter of rebellion brought a surge of illicit pleasure.

Laurel drew a deep breath and felt her lungs fill, and resolve spread through her. Kara was right—there was no time like the present. She headed for the door.

Tonight, she'd flirt with a stranger.

Two

In the elegant, embellished salon downstairs, a twelve-piece jazz ensemble was playing blues, a smoky, elegant sound. Perfect for what had to be one of the high-society weddings of the year.

Laurel hummed and did a little dance step in Kara's wake and almost skipped into Alan Sinclair, who'd materialized in front of them, holding two glasses brimming with pale, bubbling gold wine. By some miracle he managed to keep the glasses upright, while Laurel apologized effusively.

"Major catastrophe averted," he joked.

All three of them laughed.

"These were intended for you, beautiful ladies." Alan held out the brimming glasses, his hazel eyes alight with good humor.

"Only a sip for me. I'm going to need my wits about me—I need to make sure I get all the guests' names right," said Kara with a gracious smile.

Laurel took the remaining glass. "Thank you."

"I didn't get a chance earlier to give you my very best wishes," Alan told Kara. "Eli is a lucky man."

"Why, thank you, Alan." Kara beamed at him. "I certainly hope you meet the woman of your dreams soon—maybe even tonight."

Alan laughed. "I can live in hope. But maybe we should wait a while—give you time for a honeymoon—before handing you another wedding to plan."

"I'd be thrilled to do another wedding. And, for once, that's not the businesswoman in me talking. I'm so happy, I'm ready to marry everyone off."

"He's a nice man," Laurel observed as they walked away, holding their glasses.

"Thoughtful, too," Kara agreed. "He'll make some lucky woman a good husband."

They'd reached the bridal table by now, and Eli leapt up to welcome his bride, his eyes warm and devoted as he seated her.

Feeling a bit like a third wheel, Laurel slipped into the vacant seat beside her mother and set her glass down on the white damask linen sprinkled with pink and crimson rose petals. A waiter appeared to fill it up.

"Where's Cutter?" Laurel asked her mother, aware that she was sitting in his seat. The whole world had paired up—even her mother.

Everyone except her.

A wave of loneliness swept her; then she shook it off. All the more reason to follow the List and find a stranger to flirt with—and where better than a wedding?

"He spotted Harold Parsons and Mr. Larrimore and went over to greet them." Elizabeth fluttered a hand in the direction of the bar. Following where her mother indicated, Laurel could see the white-haired lawyer talking to the head of Larrimore Industries, which had recently begun doing business with The Kincaid Group, making up a little of the losses TKG had suffered when several customers defected to Carolina Shipping. Why, only this week her brother Matthew, TKG's director of new business, had heard rumblings that Jack Sinclair was trying to outbid them on an important shipping contract through backdoor channels.

Speak of the devil.

Jack Sinclair had pulled out a chair to seat himself at a table right on the edge of the dance floor. *How boldly arrogant.* He was behaving like he owned the Kincaid mansion. Laurel supposed inheriting forty-five percent of the stock in The Kincaid Group was responsible for some of that arrogance. She hadn't managed to get a handle on Jack yet. Dark, unsmiling and perpetually brooding, he made her a little uneasy. He'd certainly caused TKG enough headaches in the past few months to last a lifetime.

Then Laurel caught a sight of the smooth blond hair of his mother, Angela, seated beyond him. Something his mother said caused a ferocious scowl to mar Jack's features. Laurel shivered at the sight of his displeasure.

Why had her father's firstborn son bothered to come to the wedding, if he intended to sit there and glare? Was he only here today to fool the paparazzi into thinking he was an accepted part of the Kincaid family? Or were her siblings correct? Did Jack fear that by staying away he'd heighten the suspicion already surrounding him? Laurel didn't want to consider the possibility that her father had been shot in the head by his firstborn son.... It was too horrible.

She refused to allow Jack's presence to ruin the celebratory mood tonight. The pall that had hung over the family for months had finally lifted. Laurel intended to enjoy the occasion...and make sure her mom did, too.

Laurel caught Elizabeth's hand and gave it a squeeze. "I can't tell you how glad I am not only that you're here at the wedding but that you've been cleared of all those ridiculous charges. It's the best wedding gift Kara and Eli could ever have received."

"Today hasn't been easy," her mother confessed. "All the speculation. I'm sure there are people here this evening who still believe I killed your father. And everyone is so curious about Cutter—it's difficult for him, too."

Yet, in the way that was so typical of Southern society matriarchs, none of her mother's discomfort showed. Elizabeth's face was serene, her short, auburn hair with the elegant grey highlights was immaculate, the strain of the past four turbulent months carefully masked. Only the reserve in her green eyes hinted at the anguish she'd been through.

"You deserve some happiness." Laurel echoed Kara's words from earlier. Letting go of her mother's hand she reached for the glass Alan had given her. "And if Cutter makes you happy you shouldn't let what others think spoil that. Let's drink to happier tomorrows."

Elizabeth took a tiny sip, and then set her own glass down. "I do wish the police would hurry up and finalize the investigation. Not knowing who killed your father..." Her voice trailed away.

Her brothers RJ and Matt had some strong opinions about who might have killed her father. But now wasn't the right time to share them with her mother.

"I'll call Detective McDonough tomorrow to arrange a meeting for later in the week to find out if there has been any progress," promised Laurel. She shot the brooding interloper at the edge of the dance floor a surreptitious look. With luck, the police might finally have gathered enough evidence to toss Jack Sinclair in jail where her brothers said he belonged.

If her brothers were right, then Jack had been extremely devious—he'd made sure he had an airtight alibi, with several of his own employees vouching he'd been working late the night her father had died. Laurel didn't want to believe her half brother was capable of that kind of treachery. But as RJ had pointed out, Jack was a very wealthy man—made even richer by the forty-five percent stake he inherited in The Kincaid Group on her father's death. That kind of money could buy any alibi—particularly when the people supplying it already depended on him to earn their living. Laurel made a mental note to get an update from Nikki Thomas, the corporate security specialist the family had hired to investigate Jack Sinclair's efforts to sabotage The Kincaid Group. Laurel couldn't bear to see her mother so down, and Nikki might also have some thoughts about how to speed up the investigation—even though Laurel had once or twice suspected Nikki to be a little more emotionally invested in the ruthless man she was investigating than was wise.

Immersed in her thoughts, the touch on her arm startled her, and her head jerked around.

Eli stood there, wearing a broad grin. "Laurel, there's someone I'd like you to meet."

Glancing at the dark figure beside her former fiancé, Laurel found herself confronted by the handsome man she'd exchanged that sizzling eye-meet with during the wedding ceremony.

"Laurel, this is Rakin Whitcomb Abdellah." Eli presented him with a flourish. "Rakin, meet Laurel Kincaid, my brand new sister-in-law."

Honest to goodness, she was going to kill Kara!

Already she could feel a flush stealing up her throat.

"I've heard so much about you." Rakin held out his hand.

"Funny, that's exactly what I was about to say." Laurel set down her glass and took his hand. Her lashes swept down as she became conscious of the strength of the fingers against hers. "I'm surprised we've never encountered each other before."

"*In'shallah.*" Letting go of her fingers, he spread his own hands wide. "What more can I say? The time was not right."

Her gaze lifted and sharpened. "You believe in fate?"

"But of course. Everything happens for a reason. Today is the right time for us to meet."

Charmed, she started to smile. It looked like Eli's friend might be the perfect candidate for a flirtation with a stranger. "It is?"

"Yes." His black-velvet gaze was intent…and Laurel felt the primal power of the man.

To break the spell, she switched her attention to Eli and murmured, "You should be worried we might trade secrets—between us we probably know everything about you."

Eli chuckled. "I'm terrified."

"You're anything but terrified." Laurel glanced at Rakin, and found his dark eyes were bright with laughter

The band swung into the first bars of the first dance.

"Now there's something I am terrified about messing up. That's the bridal waltz," said Eli. "Let me go claim my bride."

Laurel couldn't help laughing as he hurried back to her sister. Conscious of Rakin's very male presence at her side as Eli led Kara out onto the floor, Laurel fell silent and concentrated on watching the dance—not an easy task with Rakin still looming over her.

A spotlight landed on the newlyweds. The guests sighed as they moved into the dance in perfect time, Kara's white dress fanning out to fill the ring the spotlight had created. They glided to the melody, and a few beats later, Laurel's sister Lily and her husband, Daniel, joined in, RJ and Brooke were next on the floor.

Laurel could see Alan smiling as he sat beside his mother at the table on the edge of the dance floor. Jack had disappeared. Laurel wished he could've practiced the same civility as the Kincaid family—at Elizabeth's request—were taking great care to show Angela and her sons tonight.

"Would you like to dance?"

Rakin's deep tone caused her to forget all about Jack's rudeness.

Silently she gave him her hand. The warm strength of his fingers closing around hers caused the return of that renegade fantasy of crushed, kissed lips, and Laurel abruptly lowered her eyelashes before he might read any of her dizzy imaginings. "Why, thank you, I'd like that."

He led her onto the dance floor and took her into his arms. The sudden intimacy came as a shock. The music swirled around them.

To break the seductive mood, Laurel said, "You met Eli at Harvard?"

"Yes, we shared some classes and sometimes went hiking together—we both like the outdoors."

"Yes. You were on the rowing team together, too, weren't you? I seem to remember hearing Eli talk about pre-dawn practices on the river."

He smiled. "Strange interest for someone from a desert country, hmm?"

"A little." She examined him. "Tell me about Diyafa."

"Ah, Eli has told you about my country?"

"Just the name. Diyafa." It rolled off her tongue. "It sounds so deliciously exotic."

"It is. The desert nights are warm and dry and the heavens above possess the brightest stars I have ever seen."

The whisper of his voice stoked her imagination. "How magical. I hate to confess this—but I've never been out of the United States."

"Never?"

She shook her head. "Never. I always intended to travel."

Item No. 6 on the List involved traveling to some far-flung exotic destination. She'd had a fleeting vision of herself standing in the center of St. Mark's Square in Venice or in front of the Sphinx in Egypt. Somewhere as different from Charleston as she could get.

She pulled a face. "Now I just have to turn that dream into reality. I even got myself a passport." Which she'd been carrying around in her purse, together with the List—and the letter from her father she'd received on that emotionally charged day when her father's will was read.

"Diyafa is a good place to visit."

Did he think she was trying to coax an invitation from him? Discomfort flooded her. "Oh, I couldn't take advantage of our acquaintance."

"Why not?"

Her lashes fluttered down. "We hardly know one another."

"I'm sure we can remedy that." He sounded amused.

Laurel's lashes lifted. Heavens, was she actually flirting with the man?

Then she examined her reaction.

So what?

Flirt with a stranger. It was on her list, and she was unlikely to ever encounter Rakin again. He might be Eli's other best friend, but before today she'd only ever heard about him. It would be at least another ten years before they met again; after all he was a busy man. Worth the risk?

Or was she going to chicken out? No. The time to act had arrived. Pursing her mouth into a moue, she gave what she hoped looked like a mysterious smile. "Maybe I will visit...one day."

An arrested expression settled in his eyes.

"You can let me know when you do." There was an intimate note in his voice.

He was flirting too!

Rakin was clearly a master at the art of flirtation. For once she was tempted to let herself go. To revel in the full power of her womanhood. This was a man she was facing, a real man with a wealth of experience with women.

"To be honest I'm more likely to visit Las Vegas—" she began with a teasing laugh.

"You like to gamble?"

Had his voice dropped? Laurel's heart beat a little faster. "I've never gambled seriously in my life. Certainly not in a casino."

Her mother didn't approve of gambling. A roguish uncle, the black sheep of the Winthrop family, had lost a fortune at poker, contributing to the dire straits the family found itself in before her mother's marriage into the Kincaid fortune. Gambling was seriously discouraged among the Kincaid children. No doubt that was why *Gamble all night* had made it onto the List....

"We'll have to change that—raise the stakes."

Yes, he was definitely flirting. If the intimate note in his voice hadn't made it clear, the gleam in his eyes confirmed it. Laurel gave herself up to the heady rush. "I wouldn't want to become addicted."

"That can only happen if the stakes are higher than you can afford."

"I'll remember that." She peeked at him through her lashes. "If I ever find myself in Vegas."

The song came to an end. She was hot and thirsty, yet Laurel found she didn't want the exchange to end. It was exhilarating. Fun. Yet risky. More than she'd ever banked on when she'd scrawled *Flirt with a stranger* on her list. The weight of Rakin's hand resting on her waist, the touch of his fingers against hers, the way his body had brushed against hers to the rhythm of the music was stealing over her senses.

"It's warm in here," she said, finally letting go of his hand and fanning her face. "I need a drink."

"There's a cool breeze outside," Rakin responded readily,

his hand sliding from where it rested at her waist to beneath her elbow. As they skirted the dance floor he picked up two brimming tulip glasses from a passing waiter with his free hand, before leading her to the open doors.

Laurel hesitated on the threshold. Outside, the balcony appeared to be deserted.

Her heart leapt as his hand touched the sensitive skin under her elbow. Rakin's voice was deep and smooth as he said, "Come. It will be quiet and cool."

And she couldn't help wondering if she'd let herself in for more than she could handle as she stepped out into the Southern night.

There was a slight breeze and the balmy night air was redolent with the sweet scent of magnolia and jasmine.

Rakin led Laurel to the shadows at the end of balcony where the sultry throb of the jazz band was fainter. Under the glow cast by a wall sconce, he handed one of the long-stemmed glasses to Laurel, then leant back against the wide balustrade. She tipped the glass up to take a slow sip, and her gaze tangled with his over the rim.

Something—lust?—locked fast in the base of his stomach.

With her tall, slender figure wrapped in a column of moonlight silk, her magnolia skin, sparkling eyes and the crowning glory of her dark red hair, Laurel Kincaid was a very beautiful woman. Any man would be aroused by having the full wattage of her attention switched on to him. And, to his chagrin, Rakin discovered he was no exception.

But he was interested in far more than the surge of attraction between them. Holding her gaze, he drank from his glass, savoring the dry bubbles against his tongue. Despite the millions he'd added to the Al-Abdellah fortune, his grandfather was threatening to toss him out of the family business if he didn't marry soon. So far, Rakin had resisted—love was not on his agenda. But the battle of wills being fought between himself and Prince Ahmeer Al-Abdellah had now erupted into open war. Marriage to the right woman might be the lesser of two evils. Eli's not-so-joking suggestion that Laurel might be the perfect bride to get Rakin's grandfather off his back was worth serious consideration.

And love would not be a factor...

One look at Laurel and his wily grandfather would ask no further questions. What man in his right mind would pass up the chance to wed such a stunning creature? Her connection to the Charleston Kincaids only served to make the deal even sweeter. But first Rakin would have to sell the idea to Laurel—she was a Kincaid, there was no earthly reason for her to agree to help him out.

Except business...

"So you'd like to gamble in Vegas?" he asked, swirling the gold liquid in his flute.

"Maybe."

He could hear the smile in her voice. Was she teasing him? He couldn't read her expression. "You've really never been?"

"Only once—as a young child. But I don't remember it, so it doesn't count."

"Such a lack is easy enough to remedy—but you shouldn't go alone."

"I only discovered recently that I wanted to go at all. A few months ago I could've invited Lily or Kara along with me. But it's too late for that—they're both married now. You may not have heard, Lily and Daniel decided to solemnize their union in a very private service just a couple of days ago—Lily didn't want to overshadow Kara's wedding. They intend to have a bigger elaborate family affair in October after the baby is born."

She spoke in a matter-of-fact voice, yet Rakin thought he detected a hint of loneliness in her voice. He was no stranger to loneliness. An only child, he envied Laurel the bond she shared with her sisters and brothers. The closeness among the Kincaids was evident in every look, every laugh.

The closest he'd come to that kind of relationship was the friendship he shared with Eli—but neither of them talked much about family...or emotions. Sport, money and business were their main lines of communication. "Marriage won't change the fact that they will always be your sisters."

Laurel moved away from the light, to the end of the balcony. She raised her glass and sipped while she stared out into the night. At last she spoke, "I know that. But now they have priorities of their own. Both of them have husbands...and Lily is going to be a mother. The sisterhood will never be the same again." Her voice held an echo of sadness. Then he caught the glint of startling white in the shadows as she turned her head and smiled. "Enough of that. I have plenty of friends with whom I can visit Vegas."

Rakin didn't doubt that for a moment. She was vivacious and breathtakingly beautiful. She'd have friends buzzing around her like bees at a honey pot.

"How did you come to be friends with Eli?" he asked.

It had puzzled him when Eli had first spoken about Laurel Kincaid back at Harvard. Initially, Rakin had thought the two must share more than friendship. With his upbringing in the traditional society of Diyafa followed by all-boys schooling, envisaging a close friendship between a man and a woman had been foreign. But Eli had made it clear he and Laurel were nothing more than friends—very close friends. When the news had come that they were engaged, Rakin had not been surprised. At some point any friendship between a man and woman would have to cross into the sexual realm. Women and men were not created to be simply friends.

Laurel's jilting of Eli, and Eli's ready acceptance of it—and his wry joke that Rakin should marry her—had astonished Rakin. So, too, had the fact that Eli's heart had not even been the slightest bit battered after Laurel's desertion.

"Growing up, we were the same age—it seemed natural that we hung out together. Now, years later, with both of us still single and such good friends, we were invited everywhere together. I guess we were linked in everyone else's minds as a couple long before the idea ever occurred to either of us." She shrugged, and light glimmered on the pale slope of shoulders left bare by her silver-gray dress. "The next step was marriage.

But clearly we're better at being friends than lovers. There was no spark."

And that would explain Eli's philosophical acceptance of the breakup. Rakin put his glass down and took a step closer to Laurel; then he murmured, "You wanted spark?"

"Doesn't every woman?"

Something leapt between them. Before Rakin could consider his actions, he lifted a hand and brushed a strand of the dark fire from her cheek. Her dewy skin was softer than any he'd ever touched—and it left him hungry to stroke again. Abruptly, he dropped his hand before he could give into the moment's madness. "Everyone seeks that elusive flame—few are lucky enough to find it."

"You mean love?"

"I don't believe in love—I'm talking about what you called spark. A tangible force that connects two people in perfect harmony only a few times in a lifetime."

She tipped her head back and drained the last of her champagne. The elegant column of her neck gleamed in the lamplight. "Spark sounds...interesting. I used to think I wanted love more than anything else in the world."

"You don't think so anymore?"

"Nope." She giggled. "That should be 'No,' clearly and politely enunciated, of course."

Rakin found himself grinning at that absurdity. The revelation that she wasn't looking for some romantic notion of love eased his conscience. Business...and maybe some sparks... might be enough to persuade her to go along with his plan.

"Pardon my giggling." Laurel moved back into the pool of light beneath the wall sconce. "There hasn't been much to laugh about lately so this feels very good."

"It must be the joy of a wedding."

She raised her empty glass. "I suspect it may have something to do with the champagne, too."

The forthright observation startled Rakin. Had he at last found a woman capable of distinguishing between realism and romance? Quite possibly. She was, after all, a Kincaid, a businesswoman. It was starting to look like he'd struck twenty-four-karat gold. "Can I get you another?"

"Not yet. I've had enough. I think I might be a little tipsy. I'm trying to remember how many glasses of champagne I've had. Three maybe." She laughed again. "That's a first."

Straightening from where he leant, Rakin took the glass from her and set it down on the balustrade behind them. "You've never been tipsy?"

She shook her head and her hair swirled about her face. "Never! My mother would be mortified, she would not approve."

At the mention of her mother, Rakin said, "I was sorry to hear about your mother's arrest—it must have been a difficult time for the whole family."

"It hasn't been easy." All humor drained from her face and Rakin found himself missing the pleasure of it. "The police are still no closer to finding a suspect. But thankfully Mom has been cleared." Laurel shivered, and he knew it wasn't with cold. "I keep replaying that last day through my mind. I was at the offices until late in the afternoon. I even made Dad a cup of coffee before I left. He glanced up when I set it down, I joked that it was hot and strong just as he liked it. He laughed—Dad didn't often laugh—and thanked me, then he went back to the documents he was reading. That's the last image I have of him. Daddy didn't even see me wave goodbye as I exited his office."

She broke off, and Rakin knew she was fighting back tears.

"But I keep thinking I should've have had some kind premonition—noticed something," she said huskily. "I saw nothing out of the ordinary. Several of the staff were still there when I left—Brooke, RJ's assistant at the time, was the last to leave."

The memory was clearly upsetting Laurel. Rakin could make out the gooseflesh rippling across the fine, smooth skin of her arms.

Wrapping her arms around herself, she walked back to the end of the balustrade. "I can't believe I never noticed anything."

"You weren't expecting anything to happen."

She fell silent. Finally she turned her head and a band of moonlight fell across her face giving her skin the sheen of silvered silk. "Out of all of us, Brooke blames herself most. In her statement to the police she mentioned while she was finishing up the filing backlog, Mom brought dinner to Dad that night. The police arrested Mom—she was the last person to see him alive and, until recently, she had no alibi. What makes Brooke feel even worse is the fact that she didn't even think to mention that earlier in the afternoon it was pouring rain and she had her arms full of blueprints when she ran for the office to avoid being drenched. A man in a hat and raincoat held the door open for her. No one has any idea who he was. Security didn't record his entry—they thought he was with Brooke. And, of course, she has no idea who he could've been. Detective McDonough thinks it's possible he hid in the building until after everyone—including Mom—left."

"And there's still no clue about who it was?"

Laurel shook her head, causing her hair to ripple over her shoulders. "Video security footage from an adjacent lot puts Jack Sinclair's vintage Aston Martin in the parking lot from late afternoon until around the time my father was shot—but he swears he was at his own office. Yet he never reported his car missing—or stolen."

The odd note in her voice made Rakin probe further, "But you think Sinclair might have murdered your father?"

"I keep hoping not. Dad obviously loved Angela—he wanted to marry her, but his parents wouldn't countenance it. Jack's clearly bitter about the situation. Fact is, he may be the firstborn son, but he's not a legitimate Kincaid. Dad tried to make it up to him—and to Angela. Yet despite the inheritance and power Dad gave him, he's behaving like he has a major grudge against the family—which makes it hard to view Jack in any kind of positive way."

"And you like to see the best in people?"

"I try." The eyes that met his held the kind of honesty he'd given up hoping to find. "But I don't always get it right. Let's talk about something else—I promised myself I wouldn't let Jack Sinclair ruin tonight. It's a celebration."

"I want to talk about you." With a sense of satisfaction, Rakin watched her do a double take. "Eli said you possess the kindest heart of anyone he knows."

It had crossed Rakin's mind in the past few minutes to throw himself at her mercy and ask her to help him out of a tight spot with his grandfather, but it went against the grain. Rakin never asked for favors. His pride would not allow it. All his decisions were based on considerations of mutual benefit—and hard profit.

She wrinkled her nose at him. "That makes me sound boring."

"Kindness isn't boring."

"Well, it's not very exciting either."

Rakin's eyebrows jerked up at that. "You want to be considered exciting?"

"I want a life." It burst from her. She looked taken aback at her own ferocity. "Goodness, that sounded much more melodramatic than I intended."

Maybe Laurel Kincaid didn't express her own wants often enough, mused Rakin. Taking two steps toward her, he asked carefully, "How do you intend to achieve the life you want?"

Her gaze shifted out to the night. For a long moment he thought she wasn't going to answer.

Then she turned her head, and her eyes glistened in the dappled shadows. "I'm going to do all the things I've never done. Things no one would expect of Laurel Kincaid, director of public relations of TKG, friend of the Library, patron of the Art Gallery—first person to join a committee for the next good cause."

Rakin couldn't suppress a smile at the self-deprecatory comment. "Like gamble in Vegas?"

"Exactly like gambling in Vegas." She lifted her chin a touch defensively. "It may not be meaningful, but it will be one brick broken out of the boundaries that are imprisoning me."

What was it about this woman that caused his heart to lighten and amusement to fill him? Leading him to feel as if he'd shed the burden accumulated over years?

Then it came to him. Under that ladylike exterior, Laurel Kincaid was a rebel. A real, genteel Southern rebel. Rakin had a feeling that she was about to throw off the constraints of a lifetime. The fates help them all. "You want to experience risk and adventure?"

"Oh, yes!"

Staring into her sparkling eyes, Rakin discovered he wanted to get to know this intriguing woman better.

Much better.

He desired her. More importantly, he liked her. It would be so easy to explain his predicament to her—he suspected she would listen. He could already visualize her head tilting to one side, her eyes fixed on his as he told her about his grandfather's threats to disenfranchise him from the company he'd worked so hard to expand. His predicament would arouse her sympathy— how could it not, given the parallels to Jack Sinclair's efforts to destroy The Kincaid Group?

Would her kind heart allow her to agree to a marriage of convenience?

Rakin suspected she just might even consider it. Eli had been right: Laurel would make him the perfect wife.

But he needed time to persuade her. Before he could check the impulse he found himself saying, "So come away with me to Vegas."

Three

"Come away with you to Las Vegas? Are you serious?"

Astonishment caused Laurel's mouth to drop open. So much for the certainty that her instilled equilibrium was unshakeable. Rakin's invitation had floored her. And, what's more, the rogue knew he'd surprised her—his eyes were twinkling.

"Absolutely serious." He'd closed the gap between them, and his broad shoulders blocked her view of the house. "You could have try your luck at the slot machines."

"I intend to do more than try my luck at the machines," she informed him. "My plan is to gamble all night—in the casino."

"That's a serious rebellion." His eyes crinkled as his grin broadened. "And I'm sure I can accommodate such a plan."

"Are you laughing at me?" she asked suspiciously, flicking her hair back over her shoulder.

"Why should I laugh at you?"

Because he considered her too staid, too much of a Goody Two-shoes to take him up on his offer? She took in his stance. His weight was perfectly balanced on both feet. In the shadows, his white shirtfront was a startling contrast to his dark, hawkish features. The rash urge to surprise him rose before she could check it. Why shouldn't she take him up on his invitation to go gamble in Vegas?

Laurel drew a deep breath and said in a rush, "My mother was a Winthrop."

She paused expectantly.

When Rakin didn't react, she said, "I forget. To people not from the South, the name is meaningless. But in South Carolina the Winthrops have always been a force to be reckoned with." She gave him a quick smile. "Sounds terribly snobbish, I know. But in Charleston they're an old, well-established family who fell on hard times. A result of bad business decisions—although the decline had started way back. My Winthrop great-great uncle was infamous for his ability to gamble huge sums on property and poker—he lost at both."

"I'm sorry to hear that."

She shrugged. "It got worse. By the 1970s the family fortune had been exhausted, but the Winthrops were still determined to hang on to a lifestyle they could no longer afford. That meant a new injection of cash to maintain their social standing—cash that came from the Kincaid shipping and—ironically—real estate profits." Laurel gave him a wry smile. "The Kincaids must've been better at gambling on property—or, at least, more astute. As luck would have it, at the same time that the Winthrop family fortune was in decline, my Kincaid grandfather was trying to scale the old money bastions of Charleston, which—despite his rapidly growing nouveau riche wealth—had proved impenetrable up till that point. So he pressured my father into marrying my mother."

He stepped closer. "You sound cynical."

"Cynicism is not a usual characteristic of mine, believe it or not." Laurel shifted back until she could feel the hard balustrade against her hip through the delicate fabric of her dress. "But I don't think the way the older Winthrops or Kincaids behaved was particularly admirable—they brokered a marriage between my parents for their own gain."

"It is how things used to be done in powerful families." Rakin shrugged. "But your parents would have to bear part of the responsibility for agreeing to the arrangement."

"My mother fell in love with Reginald Kincaid." Laurel gave

him sad smile. "He was handsome, witty—what woman can resist a man with a sense of humor?—and he had the means to restore the family fortune. A veritable knight in shining armor. She never stood a chance." She let out a shuddering breath. "Why am I telling you this? We're here to celebrate Kara's wedding, not cry over the past."

"Don't let your parents' choices in the past color your future," he said softly. "Come to Vegas—I'll take you gambling if that's what you want. Or we could just enjoy ourselves for a weekend."

Two...maybe three...days. What harm could come from a few days of pure pleasure? There was something quite wildly wicked in doing a deed that had always been frowned upon in her family—her great uncle had a lot to answer for.

"You make it sound very tempting."

"But?"

So he'd detected her hesitation. "I don't know...."

"You are getting cold feet."

He was one hundred percent correct. Despite the warmth of the balmy evening, she was most definitely getting cold feet. She drew in a deep breath, conscious of the pungent scent of jasmine on the night air. The sweet familiarity of the fragrance made the conversation she was having with Rakin seem even more surreal. "I shouldn't even be considering such a crazy invitation."

"Of course you should. It's what you want to do."

Right again.

Could he see inside her head?

Instantly all the reasons why she shouldn't go rolled through her mind. Who would follow up with Detective McDonough? With Nikki Thomas? Who would look after her mother? Her sisters? For a moment she considered that her mother had Cutter now, her sisters were both married. It would be liberating to break free of everything for a couple of days.

Enjoy herself. Have some fun. Abandon the responsibilities that were weighing her down.

Get a life.

Was it already too late? Had she forgotten how to live? Laurel

glanced up at the man who was offering her the biggest temptation of her life. His lips were still curved into a smile, the lower
one full and passionate. Her gaze lingered there. *Kiss a stranger.*
So much riskier than flirting. But oh so tempting…

She looked quickly away.

The sound of light footsteps on the balcony freed her from
making a decision. Susannah, Matt's fiancée, was bearing down
on them. Giving Rakin a curious glance, she said, "Laurel, your
presence is required. Kara's about to throw her bouquet."

Laurel's shoulders sagged with relief. Tossing Rakin a small
smile, she said, "I must go—duty summons."

"I'll be waiting for you."

He didn't need to say that he would expect an answer; that
was implicit in his intent regard. Her smile turned sultry. Flirtatious, even. She was finally getting the hang of it. "I'll hold
you to that."

A swarm of women had taken to the dance floor. Young and
old—it appeared that every unmarried woman in Charleston
wanted to catch the bouquet tonight.

Laurel's heart sank as she took in the spectacle. She came
to a dead halt. "There are already enough desperate wannabe
brides here, you don't need me to make up numbers."

"Kara specifically said she wanted you here," Susannah said
sotto voce, shepherding Laurel forward.

As they reached the outskirts of the dance floor, Elizabeth
joined them. "Hurry, Laurel. Kara's been waiting for you."

Laurel glanced from Susannah to her mother, and her tipsi-
ness evaporated. "Do I detect a conspiracy?"

"Oh, no." Though both Susannah and her mother denied it,
their eyes were stretched too wide.

Reluctantly, Laurel let her mother drag her into the center of
the group.

Out of the corner of her eye she caught a glimpse of a tall,
dark man in a beautifully tailored tuxedo. Rakin. Her head
jerked about. He was standing beside her brother Matt—and
she spotted RJ, and Daniel, Lily's husband, too. As she watched

Alan Sinclair joined them. All of them were grinning. But it was Rakin's dark gaze that brought tremors of excitement to Laurel's stomach.

I'll be waiting. The memory of his whispered words caused the excitement to rise another notch.

What answer was she going to give him?

"Laurel!"

At the sound of her mother's voice, her head whipped around guiltily.

"You need to go forward more—to the front. Kara is about to throw her bouquet."

Laurel balked. But the crowd around her had no such inhibitions. As Eli gallantly held out an arm to help Kara step elegantly onto the band's stage, Laurel was jostled forward.

From her vantage point on the stage, Kara scanned the crowd. Her gaze found Laurel, and her eyes lit up. Then she turned around.

Oh, no.

As Kara tossed the bouquet of red roses backward over her head, Laurel quickly ducked. Then she spun around to see who the lucky recipient had been of the bouquet obviously intended for her.

Elizabeth stood behind her clutching an armful of roses and wearing a bewildered expression.

"Well, congratulations, Mom, it looks like you're set to be the next bride." Taking pity on her mortified mother, Laurel placed a hand under her elbow and led her from the floor.

"Laurel, what are people going to think? Your father has only been dead for four months. Now I'm standing on a dance floor, a wedding bouquet in my arms. This is catastrophic."

Her mother needed a Get a Life list of her own, Laurel decided. She'd spent far too many years of doing the Right Thing. "Mom, stop worrying about what other people think. It's your life.... Live it. Let Kara arrange your wedding, invite your real friends to dance at it—and make Cutter a happy man. Marry him. Be happy."

"Be happy?" Elizabeth repeated. The lines around her mouth

lessened and her eyes brightened. "You're so right, darling. I will be happy. Thank you."

Laurel swallowed the lump in her throat. Was it really that easy?

Then Lily was there, too. "Great catch, Mom!"

"Oh, go on." Elizabeth's cheeks wore flags of scarlet. Yet she looked more vibrant than she had in years.

Kara arrived in a rustle of fine bridal fabric. She frowned at Laurel, who smiled back angelically.

"It was a mistake." Elizabeth shrugged apologetically to her middle daughter. "I know you intended for Laurel to catch it."

Laurel's smile broadened at the confirmation of the conspiracy she'd already suspected. Triumph at the success of her covert rebellion overtook her.

"Laurel needs a groom before she can have a wedding, so throwing her the bouquet was probably a little premature," Lily pointed out to Laurel's increasing amusement. But her relief was short-lived as Lily started scanning the men crowded around the dance floor. "Let me see. There must be someone we can introduce Laurel to. One of RJ's friends—or maybe Daniel knows someone suitable."

Again, her family was organizing her life.

"Hey—"

Kara overrode the objection Laurel was about to make. "Eli already introduced her to Rakin."

Laurel shifted uncomfortably as both her mother and Lily focused on her. "Rakin?"

"He's standing there—at the edge of the dance floor with RJ and Matt right now," offered Kara.

"Don't point." Laurel could have happily wrung her interfering sisters' necks as all eyes swung in his direction. With a touch of desperation, she begged, "And please don't stare."

"Why?" Lily was the first to turn back. "Are you interested in him?"

She flushed. "Not exactly. But nor do I want you causing the poor man any embarrassment. He's too nice for that."

"Nice? He's gorgeous!" Kara didn't mince words.

"Hey, that's the guy you were talking to so cozily on the terrace," Susannah chipped in.

"Ooh, you were on the terrace with him?" This time Brooke hounded her. "You've been holding out on us."

"I've only just met him!"

"But it sounds like you've gotten close pretty quickly." Lily raised an eyebrow.

Under the force of her family's combined interrogation, Laurel gave in. "Okay, he's invited me to go to Vegas."

"To Vegas?" It was a chorus.

"Hush, not so loud!"

"You're going, right?" That was Kara again.

"I don't know...."

"But you must."

"Or are you too busy at work?" asked Lily.

"Laurel can't use work as an excuse," piped Kara. "I know for a fact that her honeymoon was booked for the two weeks after her wedding, and I know she left those weeks open—even after the wedding was called off. There's nothing that can't be cleared from her calendar."

"I needed a break. It's been a busy few months." Laurel avoided Lily's keen eyes. She'd planned to take some time after the wedding to assess what she wanted from life. Now it looked like she was going to spend some of that time with Rakin. A dart of anticipation shafted through her. It would be fun. But what about her mother? "I promised Mom I would call Detective McDonough and arrange a meeting with him later in the wee—"

"I can do that, darling," her mother said quickly. "Don't let that stop you."

"No, I'll do it," said Brooke.

Laurel exchanged a long look with her future sister-in-law and saw the plea in her eyes. If it made Brooke feel like she was helping, that would be worth it. "That's a good idea, Brooke. Nikki Thomas might be able to help—you may want to give her a call, too."

Susannah put a hand on Laurel's arm and bowed her head

close to say softly, "I know you've been carrying a lot of the stress of the past few months, more than we probably realize. I remember it was you who called to let Matt know Elizabeth had been taken into custody."

"All of us have been under strain," Laurel responded in a low voice, so that her mother didn't hear. "I know that Matt has been incredibly worried about—generating new business to stanch the losses Jack Sinclair caused."

Susannah shrugged. "There are rumors of fresh defections all the time. But they can only be dealt with one at a time. Nothing you can do right now. You've done your bit. I know that like RJ, you've kept in close touch with the police and kept us all informed of developments. You need a break."

Then her mother was beside her. "I heard the end of that—and I agree with Susannah. Take some time off. It's your life.... Live it." Elizabeth directed a private smile to Laurel. "You deserve some fun."

"Ah, Mom." In gratitude of her mother's unexpected understanding, Laurel flung her arms around the older woman. Coming from the always correct Elizabeth, the words meant a great deal. "Thank you!"

At the back of her mind had been the thought that her mother would need her. With her other daughters now married, Laurel was the obvious choice to cosset her after her traumatic arrest for Reginald's murder. But her sisters—and Susannah and Brooke—had relieved her of the responsibility. The final—and most weighty—mental block had been removed. There was no reason for Laurel to decline Rakin's invitation.

"Now you have no excuse," Kara said with satisfaction—and Laurel didn't even try to stop the laughter that overflowed as her sister's words echoed her own thoughts.

Instead she said, "I should be mad at you. But how can I be? It's your wedding day—and you're matchmaking as many of us as you can."

Kara looked mystified at that. "What do you mean?"

"You can take all the credit—since you talked Eli into introducing Rakin to me."

But Kara was shaking her head. "Honestly, it wasn't me."
Her sister's reply left Laurel lost for words.

Laurel came toward him, her step light and buoyant, causing
the silver-gray fabric of her dress to swirl around her long legs.
Her lips were curved up and her face alight with what Rakin
could only describe as happiness. It gave her an inner glow, and
accentuated her beauty… and his heart missed a beat.

"Excuse me." Without a backward look to the group he'd
been conversing with about the state of the shipping industry,
he went to meet her. "Would you like to dance?"

She nodded.

A hand clapped his shoulder; then Matt's voice broke in.
"Rakin, we'll catch up again, I'd like to find out more about
some of those Diyafan market players."

For once, money and business were not at the forefront of
Rakin's mind. He said something to Matt that must have satisfied the other man, but he didn't take his eyes off Laurel.

He sensed he was walking a thin line.

Pleasure was threatening to overwhelm business. It would do
him well to take care and not to confuse his priorities. Then he
came to his senses. He was Rakin Whitcomb Abdellah. He controlled a billion-dollar business empire. His grandfather ruled
Diyafa. He'd never been the kind of man to let his heart rule his
head. Never.

Laurel Kincaid was business. He would not forget that.

"Let's dance," he said gruffly, and swept the most beautiful
woman he'd ever met into his arms.

The rhythm of the jazz was rich and deep, smoldering with
the passions of the South.

Laurel's body brushed against his, and involuntarily Rakin's
arms tightened. She was so soft and lush and incredibly feminine. A man could forget his resolve.

She stiffened, and he instantly eased his hold.

Business, he reminded himself.

"What's Flynn doing on the dance floor?"

She'd come to a standstill, and Rakin followed her gaze. He

might've been considering letting pleasure overwhelm him, but Laurel clearly had her feet firmly on the ground. The ring bearer from the wedding ceremony was weaving his way determinedly through the dancing guests. It hadn't been his close hold that had caused her to stiffen, Rakin realized with relief. It was the child. Wearing a pair of sky-blue summer pajamas with his dark hair slicked down, Rakin suspected the kid was supposed to be tucked up in bed.

"Hey!" Laurel slipped out of his arms in a whisper of silver satin, and caught the youngster's hand.

The boy's face lit up. "Aunt Laurel, you didn't catch the flowers Aunt Kara threw at you."

"You were watching?"

"When's Aunt Kara going to cut the cake? She said I could have some."

"This handsome rapscallion is Matt's son, my nephew, Flynn." Laurel told Rakin. Then she turned her attention back to the little boy. "I don't think they'll be cutting the cake for a while. Shouldn't you be in bed?"

He nodded, his blue eyes round with innocence. "Pamela told me a bedtime story."

"Mom's housekeeper," Laurel explained to Rakin. To Flynn, she said, "You should be asleep."

"I was excited...and I want some cake."

"So you escaped." Laurel grinned at him conspiratorially. "I tell you what, you can have one dance with us, then I'll take you back to bed. I promise I'll save you a ginormous piece of cake and give it to you in the morning. Deal?"

Flynn looked uncertain.

"Take it," Rakin advised. "You won't get a better offer tonight."

He held out a hand at a height Flynn could reach. Flynn's eyes lit up as he recognized the game. "High five," he crowed and slapped Rakin's hand.

"Deal," said Rakin.

Rakin watched with amusement as Flynn started to gyrate his limbs alongside them. He had the lack of inhibitions of the very young and threw his heart into every move. But, by the time the melody had faded, he looked exhausted.

A short, silver-haired woman hurried up to claim him.

"He gave me the slip," she told Laurel, after passing a lightning-swift glance over Rakin. "I'll put him back to bed."

As Flynn gave them a wave over his shoulder, the music struck up again. Rakin moved forward and gathered Laurel back into his arms. She didn't protest.

"Pamela, I take it?"

Laurel nodded. "Sorry, I should've introduced you, but I imagined she wanted to get Flynn off to bed before Susannah starts to worry about him."

The rapid once-over the housekeeper had given him had told Rakin that she was clearly an established part of the Kincaid family. It wasn't only Flynn and Susannah she was looking out for—there'd been a warning in that glance: *Be honorable, or have me to deal with.* Rakin smiled to himself. Pamela had nothing to fear....

Against his shoulder, Laurel murmured, "It's wonderful to see Flynn looking so much better, even though he's still thin."

Spinning her deftly around to avoid colliding with a couple who had come to a standstill in the midst of dancers, Rakin said, "He's been ill?"

"Very. For the past two months Matt and Susannah have had to be careful about allowing him out—to limit his exposure to germs. But he's had the green flag—he's well on his way to full recovery. Tonight is the biggest crowd he's been in since he got ill."

"No wonder he's excited. He's a great kid."

"I think so." Laurel laughed up at him. "We all do."

Her green eyes sparkled like precious gems. Emeralds. A sultan's prize. Rakin dismissed the fanciful notion. "Your nephew was right—you didn't catch the bridal bouquet."

He'd been amused how she'd lithely leapt out of the way of the bunch of flowers the bride had tossed at her. If he had any doubt about the veracity of her claim earlier that she wasn't looking for love, he certainly believed it now. She couldn't have chosen a more public place to make her lack of interest in romantic commitment clear. Laurel might as well have taken out an ad in the society pages to proclaim she wasn't interested in marriage.

"No, I didn't catch it."

Despite her polite smile, and the carefully enunciated "No," the dangerous glint he detected in her eyes told another story. The laugh started low in his belly. He did his best to contain it—to no avail. Her glint turned to a glare. Biting back his mirth, before they became the focus of attention of those other than her two sisters-in-law, who were trying to look as though they were not following their dance, he said, "I thought every maid of honor dreamed of being the next bride."

"Not me. I want—"

"Excitement...adventure."

That wrested a reluctant laugh from her. "You whipped the words right out of my mouth."

Rakin forgot all about her watching relatives. His gaze dropped down to her lips.

Why hadn't he noticed how perfectly they were shaped? The flowing curve of the top lip was a work of art, while the plump bottom one promised pure sin.

Instantly the mood changed, vibrating with suppressed tension. Her annoyance, his teasing, their laughter, all vanished. Rakin was no longer conscious of anyone in the room—except the woman in his arms.

Her lips parted, and she drew a quick breath.

"I'll do it," she told him in a rush. "I'll come with you to Vegas."

He hadn't expected a reply so soon.

He'd been summoning his powers of persuasion. Now there was no need. Tension Rakin hadn't even known existed eased. Had he really believed she would refuse? The way his muscles relaxed suggested he hadn't been as certain of Laurel as he would've liked.

His gaze lifted—and clashed with eyes alive with excitement. "This is only the start of the adventure," he promised her.

Triumph filled him. Laurel Kincaid was going to make the perfect trophy wife....

Four

Laurel's expression grew increasingly bemused as the limousine that had collected them from McCarran International Airport cruised along Las Vegas's famous Strip.

"There's no where else in the world like Vegas," Rakin told Laurel, watching as she tried to assimilate the staggering visual impact of the city.

"It's like a Hollywood set." She twisted around to look out of a small window. "I don't remember any of this from back when I was here as a child."

"Then I shall have to show you everything."

"I can't wait." Even under the tawdry neon lights of the limousine interior her eyes shone with excitement.

By the time the white limousine nosed into the forecourt of the luxury hotel he'd booked for them, Rakin half-regretted not reserving a suite in one of the more over-the-top resorts.

"There are more outrageous hotels." Rakin stood at the door as she emerged from the limousine. "But I thought you might appreciate somewhere more peaceful when a retreat from the madness becomes necessary."

Laurel clambered out to stand beside him. Dressed in a pair of white linen trousers and a taupe shell top she looked cool and comfortable. Pulling her sunglasses down from where they rested on the top of her head to shade her eyes, she said, "I can't imagine that 'peace' is a word one often associates with Vegas."

"Believe it or not, there are peaceful places to be found not far from here."

"Like where?"

"Eli and I came here a couple of times during vacations while we were at Harvard. The desert is vast and undisturbed. Beautiful. Sometimes we'd hike through Red Rock Canyon."

There was a long pause as she examined him.

"You were homesick," she said after a moment, a peculiar note in her voice. "You missed Diyafa...and your family."

Rakin didn't reply. But he was relieved he couldn't see her expression behind the dark, opaque veil of the sunglasses. He suspected it would be too kind for comfort. Pity was the very last thing he wanted from this woman he was determined to marry.

He certainly wasn't going to explain the complicated relationship he shared with his family. The overwhelming expectations of his grandfather that had started when he was barely out the cradle and set him forever at odds with his cousins. His father's fits of anger, which had caused his mother to weep inconsolably. His own growing resentment against his father that had increased after he'd been sent to boarding school in England. And the lingering guilt for abandoning his mother to deal with his father which had not been eased by the bravely stoic letters written in her perfect, flowing handwriting.

By his thirteenth birthday his parents had been dead—and by the time he and Eli had first hiked Red Rock Canyon they'd been buried for a decade.

So Laurel was wrong. The pilgrimages he and Eli had made to Vegas had nothing to do with missing Diyafa—or his family.

No need for her to know there were no nostalgic, happy memories for him to hanker after—or at least, not until he successfully talked her into marrying him to nullify Prince Ahmeer's latest round of threats. For now, he'd promised his Southern rebel fun and adventure—and he intended to ensure she experienced plenty of both.

Cupping her elbow, he ushered her in the porter's wake into the quiet, discreet luxury of the hotel lobby. A hostess rushed forward and offered them each a glass of champagne. Before Rakin could refuse, Laurel shook her head.

She flashed him a rueful glance. "I want a clear head—I'm not missing a moment of this."

Her humor caused his mood to lighten. "I like you tipsy," he said softly.

A flush swept along her cheekbones. "It's not gentlemanly of you to remind me."

Coming from his lady-turned-rebel, the statement caused him to chuckle. "I thought you were tired of social constraints?"

"Not so tired that I'll get tipsy again any time soon."

They'd reached the reservations desk. Laurel leaned forward to answer a question from the reservations clerk and Rakin was instantly all too aware of the taut, lean lines of her body. Her bare arms rested on the polished counter and she spread her hands drawing his attention to the rings that decorated her graceful fingers.

Her ring finger was bare. His gaze lingered on the band of pale skin that evidenced her broken engagement to Eli.

A light, summery scent floated to him. Rakin inhaled deeply. Could one get tipsy on perfume? he wondered, then shook off the absurd notion.

This was about business.

Not about Laurel's perfume. Not about the pleasure that her company brought. Hard to believe he'd only met her yesterday. It had been tough to convince her to come away today. Once she'd accepted his invitation, she'd immediately tried to buy time. She'd suggested the following weekend. Rakin couldn't risk her changing her mind. He'd pushed until she'd capitulated. He'd won. She'd agreed to two days. He had two days in which to convince her to marry him—and secure his position in Gifts of Gold, the company of which he'd been appointed CEO.

Two days...

He feared it wouldn't be enough. He'd have to tempt her to play longer.

Once they'd completed the brief check-in formalities for the penthouse suite he'd reserved, Rakin wasted no time setting his plan of attack into action. Bending his head, he murmured, "I thought we might go exploring."

Laurel had taken her sunglasses off, and without the shielding screen her green eyes sparkled up at him. "Sounds great—I can't wait."

Some of her joyous enthusiasm appeared to be rubbing off on him because Rakin couldn't stop himself from smiling back at her. "Then there's no time to waste."

Laurel very soon discovered that Las Vegas did indeed have spectacular sights.

In fact, her mind was quite boggled by the end of the first hour. The interior of the Luxor hotel was concealed in an immense black glass pyramid guarded by a giant crouching sphinx. But inside, instead of the treasures of ancient Egypt, Laurel was amazed to find the reconstructed bow of the giant Titanic complete with a lifeboat. As she and Rakin wandered through the installations, Laurel was moved by the stories of the last hours of the crew and passengers on the ship's tragic maiden voyage.

The Liberace Museum, by contrast, with its collection of resplendent, unashamed kitsch, made her giggle. The glittering mirror-tiled piano and the rhinestone-covered grand were wonderfully over the top. On catching sight of Rakin's appalled expression as he inspected the famed red, white and blue hotpants suit, a mischievous impulse overtook her.

She eyed the black jeans and dazzling white T-shirt he wore, then leaned close to whisper, "I think your wardrobe should include one of those outfits."

"It would cause quite a stir in Diyafa if I ever wore such a garment. A national disaster, in fact. There are still some conservative elements who would never recover from the sight of Prince Ahmeer Al-Abdellah's grandson sporting hot pants." Across the narrow space separating them, their eyes met, and for one charged moment a connection pulsed between them.... Then it passed and hilarity broke.

"Enough of museums," said Rakin, reaching for her hand when they'd sufficiently regained their composure. "I think we need a little more action."

A shock of surprise rushed through her as his hand closed around hers. The clasp was warm and firm. Rakin showed no sign that the gesture had affected him to the same extent—he was striding purposefully forward, seemingly unaware that they were holding hands like a pair of lovers.

She was making too much of it.

Rakin was treating her with the kind of warm friendship she craved. So why spoil it by imagining intimacies that didn't exist? She should take the gesture at face value and go with the flow. No need to overanalyze the camaraderie that was developing between them. That, too, was part of breaking free.

Easier said than done.

Laurel couldn't dampen her awareness of their linked hands, and she finally slid her hand out of his and came to a stop when a familiar skyline materialized ahead.

"New York?" The Statue of Liberty and the Empire State Building were interspersed with other landmark buildings. This was his idea of more action? But she had to admit the replica skyscrapers were impressive. "Oh, wow, there's the Brooklyn Bridge."

"The buildings are about a third of actual life size," Rakin informed her. "But it's not the sight of the buildings that will give you the adrenaline rush I promised."

"New York–New York? A rollercoaster?" she gasped moments later.

"Why not?" He shot her a taunting look. "Scared?"

Even if she had been, his all-too-male I-dare-you expression would have forced her to bite her lip. She'd told him that she craved adventure, so there was no way she was going to back down now.

She stuck up her chin. "Of course not. I love rides."

Love was a slight exaggeration. She hadn't been on a ride in years. A quick calculation left Laurel astonished by exactly how long it had been since she'd last experienced such a ride.

Where had the years gone? And, more to the point, where had her sense of fun gone? When had she let herself become so staid...so boring? When had she forgotten that there was a world out there beyond the confines of her family and the demands of public relations for The Kincaid Group?

"At least I did love them once upon a time," she added a little more dubiously, hoping that her youthful infatuation with roller coasters would return by the time they reached the start.

"The track twists between the skyscrapers—" Rakin jerked a thumb in the direction of the buildings "—rising to two hundred feet between the buildings."

"Thanks! That's very comforting to know."

"It reaches speeds of over sixty-five miles per hour—and there's a place where the train drops a hundred and forty-four feet."

The last snippet of information gave her pause. "Are you deliberately trying to frighten me?"

"I'd never do such a thing." But the twitch of his lips gave him away.

Humor rushed through her like champagne bubbles rising. "Of course you wouldn't."

"Any adventure needs a good case of butterflies to start it off—dread heightens anticipation."

That sealed it. "You are trying to scare me—wicked man!" She advanced on him, brandishing her purse.

Rakin grabbed her wrists before she could take a swing at him, his shoulders shaking with mirth. "Are you having fun?"

She stilled. Lowering her purse, she glanced quickly around. How quickly she'd forgotten to behave with the dignity that befitted the eldest Kincaid daughter. Embarrassment swept over her; then she banished it. Who amongst the hordes knew her? And who would even care? Freedom followed in a dizzying burst.

With wonder she said, "Yes, I'm having a fantastic time."

She skipped into line beside Rakin.

"The trains look like yellow New York taxicabs—complete

with hoods and headlights." She thought they looked delightful, and not at all frightening.

"We're in luck, we're going to get front seats," said Rakin, as an attendant ushered them forward.

Once seated in the front row with the restraints securely fastened, Laurel's enthusiasm waned at the unobstructed view of the red track ahead. Luck? Maybe not. As the train started forward her heart rose into her throat. "Rakin, what recklessness possessed me to do this?"

"You're going to love it." Rakin's eyes gleamed with humor.

But Laurel was no longer so sure. Ahead of them the track climbed to the height of Everest. The train chugged up, and with each foot they progressed the butterflies that Rakin had stirred up broke free of their chrysalis in Laurel's stomach and started to flutter madly.

They crested the top of the rise.

Laurel caught a glimpse of the Las Vegas skyline laid out in front of them. In the distance, hills undulated in a long curve.

The train gathered momentum.

"Oh, my heavens!"

Rakin's hand closed around hers. Before she could catch her breath, they were hurtling down. Then they were rising.... The next plunge downward left Laurel's stomach somewhere in the sky above them. Air left her lungs in a silent scream. She could hear Rakin laughing beside her.

Ahead, high above, she glimpsed a complete loop of red track.

"Noooo..." she moaned.

She gripped Rakin's hand until her fingers hurt.

The train swooped into the upward curve of the loop. Tension, tight and terrifying, clawed at her body. Laurel could hear screams behind her. For a disconcerting instant the world turned over, hovered, blue sky flashing below them in a spinning blur; then everything righted itself. They sped down into a series of tight heart-hammering curves that pressed her thigh up against Rakin's.

A wild euphoria exploded inside her.

The Statue of Liberty flashed past, and Laurel found herself laughing. Moments later the train shot into womb-like darkness.

Rakin murmured something beside her, but the sound of her heart hammering in her head drowned it out. Her hand was still gripping his, and Laurel realized her nails must be digging into his palm. Hot, awkward embarrassment flooded her.

"Sorry," she muttered, letting go.

"It didn't worry me."

"I appreciated the loan," she said lightly, and Rakin chuckled in response.

Gradually her eyes adjusted until she was able to make out lights and shapes of an underground station. Noise surrounded her—the attendant's cheery greeting as he freed her from the safety restraint, the clatter of trains on the track.

When they emerged from the front seats Laurel's legs felt like Jell-O. But sheer exhilaration propelled her forward.

"You were right, I loved it!"

Laurel didn't care that she sounded breathless as she spun around to grin giddily at Rakin through the cloud of hair that had whipped around her face during the thrill ride. Right now she felt high on joy—prepared to take on the world. Anything he wanted to throw at her, she was game for. The surge of strength—the feeling that she could do whatever she wanted— was supremely empowering. Getting a life...

Yet Rakin wasn't even breathing hard. And, what's more, not even one dark hair had strayed out of place. A wicked urge to see him look a little rumpled stole through her.

"Again," she challenged. "I want to do it again."

It was evening, and the observation deck on the fiftieth floor of Paris Las Vegas's Eiffel Tower was deserted.

Rakin felt Laurel go still beneath the hand he'd placed across her back to usher her from the glass elevator.

"How beautiful," she breathed, and gestured to the warm, dusky light that turned the observation deck to burnished bronze. "It's like being in a capsule of gold."

He watched indulgently as she picked her way along the observation deck, her high heels tapping against the steel, to take in the dramatic view of the city stretching to the purpling mountains in the distance.

Laurel came to a stop and the fiery glow of the sinking rays lit the hair piled on top of her head, throwing the elegant black strapless dress she wore into sharp relief. Against the backdrop of the sunset she looked like a goddess waiting to be summoned back from earth.

"It has been the most extraordinary day," she said breaking the spell that held him entranced. "Recklessness drove me to accept your invitation."

His gaze fixed on her, he said, "Recklessness?"

"I gave in to the temptation to break the Winthrop ban on gambling." She spread her arms wide to embrace the view. "But I didn't expect this. I've no idea how you'll intend to keep the action—and the surprises—rolling tomorrow."

"Don't worry, there's plenty more to see," Rakin told her, and closed the gap between them. "Dolphins. Sharks. Lions. We haven't even started on the animal encounters."

The sideways glance she gave him held a very human glint of mischief. "Or we could try the thrill rides at the Stratosphere Tower."

Rakin groaned. "I've created a monster. Three rides on New York-New York, not to mention braving the Speed roller coaster at NASCAR Cafe this afternoon—and you still crave more?"

"I never realized what I was missing out on—I should've put *Ride a roller coaster* on my list."

"You made a list of things to do in Vegas?" Had he left anything out?

But before he could ask, Laurel colored and averted her gaze. A gust of wind blew a tendril of hair that had escaped across her cheek, and she brushed it back. "It's not exactly about Vegas."

"But you have a list?" he pressed.

Laurel gave a small nod.

Her reticence intrigued him. "So what's on it?"

"I can't remember," she mumbled and her flush turned a deep shade of crimson.

Laurel Kincaid was a terrible liar.

"Now you've woken my curiosity."

She muttered something. Then she pointed. "Look, isn't that pretty?"

Rakin allowed himself to be distracted. Far below, the Strip was starting to light up as Las Vegas prepared for the coming night like a showgirl dressing for an after-dark performance.

"Oh, and look there!"

Rakin's followed her finger. Three rings of fountains had leapt out from the lake in front of the Bellagio, the high plumes illuminated by bright light.

A glance at Laurel revealed that she was transfixed.

"We'll see the fountains from closer up during dinner." He'd booked a table at Picasso specifically so Laurel could enjoy the display.

"From up here it gives another perspective. This tower looks like every picture I've seen of the real Eiffel Tower. It's amazing."

Rakin hadn't moved his attention from her face. Her changing expressions revealed every emotion she experienced. Wonder. Excitement.

For one wild moment he considered what her features would look like taut with desire, her dark-red hair spread loose across his pillow....

He shut his eyes to block out the tantalizing vision.

"So have you ever visited Paris or Venice? I'd love to visit both."

To his relief her voice interrupted his torrid imaginings. "Not Venice," he said, his voice hoarser than normal. "But I've been to Paris often—my mother loved Paris. She attended the école Nationale Supérieure des Beaux-Arts on the Left Bank across from the Louvre."

"She's an artist?"

Rakin nodded. "She was—she died."

"I'm sorry. I didn't mean to reopen—"

The remorse on Laurel's face made him say quickly, "Don't worry. Talking about her doesn't upset me. She's been gone a long time. Most people avoid mentioning her—it makes them uncomfortable." It ran contrary to his own need to talk about his mother, to remember her as she'd been. Talented. Mercurial. Loving. "My father died, too."

"You must miss them both."

The memories of his father were much more ambivalent. But there was no need for Laurel to discover the undercurrents that lurked beneath the mask he carefully preserved. So he focused on the facts. "My parents met in Paris."

"How romantic."

It was the conclusion he'd expected—no, led—her to draw. His mother had also thought it romantic. His father had called it fate. Neither romance nor fate had been enough in the end.

The night they'd met, Laurel had asked him whether he believed in fate....

It was Rakin's turn to turn away. The sunset blazed along the skyline.

"It was spring time." The words forced themselves past the tightness in his throat.

"Even more romantic."

Without looking at Laurel, he continued to weave the tale that had become a legend of tabloid lies. "My parents returned to Diyafa for a lavish wedding, and I was born less than a year later." That had been the end of the romance and the beginning of his mother's harsh reality. As his father had the male heir he wanted, the sheik no longer needed to woo his wife. Duty, rather than desire, had kept his parents together until their deaths.

Rakin found he had a startlingly intense need to see Laurel's face. Forcing a smile, he swiveled on his heel. Her eyes held a soft, dreamy look. "I'd love to visit Paris in the spring."

"And walk along the Seine." Rakin knew all the clichés.

"How wonderful to fall in love in a city that celebrates lovers."

"That too." His parents' story had great spin, Rakin decided savagely. The lie still lived.

She tipped her head to one side and the last rays of the sun glinted off the diamond earrings that dangled against her neck. "And I'd like to visit Diyafa, too."

It was the cue he needed.

But instead of telling her about his grandfather's plan to oust him, Rakin glanced at his watch. "Our table booking is not far off. I'll tell you more about the country of my birth over dinner—and afterwards we'll do what everyone does in Vegas—gamble."

As he'd anticipated, the dreaminess evaporated, then she said, "The higher the stakes, the better. Don't forget I have every intention of gambling the night away."

The stakes were rising for him, too. So why had he not taken the opportunity that she'd offered? Why hadn't he told her what he needed? A wife to neutralize his grandfather's threats? A part of him recognized that he was being drawn into the fantasy he'd created for a woman he found himself liking more and more with every hour that passed.

A whole day had already passed. Too soon they would be leaving Vegas and the opportunity to negotiate her cooperation would be forever lost. He could no longer delay.

It was time to return to reality.

And get himself a wife.

Picasso at the Bellagio was one of Rakin's favorite restaurants.

"Bellagio is a village on the shores of Lake Como," Rakin told Laurel after their plates from the main course had been cleared away, and dessert menus left for them to leisurely peruse. He'd secured a table overlooking a balcony and the lake beyond so that Laurel would have a good view of the fountains dancing to the music.

"George Clooney has a villa at Lake Como, doesn't he?" Laurel's smile had an impish quality as she turned from the fountains back to him. "I'd better add that to the exotic places I want to visit."

"You're that keen to meet Clooney?" Rakin wasn't sure whether to laugh or be annoyed by her mischievous interest in the movie star—especially since before his grandfather's latest threats he'd been as eager as Clooney to avoid marriage and babies. And despite conceding to marriage, babies were forever off the agenda—not that his grandfather needed to know that.

She gave him an artless glance. "Isn't every woman?"

This time he did laugh. "You're a tease!"

The artlessness evaporated. Only to be replaced with a sincerity that he found infinitely more disturbing. "Not really," she confided, leaning forward and lowering her voice. "Only with you. I've never flirted in my life—yet with you it's easy."

Her candor was disarming. And the husky note in her voice thrummed through him, playing all his nerve endings to devastating effect. He didn't dare allow his eyes to stray lower in case her action had caused the provocative neckline to reveal even more tantalizing glimpses of skin. Instead, Rakin unfolded his napkin, placed it on his lap and said lightly, "I thought all Southern women were born flirts."

"Not me." She glanced down at the dessert menu in front of her.

He could've argued that she was learning fast. Yet Rakin suspected that she had little idea of the effect she was having on him. He was more interested in her than he'd been in any woman for a long, long time. At first, his interest had been piqued by Eli's comment that she'd make the perfect wife for the predicament he found himself in. Then he'd found himself really liking her. And now—

Well, now, his interest was growing in leaps and bounds.

Impossibly long lashes fluttered up as she glanced up from the menu. "I've been attempting to flirt with you because... I feel safe."

The naked honesty of her statement shook him. All attempts at maintaining the lighthearted banter deserted him.

"Aren't you going to order dessert?"

To his surprise, Rakin realized he'd set his menu down on the table. But he couldn't stop thinking about what Laurel had said.

"You find it easy to flirt with me?"

"It must be because you're Eli's friend." This time the smile she gave him was sweet rather than flirtatious. "I know you're trustworthy."

The brief flash of annoyance he felt surprised him. "Because Eli said so?"

"Well, he never actually said I could trust you. But he wouldn't be friends with you if he didn't trust you implicitly—Eli's not the kind of man to waste time on liars and frauds."

"So you accept Eli's endorsement—rather than your own instincts?"

Laurel hesitated.

"No, don't think too much." Placing his elbows on the edge of the table, he steepled his hands and gazed at her over the top. "I want an instinctual response—not one vetted for kindness."

"I do trust you."

The expression in her eyes told him she'd astonished herself. Keeping his attention fixed on her, he demanded, "Why?"

"I don't know." She said it slowly, her gaze flickering away, then back to him as though drawn by some power she could not resist.

"It surprises you." He made it a statement.

"Yes." Again, she hesitated. Then she said in a rush. "I've never made friends easily—my family has always been enough."

"And Eli."

"And Eli," she agreed. "But that was different."

The sharp blade of envy that pierced Rakin was unexpected, and he thrust it away before the feeling could fester and turn to poisonous jealousy. "In what way?"

"We were the same age. He lived nearby while we were growing up."

"You were being kind."

"Maybe. At first. But the friendship was between equals—I got every bit as much out of it as Eli did. Remember, I didn't have other close friends."

He nodded his head. "I can understand that."

"I suppose the reason I trust you is because I feel comfortable with you. I can't remember the last time I laughed so much."

Pulling a face, he said, "I must be a clown."

"No! You are anything but a clown."

He'd been joking, trying to make her smile again. But her rapid rise to his defense made him realize that Laurel was concerned she might have offended him. Too kind for her own good. She could have no idea that his emotions had been forged in a crucible guaranteed to produce solid steel. If she had, no doubt she would not be nearly as comfortable in his company.

Nor would she be contemplating visiting Diyafa. Her comment about adding Lake Como to the places she wanted to visit probably meant her list included the destinations to which she wanted to travel. Las Vegas might only have been the start of it. He'd work on convincing her that Diyafa should be next on her list.

"It is true," she was saying earnestly before he could question her about what other places were on her list. "I can't remember when last I felt as lighthearted and carefree as I have today."

"I will take that as a compliment."

Under the weight of his gaze, he watched the faint wash of color warm her cheeks.

Laurel dropped her gaze to the menu. "You know, I've no idea what to choose."

Rakin's mouth curved into a smile. "I'm going to have ice cream."

"Ice cream?"

"Something cool in this weather. But you can't go wrong with anything on the menu."

"My meal was fabulous."

"Every dish on the menu is inspired by places where Picasso lived in Spain and the South of France."

His comment prompted Laurel to gaze at a Picasso painting on the nearest wall. "What did your mother paint?"

"She created huge abstract canvases. Mostly inspired by the desert landscape." His father had hated them. The sheikh had wanted his wife to paint realistic portrayals of the Diyafan Desert. His mother had preferred broad sweeps of color that invited the viewer to put their own interpretation on the landscape.

"Do you paint, too?"

Rakin shook his head. "I studied business—although I will confess that I majored in classical studies in my undergraduate degree so I'm not a complete philistine." A smile tugged at his mouth.

"Philistine?" She smiled back at him. "I never thought that for a moment. Why classical studies?"

The curve of her lips promised him untold delights. Rakin forced himself to glance up. "You can't grow up in a place like Diyafa and not be aware of ancient history—but I also loved the old legends. Greek, Roman, Egyptian—Diyafa has some wonderful legends, too."

"Which is your favorite legend?"

There was only one answer he could give. "In present company, I'd have to say the story of Daphne and Apollo."

Laurel wrinkled her nose at him. "Why? Didn't she get turned into a tree?"

"A laurel tree."

Her eyes brightened with laughter. "You're making that up."

Rakin shook his head. "Apollo used the leaves to weave himself a wreath—and that's how a laurel wreath became a symbol of victory."

"Not much of a victory since the woman he loved had been turned into a tree."

"And even hollower, when you consider that she felt nothing for him—she was fleeing his pursuit."

"Poor Apollo." She glanced at him through her lashes.

Heat blasted through him. And Rakin resisted the impulse to tell him that if she was any more skilled a flirt, every man in the world would be in mortal danger.

"Have you decided what you want to order?" he asked instead.

"Chocolate—rich chocolate. I'll go with the restaurant's recommendation. And then I want to gamble."

Rakin couldn't help grinning at her reckless, single-minded determination.

"I haven't forgotten—we'll gamble all night long."

* * *

The hush that hung over the casino was broken from time to time by the clatter of chips and the muted exchange of voices as bets were placed. Silent waitresses glided past with trays of complimentary drinks. By invitation only, this was the domain of the rich, the famous…and the dedicated gamblers. And Laurel was growing to dread the sound of the chips being raked across the green baize.

Around the roulette table where she and Rakin had settled, several stacks of chips were growing to skyscraper heights. But, along with the thin man sitting opposite them and nursing a whisky with increasingly desperate eyes as his pile dwindled, Laurel was losing.

And her stomach had started to churn with disquiet. She'd lost at least five thousand dollars of Rakin's money in the first ten minutes, and a fair bit of her own after she'd absolutely refused to accept more chips from him. What damage would a whole night's gambling do to Rakin's fortune—and her own? "I'm starting to think Grandfather was right," she told Rakin in a low aside.

"Your Winthrop grandfather?"

Laurel nodded. "He considered gambling a curse."

"One you hoped to break tonight?"

"Hmm." She considered that. Had she believed that by winning on the tables she'd be proving that she could break the old taboo? Had she wanted to overturn—even by a small win— the curse of impoverishment that gambling, along with bad investments, had caused the Winthrops to suffer in the past? She wasn't sure. "I don't think my reasons were quite so inspired. I was probably more determined to try something that my family disapproved of—totally the wrong reason to do anything."

Rakin chuckled, attracting a glare from the gambler losing across the table.

Leaning closer to him, she whispered, "But I've already lost far more than I intended of the chips you gave me—and what I added." Laurel gestured to what remained of the stack beside her. "I'm seeing no evidence of any return."

"Spoken like a cool-headed businesswoman."

She slid him a searching glance. "I appear to share that trait with you, too—you haven't even placed one bet yet."

"I don't gamble."

"For religious reasons?"

"It's bad business. I don't like the odds—I prefer to put down money when I am confident of a healthy return."

"Now who's the cool-headed businessman?"

They exchanged smiles.

The croupier called for bets. Laurel hesitated, then shook her head.

Rakin touched her arm. "We're disturbing the players. Time for us to move on, I think."

At Rakin's whisper, Laurel slid off the stool she'd been perched on, and picked up her purse with some relief. "So much for my grand plan to gamble all night."

"You may discover your second wind after you've had a breather."

"I doubt it." She flicked him a wan smile. "What I have discovered is how fast one can lose money on the tables. I never understood how easy it is." And it had given her some sympathy for the black-sheep Winthrop.

Once out of the stilted silence of the exclusive casino, the bustling, busy vibe of Vegas was back with vengeance. Slot machines chimed all around them, their colorful displays flashing brightly. The sick sensation in Laurel's stomach started to subside.

They found an alcove in the lounge, and Laurel sank onto a plush seat. Rakin gave an order to a cocktail waitress, then joined her on the wide cushion.

"I think my grandfather would've approved of you."

"The same grandfather who brokered your mother's marriage to your father?"

Laurel nodded. "The very same."

"And why do you think he would have approved of me?"

"According to my mother, he did his very best to repair the

Winthrop family fortune in any way he could before he hit on the idea of the marriage to a Kincaid. It was an absolute rule in my grandfather's house that none of his children were allowed to gamble. Mom said that he was furious when his eldest brother lost Captain's Watch after betting on the horses."

"Captain's Watch?"

"The Winthrop family beach house." It had been in the family since the eighteen hundreds. "Grandfather Winthrop paid Dad a visit shortly after Mom and Dad were married—and Dad agreed to do his best to buy it back. I believe it wasn't easy, and it cost him a small fortune. But it was worth every cent." Laurel could visualize the view from the wide windows of the beach house out to the sea. When her father's will was read, Laurel discovered that her father had known exactly how much she loved the beach house: he'd left it to her in his will. "We spent endless summer vacations there. It's one of my favorite places."

"Then you must share it with me one day."

Before Laurel could respond, the waitress returned with a glass of champagne and a frosted cola on a silver tray.

Laurel eyed the glass, then slid Rakin an amused glance. "You're not intending to get me tipsy, are you?"

Rakin looked a little uncomfortable, and she instantly regretted teasing him.

"No, no," he denied as he signed for the drinks. "I wanted to remind you that despite your losses on the roulette table, today is all about fun—it's meant to be a time for new experiences. I wouldn't deliberately set out to get you drunk."

Laurel touched his arm.

"Sorry, that was a joke. It was in very bad taste. Of course I don't believe you're trying to get me tipsy. Why would you?"

Laurel's perception was chillingly acute, Rakin decided. He'd hoped a couple of glasses of champagne would make her more malleable.

She leaned forward, and the movement caused light to shimmer across the bare skin above the strapless black gown. It took willpower not to let his eyes linger on the smooth flesh, the kind of willpower he'd been practicing all night.

"Thank you so much for taking the time to come with me to Vegas," she was saying, and he was conscious of the feather-light caress of her fingers against his jacket. "I am having fun."

Ignoring the urge to stroke that pearlescent skin, Rakin reminded himself fiercely that this wasn't a date—it was a business meeting. And it was past time he put his proposal to her. "Las Vegas has met your expectations?"

She lifted her hand, and took a small sip of the bubbling wine, then set the glass down. She smiled warmly at him. "It's been much better! And that makes me appreciate your company all the more. I do realize you're a busy man—and you're getting nothing out of this."

He hesitated.

The pause stretched too long, and her smile froze.

"Actually there is something I want to ask of you," he murmured.

Wariness dulled the sparkle in her emerald eyes. "You want something from me."

Rakin hesitated, searching for the right words.

"Is it sex?"

He blinked. Sex? Had he betrayed himself moments ago?

"Is that why you invited me to Vegas? Was that all that today was about?" she accused scooting away along the seat. "Softening me up to get me into bed?"

He couldn't deny that he'd been purposely softening her up. Hell, he'd wanted her to be receptive. But not for…sex.

"I thought you were different."

Laurel was already on her feet, gathering up her purse. In a moment she was going to walk away and leave him sitting here like a fool. And the opportunity would be gone.

"Not sex," he said quickly.

But she didn't halt.

"Laurel…don't go!" He reached forward and caught her hand. Her fingers were stiff with outrage. Before she could yank her fingers free and storm away, he said, "Sex is not what I'm after. Sit down. Listen to my proposition—it has advantages for your family."

Her fingers stopped wriggling. "A business proposition?"

"Yes." Rakin knew it was now or never. "I want you to marry me."

"What?"

Laurel couldn't believe she'd heard Rakin right.

Shocked, she sank back onto the padded cushions in the recesses of the alcove and stared at the stark figure in the formal suit, his shirt pristine white and collar crisp and crease-free. A beautifully knotted narrow tie completed the picture.

He didn't look insane.

He looked dark, intense...and utterly gorgeous. Her heart skipped a beat. Scanning his face she took in the taut cheekbones, the lack of humor in his eyes. There were no signs of the fun companion who'd entertained her all day long.

"You're serious."

"Completely." Challenge glinted in that enigmatic gaze as he let her fingers go.

Giving a light, incredulous laugh, she spread her hands. "I can't marry a man I hardly know."

He tilted his head back against the high, padded back of the booth, and the gaze that locked with hers held raw intensity. "Laurel, there's nothing to fear. I am a businessman—utterly respectable and a little boring."

She didn't fear him. But to take a risk and marry a man she barely knew...the grandson of a Middle Eastern prince? Laurel wasn't so sure about the wisdom. "You're not boring," she said at last.

The warmth that seeped into the dark eyes caused a funny stir deep in her chest.

"Does that mean you will agree to marry me?" he asked softly.

Tipping her head to one side, Laurel tried to ignore the way her heart had rolled over and considered him. "You don't even mention love."

"So you want love? A proposal wrapped up in sweet words? Should I kneel on one knee before you?"

She shook her head slowly. "If I still dreamed of that kind of love I would've snatched the bouquet that Kara tossed at me."

Rakin gave her a slow, appreciative smile. "You're a realist. We haven't known each other long at all. . . and although I would like to think we've discovered much in common, I wouldn't insult your intelligence by talking of love so soon."

"Thank you—I think."

She was still trying to make sense of his bombshell proposal. He'd said that her family would benefit from the proposition. But what was in it for him? Her mind leapt from one scenario to the next. But none of them made any sense.

"You've asked me to marry you, but I still have no idea why."

The smile still lurked in his eyes. "You're a very beautiful woman, you must know that."

She could sense that he was prevaricating, even as she countered, "Beauty doesn't guarantee that a marriage will succeed—you only need to look at my mother's marriage to know that. You implied you were putting a business proposition to me—I didn't expect a marriage proposal."

"My marriage proposal *is* a business proposition."

Laurel started to laugh.

He sat forward, and his knee pressed against hers. "Believe me, it's not as crazy as it sounds. My grandfather has been threatening to change his will and disinherit me for years for not forming an alliance with the various women he has picked out for me—each time I have ignored his threats, because he is an irascible old man with plenty of life still left in him. He will cheat death for a while yet. But recently the threats have intensified. He no longer merely threatens to disinherit me on his death—now he has vowed he will force the board to vote me out as CEO. And, not satisfied with that, he will also transfer the controlling stocks he holds in the Abdellah business empire to my cousin. All this will be done if I am not married by my thirty-sixth birthday. It is no longer a matter of waiting until he dies to find out whether he has made good on his threats—he intends to disenfranchise me within the next year."

Rakin's face was a study in frustration.

"I have no intention of being robbed of the company. I have spent many hours of my life working to expand the Gifts of Gold division until it has become a first-class supplier of soft furnishings and luxury linens."

She knew from listening to Eli rave about his friend that every word Rakin spoke was true. He'd built up a network of clients across the finest hotel chains and resorts in the world, including Eli's.

"So I need a wife."

At that, Laurel couldn't help being conscious of the solid weight of his leg resting against hers. Even through his trousers and the sheer stockings that she wore, she could feel the warmth of his flesh. But she didn't shift away. "Will your grandfather really go through with such a pointless threat? Surely it would harm the family as much as you?"

"It's not pointless to him. He's a proud man—and he's accustomed to having things his way. Right now he doesn't care about profits. He wants me to marry, and this is the way he intends to bend me to his will."

"Who will run the company if he wrests control from you?"

"Ah, my grandfather already has that sorted out. The cousin to whom he is transferring the controlling stocks on my thirty-sixth birthday will be ushered in as the new CEO of Gifts of Gold. None of the board would dare act against my grandfather's orders."

"This cousin is married?"

"He is engaged—to a woman my grandfather handpicked for him." Rakin's lip curled up.

Understanding dawned. "You and your cousin don't see eye to eye?"

The sharp incline of his head confirmed her suspicion. "Zafar hates me. He would destroy me if he could, and I would die before I allowed Zafar to take this from me...so I will be married first."

"Wouldn't it be more advantageous for you also to marry a woman your grandfather had chosen for you?"

Rakin's eyebrows drew together, giving him a formidable air.

"That would give him too much power over me." The frown relaxed. "Besides, even if he scoured the whole earth, my grandfather could find no better candidate than you."

Laurel could feel her cheeks heating. "That is shameless flattery!"

"Not at all. You are beautiful and presentable. You are well connected…and incredibly gracious." Leaning farther forward he captured one of her hands. "And, to make sure you are equally happy, I will also make sure that our marriage will lead to benefits for The Kincaid Group."

Laurel jerked upright at his touch. "What kind of benefits?" He had her.

Rakin was certain of it. She was going to agree to marry him—exactly as he'd hoped. He let her hand go and sat back. Not far away he could hear the chiming of a slot machine announcing a winner, the whoops of celebration that followed.

He focused on the woman beside him, the woman he was determined to have as his wife. "There are many exporters and importers in Diyafa—they rely on shipping containers to transport their products around the world. I will see to it that they are introduced to your family's business. I will do everything I can to expand the profile of The Kincaid Group within my circle."

"You wouldn't expect me to give up my role in the company?"

Laurel was even starting to speak as though their marriage was a fait accompli. Satisfaction spread through Rakin. "Our marriage would be temporary—such a drastic sacrifice would not be required."

"How temporary?"

Rakin shrugged, impatient with her insistence. "Once we are married, my grandfather will sign the stocks over to me, I will have control of the company…and you will be free to leave—to return to Charleston, and your family, for good."

She shifted to the edge of the seat, and the rogue tendril of hair fell forward. She brushed it back impatiently, and the pendant lights illuminating the alcove turned her diamond drop earrings to a cascade of sparkles. "But you would expect me to live in Diyafa, right?"

He nodded and crossed one leg over the other, keeping his pose deliberately casual, taking care not to spook her. A few minutes more…that was all it was going to take. "Otherwise my grandfather would not accept that our marriage was legitimate—and I cannot afford him to doubt the veracity of our union. But there would be compensations for living in Diyafa for part of the year. I travel a lot—and I'd expect you to be by my side. I make regular business trips to the United States, so you would see plenty of your family. You could continue doing public relations work for your family's business. I would never stop you. The technology in Diyafa is groundbreaking; you could work there with everything at your fingertips. I travel to many countries, too. Think about it, you would be able to work through that list of yours."

"What do you know about my List?" Laurel was staring at him, green eyes wide with shock.

He tried to keep the smugness out of his smile. It hadn't taken him long to fathom what was on her list. "It's obvious that you have a list of places you want to travel to. I know Vegas is on there for certain, you mentioned adding Lake Como—and you may even have considered Diyafa."

Rakin got the feeling she was debating something.

He certainly couldn't afford for her to have second thoughts now.

"Laurel, I will take you everywhere you wish to travel. We would visit the Taj Mahal, I would take you to the Tower of London. You could sip French champagne beside the Seine in the spring time. You will never regret the adventures you will experience."

The doubt vanished and her expression filled with yearning. "That's not fair. You're chipping away at my weakest point."

Of course, he knew that. For someone who had confessed to never having traveled much and always wanted to, he was offering the dream of a lifetime.

"It's not a weakness to have a dream."

There was an expression in her eyes that he did not recognize. "You're offering to fulfill my dream?"

He didn't need her romanticizing him. He was, after all, not the love of her life that his mother had thought his father to be. He wanted no misunderstandings. He was, after all, only a man. "It's not one-sided. Don't forget that I will get what I need, too."

"So this will be a win-win deal?"

She understood! He couldn't have chosen better if he'd spent the whole year searching for the perfect wife.

"Exactly," he purred. The dazzling smile Rakin directed at her was filled with triumph. "Why not accept my proposition?"

Proposition.

The word dragged Laurel back to what Rakin was offering: a business deal...not the dream of a lifetime.

Restlessness flooded her, and she leapt to her feet. "I think I've found my second wind. Let's see if I can break that Winthrop curse."

Rakin rose more slowly and blocked her escape. "You want to gamble more? Now?"

She shot him a look that could never be described as flirtatious. He was the cause of this...this turbulence that was turning her inside out. "You're asking me to take the gamble of a lifetime by marrying you—what difference is a few minutes going to make?"

He raised his hands in a gesture of surrender.

"Take all the time you need." The look he gave her was full of masculine confusion as he stepped away so that she could pass. "But it's hardly for a lifetime. It's not a permanent arrangement."

But Laurel didn't move past him. "I want a sign."

"A sign?" The confusion evaporated, leaving frustration clouding his eyes. "What kind of sign?"

"That marrying you is the right thing to do."

"And what would you consider a good sign?"

Laurel thought about it for a moment. "Winning back the money I lost on the roulette tables—losing it was very bad luck."

"But your family never wins." Rakin looked fit to burst.

A wave of amusement swept Laurel along as she headed for the gambling area. Now perhaps he felt as off-balance as she did. Over her shoulder, she tossed, "I'm going to stick to the slot machines this time. So chances are if I do win it would be an excellent omen."

Rakin made a peculiar sound.

Laurel turned, in time to see him produce a coin from his pocket.

"Heads or tails?" he demanded.

The absurdity of it struck her as she came to a stop. "You're asking me to make what might be one of the biggest decisions of my life on the flip of a coin?"

"You're about to risk it on a machine that pays pittances on pairs of cherries. I prefer these odds," he said grimly.

"I prefer the cherries."

He didn't even smile.

"You've got no intention of saying 'yes' to my proposal, have you?"

Laurel didn't answer at once. To be honest, she was confused—Rakin had turned her world upside down with his proposal. It was far more disorientating than the roller coasters they'd shared earlier. Or the flashing lights and loud chimes of the nearby slot machines.

Part of her wanted to leap in and say yes.

No doubt about it, marriage to Rakin would be an adventure. A chance to experience things she wouldn't otherwise. It certainly made good business sense. The Kincaid Group couldn't afford to turn away opportunities for new business—particularly not with Jack Sinclair still causing all kinds of mayhem.

But the more cautious side of her, the old carefully and conservatively raised Laurel Kincaid, warned that she didn't know Rakin terribly well, that this was an extremely risky proposition, one she should avoid at all costs.

All reason evaporated when he strode up to her and put his hands on her shoulders. "I should've asked you to marry me back on the balcony last night—I'm starting to think you might have been more likely to say yes back during the wedding."

His touch against her bare skin was...disturbing. Laurel struggled to think. At last she shook her head slowly. "You were a stranger then, I know you so much better now."

She realized it was true.

In the cocoon formed by his arms, for her benefit as much as his, she ticked off on her fingers what she'd learned. "One, you're fun to be with—I've never laughed so much in my life as I did today. Two, you're kind—you held my hand when you thought I might be scared that first time on the roller coaster. Three, you love the world around us—I discovered that at the top of the Eiffel Tower. Four, you're good with children—"

"You can't possibly know that!"

His hands dropped away from her shoulders, and her flesh felt cool where, an instant before, his fingers had rested.

"I do," she insisted. "You patiently humored Flynn at the wedding."

"Then marry me!"

His eyes drilled down into hers.

"Only if I win."

She swung away. From her purse she extracted a roll of coins. Tearing the wrapper with the casino logo from the coins, she fed them into the first slot machine she came to and hit the play button.

The patterns spun crazily.

When they came to rest, nothing lined up.

Not even a pair of cherries.

The same thing happened on the next play.

Laurel's heart felt hollow. It was ridiculous to feel so flat, like a loser, simply because she couldn't even hit the cherries.

Get a life. ...

She hadn't felt this flatness earlier. She and Rakin had connected; they'd enjoyed each other's company. The day had been filled with joy. Her intuition told her they'd make a great temporary team—The Kincaid Group would benefit and so would Gifts of Gold.

It wouldn't be crazy to marry him—she liked him.

And the man didn't even gamble.

She stared at the rows lined with pictures and numbers. What was she doing? Rakin was right: she didn't need some arbitrary sign. This was a solid business decision. It made perfect, logical sense to accept his proposal.

She didn't need to prove that she could win.

Laurel knew she was going to say yes.

She hit the play button for the last time, and turned to give him the answer he was waiting for.

The cacophony of bells and electronic chimes rising in a hysterical crescendo caused her to whip around to stare at the slot machine.

In disbelief she read the flashing letters instructing her to call an attendant.

"The lights are flashing," she said, as numbness invaded her. "I've won."

Rakin was laughing.

"I've won," she said again.

But Rakin wasn't looking at the crazy, psychedelic fireworks above the slot machine. He was coming toward her his arms outstretched. "Looks like you've broken the Winthrop curse. You've hit the jackpot."

Her eyes lifted to the amount in white lights at the top: $22,222. It wasn't a fortune, but it more than covered her earlier losses. And it was definitely a jackpot. "Two must be my lucky number."

Then she was being swept off her feet into Rakin's arms. He spun her around as colors flashed crazily around her. By the time he set her down, the numbness was starting to recede as feeling returned...and with it, euphoria.

She grinned up at him. "I feel..." How best to describe it? "...lucky."

"We'll be lucky together." Rakin's gaze blazed into hers. "We will be married tomorrow."

Five

Today was her wedding day.

Laurel freed herself from the sheet that had twisted around her limbs while she slept. In one lithe movement, she swung her legs out of the bed and sat up. Hooking a finger under the narrow strap of her cream silk nightie that had slithered off her shoulder, she righted it.

On the bedside table the rose that Rakin had organized to be delivered with the check for her winnings rested in a glass of water.

Laurel's gaze fell onto the crumpled letter with the card tucked beneath that she'd placed on the nightstand beside the rose last night. The two documents that were dominating her life: her father's letter—and her Get a Life List.

She reached for the List first.

No. 1 Jilt Eli.

Laurel shut her eyes. No need to feel guilty, Eli was much happier married to Kara.

No. 2 Wear red lipstick. Check.

No. 3 Flirt with a stranger. Check. She'd done that with vengeance… and look where it had gotten her. Now she was marrying him. Even though she hadn't even kissed him yet.…

Laurel was smiling when she read the next item.

No. 4 Eat ice cream in bed. An absolute taboo in the Kincaid household. And last night when Rakin had ordered ice cream for dessert, she'd immediately thought of her list... and the visions that had flashed through her head had been dangerously X-rated. All too easy to imagine herself doing plenty of things she shouldn't even be considering with the dark stranger to whom she was growing curiously addicted.

Well, she certainly wouldn't be eating ice cream in bed with Rakin any time soon....

No. 5 Gamble all night.

Laurel read the entry again. Last night she'd proved—forever—that she had no need to gamble all night. It gave her a curious sense of peace. She was a winner in her own right.

No. 6 Travel to far-flung places.

Check. She would be going with Rakin to Diyafa. There would be more journeys beyond that. The passport she carried with her was about to be put to plenty of use.

Her face broke into a smile as she glanced down the remaining items.

She was well on track...even though the tasks grew tougher toward the end.

Laurel placed the list back on the nightstand. By contrast, the much-folded paper that her father's letter was written on had the texture of tissue paper between her fingertips. Laurel unfolded it, her eyes immediately drawn to the salutation and the first line.

My dearest Laurel,
If you are reading this, I am no longer with you.

Even though she knew the contents by heart, the words still had the power to clog her throat with emotion.

Her father had been gone for nearly five months, yet it was still hard to accept that she would never see him again. She read the letter through to the end, then set it down with a profound wish that they'd never discovered that her father possessed feet of clay. Discovering her father's secret life with Angela while he was still married to her mother had turned her belief in their happy marriage on its head. Had everything she believed about her parent's love simply been a lie?

Rakin might not be offering her love...but at least he was offering her honesty.

The benefits would be very real.

What he was offering would tick off the boxes of the shopping list of wants she'd scrawled before jilting Eli.

By marrying Rakin, she'd be actively fulfilling more of her dreams. At the same time, she'd also be able to source leads for new business to refer to her brother, Matt. That way she'd also be working actively on No. 9 on the List: *Help save TKG*. Rakin would be getting something he wanted—needed—out of the deal, too.

She had nothing to lose.

At the marriage license bureau it took only minutes of standing in the queue before Laurel found herself signing the application in the space beside the bold slash of Rakin's signature. She stared at the word printed in bold type below her signature: *BRIDE*.

Bride? For one wild second panic surged through her. A month ago she'd been engaged to her best friend. Someone she knew. Someone she was fond of. Someone she understood. She'd certainly never had any intention of marrying a man she'd only just met—and a sheikh at that.

Then her nerves steadied.

She liked Rakin. She trusted him. He needed a bride; the Kincaid Group needed more business. And he was going to help her become the woman she'd always wanted—secretly—to be.

Her pulse slowed down as the panic subsided. Behind the counter, the clerk handed Rakin a duplicate form.

"Cheapest place to get married is the Office of Civil Marriages. It's on Third Street, on the right-hand side, only a short walk away."

"We'll do a bit of research—but thank you for your help." Rakin flashed her an easy smile.

"Some of the hotels on the strip are mighty expensive." The clerk gave Rakin a once-over. Then she gave a wistful sigh. "But maybe that won't matter." The look she cast Laurel held a glint of envy. "Have a wonderful wedding...and good luck."

Laurel smiled back. "Thank you."

They exited through smoked glass doors.

Laurel caught sight of the signboards for lawyers and paused. It started her thoughts down a path not easily stopped. What would her family make of her impulsive wedding? Before she'd told Eli she couldn't marry him, she'd spent months talking to her family's attorneys negotiating a prenuptial agreement that the lawyers were confident protected both her and The Kincaid Group. Eli's lawyers had worked equally hard to ensure that the prenup was fair to him, too.

If her father were alive, he'd be having a stroke at the thought of any of his daughters marrying a man the family hadn't inspected, without a prenup, exposing The Kincaid Group to all manner of risks. No prenuptial agreement was a sin worse than unprotected sex—and that was calamity enough—in her father's opinion.

So she slid Rakin a sideways glance. What did she really know about him—beside the fact that he was Eli's friend? And she liked him. A lot. He could be a gold-digger—a gigolo—for all she knew. Quickly, she checked her thoughts. Told herself she was being ridiculous.

Rakin Abdellah was clearly a very rich man. Even the clerk had noticed the patina of wealth that glossed him, separating him from the average romantic swain who turned up in the marriage license bureau.

But the lessons of a lifetime caused her to say, "We should've signed a prenup. My family will kill me when they find out...." Her voice trailed away as Rakin took her elbow. "Where are we going?"

"To see if we can find a lawyer. I don't want you having any sense of guilt, or any reservations about this."

"I must sound like the biggest party pooper ever."

"Never." He was smiling down at her, and it eased the butterflies fluttering around in her stomach. "How could I think that? I admire you for being so clear-sighted—for thinking about protecting your family—and their livelihood."

In some childish, hidden corner of her heart, Laurel wished that he'd dismissed the caution she'd voiced, and swept her up in his arms, then charged into the Little Red House of Love to rush through their temporary vows.

At least, that way, she wouldn't be held accountable for what happened next.... That way she could blame him for whatever the outcome was.

And maybe the disturbing little niggle of doubt that had taken hold would've evaporated in a puff of smoke....

They caught the lawyer closing up his offices.

The slight, dark-suited man started to object, but one glance at Rakin's determined face convinced him to welcome them instead. A raised hand stayed the last-remaining paralegal who was about to slip out a side door.

With the recent negotiations with Eli so fresh in her mind, it didn't take Laurel long to explain what she needed. Rakin took even less time to get his requirements across. It reinforced what Laurel was starting to realize—under the handsome, charming facade lurked a tough negotiator.

A tiger, rather than a pussycat. With a tiger's feral instincts. Something she would do well to remember.

"You need to be aware that a prenuptial agreement entered so near in time to a wedding date can be held to be void for duress," the lawyer told them once they were seated around a conference table with plush, padded chairs in the privacy of his offices.

It was hardly the time for Laurel to confess that Rakin had proposed a temporary marriage—a mad adventure for her with some fringe benefits for her family's business thrown in—and a sane solution to Rakin's problems.

Laurel got the feeling that if the lawyer knew about the reasons for their marriage he'd consider them both a little mad—and advise them they were headed for trouble.

"Do you want to wait?" Rakin's murmur, loud enough for

her ears only, broke into her speculative thoughts. She turned her head and looked into eyes that mesmerized her.

"Wait?" She raised her eyebrows.

"Take some more time to think it through." He gave her a tender smile that probably convinced the lawyer seated across the polished conference table that this was a love match.

Laurel almost grinned back. The misgivings that had settled over her began to lift. In their place, recklessness danced a wild waltz through her. She'd made her decision—she was ready for the adventure of a lifetime.

She was done being careful.

"No need to wait." Who was this stranger who had taken up possession inside her skin? With a defiant toss of her head, she spoke directly to the lawyer, "No one's forcing me to do anything I don't want."

"Laurel wants to make sure we both understand exactly where we stand—especially given that we both have family businesses to consider," said Rakin.

"Very wise." The lawyer pulled his yellow legal pad closer and uncapped his pen. "It may not seem like a very romantic thing to do, but it certainly shows you both agree on many basic things—very important for building the foundations of a lasting marriage."

When the lawyer suggested that each of them might want their own counsel, Laurel waved his concerns away. She'd been through all that once already with Eli. She knew what would be said, the cautions, the ifs and the buts that she'd considered so carefully the last time round. She knew the pitfalls, what safeguards were required.

It didn't take him long to make a note of what those concerns were. Or for the paralegal to reduce the terms to a draft both she and Rakin perused. Once the agreement was executed and the lawyer had arranged where to send the bill, the meeting was over.

"I wish you the long and happy marriage I am sure you will enjoy."

Laurel decided to leave their adviser with his illusions.

Clearly, he'd concluded this was a love match. A meeting of true minds. And who was she to disabuse him of that romantic notion?

Entering the hotel suite a short while later, Laurel kicked off her shoes and sank into the welcoming comfort of a plush L-shaped sofa with a breathy laugh. "Well, I'm glad that's done."

"Soon you will be Mrs. Abdellah."

Rakin extracted a bottle of champagne from the depths of the bar fridge.

"I'll help myself to a cola in a little while," Laurel said quickly. "Otherwise you might railroad me into more propositions."

He gave her a wry smile. "You're never going to let me live that down."

"Never is a long time." Lazily, she stretched her arms above her head. "I should take a shower."

"Relax for a few moments, there's still plenty of time to get dressed."

Dressed? Laurel gulped as her thoughts homed in on one overwhelmingly feminine worry. A dress. A wedding dress. She didn't have a dress. What was she to wear? With dismay she thought about the strapless black dress she'd worn to the casino last night. Black wouldn't do for a wedding. Even if it wasn't a marriage for love—there should still be some element of romance about the occasion.

"I don't have anything remotely suitable for a wedding," she confessed as Rakin closed the door of the bar fridge.

"Have no fear." He gave her a smug smile. "It's all been taken care of."

"All been taken care of?" Laurel echoed.

At his look at satisfaction, it fell into place.... Rakin had already bought her a wedding dress.

He'd clearly thought of everything—Kara would've been impressed.

The doubt devils returned. What if the gown didn't fit? Or,

worse, what if she hated the design he'd chosen? How was she supposed to tell him that when he'd clearly been thinking of her?

If only Kara were here to help…

An image of the dress Kara had picked out for the-wedding-that-had-never-happened flashed into her mind. The perfect dress. An elegant fitted white lace bodice with a full skirt. She'd had more fittings than she'd wanted to get the fit just right.

But Kara wasn't here.

Besides the last dress Kara had picked out had suited the old Laurel. Perfectly. The Laurel who did exactly as everyone expected. Not the woman with an unquenchable thirst for adventure that she'd become.

Rakin had called her a rebel.

Suddenly she found herself looking forward to seeing what Rakin had chosen. Laurel found her lips creeping up into a smile as he settled on the sofa beside her. "You've bought me a wedding dress, haven't you?"

"Not quite."

Before Laurel could question what that meant his cell phone buzzed. Rakin reached for it. After a brief exchange, he killed the call. "Macy and her assistant have arrived."

"Macy?"

"She's a shopping consultant who came highly recommended, and she's picked out a few dresses you might like. But you'll need to make the final choice."

Laurel suppressed the ridiculous thrill of pleasure that gave her. He'd left the final decision down to her. For too many years she'd allowed other people to make decisions for her.

Rakin wasn't doing that.

A buzz signaling the arrival of the private elevator sounded, and seconds later the doors slid open. Macy turned out to be a tall, angular brunette with sharp eyes, and she was followed by a shorter woman who Laurel assumed must be her assistant. A bellhop brought up the rear, wheeling in a cart of boxes emblazoned with designer names.

"The wedding is tonight, right?" Macy radiated efficiency.

"Um…maybe," said Laurel thinking about how long all the

details for her wedding to Eli had taken to arrange. "But I'm not sure everything can be done in such a short time."

"No maybe about it," Rakin corrected. "Our wedding will definitely take place tonight—I will make sure of that." His wicked grin caused Laurel's heart unexpectedly to contract.

"Then we don't have any time to waste." Macy's clipped words broke the spell. "Katie, let's get those dresses out of the boxes." The assistant sprang to action and a swathe of fabric emerged in a shower of falling petals.

Laurel's breath caught. "Oh, my!"

"There are some things I need to take of." Rakin crossed the floor to tip the bellhop for his help, then made his way back to Laurel. "If you'll excuse me."

As he came closer Laurel found that her pulse had started to race. There was a glint in Rakin's dark eyes. Her heart slammed in her chest.

He was going to kiss her.

But when the kiss came, his lips brushed her cheek instead of her mouth. A perfunctory, too brief caress.

Then he was gone, the door to the suite's elevator sliding shut behind him.

Laurel slowly let out a breath.

"By the time he comes back you will look like the woman of his dreams," Macy said from behind her.

The woman of his dreams.

Being the woman of his dreams wasn't what this marriage was about. But Laurel didn't have the heart to smash the other woman's illusions. Laurel responded absently to the bellhop's goodbye when he and the cart departed, and then only she, Macy and Katie remained in the spacious suite.

But there was no question of any awkward silence as Macy conjured dresses out of their boxes along with accessories. The personal shopper's enthusiasm was contagious. Laurel glimpsed slips of lacy lingerie, gloves, stockings…and shoes with high, delicate heels.

But her gaze kept coming back to the dress Macy had unpacked first.

The fabric appeared to have been created from white rose petals. The design of the dress itself was deceptively simple, no flounces, no bows. It relied on the beauty of the fabric and the stark simplicity of the cut.

"Would you like to try it?" Macy was sizing her up with an air of an expert. "Your fiancé is a good judge of size—it should fit perfectly."

Laurel tossed caution aside. "I'd love to."

The dress slid over her head in a whisper of fine cloth. When Laurel opened her eyes she gasped...and blinked.

This was no conservative Southern lady that stared back at her from the mirrored cupboard doors. She looked sexy. So sexy. Yet still tasteful.

Laurel examined herself in the mirror.

"We'll leave your hair loose at the back, but these bits can be swept up." Macy was there, matching her actions to her words. "And perhaps a small spray of flowers here."

Laurel thought her eyes looked huge in her face. And her cheekbones were thrown into prominence.

"Katie's a magician with makeup. But not too much—you don't need it. A touch of eye-shadow and some mascara on those incredible lashes—this will not take long."

Laurel waited as the front strands of her hair were drawn up and pinned back.

"A ribbon, I think." Deft fingers wove the silk through her auburn hair. "Your complexion is so creamy."

By the time her hair had been arranged and her makeup applied in soft shades, Laurel felt like a siren. And when she finally heard Rakin's voice outside the bedroom door, her heart jumped into her throat. She swung around...and gasped.

Her groom stood framed in the doorway.

He was wearing a tuxedo that made him appear dark and formidable. And, in sharp contrast to his masculinity, a white rose was pinned to his lapel.

And, he was inspecting her with equal interest.

Laurel didn't even notice Macy and Katie file past him. All she was aware of was the touch of Rakin's eyes. On the V of skin between her breasts. On her mouth. Before his gaze swept up to meet hers. There was heat...and something more.

Suddenly it hurt to breathe.

This was crazy!

She shouldn't be feeling like this. Trembling. Like a teen on her first date.

She was a grown woman getting married to a man who'd turned her legs to water just by looking at her. This was supposed to be a business arrangement that would benefit both of them. It was a temporary fix. It certainly wasn't about this... this shaky, trembling sensation that she couldn't even name.

Whatever it was, it had made it hard to breathe. To hide what she was feeling, Laurel gave him her most charming smile.

He smiled back. She couldn't help noticing that he had a beautiful mouth. The upper lip had been formed by a master hand; the bottom lip was full, promising passion—

Get a grip.

Laurel searched for something appropriate to say. "You've changed already," she said finally. He'd showered, too. The smooth line of his jaw told her he'd shaved.

"You look exquisite." His voice was deep.

"Thank you." Laurel felt a blast of pleasure. All her life she'd been told she was beautiful: She'd been told in tones laden with envy, and she'd been told factually as if it were to be expected that Elizabeth Kincaid's eldest daughter should follow in her mother's footsteps. Yet never had she derived so much pleasure from hearing the words. Under the heat of his gaze, Rakin made her feel more like a woman than she'd ever felt in her life.

He was taking something from his pocket. "I brought you a gift."

"A gift?"

"A keepsake—to remember our wedding by."

He opened a slim, black velvet box to reveal the gold chain looped inside. As he hooked his index finger under the chain to extract it from the box, blue fire flashed in the light. A diamond pendant swung from the end of the chain, but Laurel lost sight of it as Rakin moved behind her. A moment later she felt the pendant drop into the valley between her breasts and then Rakin's fingertips brushed her nape, as he closed the clasp. A sensation of delicious delight thrilled through her.

Standing behind her, thankfully, Rakin wouldn't have noticed the electric surge of awareness. When his hands closed on her shoulders, Laurel stilled. But he was intent on steering her toward the mirror.

She breathed again.

"Do you like it?"

"It" was a flawless single diamond suspended in a simple gold setting to show off the glorious stone that nestled against her skin.

"I can't accept this!"

"Why not?"

"It's too…" Laurel groped around for the right word. Finally she settled on, "It's too much."

"You don't like it."

"No!" she sputtered. "I mean—of course I like it—it's beautiful."

"Then stop pouting and say a pretty thank you."

"I don't pout." Feeling awkward and horridly ungracious, she gathered her composure. "Thank you, it's truly lovely." A discomforting thought struck Laurel. "I didn't buy you a gift."

"I never expected one."

In the mirror, the reflection showed a sophisticated woman in a petal-strewn white dress with a dark, smiling man behind her. Her gaze homed in on where his hands still rested on her naked shoulders, the long fingers dark against her much paler skin. Laurel shivered. There was something so carnally sensual about the contrast of male and female, yin and yang, that it caused her latent awareness of him as an attractive man to rocket.

Her gaze lifted to his. In the mirror, their eyes met. After the beat of a charged second, Rakin let his hands fall from her shoulders. Laurel's breath hissed out.

"We should leave now," he said.

"Yes, of course." Laurel was only too grateful to bolt for the door—for, despite its size, the suite had become unexpectedly oppressive.

When next they returned to the hotel, they would be married.

Six

"The Venetian?"

Laurel flung her head back to read the name spelled in vertically arranged letters down the outside of the hotel's facade.

Her groom gave her a very white smile. "We're going to have photographs taken—we'll want something to remember the occasion by."

She'd been wondering which of the popular chapels Rakin had chosen for their wedding. Now Laurel flicked through the possibilities in her head. The Chapel of Bells or the Little White Chapel. Or even a wedding out at Red Rock Canyon—but then they'd hardly be coming to the Venetian for photos. Now she couldn't help thinking what others in the resort would make of the white petal-dress that pronounced romance—and bride.

Then she shrugged her self-consciousness aside. This was Las Vegas after all. Couples got married all the time. Most likely, no one would cast them a second glance.

That smile still played around Rakin's mouth. "You said you wanted to one day visit Venice."

Laurel smiled back.

But that turned to a gasp of awe as they entered the Venetian's lobby with its high, vaulted ceilings and ornate gold-framed painted frescoes that stretched across the vast space. "Oh, wow."

"A ride on a gondola perhaps? Would that be enough of an adventure?"

"A gondola?" A gurgle of laughter rose in her throat. "Yes, please! I can think of nothing more romantic to do on my wedding day." And Rakin had promised there'd be photos to remember the occasion by. Kara would be impressed!

"Good."

Laurel was even more astonished when they reached the waiting gondola. White and gold, it floated in a canal surrounded by buildings that looked like they'd been transported from Venice to be set along the cobblestone walkways beside the canal. Looking up she could see balconies with pillars and arches and intricate wrought iron, all capturing the detail of a far-away place.

A woman stepped forward offering a bouquet of white roses with sprigs of orange blossom.

"That's a bridal bouquet," said Laurel. Then she got it. "For the photographs?"

Rakin introduced her to Laurel as the hotel's wedding planner. The next surprise turned out not to be a photographer as she'd half expected, but a distinguished-looking wedding celebrant in a dark suit with a flowing robe over the top.

Laurel gasped as it all suddenly made sense. This wasn't just about wedding photos...

"We're getting married here?"

Everything was happening so fast.

The celebrant was already shaking Rakin's hand. Then Rakin placed his hand beneath Laurel's elbow and steered her to the waiting gondola. White petals drifted over them, filling the air with fragrance. As they landed on the pathway, Laurel trod carefully over them, loath to spoil such beauty.

Once they were seated the gondolier pushed off behind them, and the gondola glided along the glass-like water of the Grand Canal.

The space in the gondola was surprisingly intimate. In front of them was the celebrant, his robes giving him a majestic appearance. The limited space forced Rakin's thigh up against hers; and the taut pressure of the hard muscle caused a wave of warmth to spread through Laurel.

The celebrant began to speak. Laurel turned her head to find Rakin watching her with hooded eyes. Her heart thumped.

Excitement churned in her stomach.

When the celebrant started to recite the wedding vows, Laurel discovered that her voice shook a little as she repeated the words in the intimacy of the gondola. She was marrying Rakin Abdellah. Not for love...but for much more sound reasons.

When he took her fingers between his, she felt a little shock at his touch. Up until now this had been so businesslike, but his touch changed that...bringing a flare of heat.

The glint of gold gave her some warning as he slowly slid the plain, unadorned band onto her fourth finger. Her eyes leapt to his in surprise. She started to apologize for not getting him a ring, but the intense focus in his eyes silenced her. Her heartbeat quickened.

"You are now man and wife."

Man and wife.

Laurel swallowed, the daze of disbelief and disconcertment growing more acute.

A month ago she'd been contemplating marrying Eli; now she was married to a man she hadn't met until only a few days ago. A man who had promised her adventure and business opportunities—not love—and in exchange she would pretend to be the wife he needed to nullify his grandfather's threats. A man who had taken over her life...her thoughts...in a way she'd never anticipated.

Behind them the gondolier broke into song. The soulful strains of "O Sole Mio" wound their way around Laurel's heart and tugged tight. Her fingers convulsed beneath Rakin's. For an instant she wished this had been a real romance—the wedding of her heart.

But it wasn't.

It was a convenient arrangement—for both of them. Yet Laurel knew there was more than that to what was passing between them. Rakin had promised her experiences she'd never had…and he was delivering on that. Her world had shifted. And somewhere in the change, she hoped to find herself. Someone who didn't live to please others, someone who took joy in her own life: the Laurel Kincaid she'd never allowed herself to be.

"It is customary for the bridal couple to kiss beneath the bridges." The celebrant offered them an indulgent smile.

Before Laurel could graciously tell him that a kiss wasn't necessary, the gondola swept into the shadows under the bridge and Rakin's head swooped.

His mouth closed over hers and the bottom dropped out of her world.

Rakin's lips were firm—very male—brooking no resistance. She tensed under the unexpected arousal that spread through her like wildfire, and kept her lips firmly pressed together, telling herself Rakin was only doing this to indulge the celebrant. Yet he made no attempt to press further for a more intimate connection. Instead, after a pause, he brushed a row of flirty kisses along the seal of her lips.

With a final kiss on the side of her mouth, he whispered, "That dimple has been driving me crazy."

And then the bridge was behind them, and they were out in the light.

Laurel couldn't respond with a light laugh; instead she bit back a moan of feminine frustration as he lifted his head and put inches between them. But his eyes still held hers, radiating purpose. It took Laurel only a heartbeat of time to realize that his kiss had nothing to do with the watching celebrant, and everything to do with her.

He'd wanted to kiss her.

Flutters of apprehension stirred within her. Once again, her perceptions of their relationship had shifted.

Rakin bent his head toward hers. "Now the adventure starts for real."

A frisson of excitement feathered down Laurel's spine. Not

for the first time she realized that Rakin was a devastatingly attractive man.

To catch her breath, and gain time, she tipped her head back and closed her eyes. Yet still she left her fingers tangled with his, reluctant to break the remaining link between them. The rich serenade of the Neapolitan love song swirled around her, causing a flood of long-banked emotions to overflow.

This was supposed to have been a lark, mixed up with a bit of business. So how had it become the most romantic experience of her life? When she opened her eyes again, she found herself staring blindly at the stars overhead.

"They're not real," volunteered the celebrant. "If you watch carefully the sky keeps changing."

Of course they weren't real! Nothing about this crazy, wild ride with Rakin was real. It was an adventure. A fantasy. Her fantasy.

Yet in another way it was the most real thing that had ever happened to her. She was taking risks. Risks she would never have contemplated before she'd taken a leap into the unknown, out from the safe world of being one of the Charleston Kincaids, to do things that Laurel Kincaid was never expected to do.

Like marrying a sheikh she barely knew.

"The next bridge is coming up," the celebrant's warning broke into her thoughts.

Instantly every nerve ending sprang to alert. Laurel's heart was racing even before she met Rakin's gleaming dark eyes.

As the gondola glided into the shimmering shadows beneath the bridge, Laurel braced herself. Yet no amount of bracing could prepare her for the kiss that finally came. It knocked the breath out of her soul.

This time, Rakin took his time.

And this time the kiss was different.

Laurel gasped as Rakin tasted her, his tongue sweeping over her parted lips into the moistness beyond. Her senses leapt, and she found herself responding with wild ardor, kissing him back, linking her fingers around his neck.

Laurel forgot about the celebrant—forgot about the gondolier punting behind them—and gave herself up to the passion. Hot and fiery, it ignited and burned along her veins until her heartbeat thundered in her head. And all the time "O Sole Mio" washed over them. She'd been transported to another universe, an exotic world light years away from anything she'd ever known.

Nothing was ever going to be the same again.

Laurel had said very little since they'd alighted from the wedding gondola after exchanging vows.

Rakin was starting to wonder what was keeping her so preoccupied. When they'd returned to their penthouse suite a feast was waiting. But Laurel had only picked at bits of smoked salmon and some melon; she hadn't touched the sparkling wine Rakin had poured for her.

Now she blocked the open doorway leading out to the balcony that overlooked the acres of hotel gardens.

"You're very quiet," he said at last, coming up from behind her and placing a hand on her bare arm. "Don't you want something more to eat?"

She drew a deep breath, then said in a rush, "You promised this marriage wouldn't be about sex."

He did a double take. Had Laurel thought his concern for her was a come-on? "It isn't."

"Then why…" She cocked her head and dropped her eyes to rest pointedly where his hand lingered on her forearm ". . .that?"

His gaze followed hers. *Ah.*

"I like touching—I'm a very demonstrative man."

"Always?"

"Not always," he admitted.

"Then when?"

When he liked someone. When he was attracted to someone. And both applied to Laurel.

He made a sound that was half sigh, half laugh. "Busted. It seems that some sex might be involved after all."

But Laurel didn't laugh along with him. Instead, her gaze

lifted to his face. "Frankly, I've never known what the fuss is about."

She said it with innocent artlessness that was an affront to his prowess. Rakin was utterly certain he could change her mind. Arousal leapt through him at the very notion of teaching Laurel about the adventures of love. Huskily he said, "I could show you exactly what the fuss is about."

That evoked a startled look. The flush spread along her throat, down over the décolleté that her exquisite white wedding dress left exposed. She tried to laugh—it came out a strangled croak. "No, thanks."

But her eyes dropped to his bottom lip, lingered for a long moment, then leapt back to meet his before scuttling away. And in his trousers his erection grew rigid. Laurel was curious. And, forget killing the cat, her curiosity was going to be the death of him.

"Okay. No sex, only marriage," he promised, and wondered how the hell he was going to keep such a stupid vow.

Her tongue moistened her lower lip. "I wasn't even thinking about sex."

Who was she kidding? She'd brought the damn subject up! Lowering his gaze to her lush, red mouth, he said softly, "Of course you were. You're a very beautiful woman. You must fend off propositions all the time."

"I try to head them off before they happen," Laurel said with blunt honesty.

That brought his gaze back to her face and he searched to read what she was telling him. "You freeze them out?"

"Freeze sounds so...cold. I try to be a little kinder."

He gazed at her for a very long moment. The green eyes were more vulnerable than he'd ever seen them. They'd turned the soft, delicate shade of spring leaves dampened by rain. Rakin got the impression he was seeing a side of Laurel that few people ever did.

"What are you thinking?"

He shook his head, doubting Laurel would be comfortable with his observation. "Eli was right."

"About what?" she asked suspiciously.

"You really are a very nice woman."

Her lips curved up. "The feeling is mutual. I think you're a very nice man. So if it's not for sex, then why kiss me like that in the gondola?"

Rakin placed a hand on the doorframe on either side of her. "I could say to seal the terms of our agreement."

"It's a business agreement—it didn't need a kiss to conclude it, and it definitely didn't need two kisses."

He restrained himself from pointing out she hadn't rebuffed either kiss.

"I'm not going to lie," he settled for saying instead. "I would very much enjoy making love to you. It would be an intensely sensual and pleasurable experience for both of us. Another adventure—more for you to discover, I have no doubt about that. But if you wish sex to play no part in our arrangement, I will respect that."

But it would not be easy.

When she didn't respond, he grew more serious. "What are you waiting for? Do you believe there's someone out there in the world just for you? Someone who you won't want to freeze out?"

"Honestly? Love's been more than a little elusive. I'm not sure I really know what it is—even though I know there is a great deal more to it than sweet words. Kara and Eli have proved that to me." She shrugged. "Frankly, I'd settle for a marriage with the promise of adventure rather than love."

Relief filled Rakin, and the tension twisting his gut that all that talk about love and babies always brought drained out of him. "Adventure I can give you."

"Ah, but what's the catch? Are we still talking about sex?"

"No catch." Laurel raised her eyebrows so sharply that Rakin gave her an amused smile. "Not that kind, anyway. Not sex. At least, not if you don't want it, too." His smile became taunting. "Are you sure you want to close the door to the opportunity to explore something wonderful that might exist between you and me?"

Then he steeled himself for her rejection.

But instead of rejection, her eyes filled with curiosity. Her gaze touched his face, dropped lower, then came back. "Exploring anything between us? I just don't know...."

And her indecision left him in a worse, far more frustrating place than outright rejection.

"I'm going to take a shower," he said, his voice rough with frustration.

Talking about sex had made it hard to even think about sleep.

Laurel had showered in the luxurious bathroom off her room. She should've changed into the nightie that Kara, in her role as sister and wedding planner, had once upon a time chosen for Laurel's honeymoon. What on earth had possessed her to pack it? It seemed wrong to wear it now—because it had been picked out for her honeymoon with Eli.

And tonight was her wedding night...with Rakin.

So the sexy garment lay abandoned on the bed, and Laurel didn't feel like crawling into a comfortable T-shirt. She was far too wired.

Which was why she was sitting on the stool in front of the dresser in a one of the *HERS* monogrammed terry robes that the hotel supplied, thinking about her provocative brand-new husband. Because of him, the idea of a marriage in name only was proving to be a little disappointing.

Why not turn the relationship between herself and Rakin into a journey of exploration, too?

Laurel stretched sinuously. In the mirror above the dresser she caught sight of her neckline, which gaped open, revealing the rising curve of her breast. When she looked up, she caught sight of her eyes sparkling with interest and excitement.

Rakin promised to be an accomplished lover. Why shouldn't she take advantage of his suggestion?

Rakin came out the master bathroom toweling his hair, his body still damp from the shower he'd taken. He flung the wet towel onto the king bed.

He heard a gasp, and glanced up.

Laurel stood in the doorway to the master suite, her eyes wide at the sight of his nude body.

No point trying to cover up—it was far too late.

"What are you doing here?" he asked instead.

Her eyes gave her away. And instantly he was aroused.

He moved toward her. "You came for this."

She didn't protest as he took her into his arms. He kissed her, and her lips parted.

He paused, aware that once he started, he wouldn't stop. "Are you certain?"

Her nod was a quick, jerky movement. Rakin smoothed his hands along the front of her bathrobe, then slid them underneath. He caressed her arms, but the terry cloth hindered him. He pushed it back. It fell from her shoulders, then to the floor.

She, too, was now naked.

Rakin drew her down to the wide space of the bed, and came down beside her. He caressed her with long slow strokes, and she relaxed with a soft sigh. His thigh brushed hers apart, and he placed his mouth over hers.

This time the kiss was ravenous.

Rakin was breathing hard by the time it came to an end, and Laurel's eyes were wild.

Reaching out a hand, he stroked her belly; then he reached down farther...and touched her. A keening sound broke from her throat. Rakin stilled.

Laurel didn't move. Her eyes were closed and her teeth had bitten into the soft bottom lip that he'd kissed so thoroughly. She appeared to be waiting.

Gently Rakin stroked again. Her spine arched, and her harsh gasp broke the silence simmering between them. Her eyes popped open.

"Sorry."

Rakin took in the flood of pink on her cheeks.

"Relax," he urged. "Don't apologize."

"That moan..." Laurel looked uncomfortable. "It wasn't ladylike." She rolled over and buried her face in the pillow. "And describing it sounds much worse. Forget I said…whatever it was."

Rakin leaned forward and took her hands in his and gave a gentle tug. When she finally lifted her head, he said, "Listen to me. I don't need you to be the perfect lady. I want you to be yourself."

She gave him gentle smile. "Then there's one thing you need to understand: I am a perfect lady—I don't think I could be an imperfect lady."

He adored her sense of humor, the way she could laugh at herself…at the world…with him.

"Oh, I understand that."

"It's—" She broke off and her eyes slid away from his. She gave a breathless laugh. "I'm embarrassed."

He knew that too. And it was holding her back. Rakin threaded his fingers through her hair and tipped her head so that he could look down into her eyes. "Why?"

"Everything feels so much…more."

"More?"

"Stronger. More intense." She laughed again. "Do I sound crazy or do you have this effect on all women?"

Rakin didn't want to talk about other woman.

His bride was the only woman who interested him—and what she'd just revealed had pleased him. Maybe she wasn't holding back at all; maybe she was progressing in leaps and bounds.

Euphoria drowned him. "Then I'll have to prove there's still more to come," he growled throatily.

Her eyes glazed over in shock. "More? Is that possible?"

Laurel was a grown woman, but clearly she'd never encountered the right man to unleash her passion. Triumph swept him. He intended to change that. Lessons in seduction. She'd prove to be an eager student. He couldn't wait.

With a slow, deliberate smile he said, "I think there's more about adventure for me to share with you. But first I want a promise."

"A…promise?"

He nodded. "I want you to let yourself go. No restraint. No holding back."

Wariness shadowed her eyes. "What are you planning to do?"

The way she looked at him caused Rakin to give a crack of laughter. "Nothing too wild. All I want you to do is enjoy yourself."

"Enjoy myself? You mean..." She spread her hands helplessly. "What exactly do you mean?"

Rakin took pity on her and he lay back on the bed, propping himself up on one elbow. "Let yourself go a little.... Don't stress or feel awkward. Most of all I want you to forget all about being a Kincaid. You're you. Focus on being the woman you want to be. Above all, trust that every bit of pleasure you experience, I get to live it, too."

Laurel's eyes brightened. "I can do that."

"Now roll over—so that I can pleasure you."

She must be intoxicated, Laurel decided as she drew a deep, steadying breath. But this time not tipsy from the effects of too much wedding champagne as she'd been at Kara's wedding. Or even from the French champagne that Rakin had poured into slim crystal goblets when they'd walked into the suite. This time it was the impact of Rakin's closeness.

He filled her senses.

The rich warm gold of his skin, the way the light caught the high blades of his cheekbones, the dark velvet eyes that could be so forceful and compelling one moment, so kind and compassionate the next. And when his hand touched hers...sensations she'd never felt before prickled through her.

His lips whispered across the soft silk of her throat. Laurel arched her neck and he rewarded her with a row of kisses until his lips reached the hollow at the base of her throat. The lick of his tongue against the tender skin caused her to arch farther, her back coming off the bed.

The sound that broke from her suddenly dry throat was raw and without restraint—and definitely not what could be expected from a Southern lady—especially not a Kincaid. Laurel was trapped in the mindless web of pleasure where nothing existed.

Except Rakin.

And the shattering pleasure she was experiencing.

Twisting her head, she closed her eyes more tightly, her fingers twisting through his hair. Rakin covered her skin again with open-mouthed kisses that inflamed her further.

Her breath caught in the back of her throat as his lips closed over the tip of one sensitive breast. The sensation that forked through her was incredible. Hot. White. Spears of pleasure pierced her. Between her fingers his hair had the texture of rough, raw silk. When he broke off the caress, a sigh of denial shook her.

"Slow down," he murmured, before giving the other breast the same treatment, trailing a row of fresh kisses over the skin he'd uncovered.

How was she supposed to slow down when he was driving her mad?

Her hands dropped from his head and dug into the counterpane, and her back arched off the bed. She fought to keep her breathing even. Not to let it escape in the great gasping pants that instinctively seemed to want to happen.

Rakin, too, seemed to lose the race. His heart was pounding against her breasts, as he moved over her. Her legs parted, and she welcomed him, her arms closing around his back, reveling in the smooth satin of his skin against her palms.

It didn't take much more, before he came apart in her embrace.

Rakin rested his arms on the balustrade. The blackness of night enfolded him, while overhead the star-studded sky twinkled. In the master bedroom he'd silently sneaked from, Laurel slept.

He was restless.

The earth-shattering pleasure he had just experienced was not what he'd expected from his bride of convenience.

Foreboding rolled in the pit of his stomach as he stared out into the darkness.

Rakin was not accustomed to the unexpected. Despite what he'd told Laurel about letting go, every facet of his life was meticulously plotted, with careful consideration given to the outcome of each action he undertook. Being swept along by the force of the unknown was not part of his plan. It was Laurel who should be experiencing the thrall of adventure…not he.

He'd thought himself immune from the excitement of novelty. World-weary. Cynical. Not the kind of man to lose his head over a woman—not even one as beautiful as Laurel. After all, he didn't believe in love. He'd been immunized against that lethal condition from a very young age. Not that it stopped him from appreciating—or enjoying—women.

What he didn't do was go crazy over them or fall in love—that way led downhill to destruction.

And, even though he wouldn't call it going crazy, he was thinking way too much about his new bride.

The softness of her skin, the curve of her cheek…the sweet taste of her mouth. And that was before he got to the passion of—

Rakin censored his wayward thoughts. He didn't want her to stir again, not until morning.

For the rest of the night, he would let his bride sleep.

While he reminded himself why he'd married her. For business only.

Seven

Last night had been a mistake.

While Rakin had been courteous at breakfast this morning and unfailingly polite during the journey to the airport, Laurel detected a distance between them that she hadn't encountered before.

She wasn't imagining it.

Since they'd boarded the Learjet, she'd made a couple of light attempts to engage him in conversation, but he'd remained aloof and eventually he'd settled down on the sofa opposite and picked up the business section of the newspaper.

Her humorous, patient companion of the past few days had vanished without a trace.

And Laurel wanted to know why.

Pretending to be engrossed in a magazine, she flicked through stories about the latest celebrity scandals. But her brain couldn't stop buzzing. Had Rakin wanted a marriage in name only? Had he felt pressured to provide a sexual adventure for her benefit last night? Or was the passion they'd shared last night what he wanted? The notion was far too awkward to broach.

The lack of a clear answer left her feeling terribly unsure.

"Would you like a glass of champagne, madam?"

The attendant's voice jerked her out of her reverie. "No

thanks." Champagne was the last thing she needed. And with Rakin in this mood she couldn't even joke with him about trying to get her tipsy....

"Maybe orange juice?" suggested Rakin, looking up from his papers to her immense surprise.

"That would be nice." Laurel smiled her thanks as the attendant poured the juice and set the glass down on the coffee table.

"Don't hesitate to call for anything you need," the attendant offered before disappearing through a set of heavy curtains.

The touch of Rakin's eyes was distracting, especially with the silence that hung over them now that they were alone. Laurel swallowed. "Okay, so I know you have a grandfather who is a tyrant and a cousin. Tell me about the rest of your family."

"There's not much to tell. I'm an only child. My parents died in an airplane crash when I was twelve. My mother was American, my father was the eldest of two sons and four daughters all born and raised as part of the extended royal family in Diyafa. My grandfather is the youngest brother of the ruling prince." A glint appeared in his eyes as Laurel reacted in surprise. "But never fear, I am far enough removed from the throne for the internecine politics not to rule my life."

It was starkly delivered. The barest of information. Some of which he'd already told her. Heavens, she'd gleaned more color about him from what she'd heard from Eli over the years. Rakin had been enrolled in an English boarding school, where he'd remained in the traumatic aftermath of his parents' sudden death. Once his schooling was finished, his grandfather had sent him to university at Harvard—which had brought him in touch with Eli...and ultimately into her life.

Yet the bare recital of facts gave her little insight into the people she was about to meet, and no glimpse into the man behind the suddenly guarded facade.

"Tell me more," she insisted before he could retreat again. "I'll be meeting your grandparents. I want to make a good impression."

"You will meet them at a formal reception where it will be difficult to engage in intimate conversation, so it won't matter if you don't know all about my family. Try not to worry about making a good impression—just be yourself. They're going to love you."

Just being herself was easier said than done.

Laurel was starting to realize that she'd spent much of her life trying to be the person she thought other people wanted her to be. For her father she'd been the talented pianist, and later, the PR expert that The Kincaid Group needed. Her mother had brought out the responsible eldest daughter. With her sisters she'd been the role model. Only her childhood friendship with Eli had been free of all the posturing. Yet even that had changed once all their friends had started pairing up. . . and suddenly Laurel had again found herself playing to the expectations of others—that she and Eli should make a match of it.

It was curiously liberating to realize that with Rakin she could simply be herself.

He'd been completely honest about what he wanted from her: a wife who his grandfather would accept so that Rakin could gain control of the family business and stop it from being signed over to his cousin. Yet he was making it clear that he had no wish for her to pretend to be anyone other than the woman he'd promised to induct into a world of adventure.

She could still be herself.

And, the best thing about their deal, was that she'd had more adventure in the past few days than her somewhat staid, buttoned-up life had afforded her in the last three decades.

Raising his glass, he said, "Here's to new friends and new destinations."

It sounded hopeful as well as adventurous, and Laurel felt her enthusiasm rising. "I'll drink to that."

Their glasses filled with juice clinked together, and their eyes met over the rims in silent intimacy. The impact of it was profound. Laurel forced herself to glance away, not to reveal her sudden burst of confusion.

As the Learjet started its descent, Laurel caught her first glimpse of Rashad, the capital city of Diyafa from the air.

The city was built on a hilly outcrop and all around stretched an endless sea of sand as far as the eye could see. Shades of ochre and soft pinks with blocks of red clay dominated the city. Domed roofs and towering minarets gave the city a spicy exoticism. Yet interspersed between the traditional domes, Laurel could also see tall, modern structures of towering glass thrusting into the sky. A mix of ancient and modern.

Excitement surged. She swung around to Rakin, only to find he wasn't looking out the window but at her. The divide between them appeared to have been bridged. There was an expression in his midnight-black eyes that caused all her reservations about what had happened last night to evaporate, and her face broke into a wide smile.

"It looks like something from *Aladdin*—or rather, *Aladdin* meets the twenty-first century. I can't wait to see everything!"

The formal reception that Rakin had warned her about was held at a palace in the center of Rashad that resembled something out of *Arabian Nights*.

Laurel had never seen anything like it.

The floors in the immense reception room were made of colored marble arranged in intricate patterns. Gilded paneling carved by a master hand decked the walls, lit by sconces that cast a glow over the crowd. Around the edges of the immense room, large ancient urns added to the grandeur while lush arrangements of flowers gave the room extra bursts of color and a heady scent. The sheer luxury of the palace's interior took her breath away.

Its owner, Rakin's grandfather, was equally imposing.

Facing the man with his flowing robes and fierce visage, Laurel found herself unusually tongue-tied. Their meeting was brief, and Laurel felt as though the old man's sharp eyes were staring into her heart.

It was a far-from-comfortable experience.

Tula, Rakin's grandmother, was more approachable. Her wrinkled face bore the evidence of a lifetime spent smiling. And the hug she gave Laurel was as warm as her husband's greeting was suspicious.

"You have known my grandson long?" Prince Ahmeer Al-Abdellah demanded.

"Long enough for her to know she wanted to marry me," Rakin answered for her.

Determined not to be put on the defensive, Laurel smiled at Tula. "Your home is magnificent."

Tula nodded. "We have spent many happy years here."

"We should circulate among the guests. I have promised Laurel that I will introduce her to many people so that she can make friends," Rakin said, stretching the truth, "I will bring her to visit again when you are alone, perhaps tomorrow?"

"Rakin, I wish to talk to your bride!" scolded Tula. "You have made us wait for so many years. Now that you are finally married, you cannot drag your wife away from us so soon."

Laurel shot Rakin an I-told-you-so glance, which he ignored.

"Rakin tells me that your family is of some importance in America." Prince Ahmeer went straight to the heart of the matter.

Laurel nodded. "My mother's family has lived in Charleston for centuries."

Prince Ahmeer nodded in approval. "Your family has roots—like we have in Diyafa."

"Yes."

Before long, he was asking shrewd questions about the business interests of The Kincaid Group. His knowledge of container shipping was extensive, and Laurel was challenged to answer his questions. Within minutes, he was smiling and nodding, looking much more at ease.

Finally he clapped his hand on Rakin's shoulder, "I was concerned when you called to let me know you were married. But it appears that you have chosen well. I am satisfied. You may visit us tomorrow alone."

As the sheikh and his sheikha strolled away, Rakin murmured to Laurel, "My grandfather is not easily satisfied—you have worked a miracle." His mouth curved up. "But then I never doubted for a minute that you would."

And then there were the guests....

Men wore a mix of European-tailored suits, a sprinkling of tuxedos and dishdashas with white headdresses embellished with beautifully knotted cords. Most of the women wore Western fashions—only a handful in traditional dress. The women were beautiful, dressed in the finest designs that made Laurel feel almost dowdy. She'd played it safe in a black halter-neck gown, adorned only with the diamond pendant Rakin had given her to celebrate their wedding. She felt as wide-eyed as a child in this lavish gathering.

Half an hour later, Laurel found herself alone for the first time. She'd been fed delectable morsels of Diyafan food. And she'd been introduced to dozens of people—and her face hurt from smiling.

Rakin had been swept away by two men to meet a third whom he'd invited here tonight. He'd promised to return in minutes, and Laurel had urged him to go, assuring him she would be fine without him.

"You are Rakin's new wife."

She turned at the statement. A tall, dark-haired man clad in traditional robes was standing behind her. He stepped forward and smiled. "I am sheikh ibn-Ahmeer."

Laurel found herself smiling back.

"Yes, I am Rakin's wife."

"I had not heard about you before I was invited to welcome you—how did you meet Rakin?"

She should have foreseen this. She and Rakin had not agreed on the fiction that they would spread. Telling this man that they'd met for the first time, less than a week ago, would not do. Desperately she cast her gaze around the room searching for inspiration—or Rakin's return.

Rakin was no longer with the trio of men; instead he was talking to his grandfather, and it looked like the conversation had grown stormy. His grandfather was frowning, and Rakin's body language told her that he, too, was tense. That worried Laurel. She was getting the sense that he and his grandfather did not have an easy relationship...and that did not augur well for Rakin's plan to stop his grandfather from ousting him.

"So how did you meet?"

"Oh, I'm sorry, I didn't answer your question."

Laurel focused on him.

He was only a little shorter than Rakin with dark, liquid eyes that had a way of connecting to make her feel like the only woman in the room. After the way Rakin had ignored her and caused her to be a little hesitant, to be listened to, to feel interesting was a balm for wounds she hadn't even known she nursed.

She stuck as close as she could to the truth. "We have a friend in common." Let him believe that Eli had introduced them.

"So you have known Rakin for a while then?"

Help! How was she supposed to answer that? And, more to the point, what had Rakin led his grandparents to believe? Laurel did not want to contradict his version of their romance, but nor did she want to tell an outright lie, so she compromised by avoiding his question.

"It was at my sister's wedding that we finally realized we were fated to be together."

He gave her a searching glance. "Rakin is a fortunate man."

The expression on his face warned her that "fortunate" hadn't been his first response. Did this man suspect that her and Rakin's marriage was a sham?

Or was she being paranoid?

"Rakin and I have something special."

That was certainly true. No man had ever made her laugh, shown her what her life was lacking, in the same way as Rakin had. He appeared to accept her statement and their conversation became more general as she recounted her impressions of Diyafa.

Within minutes, they had discovered common ground. Her new friend had a sizeable property portfolio, and with her family's interests in developing the old container yards down on the battery, Laurel found herself telling him about the plans for the new development. A development that was currently stalled due to Jack Sinclair's interference which had resulted in a loss of investors.

"The returns will be good," she said enthusiastically. "The whole area is coming to life, being regenerated."

"You do know about the business."

She gave him a questioning look. "But of course. I'm the director of public relations for the company."

"Forgive me, I assumed it was a puppet position when you first told me what you do, a role without any real meaning."

For a moment she felt affronted; then it passed. "At least you are honest. No, I worked hard to get where I am today."

A flicker passed over his face, and Laurel wished she hadn't been so sharp in her retort. Then she shoved her regret aside. Wasn't this exactly what she was trying to get over? It was time to be her own woman, not to worry about what everyone else thought of her.

"Then I must certainly apologize for my rude assumption. You must be thinking I am a chauvinist."

It had crossed her mind, and Laurel held off politely denying his charge—as she might have in the past. Instead she said, "If you are interested in learning more about the project I can put you in touch with my brother, Matthew—there is money to be made."

"Yes, please do have him contact me." He fell silent for a moment as he studied her. "I think Rakin has chosen very well. You are going to be an asset to the Al-Abdellah family."

Where did he fit in to the family? But before she could ask, Laurel sensed Rakin's dark presence behind her.

When he spoke, his harsh tone jarred. "I see you have met my cousin."

"Your cousin?" She glanced between the two men with some confusion. "But I thought your surname was Ahmeer—not Abdellah."

"Zafar ibn Ahmeer is the name I go by within the family—in honor of my grandfather. But I am also Zafar Al-Abdellah."

This was the man who Rakin's grandfather had threatened to give control of the family business to if Rakin did not produce a wife? Zafar had been civil, pleasant even. He'd made her laugh—he was nothing like the ogre Laurel had expected. She cast her mind rapidly back over their discussion to check if she might have been indiscreet. Then she stiffened her spine.

Why was she worrying? There was no earthly reason why she shouldn't promote The Kincaid Group to anyone she met in Diyafa. Hadn't Rakin assured her that by marrying him she would gain access to his business contacts? And didn't she want to help her family protect TKG from any harm Jack Sinclair might do by gaining as many new clients as possible? Zafar's business interests dovetailed with that of The Kincaid Group. If he wanted to invest, his money would be welcome.

An aide appeared behind Zafar and murmured something to him in Arabic.

"I will ask that you excuse me, I have something to which I must attend." He dug into the voluminous dishdasha he wore. "Here are my contact details." He handed Laurel a card. "We will have plenty of time to talk again later, I am sure."

With an unsmiling nod in Rakin's direction, he followed the aide.

Rakin glared after his cousin, and it gave his features a harshness Laurel had not seen before.

Since their arrival in Diyafa, Rakin had changed.

At first Laurel had not been able put her finger on exactly how he'd changed; she'd only known that the difference was marked.

He was distant. He was aloof.

And it was not merely the tension between them as a result of the night they'd shared together in Vegas. This was different. It was complex. He'd lost that lightness of spirit that had captivated her, made her laugh, and assumed a mantle of authority and become increasingly remote.

Now, having met his autocratic grandfather, Laurel was starting to fathom what was happening.

Diyafa was his birthright. He was part of the ruling royal family. With his return, Rakin's persona had changed. He'd become more than a man; he'd become a sheikh.

* * *

The sight of his cousin staring into Laurel's eyes had goaded Rakin into returning to his bride's side. He'd cut his grandfather's complaints short, and hastened over to see what mischief Zafar was wreaking.

"What were you two talking about?" Rakin growled into Laurel's ear as he watched his cousin depart in a hurry. "Why did he give you his card to contact him?"

His wife's chin came up in a gesture he was starting to know too well.

"We were talking about real estate."

"That is all? Then why did he rush off as I arrived?"

"He didn't rush off, he was called away. You're seeing a conspiracy where there is none."

Her exasperation only made the knot that had started to form in his stomach pull tighter. "I have plenty of reason. You do not know Zafar like I do."

Her expression changed instantly. "He has done you harm?"

Rakin hesitated. Almost reluctantly, he said, "He has always been my foe."

He could see his response had surprised her. "Always?"

Wishing he'd kept silent, Rakin said with even greater reluctance, "From childhood we have been in conflict."

"You look like you are near in age."

"I am three months older." But he'd been sent away to England—while Zafar, his grandfather's favorite, had stayed.

"How sad! I would've have expected you to be friends."

"We were never encouraged to be friends." The brusque statement was not intended to illuminate the tensions that had existed between him and his cousin. Rakin waved a dismissive hand. "Talking about Zafar is of no interest. I came to find you because I want you to meet Ben Al-Sahr. He imports large quantities of cotton from the United States. Presently he ships mostly from other areas, but if the Kincaids can introduce him to a supplier in Charleston, that could change."

"Thank you, Rakin. I would certainly like to meet him—and I'm sure Matt would love to connect with him, too. I'll have to let him know to expect a call." She placed her fingers on his arm, and the smile she gave him was brilliant.

"Matt? It's Laurel." Across the world, her brother sounded half asleep. "What time is it? Did I wake you?"

"It's okay." His voice sharpened. "Laurel? Is something the matter?"

"No, no. Nothing's the matter." She crossed her fingers. "I got married."

She shut her eyes...and waited.

The eruption she'd anticipated wasn't long in coming. "You got married? When? To whom?"

"To Rakin. In Vegas." Before he could interrupt she added in a rush, "But we're in Diyafa now. Rakin wanted to introduce me to his family."

There was a long silence. Laurel found herself staring out of the window, over the planted garden outside the palace windows. The rosebushes were in bloom. Red. Yellow. Orange. All the fiery colors of a desert sunset.

"Does Mom know?" Matt spoke at last.

The pointed question caused a stab of guilt. "It happened so suddenly. You're the first to know."

"Oh." Matt fell silent.

"I'll call Mom next," she said quickly as the pause again expanded beyond what was comfortable. "Then I'll call Kara and Lily—and RJ."

"Kara and Eli have gone away for a few days."

"Oh." It highlighted how out of touch she was. It felt as if more than a few days had elapsed. Why should it surprise her? After all, more than the view out the window had changed—her whole life had changed.

"Why?"

This was the question she'd been dreading. Somewhere outside she could hear children laughing. "Because he's an attractive man?" she suggested tentatively. "Because—"

"Not why did you get married—why are you telling me first and not Mom or RJ?"

Relief filled her. At least the answer to that was easy. "Because Rakin introduced me to a business associate of his. He's a cotton importer and Rakin has convinced him he'd be better off buying in Charleston and using TKG for shipping. I wanted to warn you that he'd be calling soon."

"You get married and that's what you call to tell me? That your new husband may have sourced us new business?"

Matt sounded mad.

But why?

And why did men have to make it so difficult to understand them? She'd thought Matt would be thrilled—both at the news of her marriage and at the idea of the contacts she was making for TKG.

Finally Laurel settled for, "Yes."

"Since when did business become the most important thing in your life, Laurel?"

"What do you mean?" Bewilderment flooded her, quickly followed by a tide of sisterly annoyance. "For months all we've talked about is what's going to happen to The Kincaid Group. And sure, the position is a lot easier since Susannah's grandfather came on board with Larrimore Industries, but we're not out of the woods yet, Matt. The last thing I heard at the wedding before I left for Vegas with Rakin was that Jack Sinclair was causing trouble again—and that you were worried. I might not be there, but I can still do my best to help."

"Laurel, calm down."

"No, listen—"

"Calm down! No one is doubting that you do everything for this family—it's the reason everyone was so keen for you to take a break. You've been carrying a lot of stress—"

"So has everyone else!"

"I'm not arguing, but one of the things I realized when Flynn became ill, when I reconnected with Susannah is that there is more to life than business." His voice softened. "You've gotten married, so you've discovered that, too. The news of your marriage to a man you've fallen for is way more important than a new business contact."

Laurel couldn't come up with a single argument against what Matt was saying. Every word he spoke twisted deep in her chest. Her baby brother had become a romantic.

But what Matt didn't understand was that she and Rakin hadn't married for the same reasons as he and Susannah.

"Okay, I take your point," she said slowly. "But before I call Mom, RJ and Lily, you need to know that you might also get a call from Zafar ibn Ahmeer Al-Abdellah. He's interested in investing in the battery development. Look after him, he's Rakin's cousin."

"Family *always* comes first."

Laurel was still smiling when she set the phone down, Matt's words ringing in her ears.

Eight

The rest of the week passed in a haze of engagements.

Rakin kept his word. He'd introduced Laurel to a host of his business contacts. In return, she made sure that the fiction of their loving marriage was firmly in place whenever his family or the extended network of relations—was present.

There had been no repeat of that steamy night in Las Vegas.

And Laurel wasn't sure whether to be relieved or disappointed about it. Despite her inner tension about her increasing awareness of him, her respect and even affection for Rakin was growing in leaps and bounds. Yet there was still a part of him that she couldn't reach, a part that was closed away and tightly controlled.

They had been watching the sunset from one of the many balconies of the palace, when she took the plunge and asked Rakin, "Will we get a chance to see the desert any time soon?"

It was something she'd been hoping he would show her. In part, because the presence of the vast Diyafan Desert surrounded them in Rashad, but also because she had the strong sense that Rakin had been defined by the harsh beauty of the world beyond the city. It was part of his psyche. By understanding his relationship to the ancient desert, she hoped to learn more about what made him tick.

Understanding Rakin had become increasingly important to her. Laurel was beginning to realize that he would forever be more than a stranger who had introduced to her to a world beyond her imaginings. Yet she could not yet put a name to the complex emotions he roused. There was liking...and laughter... and desire.

And something more.

Something that hovered maddeningly out of reach, defying her need to capture it...contain it...name it. It was something that had crept into her soul by small degrees until it was part of her.

"We could go any time you want." Rakin rose from the carved olive wood chair where he'd been seated and, moving past her, he leaned against the stone balustrade, his back to the sunset. From this angle he formed a dark silhouette against the flaming sky. "You are eager to visit the desert?"

"Absolutely!" She nodded enthusiastically.

"Then we will go tomorrow."

"But only if it suits," she said quickly. "Only if your grandfather—"

The interruption was immediate. "I have done everything my grandfather could expect of me—and more." There was pent-up frustration in his voice.

He'd even married her for his grandfather.

Rakin might not have said that, but the truth of it lay between them, a silent divide.

She glanced away before he glimpsed her thoughts.

The palace gardens were cloaked in falling darkness. Only the distinctive outlines of palms stood out against the pale gold of the desert sky. The first star had appeared, and a longing to explore the world that lay beyond the city walls once more overtook Laurel.

"It will be my pleasure to show you our desert. I didn't offer to play tour guide back at your sister's wedding out of politeness." Humor filled his voice, and it warmed Laurel as he drew her gaze back to his dark shape. "I wish to see it through your eyes—it will be a fresh glimpse. My own personal retreat is near

Dahab, a settlement in the heart of the desert," he added. "We will go there."

"Another adventure!"

He inclined his head. "Of course. And I promise you it will be far more authentic than a black-glass pyramid fronted by a crouching sphinx."

She gave him an amused look. "You didn't find that exotic?"

Rakin shifted, and the sinking sun caught the movement as his mouth tugged into a smile. "Exotic maybe. Authentic, no."

Gratitude for the experiences that he had already offered flooded her. Laurel found herself on her feet, in front of him. And, before she could consider her actions, she was saying, "Thank you."

An eyebrow raised. "For what?"

"For giving me the opportunity to break free."

"If it was important enough, you would've done it anyway."

Laurel was shaking her head. "I'm not so sure I would ever have found the courage."

"Because your family needs you?"

She looked down and didn't answer.

Rakin could understand the pull of duty. It had dominated much of his life. "What about what you need?" he asked quietly, above her bowed head.

Her shoulders hunched up. "My needs...?"

"Yes. You have needs, too."

The words reverberated through his head, assuming a double-edged meaning Rakin had not intended. A wild, sensual glimpse of needs very different from those he'd been alluding to taunted him. The memory of her face alight with excitement after the roller coaster ride flashed through his mind. The wild sounds she'd made when they made love...

She'd been animated in a way he'd never seen her. Alive. Held in a thrall that turned her beauty into something far more primal and caused want to leap through him.

"My needs are not important." She spoke with a finality that told him she considered the topic closed.

Letting out the breath he'd unconsciously been holding,

Rakin placed a hand beneath her chin and tilted her head up. Her eyes were turbulent with emotion. He forced himself to ignore the want that flared, and concentrate on the yearning in her eyes. "Your needs are very important. It's time you start to put yourself first."

Her gaze clung to his. "What do you mean?"

"I think you know." The evening sun had turned her hair to a nimbus of auburn flame, and she looked breathtakingly lovely. But Rakin couldn't allow himself to be sidetracked. "Eli said kindness is one of your best traits, but it may also be one of your greatest shortcomings, too."

"That's contradictory."

Despite the dismissive words, all her attention remained fixed on him.

"No, it's not. You've always done what everyone else wanted—even when it wasn't best for you." He heard her breath catch. "You haven't been very kind to yourself."

"It would be selfish to think of my own needs at a time my family should come first."

"Only you can decide whether it would be selfish—because only you know what you really want. Staying in Charleston, going through the motions of a life that isn't what you dream of would've been condemning you to a half life." His fingers still rested against her chin, and her lips parted. He ached to capture the softness of that sweet mouth. He thrust his desire down. Relentlessly he pressed on. "You need to be true to yourself."

There was a pause. Finally she said in a low voice, "You're saying that by doing what's best for my family I've been dishonest."

"I think that all your life you've done what you think others want—rather than what you truly desire."

"I love my family—I love my job," she protested.

"I'm sure you do. I'm not saying that you don't," he said gently, his fingers straying along her jawline in a caress. He wondered if she'd realized yet that she'd allowed that love to become a trap that was draining her of her vitality and life force. "But what you've proved to me is that you feel a need to escape from everyone's perception of who Laurel Kincaid is. That can only be because you have a different vision of the real Laurel Kincaid. Don't forget it's your vision that matters." Rakin knew she was still defined in terms of the Kincaid name. He bit back the urge to tell her she was an Abdellah now. His wife. And that he placed no constraints on whomever she chose to be. "Your vision. Not your mother's. Not Eli's. Not mine. Only yours."

This time he watched her throat bob as she swallowed.

But what she said next startled him. "And you, Rakin? Are you loyal to the vision of what you most want?"

The helicopter descended to the desert below.

Rakin had wasted no time in putting the plan for them to visit Dahab into action. Through the bubble windows the gold expanse of the sand rose up to meet them. What from the air had appeared as a barren stretch of nothing, now rearranged itself into a myriad of colors. Rocky outcrops with bent tamarind trees nestling at the base. Ahead, stone battlements clawed their way up against the outcrop.

Laurel spoke into the microphone built into the headphones that had muffled the noise of their journey. "This is your retreat? Good heavens, it looks like a fortress."

"It was originally a fort."

The helicopter cleared the high walls surrounding the edifice and dropped onto a helipad. Minutes later, the pilot came around and opened the door, and Laurel clambered out, keeping her head down until she'd cleared the slowing rotor blades.

Outside, the desert heat was dry and dusty.

She gazed about with interest.

Closer to the house—fort, she amended—water cascaded over rocks into pools adorned with lush plantings.

"It looks like an oasis."

"It is an oasis. Come." Rakin placed his hand under her elbow. "It will be cooler inside."

"What's that?" Laurel pointed to a building jutting out in the distance.

"That's the stable block."

"Stables?" Laurel came to a standstill. The face that tilted up to him was radiant. "There are horses? Or are the stables empty?"

"There are horses. Not many—the royal stud is located closer to Rashad. But I like to ride when I am home so there are always horses."

"Can we ride?"

Rakin nodded.

Joy exploded in her eyes. "Tomorrow?" At his nod, she said, "Do you know how long it's been since I've ridden a horse?"

That startled him. "You can ride?"

"All Winthrops can ride—we were taken for our first lesson before we were five." Her beatific smile told him she'd clearly loved every moment.

"Then why stop?"

"So much else to do. My brothers carried on—they still play polo. But, as the eldest daughter, mother insisted I learn to play tennis and do ballet and piano so that my sisters would follow in my ballet slippers." She grinned, but Rakin detected a forced gaiety. "And Winthrops fish and shoot and hunt, too, so there was little time left for the demands of horse-riding lessons."

"You shoot and hunt?"

"I don't hunt myself, but I'm a crack shot."

Rakin knew he shouldn't have been surprised. Yet he couldn't help it. Laurel was so intensely feminine and ladylike he didn't expect the more physical side of her. Then he remembered what she was like in bed. More tiger than lady. Instantly desire stirred.

He overrode it.

"We will take the horses out tomorrow."

"I can't wait."

"Now, let me show you my home."

The ride surpassed everything Laurel had expected.

They rode out of the dark stable yard while it was still cool. It was the only way to escape the relentless heat of the day, Rakin told her, his stirrup chinking against hers as they rode abreast.

The mare she was riding, a gray with small pricked ears and the delicate dish face so characteristic of an Arabian horse, had an easy gait. By contrast, Rakin was mounted on Pasha, a strong stallion with a high-held tail and long mane.

For a while they rode in utter silence, the clip of the horses' hooves muffled by the desert sand. Laurel shifted in the saddle and inhaled the dry, already hot air. To the east, the first bright slivers of dawn had cracked the jet-black sky. All around them the desert was coming to life.

To Laurel's right a dark outcrop had taken shape, and now the first rays of the sun struck the rockface.

"What is that?"

"Jabal Al Tair. The mountain of the birds," Rakin translated. "We will make our way up as far as we can and watch the sun rise from a higher vantage point."

The stony path climbed steeply until they came to a place where the rise leveled out between two imposing rock faces.

Rakin dismounted first, then came to hold her mare's head as Laurel swung her leg over the back of the saddle and slid down to the ground. Handing the reins to Rakin, she watched as he tethered the two horses. Then she followed him along a winding, narrow path between the cliffs.

Once through the fissure, the path opened up into a broad rock platform.

"Oh, wow!"

They stood on the edge of the world.

In front of them the gold desert sands stretched to meet the rising sun.

"Dahab means gold. You can see where the name comes from."

"Yes." Laurel didn't even want to breathe to break the awe of the moment.

"Look," Rakin pointed.

She followed his arm. A hawk circled in wide swoops. "He's hunting."

"Yes," Rakin agreed, his eyes narrowed as he watched the

bird swoop down to the desert below. "See that blur of movement? That's a hare he's after."

The hawk rose, a silhouette against the rosy sky, the hare clutched between hooked talons. Ascending to the sheer walls above them, the big bird disappeared from sight.

Gesturing to the vista spread out in front of them, Laurel said, "It looks so empty, yet it's an entire ecosystem. It just took the sun coming up to reveal it." She shot Rakin a look that caused him to want to pull her into his arms and seal her smiling mouth with his. "Apollo driving his fiery chariot into the sky to meet the new day," she murmured.

Before he could turn thought to action, one of the horses whickered behind them. Laurel started to laugh. "You want to be up there, too?"

"It would be hard, hot work galloping that course every day," replied Rakin, leashing the rush of raw desire that she'd evoked. "Only an Arabian could keep up."

"Apollo himself would have to be pretty fit." Laurel let her gaze drift down Rakin's lean length. "A horseman with years of skill."

Rakin grew still.

"I want you," he said roughly. "Now."

"Now?" Laurel could feel herself flushing. "Here?"

"Yes."

The bald statement caused her to blink. Twice.

His cheekbones jutted out in hard angles from his rigid face.

"But it's morning." She heard herself, and shuddered. She sounded like a naive virgin. Both of them knew she was not that.

"It makes you shy to make love in the daylight?" he asked, and touched her. One finger trailed down her cheek. "Still? Despite what we shared that night in Las Vegas?"

Her heart contracted at his mention of love.

This marriage had never been about love...yet Laurel was starting to think increasingly about love. It wasn't something she had ever discovered. Her lashes sank hiding her eyes from his all-too-perceptive gaze. What she shared with Rakin had a depth and intensity beyond what she'd felt for men in the past.

This was different.

Could it be love?

She started as his hands closed on her shoulders.

"Laurel...?"

The husky sound of his voice caused her look up. Taut tension radiated from him. A rush of desire bolted through her veins. She knew he was going to kiss her...and she did nothing to stop him. Instead, she waited...and welcomed the surge of heat as his mouth opened over hers.

His tongue sank in. Hungry. Possessive. Laurel's hands came up to grasp his forearms and she held on tight, her response desperate with pent-up passion. At least she hoped it was passion. Not—

Or was this...hunger...this desperation...this powerful emotion possibly...love?

Fear of the answer finally made her break away.

Rakin's chest rose and fell as he sucked in a rasping breath—but he let her go.

After a beat he said, "So? You're certain you don't want to risk making love in the daylight?"

There was humor...and a dark passion that tempted her at the same time that it terrified her. "It's the idea of..." She swallowed, then carefully imitated the wording he had used ". . . of making love outside—where anyone might see us. What happened in Vegas was under the cover of darkness." Mostly.

He scanned their surroundings. "Who will see us? We are far above the desert. There is no one near." And he came closer.

So much for her thirst for adventure, her craving to break free.

"I know, I sound ridiculous. I can't explain it." She backed toward where the horses were tethered. And she damned all her inhibitions.

There was a glint in his eyes, as he murmured, "So my rebel is not such a rebel after all."

Laurel wished she had the gumption to pick up the gauntlet he had thrown down. "I'm not ready for such an adventure."

Nine

They were almost home when a boy came running toward them.

Rakin checked the stallion, and brought him to a halt beside the boy.

"Give me your hand." Leaning forward, he grabbed the boy's hand and scooped him up onto the stallion in front of him.

The horse started to stride out, neck arched and head held high.

"I am riding Pasha." The child's back was rigid with pride. "He's much better than Halva."

Rakin laughed out loud. "Don't let Halva hear that—her feelings will be hurt, and she might buck you off."

"Pah." It was a sound of disgust. "Halva is too old to buck."

Rakin shot Laurel a conspiratorial look. "Halva is kind with the sweetest nature in the horse kingdom. Nothing wrong with nice. And don't forget I learned to ride on Halva's mother."

They turned into the stable yard. An elderly man with a sun-beaten face came out of the nearest stable.

As Rakin reined the stallion to a halt, the boy muttered something and slid off the horse. By the time the stable manager had hobbled up, the boy had disappeared.

"That boy, he is a nuisance." But there was pride in the old man's eyes.

"Your grandson will be a fine rider one day—like his grandfather."

The pride grew brighter. "He does well at school. He learns more than his father or his grandfather ever did. English. Computers. All the villagers say we are blessed."

Rakin waved his thanks off. "It was time."

The more she learned of Rakin, the more complex he became. The news that he was responsible for educating the youngsters. His gentleness with the boy and his grandfather made Laurel forget the reserve that had distanced him from her. Instead, she found herself melting inside at his connection with the pair. The discovery of this softer side of her husband moved her more than she would've expected. Rakin's gentleness…his social conscience were more facets to admire about a man who was starting to occupy an awful amount of her life.

He would make a wonderful father one day…and a perfect husband.

One day…

When she was long gone. Looking away from the man who'd taken over so much of her life, Laurel reined the gray in and swung her leg over the back of the saddle to dismount. She slid to the ground, then walked to the horse's head, taking care not to glance in Rakin's direction.

Their marriage had not been forged for love or family. It was purely a temporary proposition. She was nothing more than a temporary wife.

And, despite the heat of the day, that reminder caused a chill to settle around Laurel's heart.

It was the final day of their getaway. Tomorrow they would be leaving as Rakin had a board meeting in the capital.

They'd retreated to Rakin's library after sharing a late dinner as they'd done each night. The past four days had been a time that Laurel knew she would treasure even after their marriage was over.

Today Rakin had taken her deeper into the desert to explore its magic. They'd explored towering rock formations where wadis—water paths that brought life to the desert—hid. He'd taken her to visit villages with markets that had delighted Laurel with their character.

She should've been exhausted.

Yet she was too wired to sit. Her mind was still whirring, stimulated by the color and excitement of the day. Instead of joining Rakin on the wide, overstuffed daybed, where heavily embroidered cushions added an exotic touch to the huge room, she made for the floor-to-ceiling bookshelves.

Every subject under the sun was covered.

Politics. History. Books about Diyafa; about deserts; about ancient cultures. In addition to the leather-covered books and coffee-table hard covers, there was a large selection of well-read paperback fiction. Modern literary novels and a selection of popular crime fiction. The collection revealed the breadth and scope of Rakin's interest.

"There's a large number of travel books both ancient and modern," Rakin said from the couch.

"I can see."

"Their journeys were fascinating—they were men driven by more than action, by a vision of what they wanted from life."

She was on her own odyssey, Laurel realized. And it was far from over. Blindly she stared at the shelf in front of her. Then her gaze fell on a shelf of smaller tomes. Poetry, she saw. One was a volume titled simply *Pleasures* in faded gold lettering on the burgundy leather spine.

Laurel drew it from the shelf, the calf binding soft against her fingers. As she opened it, the yellowed pages with a flower-printed border were revealed.

A verse caught her eye.

My love! Sun of my Dark Heart, brighten my Day,
Bring life to stone-dry Desert, warm me with your Fire;

As surely as Dawn follows the Star-scattered Night
And floods the Perfumed Garden of my Desire.

Love poetry. Oft read from the way the pages fell open.
Read by Rakin?
"What are you looking at?"
It was as if her thoughts had conjured up his voice.
"A collection of poetry."
She flipped the page over, and her eyes fell on an illustration. It caused her to gasp. A pair of lovers, entwined on a bed under a tree. The woman lush and voluptuous, her lover dark and powerful. Laurel stared down at the undoubted beauty of the naked flesh that the artist had painted.

Normally she would've felt awkward to be faced with such material. The man's head was flung back, a look of unrestrained passion on his face, while the woman looked utterly satisfied.

Heat balled in her stomach.

What would she give to see that look on Rakin's face?

She shut the book and slid it back into the empty space; then she crossed to where Rakin sat and dropped down on the wide sofa arm.

"Thank you for a wonderful day," her voice sounded hoarse. She couldn't look at him yet, in case she gave herself away.

His finger touched the tip of her chin, with a gentle pressure to turn her head. She resisted. His fingertip moved to touch her lip.

Then he said softly, "You must be tired—ready to go to bed?"

Was that a question in his voice? A suggestion? The heat in her stomach blazed through her veins. Her gaze dropped down to connect with his. And a spark leapt between them.

"Come here," he groaned.

Laurel couldn't have said who moved first, but she was in his lap, his mouth replacing his fingertip on her lips, and they were kissing fiercely. The fevered heat was soaring. Raging. Within a minute her control had shredded.

Their clothes came off in a hurry, and there was little time for preliminaries before Rakin pulled her astride him.

It was fast and furious.

With every pleasure-increasing stroke, she watched him. Every flicker of his eyes. The way his throat tightened as he swallowed and the moment his eyelids closed as a moan broke from deep in his throat.

There was something sinfully wonderful about having this much power over a man—especially one as strong and unyielding as Rakin. So far he'd called all the shots in this game of chess between them. Back in Las Vegas, he'd reduced her body to quivers, played it like a virtuoso until she'd learned hidden secrets about her psyche that she'd never imagined lurked behind her conventional ladylike exterior.

He'd unleashed passions she'd never suspected existed, awoken desires that she'd never considered would come to play across her mind every time he walked into a room.

But now it was her chance to turn the tables.

Rakin was every bit as hungry for her as she was for him.

When it came, the explosion of pleasure was sudden and satisfying.

And afterward Laurel dropped her head onto his chest, and the pounding of his heart told her that his composure was as stripped as hers.

He'd seriously miscalculated.

Rakin had left Laurel asleep, sprawled across the enormous bed in his bedchamber, and he'd come outside to the pool for a swim to calm the turbulence in his head.

Who was the fool who'd said business and pleasure didn't mix? Then broken the rule he'd created? Not once, but twice. Worse, Rakin suspected that it would soon be broken a third—even fourth—time and beyond.

He swam a length, then back, searching for the tranquility, the clear head, that cutting through the water had always brought.

But this time it didn't.

He stopped at the far end, grasped the rail and tipped his head back. The pool was lit up by the golden coin of the full moon.

Not even the beauty could capture him. Emotions churned inside him, too hard to separate—or even identify.

The click of the latch on the wooden gate set in the wall surrounding the pool, followed by the sound of a footfall caused him to turn his head and squint through the darkness toward the arch.

He caught a glimpse of something in the shadows; then the moonlight moved on white silk.

His wife.

At the edge of the pool Laurel stopped. She'd woken to find Rakin gone—and she'd come looking. She'd suspected she'd find him here in the pool garden behind the high walls. She made out his dark shape swimming toward her, his arms cutting through the water with quiet strokes.

He rose in the shallows, and the moonlight rippled across his wet shoulders. "Join me for a swim?"

"Oh, I intend to."

Laurel dropped her white silk robe. Beneath, she wore nothing. She stepped into the water.

Conscious of his eyes caressing her, she came down the steps, head high, shoulders back, proud of her nudity. The water was silken against her knees. Another step brought it swirling around her thighs and her fingers trailed over the calm surface. By the time she reached the bottom, Rakin was waiting for her. He rose from the dark pool, his hair slicked back, water streaming over his body. Her breath caught.

He was magnificent.

Pagan. Masculine. And too darn sexy for words.

Moonlight fell on his face, bringing his angled cheekbones into sharp relief, casting light on the fullness of his bottom lip. Her gaze dropped down…farther…skimming his broad shoulders, resting on the amulet that hung on his chest and back up to his mouth.

Desire twisted her in stomach.

She wanted him.

Again.

It should've shocked her. But it didn't. This feminine hunger for her mate was the most natural thing she'd ever experienced. Under the veil of the hot desert night, she'd shed her inhibitions. She reached out, stroked the side of his face. His chest rose in a groan, then fell as air rushed out. Her hand swept down... running along his jawline...and came finally to rest against the water-slickened skin at the side of his neck.

Against her fingertips, his pulse reverberated.

So he felt it too...this powerful hunger. Too strong to control.

Lifting her hand away, she reached out with one finger, touched the center of his lip as he had done to her hours earlier.

His lips rounded, and he sucked.

Laurel's nipples hardened, and a sweet pain contracted in her stomach with the erotic play. The liquid heat of arousal filled her.

"Yes," she murmured.

When he released her finger, she trailed it across his lower lip, leaving traces of moisture. Then, unable to resist, she stood on tiptoe and placed her mouth on that same spot.

His mouth became passionate, his tongue sinking past her lips, ravishing her. Promising her that what she'd started would be good.

The want twisting inside her leapt higher.

She shifted restlessly...and brushed against him. With a sense of shock she discovered he was naked...and already aroused. Her heart turned over at the discovery and her pulse started to hammer. His breathing had quickened, filling the silence of the night where only the soothing sound of the water trickling over rocks broke the dark spell.

"What do you want?" he whispered.

You. But she said nothing, only brushed herself up against him, in a language older than time. Her body telling him more clearly than words.

Embracing her, he dragged her through the water to him. Corded muscled met her feminine softness. A sigh whispered in the night.... It sounded as though it came from a long way off, not from her. The stroke of his hands down her back caused shudders to sweep her in torrents. When his strong, male hands closed over her buttocks, his fingers flexing into the rounded mounds...it was ecstasy.

Laurel arched against him, panting against his mouth, all too conscious of the rigidity of his erection. One rock-like thigh drove between her legs, forcing her stance to widen, giving him space to maneuver closer still.

She flung back her head, surrendering herself to the pleasure of his hands...his touch...gazing up into his face, that dark mask silvered by moonlight.

For a beat of time he looked like a stranger. His face taut with desire. No sign of the good-humored man she'd come to...like.

His hands speared through the tangle of her hair. He drew them through, fingers sensually combing the long strands. Her eyes closed. Was this how mermaids of old had felt? This primal passion for their all too human lovers? Caught up in the mood of the moment, Laurel leaned into him, inciting him...not caring that she was driving herself—him—crazy.

The shackles had been shaken off.

This last week, for the first time in her life, she'd been free. Free of restraints, free of all the expectations that came with the Kincaid name. It had taken action on her part to step from the existence that had been so familiar into the fear of the unknown. But the reward was infinite. She'd become someone... more.

Someone she no longer recognized.

The old Laurel would never have undressed and entered the pool, naked, with such abandon. Would never have pursued her wants...her needs...so blatantly. So wantonly. Even a few days ago it would've been too much.

Yet in her heart she knew what drove her tonight was more profound than raw passion. Their time together—this adventure—could not last.

It would come to an end too soon.

An emotion to which she had not yet put a name overwhelmed her. It was more than liking . . more than friendship...

or even respect…much more than all the other things she'd been telling herself she and Rakin shared.

She dared not use the word love…

Get a Life.

Under the water, the smooth friction of his leg against the sensitive skin of her inner thigh caused her to gasp. Her eyes shot open. The pressure increased, rubbing against her. Then his fingers were touching her, peeling back the petals to find the sensitive bud that bloomed within.

Heat roared in her head. She fought the shivers that threatened to break, to bring the escalating excitement to completion. She wanted to stretch this time…to savor it…to never let it end.

His blunt length replaced his fingers. The pressure increased. Then he was sliding into her with slow strokes. Laurel gripped his shoulders and squeezed her eyes shut, giving herself up to sensation.

It rolled over her, in hot, endless waves.

A final thrust and she felt the quivering tension take hold of Rakin. He froze. A harsh, rasping sound broke from his throat as his control shredded. It was what Laurel had been waiting for.

She let the tide sweep over her, allowed the shivers of satisfaction to take her. But she had a blinding insight that this was far from the end. This was only the beginning.

The power of the emotion that had been confounding her had to be love.

Joy bubbled up.

She was in love with her temporary husband.

Laurel shifted restlessly against him in the water, and Rakin tightened his embrace. The blood still thundered in his ears.

"Cold?" he asked, nuzzling her neck.

She shook her head.

But he lifted her up into his arms and headed up the steps to a lounger, where his towel waited. Once he was seated with Laurel on his lap, he drew the towel around her. Using a corner, he patted her face dry. She closed her eyes and didn't resist.

She hadn't said a word since that shattering experience in the pool.

To his surprise, Rakin discovered he wanted—needed—for her to say something.

Placing a finger beneath her chin, he raised her face. Her eyes remained stubbornly shut.

"Laurel?"

Finally her eyes opened. But these were not the sparkling gems he'd grown accustomed to; there were only shadows in the jeweled depths.

"What is it?" he asked. "What is the matter?"

"What could possibly be the matter?" Her lips curved into a smile. "I've just experienced possibly the best orgasm of my life."

"Good," he purred, and relaxed a little, relieved he'd been reading a problem where none existed. "It was pretty damn fantastic."

"Yes."

She was still smiling, but he couldn't shake off his concern that she was troubled. "Are you sure you're all right?" A nasty thought struck him. "I didn't hurt you?"

He'd been so hungry for her—and he'd been sure she'd been ready for him, despite the barrier of the water.

"Of course you didn't!" The smile had vanished, and she gave a little sigh. "I'm just tired."

Instantly he was contrite. "It was a long day...yesterday. I will take you back to bed."

"No, wait." Her words stayed him. "It's so beautiful here tonight. The moon—" she gestured "—the water. Let's stay a little while."

Rakin realized what must be troubling her. "It's our last night. We go back to Rashad tomorrow." It filled him with regret, too. The board meeting he'd been pushing for, for so long, now didn't necessarily seem so important. Giving in to the kind of impulse he seldom acted on, he said, "We could stay longer, if you wish."

She shook her head. "No, you'd miss your meeting—and your family is expecting you for dinner. We must go back."

"We will return here soon. Have no fear."

Yet even as his mouth swooped to claim hers, Rakin realized that in the shadows of her eyes there was something akin to fear.

Ten

Laurel had imagined that it would be a small, intimate dinner. But at least twenty places were set on the long table in a reception room with rich hand-painted friezes on the ceiling. Platters spread with kofta, parcels of rice and nuts wrapped in vine leaves, and mechwya—grilled vegetables dusted with paprika and ginger and speared on iron skewers—as well as an array of morsels with which Laurel was still unfamiliar had arrived on the large table. The dinner guests were beginning to gather around, with the exception of the men of the family, who were currently closeted in the royal salon discussing the future of Gifts of Gold.

Laurel's nerves were frayed with waiting to learn the outcome.

Had marrying her gotten Rakin the control of the Gifts of Gold as he'd wished? Would Prince Ahmeer permit Rakin to remain as CEO and pass the controlling stocks to him as promised? Or would the prince renege by giving Zafar control of the company—or even changing his will and making Zafar heir to those all-important stocks? Laurel didn't want to even contemplate what that would do to Rakin.

Her gaze kept straying anxiously to the huge double doors leading into the dining hall.

When the doors finally opened and a phalanx of men entered, her eyes went straight to Rakin. He carried himself with such authority it was easy to distinguish him from the crowd, but no sign of what had transpired showed in his inscrutable expression. Laurel knew she should not have been surprised.

Then his gaze found hers, and his expression softened.

He broke away from the others and came toward her. Conscious that they were not alone, she offered him a tentative smile. He settled down beside her.

Leaning toward her, her murmured in her ear, "Success. I am now the major stockholder in Gifts of Gold—the contract has just been signed. Now all that remains is for the shares to be physically transferred, which should happen in the next two days."

She couldn't restrain her joy. "That's wonderful."

He came closer. "Thank you."

This close he smelled of peppermint and aftershave, fresh and heady.

Then the significance of what he was telling her hit. Rakin no longer had any need to remain married. Had his grandfather only changed his will, he could've changed it back at any time. But a contract for the transfer of stocks provided far more certainty—no doubt that was why Rakin had pushed for a resolution.

It meant they could part ways sooner.

No need to wait. A couple of days and the transfer would be registered. Divorce proceedings would begin soon.

The joy that had filled her only moments earlier drained away, leaving her with an acute sense of loss.

It was a task to eat the beautifully prepared meal. Roast lamb accompanied by root vegetables fragrant with cumin and coriander. No doubt the tastes and textures were exotic and delicious—but it might as well have been straw. Laurel found herself wishing she and Rakin were still at Dahab, eating simple dishes out on one of the balconies overlooking the desert.

She loved her husband; she was not ready for this divorce.

Glancing at Rakin, she took in the dark business suit he wore with a tie; his only concession to traditional dress was the head-dress he wore. He caught her staring and gave her a warm smile that lit up his face.

Caught by that warmth, she began furiously to hope.

Surely Rakin felt it too? They had so much in common. They liked each other, they laughed together—and she knew that he desired her. It was more than many couples had going for them. There was no reason to get divorced—instead of a temporary proposition their marriage could become real.

She touched his arm. "Rakin—"

An aide appeared on his other side. Murmuring an apology, Rakin turned his attention to the aide who said something in Arabic. Rakin's reply was brief. Pushing back his chair, he said to Laurel, "I won't be long."

A hand touched her shoulder. Laurel pasted on a smile and readied herself for the next round of civilities. She turned, and found Rakin's grandmother beside her.

"You have eaten enough?" Tula slid into Rakin's chair and rearranged her black flowing robe around her.

Laurel bowed her head. "Thank you. Everything was delicious."

The sheikha gave her a bright smile. "That is good. You must look after yourself—we anxiously await your news."

Blinking at Tula, Laurel said, "News?"

The older woman leaned across and patted her stomach. "Of a baby."

"A baby?"

Laurel knew she must sound ridiculously like a parrot. Yet she couldn't help herself. It was strange to be holding such an intimate discussion with Rakin's grandmother—especially given that she and Rakin had barely had time to get to know each other, much less plan a baby. Yet she couldn't help remembering that she and Rakin had not practiced much caution...a baby was not out of the question.

A shiver slid down her spine.

Unaware of the unease spreading through Laurel, the sheikha

made a sweeping gesture.. "You and my grandson will have beautiful babies."

How to respond to that?

Laurel laughed awkwardly.

"It is important for you to get pregnant."

Of course. This was about succession rather than beautiful babies. Feeling the heat rising in her cheeks at the deception she was about to weave, Laurel said, "We're taking a little time to get to know each other first."

The older woman shrugged. "You are married. Becoming acquainted with each other will come with time—you will have many years to do so. I, too, was once a new bride. I'd never met his grandfather before the ceremony. My husband always says he fell in love with me the day I delivered my first baby—Rakin's father." Tula beamed at the memory. "Rakin is very wealthy and now he has the responsibility of running Gifts of Gold. He will need a son to follow in his footsteps."

Staring at Rakin's grandmother in shock, Laurel knew there was no way she could expect the sheikha to understand that the marriage between her and Rakin was not about progeny.

Unless, of course, she could convince Rakin to make this marriage permanent.

Once again hoped surged. Rakin would want children, and why should she not be the woman to bear them? She loved him, they were married....

Laurel was starting to feel a whole lot better about persuading Rakin that it made no sense to get a divorce.

If only he loved her...

That would make it all perfect.

She could be patient. And there was the chance that perhaps he was already falling in love with her. The warmth in his eyes when he'd walked into the great reception room was a good start.

"It is not good to wait—you are not getting any younger," Tula was saying. "If you leave it too long you may become unable to bear children."

That was a reminder Laurel did not care to dwell on, and

it could ruin everything if, as she expected, Rakin wanted children.

In some secret compartment of her brain she'd been unconsciously clocking the march of time. It was one of the reasons why, when a procession of her school friends had trooped down the aisle, she'd been so eager to settle down with Eli. But it wasn't the reason she'd married Rakin.

A stab of regret pierced her.

The irony. Since her discovery that she loved him, she could envisage having children with no one but Rakin. He was the man she wanted to share her life with. He was the man she loved. He was the man she wanted to father her child—her children. He was the man she wanted beside her to watch them grow up.

She wanted more than a temporary arrangement driven by business and pleasure.

Even adventure was no longer enough. It tasted like ashes in her mouth. She wanted so much more.

"This subject is too difficult for you to address with your new groom? You are...shy?" The sheikha looked satisfied with what she clearly viewed as Laurel's modesty. "Then I will speak to Rakin's grandfather and he must tell Rakin he must do his duty."

"No!" Laurel couldn't bear the idea that the one area of their life where they shared intimacy might become riddled with conflict, or wrecked by expectations outlined by his grandparents. "That will not be necessary. I've taken note of your concerns and will discuss them with Rakin."

"My grandson has chosen well." The other woman's face was wreathed in smiles. "You are a sensible woman who understands what is important—your cooperation does not go unnoticed. You have brought great happiness to our family."

Little did Rakin's grandmother know that it had nothing to do with being sensible or cooperative and everything to do with her own eternal happiness.

"Rakin, your grandmother cornered me last night."

"Hmm?" They'd made love last night in their boudoir, after

the interminable evening finally drew to a close. Freshly show-ered, with the sun already rising for a new day, Rakin was ready to make love to his wife again, already eagerly admiring her scantily clad form.

He paused beside the bed where she lay and stroked her hip with meandering fingers, admiring the feminine curve, while trying to recall whether he'd already kissed the spot. What did it matter? He'd kiss it again before the sun was high to be cer-tain—he'd intended to leave no part of her uncherished.

"Rakin? Did you hear what I said?"

"My grandmother wanted to talk to you." He lifted his head and gave Laurel a slow, satisfied smile, already planning out how every bliss-filled minute of the next hour would be spent. He tugged the damp towel off and threw it onto the ground, leav-ing him naked. Then he sank down onto the bed, and reached for his wife. "Was she trying to persuade you to help organize her French film festival? It is her passion."

Laurel's eyes held a strange expression. Then she moved and the illusion vanished, forcing Rakin to decide he'd imagined it. "No, no—nothing like that. She only thought I should know that it was important for me to get pregnant as soon as possible. Ap-parently you are in dire need of an heir."

Had she expected him to laugh? If she had, she'd miscalcu-lated. Rakin rolled away from Laurel and sat up, raking his fin-gers through his hair before pulling the covers over his nudity.

A moment's silence followed in which he could hear his heart thudding in his chest. From behind him Laurel said tentatively, "Rakin?"

He turned his head.

"Is something wrong?" She'd come up on her knees in the bed. Her hair lay in long flags down her shoulders. Desire stirred. He suppressed it ruthlessly.

"I've never wanted children."

"You haven't?"

He shook his head.

"Then that's the one thing on which we differ. I've always known that one day I would have children. A family." She spread her hands. "Your grandmother spoke the truth—I am getting older. From her perspective, if we're going to have children we can't afford to delay too long. The sands of time will soon start to run out."

She offered him a pensive smile.

Her intransigence caused him to say more harshly than he intended, "I don't want a child—I never wanted a wife either. But I was given no choice. The charade of a temporary wife was my best solution."

A deep emotion flickered in her eyes; it was gone too fast for him to identify it.

Already she was turning away, reaching for the white silk peignoir at the foot of the bed and donning it. Rakin felt a piercing stab of regret. He let it pass. He'd never deceived her. Theirs had always been a marriage of convenience—and a temporary one at that. Laurel knew that. He'd never promised more than fun and adventure—and the added bonus of exposure to his business network There was no need to feel as though he'd let her down in some inexplicable way.

"Ours was never a union intended to produce children." He made his position clear with repetition.

Her shoulders straightened. "I know that."

She tossed her head and the dark auburn hair rippled like tongues of flame in the golden morning light.

But he couldn't let it go. There was a deep need to assuage the roar of guilt. "I promised you the adventure of a lifetime—not family bliss."

Her head twisted. "I'm well aware of that, and you've delivered on your promise. I'm not arguing that you didn't satisfy my need for every kind of adventure."

Surely, she couldn't mean what he thought she was implying?

Her gaze dropped down to where he'd drawn the sheet over his nakedness. Arousal blasted him. Heat rose in his face. "I am *not* a gigolo."

Her gaze touched the flat planes of his stomach, drifted over his bare chest, lingered on his lips. Finally she met his gaze and gave him a slow smile. "You could be. My own personal love slave. I rather like the idea."

"I was talking of other adventures," he bit out.

"Like bathing in the pool under the starlight?" There was a gleam in her eyes that he did not like. "Or sex in Las Vegas?"

He didn't like the bald way she referred to what had been a shattering experience simply as sex.

"Like bringing you to Diyafa, opening my home to you, showing you the desert, the ways of my forefathers," he bit out. "Like exploring places where few people have trodden. Like venturing forth on the horses...and bargaining with Bedouin. Adventures that few will ever experience."

He'd shared his soul with her.

"Ah, *those* adventures."

"Yes!" But he couldn't stop imagining the more erotic visions her wicked words had evoked. Rakin fought to keep his head cool and his voice level. "And I kept my part of the bargain about setting up business opportunities for The Kincaid Group. Already Ben Al-Sahr has been in touch with your brother Matt to find a cotton supplier in Charleston."

"Yes, I told Matt about that."

"Your brother has been in touch?"

She shook her head. "I called him. We've spoken several times."

"I knew you'd let your family know of our wedding. You did not tell me you were discussing business with your brother."

She gave a light laugh. "As you have made clear, this is very much a marriage of convenience only. We are hardly joined at the hip, Rakin."

She was smiling, but Rakin suspected underneath there lurked something else. Hurt?

"You are upset."

She tossed her head. "Why should I be upset because you choose not to have children? It's your decision, not mine."

That made him certain. She was most definitely upset. When a woman said things like that it left the matter in no doubt.

* * *

She had been such a fool!

Rakin had warned her from the start that theirs was nothing more than a temporary marriage of convenience. She'd known that. It had never been about love. It had never even been about sex—that had been an adventure he'd provided in addition to the rest.

Today Rakin had gotten what he wanted out of the deal—he still controlled the board of Gifts of Gold and soon his grandfather's majority stockholding would be signed into his name. He no longer needed her.

Scratch that. He'd never needed her.

He no longer needed a wife.

Any wife.

As far as her husband was concerned, the need for their temporary marriage was over. Yet, with her discovery that she loved him, from her point of view, their marriage had only just begun.

"You're heartless." The words burst from her before she could stop them. Instantly a sense of release swept her. It was true—he was heartless.

The skin had drawn tight across his cheeks.

"Not heartless—simply a realist."

Simply? Nothing about this relationship was simple anymore. Laurel couldn't believe she'd ever convinced herself that marriage to this man could be a lighthearted adventure. Fun. A carefree romp to break free from the drudgery that her life had become and help her complete her Get a Life List. It had all turned complicated—and come back to bite her in the ass. "I don't want to live my life in your reality."

He shrugged. "You don't need to. That's the advantage of our temporary marriage."

His attitude brought home how little he cared. About their marriage. About her. Rakin had what he wanted, and now he expected her to walk away from their marriage unscathed. Unchanged.

But she couldn't—because for her everything had changed.

The aftershock of the pain was devastating.

She loved Rakin.

He didn't love her. She had to face that, accept it and move on. This marriage was over. He'd just made it heart-wrenchingly clear he didn't even want to be married to her. Laurel couldn't fool herself that he was ever going to love her in the way she wanted—needed—to be loved.

"So what happens now? You clap three times, and our marriage is formally dissolved?"

"Do not be sarcastic," he said coldly. "It does not become you."

She drew herself away. "I need some fresh air—it's gotten a little claustrophobic in here."

He rolled away from her on the bed and closed his eyes. "I'm weary—I didn't get much sleep last night. We will finalize the matter later."

As the bedroom door closed softly behind his wife, Rakin's eyes opened.

There was no point storming after Laurel and bringing her back to heel with harsh words. He stared blindly ahead. It was better to let her cool down first—they could talk later.

Rakin had witnessed too many such confrontations between his parents as a young boy that had ended with shouting and slammed doors. He was proud that he had not allowed this confrontation to escalate in a similar manner. It had taken all his willpower not to tell her that she was being ridiculous. Their marriage would not be ended by a few claps.

If it was to happen it would be ended properly. Formally. Legally. Civilly.

They would remain business associates—even friends.

He didn't want to lose her friendship because of an outburst. And there was no reason for their liaison to end...even if their marriage did. The passion they shared was magnificent. He wasn't risking losing that. His preference was for their relationship to continue as it was...with no mention of children.

He would give her time to realize that what he spoke was nothing less than the truth.

Laurel was a mature woman. She would come round.

By the time lunch time came, she would have calmed down. Then he could comfort her—if that was what she really wanted. Or they could make love.

Right now he needed some rest. Shutting his eyes against the bright sunlight, Rakin drifted off to sleep satisfied that he had handled the problem in the best way possible.

Laurel let herself out a side door and stepped out into a walled garden she hadn't seen before.

It was an orchard. Even before she caught sight of the bright globes of fruit, the fragrance of orange blossom on the warm desert air confirmed it. The sweet scent evoked visions of her wedding to Rakin.

Their first kiss under the bridge in the gondola, the moment when her growing awareness of him as a man had crystallized into passion.

A passion that had culminated into the pain she felt now.

Well, she'd certainly made up for her reticence in the past. She'd had the fling of a lifetime. And now it was over.

It was time to come back down to earth and pick up the pieces of her life. Her real life. Not this romantic fantasy that she'd been playing out with Rakin. Laurel clenched her fists and moved into the dappled sunshine between the trees. Deep in her heart, under her anger at herself—at Rakin for disappointing her—pain splintered into sharp, piercing shards.

She ached. With disappointment. With loss. With loneliness at the idea of facing the future without Rakin.

The knowledge was growing that her escapade—her walk on the wild side—was over.

If there was one thing that had solidified in the past hour, it was the knowledge that Rakin did not love her, would never love her. But she'd fallen in love with him.

Big mistake.

His proposition had never contemplated that—nor had she

ever expected to fall head-over-heels in love with a charming stranger. He'd made her laugh. He'd encouraged her to experience the adventure she'd craved and launch herself headfirst from her safe existence.

She'd taken risks and been rewarded by joy. But now she was also living through more pain than she'd experienced in her life.

If this was what love was like, she wasn't going to endure it.

One thing last night had proved to her was that she wasn't the genteel Southern lady who could be trapped in a loveless relationship—even if she loved her husband. Uncurling her fists, Laurel reached for a spray of blossoms from the closest tree. Once she'd plucked it, she bent her head and inhaled scent of the crushed sprig. She'd been Rakin's bride, but she would no longer be his wife.

A pang shook her as she remembered laughing with him in the Liberace Museum in Vegas. That moment when she'd clutched his hand on the roller coaster and her stomach had fallen away when the train had dropped into a void. Just as her father had appeared so handsome and witty to her mother, Rakin had appealed to everything she'd thought she needed with his sense of humor, his readiness to lead her to the adventure she craved.

But it was a mirage.

It could never be real—because he didn't love her.

Her pride would not let her stay. Beg for whatever he could offer. She had to leave. Today. She would go back to the life she knew, the life with her family and The Kincaid Group.

A life that was safe…

Laurel dismissed that fleeting rebellious thought that she was running away. There was nothing for her to stay for. Rakin had made that abundantly clear.

She would walk away with her head held high.

By the time Rakin came down for the midday meal Laurel was gone.

"She told me it was a family emergency," his grandmother explained as Rakin stood glaring at his grandparents in the great anteroom in the palace. "You were still sleeping. I organized one of the royal drivers to take your wife to the airport. She was sure everything would be sorted out in a couple of days."

Sorted out in a couple of days? She'd been buying him time, so the transfer of his grandfather's stock into his name would go through and not be canceled.

Hands on hips, he fumed inwardly. "You didn't consider checking with me?"

"Family emergencies are women's work—not for you and your grandfather to trouble your heads about." His grandmother stared at him with bewildered eyes.

He wouldn't have wanted Laurel to face an emergency alone—if there truly had been one.

"Is something the matter, Rakin?" This time his grandmother's tone was laden with hesitation. "Is there something wrong other than a family emergency? Laurel appeared so happy last night."

Rakin let out his breath in an impatient sigh. "What could possibly be the matter?"

He swung around on his heel. His bride had been happy— until his meddling grandmother had started talking about heirs. Now she'd interfered again—and helped Laurel escape.

Maybe he was jumping to conclusions. Perhaps there was indeed a family emergency. The first step was to make sure that there was no family crisis, that she had indeed fled.

And that meant a call to Eli.

Which brought an unwelcome thought. She'd walked away without a backward glance from her engagement to Eli because she didn't love him. Rakin had been so certain he never wanted marriage...a wife. But now that his wife had run from him, making it clear that she felt nothing for him, he was surprised to discover he wanted her back.

There was no other woman he wanted more than his wife.

Eleven

Sunday afternoon Charleston welcomed Laurel back with warm, scented arms.

At the Kincaid mansion on Montagu Street, Pamela, the family housekeeper, opened the front door and greeted her with an enormous hug.

Instantly Laurel felt the pent-up tears pricking at the back of her eyes.

"Now, now my child. Why the tears?" Pamela drew her in and shut the door behind them.

"I've missed you all," Laurel said truthfully.

Halting at the foot of the white-carpeted, marble stairs that curved upward, Pamela told her, "Miss Elizabeth is upstairs. That nice detective just left."

"Detective McDonough?"

Pamela nodded. "That's the one."

"Has any progress been made with Dad's murder?" Laurel couldn't stop a flare of guilt. In the past two weeks she'd barely thought of her father's murderer.

"You'll need to ask your mother that." Pamela still hadn't started up the stairs. "What I can tell you is that we've made a start on packing up your father's clothes."

Her poor mother. Laurel exchanged a long look with the housekeeper. "How is she handling it?"

"Much better than I expected. How about I go and make a pot of coffee and let you see for yourself?"

Upstairs, Elizabeth was kneeling on the floor beside a pile of clothes and carefully placing a folded cable-knit sweater in a box. She stilled as Laurel came in. "Laurel! What are you doing here?"

"I've come home."

Elizabeth glanced past her to the doorway. "Where's Rakin?"

"I came alone. He's still in Diyafa."

"I'm surprised he let his new bride go off alone so soon."

Laurel sought for a way to break the news. Nothing could blunt the truth. Finally, she said baldly, "I've left him, Mom."

"Oh, my dear!"

Elizabeth was instantly on her feet. She folded Laurel into an embrace filled with warmth and the familiar scent of lavender.

Laurel closed her eyes, drawing comfort from her mother's arms. She felt like a little girl who'd rushed into the house to find her mother after roughhousing with RJ had led to scraped knees. In those days her aches had been fixed with a bandage and a mother's make-it-better kiss.

This time it was her heart that ached—and that couldn't be fixed so easily.

"Do you want to talk, my dear?"

The sympathy nearly undid her. Opening her eyes, she inhaled deeply and stared over her mother's shoulder. Did she want to talk? It came to her that there was probably no one who would understand what she was going through better than her mother.

After all, like Laurel's marriage to Rakin, her mother's marriage to her father had originally been brokered for business. Until Reginald had swept Elizabeth off her feet. Laurel shuddered. And, in a case of history repeating itself, she too had fallen for her convenient groom.

The major difference was that Reginald had convinced her mother he loved her. While Rakin made no such promises of devotion. In fact, he'd made it brutally clear that he didn't want a wife...or a child.

"There's not a great deal to say," she told her mother. Laurel sank down on the edge of the bed. "Come sit next to me and tell me what you've been doing while I've been gone."

"That lovely Nikki Thomas has been to visit me—and she's been talking to the police, too." Elizabeth gave a gentle sigh as she settled down on the bed beside Laurel. "In fact, the detective just left. His suspicion is firmly on Jack Sinclair. As you know, the only problem is that Sinclair has an alibi—his office staff say he was working late that night."

Laurel laced her fingers through her mom's. "But surely that doesn't count? I mean, he could've bribed them to say that." Laurel couldn't believe the police were no further with the matter than when she'd left for Las Vegas. Her mother had been right; it hadn't been necessary to stay. "And then there's also the small matter of his car parked in the lot near the TKG offices."

"But he denies parking his car there, too."

"How very strange." Laurel paused. "He must be lying. What does Nikki think?"

"She says she still wants to do more research—but she's determined to find the culprit."

Laurel had been too. She thought about the final item on the List. No. 10 : *Find Dad's Murderer.* The toughest task of all. And she'd made no headway on that. Laurel brushed her hair off her face with her free hand. Nikki would probably do a far better job solving the case than she ever could—so long as Nikki didn't let her heart rule her head.

"If the police aren't getting anywhere, maybe Nikki's going to be the best person to crack Jack's alibi." She gave Elizabeth's hand a squeeze. "The sooner he is arrested, the sooner you'll be able to get your life back together." And once Jack Sinclair was arrested, any chance that he'd be elected President of TKG at the June meeting would be scuttled for once and for all. Laurel knew that not only her mother, but she—and her siblings—would all breathe a sigh of relief.

Her mother interrupted her thoughts. "I'm getting my life together now. I've asked Kara to help get my marriage to Cutter planned. We'll probably be married in a month or two."

"Oh, Mom, that's such good news." Sadness touched Laurel. She certainly hoped that her mother would have better luck with marriage than she'd had. Just thinking about her marriage—the problems—was enough to make Laurel feel like sobbing her eyes out on her mother's shoulder.

As dusk fell, Laurel stayed on at the Kincaid Mansion to attend the weekly family gathering. Even though they were very surprised to see her, her family's support was immediate. Matt was there with Susannah—Flynn had wandered off to discover whether Pamela had any treats in store for him. RJ and Brooke were coming later.

Secure in the bosom of her family, amidst their concern, their love warmed her.

Lily and Daniel had eyes only for each other.

Kara was utterly radiant, so beautiful, and exchanging secret looks with Eli, the two of them clearly in their own world. Laurel envied them the intimacy. That was the kind of marriage she wanted—and it was not the kind of experience Rakin would ever provide.

But one thing stood out as they were finishing the meal that Pamela had prepared for the family—the relationship between herself and Eli had changed. He was her brother-in-law now... no longer her best friend. The ability to talk to him with the old ease had gone forever.

And besides, how could she talk to him about Rakin? It would be unfair. Rakin was his other best friend.

Yet Eli looked wretched, and she soon discovered why.

"Rakin called me," he told her from his position across the table from her.

"Rakin called you?" Laurel stared at him. "When?" *Why?*

"He seemed to think we had some kind of family emergency. He wanted to make sure everyone was all right."

She glanced away, her face warming, and a twinge of guilt

twisted her heart. "I didn't think he'd care," she muttered. "I suppose that means his heart isn't a block of ice."

"Rakin has a heart," Eli told her.

"You think?" Her mouth twisted as she glanced at him. "I'm not so sure."

It didn't need Eli's slanted look to know that she was being unfair. Despite her bitterness, Laurel knew he had a heart. After all, she'd seen glimpses of his kindness to children and the elderly. What Rakin didn't have was space in his heart for *her*. And that would never change.

"This is my fault."

Laurel waved a dismissive hand. "Nonsense. Don't blame yourself for introducing us, Eli. We would've met sooner or later."

"You don't understand."

Laurel's heart dropped like a stone at the haunted darkness in his eyes. "What don't I understand?"

Eli looked around. Everyone else was engaged in conversation. He lowered his voice. "I suggested to Rakin that he marry you."

"*You* suggested?" Laurel fixed her gaze on the new brother-in-law who had been such a close friend for most of her life and who she had until not long ago thought she knew better than any other man on earth. "When?"

"After you jilted me."

"Why would you do such a thing? Why?" It was a cry from the heart.

Along the table Lily stopped talking to Brooke and turned her head. Laurel quickly flashed her sister a reassuring smile. After a moment Lily smiled back, and when Brooke spoke to her she turned away resume their conversation.

Laurel exhaled in relief. That had been a close call. The last thing she wanted was her sister's concern.

Shifting uncomfortably, Eli murmured, "Rakin had a problem. I told him you might be the solution."

"Just like that?" How typical. How very male. "And he agreed?"

Eli gave an awkward chuckle. "What man wouldn't? I told him you were beautiful and smart and he couldn't go wrong."

Like a horse trader showing off her good points. Laurel spoke softly through gritted teeth. "Thanks, Eli!"

He looked as guilty as sin at the unfamiliar edge to her voice. "You're furious—in all the years I've known you I've never seen you furious, do you know that?"

What on earth was she supposed to say to that? Laurel didn't even try answering.

As the seconds stretched into an uncomfortable silence, Eli said hesitantly, "I could try to fix it."

"How?" she demanded.

"If I called him—"

"No!" She shook her head. "Absolutely not. I don't want you trying to help."

"I'm sorry. I've hurt you. I never thought..." Eli shook his head and let his voice trail away.

Laurel gave a most unladylike growl of frustration.

"That's the problem. Men just don't think about the problems they cause!"

Lily had turned her head again. A frown creased her forehead. Clearly she'd sensed discord. To allay her sister's suspicions, Laurel gave her sister the sweetest smile she could summon, and Lily's frown cleared.

"I can't be pregnant."

It was Monday morning, and the day was already to starting to deteriorate.

The doctor glanced up from the results in front of her. "You have not engaged in any sexual activity?" Concern glinted behind her spectacles.

"I got married—and yes, we did make love." Despite Laurel's embarrassment, the doctor looked relieved. "But I never meant to get pregnant—we took precautions. Except once," Laurel added, remembering the night in the pool.

"They are not always failsafe."

The urge to laugh hysterically rose. "I know that. Mother

had that talk with me when I was fifteen and went on my first date with my best friend at the time's brother. What I meant is this cannot be happening to me. I'm a grown-up. I'm sensible." Even Rakin's grandmother had thought so. "I'm certainly not the kind of woman who gets pregnant by accident."

The doctor grimaced. "Accidental pregnancies happen— even to sensible, grown-up businesswomen. Treat it as a blessing. Because I have even more sensible grown-up patients who would love to become pregnant by accident."

Those words struck home.

A lump formed in Laurel's throat.

She was not going to cry. Absolutely not. Instead, she said, "I always planned to have a family. One day. Of course, I planned to have a father for my children too—a traditional family."

The doctor looked confused. "I thought you said you got married."

Laurel shifted in her seat in front of the desk. "Yes, in Vegas. But it's already over. I served my husband with separation papers this morning." Ignoring the other woman's startled expression, Laurel thought about her mother betrayed and left loveless. About her father murdered in the prime of his life. "But we don't always get quite what we thought we wanted in life, do we?"

At least her father had left her the beach house. She still had that. Suddenly Laurel had an overwhelming need to be surrounded by the solace of the huge house.

As always, Captain's Watch, the great old house on the beach, stood unchanged.

Built in the late eighteen hundreds when the great families of the area had discovered the beach, it had stood for more than a century watching the ebb and flow of the tides.

Opening the heavy weathered wooden shutters to let in the May sun, Laurel felt a surge of renewed pleasure as she looked out onto the strip of beach where she had spent so many hours first as a child, and later as a teen with her dates and friends. Her hand rested on her stomach.

"You'll have that too, my sweetie, I promise."

The great house and the acreage around it were hers. Her father had known how much she loved it here. Leaving the window, she made for the large hand-hewn timber table where the family had eaten countless meals and played board games on rainy days. In the center of the bleached wood lay the List—and the letter from her father.

Laurel knew she no longer needed the Get a Life list. She had a life. A life with a job, a family, and soon a baby, too. But she couldn't bring herself to throw the List away. Laurel poured the last bit of sparkling mineral water into her glass, and took a sip. The List had changed her life—or rather, it had caused her to re-evaluate what she wanted from life. She had grown, undertaken *experiences*—the word *adventures* reminded her too painfully of Rakin—and found a deeper understanding of who she was. She would never regret that.

Her gaze fell onto the empty water bottle.

Then she picked up the List. She read through it one last time. Only item No. 10, *Find My father's murderer*, remained incomplete.

And No. 4. But the idea of eating ice cream in bed seemed suddenly childish.

For now.

Maybe Nikki Thomas would have better luck than she in getting leads that would result in Jack Sinclair's arrest. She folded the card on which she'd scrawled the List in half, then in half again. Her left hand reached for the water bottle and closed around the smooth, cool glass. Laurel pressed the folded card into the narrow mouth of the bottle. It dropped into the belly with a plop. She let out a sigh.

The List had done its job.

Drawing out the letter that had been opened, read and refolded so many times that it had the soft texture of crumpled tissue paper, she unfolded it and took in the words that her father had written.

My dearest Laurel,

If you are reading this, I am no longer with you.

But Captain's Watch is forever yours. For days your excitement before we arrived each summer at Captain's Watch would vibrate around the family, infecting everyone. You once told your mother that was because, even though the beach house never changed, no day was ever the same, that time spent at Captain's Watch was a summer-long adventure.

In the beach house there is a photo of you celebrating one such adventure. You are kneeling beside a sandcastle decorated with shells. I remember you persevering all day long after the other children had given up and moved on to other games. You stayed out there until, as the day was drawing to a close, I came to find you.

The sandcastle was finished and you were gazing at it with a look of such contentment on your face that I knew the time had been well spent. The following morning, you rushed out as soon as you awoke only to find that the tide had washed it away. You never cried. Instead you started building again, but this time you moved above the tide line.

I leave you Captain's Watch in the hope that it will bring you many more adventures through the course of your life. I know that your kind heart will open the doors to all the family who may want to join you at the beach each summer.

Happy family vacations always.

With my love,

Dad

Through the blur of tears, Laurel traced the flourish of her father's signature across the page with her fingertip.

The discovery that he had another family, other children, had been devastating to all of them—particularly to her mother.

But Rakin wasn't like her father in that way. He didn't already have another woman...or another child. To the contrary he'd told her he'd never wanted any children—or a wife.

Nothing changed the fact that he didn't love her.

But he needed to know that they'd created a child together. For the first time Laurel felt an inkling of empathy with Angela Sinclair. Angela had done the right thing. Laurel knew Jack's mother had tried to contact Reginald once, many years ago, to tell him she was pregnant—and failed in her quest.

The tears that had blurred Laurel's vision spilled over and tickled her cheeks as they trailed down. Holding the letter in her hand, she cupped her still-flat belly. Unlike Reginald, Rakin would have every chance to be part of her baby's early life.

Laurel could not even begin to think of how painful it must've been for her father to discover a decade later that Angela had borne him a son. A son who had grown into a bitter, brooding man, hating their father enough to one day kill him.

If only Jack could've known that his father had loved him enough to leave him forty-five percent in The Kincaid Group, Reginald's life work.

Perhaps if Jack had known that, it might have been enough to turn his hatred to hope.

But they would never know....

With gentle fingers Laurel folded the letter from her father and then placed it back into her purse. When she was finished, she reached for her cell phone.

After marshaling her thoughts, preparing what she was going to say to Rakin when he answered, she was almost disappointed when it diverted to his voice mail message. After a moment's hesitation, she killed the line.

She couldn't leave a message. This was something she needed to tell him herself.

In an hour she would call again—and if she couldn't reach him, then she'd just have to book a flight and go back to Diyafa.

Rakin needed to know they were going to have a baby.

Twelve

The sea sucked at her toes.

Laurel watched as the swirl of water disappeared when the tide sucked out again. The bottle with the Get a Life List bobbed on the surface about twenty yards out.

She knew she was procrastinating. Ever since putting the phone down earlier, butterflies had fluttered in her stomach. She'd been finding excuses not to call Rakin again. *Coward!*

This time she would leave a message for him to call her back. And if he didn't call back, she wouldn't leave it there, she would call again.

And again.

Until he knew.

Distracted by her thoughts, she didn't see the next wavelet until it washed over her feet. She yelped. The high tide was about to turn—and she didn't want to get the jeans she wore wet. Another wave came rushing in.

She backed up in a hurry—right into a hard body.

An apology ready on her lips, Laurel spun around.

Then froze when she saw who stood there.

Rakin.

"I called you just over an hour ago," she said, disbelief filling her. Had she conjured him up like a genie?

"I saw I'd missed a call from you—it must've come through not long after I landed. But I figured I'd show up instead of calling back."

"What are you doing here?"

His face darkened. "You can ask me that? After you arranged a legal separation?"

He must have flown from Diyafa the instant the papers were served. Her heart soared—that could only be good. Then crashed. Rakin didn't love her. There was nothing to hope for. He probably wanted to sign the paperwork off as quickly as possible. "There doesn't seem to be any point—"

"How can you renege on our marriage?"

The set of his face was frighteningly remote. A chill swept her. He looked more distant than he'd ever been. What would it take to reach him? Certainly not the news of her pregnancy.

"Rakin—"

"Nothing has changed. You knew the ground rules."

"It was temporary…that has not changed." But hope flared within her.

A dark eyebrow shot up. "Did I ever agree to end our marriage? Did you bother to ask before you took off while I was sleeping?"

Rakin was annoyed because she hadn't asked? The flicker of hope went out.

She loved him, and she couldn't carry on pretending that this was nothing more than a convenient arrangement.

She wanted more.

Much more.

"You don't need me anymore," she said. "You've gotten what you married me for—your inheritance. You even got it early."

Rakin gazed down into the pale face of the woman before him.

A shaft of afternoon sun fell across her skin, suffusing the fine creamy texture with a golden glow. Yet her eyes were dark and wary. A gust of breeze from the sea fingered strands of her dark red hair, spreading them across her cheek. Rakin reached forward to stroke the recalcitrant strands off her face, but she ducked away from his touch.

He dropped his hand to his side.

"You ran away." He had not expected the numbing emptiness that followed Laurel's departure. Suddenly the threats of disenfranchisement that his grandfather had been holding over his head for years hadn't seemed so important.

"I didn't run. I walked. One step at a time."

"You told my grandmother that you had a family emergency."

"A lie—I didn't want to tell her the truth: that I could no longer stay. Nor did I want to cost you your future by telling her the truth."

A cold fist gripped his heart. He wasn't reaching her. He was going to lose her....

Where was his warm, loving, sexy wife? Terror filled him. Was this how his mother had felt about his father? Was it this fear of life without him that had driven her to stay with a spouse who didn't love her?

Unrequited love was Rakin's idea of hell. He'd sworn never to repeat his mother's mistakes.

But living without Laurel would be infinitely worse....

He tried a business bribe. "You're going to have to come back to Diyafa. Ben Al-Sahr has a brother with another proposition for you."

Laurel shook her head. "No, I'm not. Matt can handle it. I'm going to stay here."

The terror doubled. She'd never refused an opportunity to benefit The Kincaid Group. She wasn't coming back to Diyafa. Ever.

The hollowness of the future faced him.

Unbidden, the legend of the laurel came back to him. Daphne had fled from Apollo, and when the sun god had caught up with her, embraced her, she'd turned into an inanimate laurel tree rather than stay with him.

It gave Rakin a terrible sense of déjà vu.

He had no taste for the hollow victory that lay in a laurel

wreath. The time had come to throw everything into it...renegotiate with whatever it took to get her back.

Drawing a deep breath, he played his ace. "We can try for a baby if that's what you want."

The shock in her eyes was unfeigned. "A baby? Of all the things in the world, why suggest that now?"

Her further withdrawal caused him confusion—panic even. He'd been so certain she wanted a child. Shaking his head to clear it, he said, "That's what you want, isn't it?"

Laurel didn't respond.

His panic and confusion grew. The reason she'd left was because he'd told her he'd never planned to have children, wasn't it? He'd been deeply shaken to find her gone. Devastated. But he would never tell her that. Exposing his heart in such a way was a risk he would never take.

Nevertheless he murmured huskily, "I'd like to father your child."

Instead of opening her arms to him, Laurel wrapped them across her chest and stared at him with accusing eyes. "This is a temporary marriage—based on sex and business. That's what you said. Remember?"

"I said many foolish things." He reached forward and stroked her arm, the satin skin soft beneath his touch. How he longed to touch the other, even softer places he'd discovered. "Men do that when they are afraid."

"What were you afraid of?"

Rakin dropped his hand.

Dear Allah...what did she want? Blood? *His* blood?

"You don't have to tell me if you don't want." She glanced away. Sunlight slanted off the sea, and Rakin caught the reflection of silvery tears in her eyes.

"Please don't cry." Reaching clumsily for her, he hesitated, then stuck his hands into the pockets of his jeans instead.

"I'm not crying." But tears spilled onto her cheeks as she turned back to face him, refuting her words. "At least, not really. Not sad tears. If you know what I mean."

No, she'd lost him. Rakin wondered whether he'd ever understand her. "Then why are you crying?"

She blinked, her eyelashes fluttering. "I'm relieved—thankful. I thought you didn't want children."

He'd never had much to do with children, and it was true he'd never wanted any of his own.

"Aren't you going to ask why I called you?"

Rakin wanted to hold her close, not worry about questions to which he didn't know the answers. But she was holding her breath, waiting for his reply. He sensed his response was important to her. "What were you calling to tell me?"

"That I'm pregnant."

"Pregnant?" Rakin felt the blood drain from his face.

She nodded, her eyes wide and expectant. What did she expect him to say? That he was thrilled?

Of course she did. Hadn't he just told her he'd like to give her a child? Hadn't she just told him of her fear that he didn't want children? Rakin closed his eyes, and tipped his head back. Trapped. In a noose of his own making. He swallowed and found his throat was thick. Now came the moment of truth.

"Rakin, are you all right?"

"I'm sorry." He opened his eyes. "It's a shock."

Her expression changed, became drawn. "You're not pleased. You didn't mean that about having a baby, did you? Not really."

She turned away from him, her shoulders slumping as she walked away with the tired gait of an old woman.

The pain of it made him call out, "Laurel, wait."

She froze, her shoulders drawn tight.

Coming up fast behind her, Rakin slid his arms around her, linking his hands below her breasts, over her belly where his child lay. Gently, ever so gently, he tugged her around to face him.

"Laurel…" The words dried up.

He stared at her. Frustrated. Hurting. Exposed.

Her shoulders sagged.

How could he say what she wanted to hear when the sentiments were nothing but lies? He wasn't pleased about the baby.

Not now. Not before they'd sorted their own relationship out. He didn't want her choosing to stay married to him because of the baby.

He wanted her to stay because—

Because he loved her.

This was like a terrible echo from the past. His mother had adored his father, but all his father had wanted had been an heir. History was repeating itself. Except this time, in a reversal of roles, he was the one who loved—and Laurel was the party who wanted a child. He loved her. It was unwelcome. It hurt like hell. He didn't need this.

All he could think was that, like his mother, he was not loved.

Pain tightened his chest.

He tore his gaze from her face. Rakin didn't even notice the wave that splashed around his feet, soaking his expensive sneakers as he stared blindly out to sea. The sunlight danced across the water glittering like diamonds. This must be how the sun god had felt pursuing Daphne after Cupid had wreaked his havoc. Unrequited love. His worst nightmare had come true.

Of course, in one of life's great ironies, his grandparents were going to be delighted.

Laurel was pregnant. He would have an heir. A successor for the business empire he was amassing would be assured.

Yet there was no joy. No stunning delight. Only endless dread.

He would be married to a woman who did not love him. Tied forever to Laurel with the strong, silken bonds of a child. Inescapable. He might has well have been imprisoned in the shape of a tree.

He couldn't let her go either.

Yet he knew he would never have the happiness he'd glimpsed too briefly in Dahab, the days and nights of pure joy. There would be duty and unfulfilled desire...and that would have to be enough.

He was trapped.

In'shallah. This was to be his fate.

* * *

Laurel didn't know what was wrong.

She only knew that Rakin had retreated. He'd been brooding ever since they'd come in from the beach half an hour ago. He'd given the interior of the beach house a cursory glance before heading for the comfortable leather chair her father had always occupied in front of the glass doors that looked over the beach.

At first she'd given him time to adjust to the revelation of her pregnancy. From her vantage point on the couch, where she was pretending to page through magazines, she kept sending him little sideways glances, but his mood had not relented.

He was thinking too much. It could not be good.

She'd known he would not be pleased about the baby given the sentiments he'd expressed back in Diyafa. But after he'd offered to give her a baby, she'd felt a lift of hope.

But his reaction had confounded her.

Was he hurting?

Laurel had had enough. She was hurting, too.

"Do you intend never to talk to me again?"

"What?" He gave her a blank look.

"Do you realize that's the first thing you've said to me since we came inside the house?"

"No." He shook himself and blinked rapidly. "I apologize, I have been rude."

"This isn't about good manners." She'd had enough of social expectations to last her a lifetime. It was ingrained in her family's genes. "This is about the fact that it hurts me when you wall yourself up behind that mask of self-control."

He stared at her.

This wasn't working. Laurel sighed. Perhaps she could shock him enough to drop that polite, urbane mask. "I'm going to need a pair of handcuffs."

"Handcuffs?"

"Yes. Handcuffs!" Her pent-up frustration was showing. "Sex seems to be the only way I can get you to lose your cool."

A flush darkened Rakin's cheeks. "There is no need for handcuffs to do that."

His murmur had caused her pulse to start to pound. "What do you mean?"

"It's not sex. It's you who makes me lose control."

The words were so soft she only just made them out. Her heart started to hammer. His honesty was more than she could ever have hoped for. Laurel went to sit beside him on the arm of the great chair. "Show me," she invited.

But the kiss was not raw with passion. Instead he brushed her lips gently with his.

Tender. What did this mean?

Finally he lifted his head and looked down at her. "I am terrified," he admitted softly.

It was true. There was fear in the depths of his onyx eyes.

"Why?" Then it came to her. This was about the baby. "You're worried for the baby? I know I'm an older mom, but lots of women wait until their thirties to have families now. I'll get the best medical care money can buy. It will be fine."

"No. Not that—my fears are much more selfish."

"What is it?" Now he was frightening her. "Tell me," she insisted when she'd had enough of empty, polite silences.

"Despite what I led you to believe, my parents' marriage was far from perfect. It wasn't the romance of a lifetime."

"Is that all?" Relief flooded her and she shifted closer to him. "Well, it turns out that my parents' marriage must've been far from perfect, too. But we're not our parents, Rakin. We don't need to repeat their mistakes."

His eyes locked with hers.

"My father never loved my mother," he said flatly.

Pain shot through her. He was telling her that he could never love her. He'd told her it was over between them. She'd already accepted that, so why was she letting the wound tear open again? Laurel squared her shoulders. "Even though my mother claims my father loved both her and Angela, I'm finding it very hard to reconcile my father's behavior in having a second family with any kind of meaningful love for my mother—it's certainly not the kind of love I want."

"But if he made your mother happy—"

"Exactly! And he was a great father. To all of us. And I can never forget that." With that off her chest, Laurel felt a lot easier. Now she had to come to an understanding with Rakin. One they could both live with. "After the divorce we can work at our relationship—and make sure the baby is well adjusted. We certainly don't need to keep each other miserable in an empty shell of a marriage. And we will both love the baby."

Rakin's gaze drilled into her. Then he said, "It wasn't only my mother that my father didn't love. He had high expectations of me. He was proud of me. But he never loved me."

Her heart melted. "Oh, Rakin—"

"What if I can never love this child?"

The terror was back in his eyes. Her heart ached. This was what he was afraid of?

"I've seen your patience with Flynn—"

"That's different." He waved her reassurance away.

Laurel persisted. "I saw you pull that boy onto Pasha—the way you gave him what he most dreamed of."

"Who wouldn't?"

"A person who didn't like children." Laurel wanted to throw her arms around him, hold the little boy in him close. "Believe me, if this is your fear, I assure you it is groundless."

He shot her a veiled look. "It is not my only fear."

"So what else do you fear?"

He shook his head.

"Rakin!" Laurel let a little of her exasperation through. "How can I help when you won't even let me know what you're thinking? Let go!"

"Letting go is the hardest thing you could ever ask of me." He drew a deep breath. "All my life I have been raised to be proud. To be restrained. To behave like a member of the royal family. To honor the Abdellah name."

Laurel couldn't help making the connection.

"Some men shouldn't be fathers. Yours may have been one of them." The uncertainty in Rakin's eyes caused her heart to contract. "Your treatment of Flynn at the wedding, of the boy who you put up on your horse is different from how your father would've responded. You are *not* your father."

Rakin shook his head. Laurel watched him rise to his feet and walk across the room to stare out the windows overlooking the sea. She sensed he was facing the most important challenge of his life.

And he was terrified.

"I love you."

The sound of the words was as soft as the whisper of a gull's wing on the wind. Yet it roared like a tornado through Rakin's brain. He wheeled around in disbelief.

"What?"

Despite the summery sunshine that streamed in through the windows, she stood with her arms folded protectively around herself, clearly steeling herself for his rejection.

Then she said it again. "I. Love. You." More slowly for sure, but still the same world-changing words. He hadn't misheard.

Rakin took a step forward. Then stopped.

Did she mean them?

Or was this obligation speaking…for the sake of their child? He despised himself for the moment of doubt as soon as he saw the sheen of emotion in her eyes. Relief buckled his knees; then strength and confidence flowed back through him.

She meant it.

Laurel loved him.

And this beautiful woman was so much braver than he. She'd risked all, baring her heart, risking his rejection.

He swallowed. Then demanded, "Say it again."

The green eyes he adored sparkled at him. "I love you."

Rakin didn't wait for a silence to follow. He gathered the strength that her words had given him and, taking a quick breath, he shut his eyes and forced out a whisper. "I love you, too."

Then, needing to see her reaction, he opened his eyes. Moisture glimmered back at him.

"I'm not going to cry," she said determinedly.

"No, you're too happy to cry."

That wrung a laugh from her.

"I want to get married again," he said.

Joy blazed in her face. "Yes."

For a moment Rakin couldn't absorb it. "You agree?"

She launched herself into his arms. "Of course I agree."

"So where are we going to be married?" she asked a little worriedly her head resting against his shoulder. "I'd love to be married here with my family present. But it would be a little odd because we're already married. And wouldn't your grandparents expect us to be married in Diyafa?"

"I don't care where we get married—or who attends. The only person I want there is you." Rakin kissed the top of her soft, sweet scented hair.

"Like when we got married in Las Vegas."

Leaning back so that he could see her face, he said, "Except this time will be different. This time when we exchange vows I will know you love me. You will know I love you. That is what this marriage is about—celebrating our love for each other."

The wrinkle on Laurel's brow cleared. "We don't need anyone else there. As far as the world is concerned we're married already. This time is for us alone."

Rakin nodded.

"I feel free. I don't need to worry about what people think." Laurel mouth curved upward. "I loved the romance of our Vegas wedding."

"Then we will be married on the Grand Canal."

"We're going back to Las Vegas?"

Rakin gave her a smug smile. "I thought you might enjoy the real thing this time—a wedding in Venice."

She threw herself into his arms. "Oh, Rakin." Then she sniffed and laughed. "We're going to come back here every summer."

"Whatever you want." Rakin grinned, ready to agree to anything.

"I'm serious."

"So am I." His grin widened.

"You don't look very serious."

"I'm happy."

That got him another—more passionate—kiss. And for a few moments there was silence. When it was over, she said, "I want our child, our children—"

Rakin's eyes blazed. "Good. I'm glad we're in agreement. I do not want only one child."

"Yes!" Laurel knew what was bothering him. He had been an only child. "I want our child to have siblings. And every summer we'll come back here to the beach house. My brothers and sisters and their wives and husbands and children will be welcome, too." As her father had known they would be when he had left her Captain's Watch.

"That will keep you close to your family. But it's not like you'll be separate from them forever. We can jet over to visit them any time you like. And you'll still have your public relations work."

At that she flung her arms back around his neck. She'd half-expected him to demand that she give her work up. Relief filled her that it was a battle she didn't have to fight. "I love what I do."

"I know that."

"And as my wife you will have even more opportunities to gain connections. You may, in time, want to talk to your siblings about outsourcing the PR. That way you could set up your own consultancy, still work for The Kincaid Group, but you'd be able to source other clients as well."

"That's not a bad idea."

"I know," he said smugly. "I'm simply full of good ideas."

Laurel wrinkled her nose at him and laughed.

"I love it when you laugh. You hold nothing back. And you become more beautiful than ever."

"How can I help it? You make me happy."

Relief filled him. He was not his father. His wife would not become a miserable shadow of herself. She loved him...and he loved her.

Their children, too, would be loved.

Epilogue

The doorbell sounded.

Elizabeth Kincaid glanced around at the family who'd already gathered in the salon for pre-dinner drinks. "That should be Laurel and Rakin."

"I'll let them in." Pamela disappeared to open the front door.

When Laurel appeared in the doorway to the salon with her lean, dark husband behind her, Elizabeth immediately saw that her eldest daughter was not the sad character who had visited only a few days ago—she glowed. Rakin's arm was settled possessively around her waist, his lean length complementing her fiery beauty.

After they'd all exchanged hugs and greetings, Laurel announced from the circle of her husband's arms. "We've got news for you all."

Silence fell over the room.

"We're expecting a baby!"

Excitement erupted. Kara squealed. Lily, blossoming from her own pregnancy, was the first to leap to her feet and give Laurel a hug. Susannah wiped away the tears of joy that had sprung to her eyes.

And Brooke rushed to give Laurel a kiss. "RJ and I aren't

having a baby just yet. But this is almost as exciting as being pregnant myself."

Laurel hugged her sister-in-law. "Don't take too long—it will be fun for our children to have cousins the same age."

Elizabeth swallowed as Brooke gazed across at RJ. "I don't think it will be long."

Everyone started talking at once.

His arm around Kara, Eli edged them both forward to stand beside Laurel. Then he said, "I take it this means I'm forgiven?"

Laurel took his hand in hers, and Elizabeth's heart swelled at the sight of the gratitude on her eldest daughter's face. "If it hadn't been for you, Rakin would probably never have proposed, so I owe you a thank-you from the bottom of my heart."

Kara retorted, "There's a certain déjà vu feeling about this. I seem to remember my gratitude to you for jilting Eli."

Her middle daughter's forthrightness made Elizabeth gasp. But everyone else laughed. Soon Elizabeth was laughing, too. It brightened her face and she caught a tender look from Cutter.

He was her rock. She had a second chance at happiness and love. The future was already brighter than it had been for a long time. If only the questions surrounding Reginald's death could be settled, everything would be perfect.

She spared a thought for Angela Sinclair. It couldn't be easy knowing that the police had your son under suspicion for his father's murder. Elizabeth looked around the room at her sons. RJ was shaking hands with Rakin. Matt had pulled Flynn onto his knee and was stroking his son's dark hair while he talked to Lily and her fiancé Daniel.

She had her family. They were safe and happy. It was Angela's world that was about to turn upside down—

Pamela's voice interrupted her thoughts. "Ten minutes until dinner will be served. Flynn, come wash your hands."

Crossing to the bookshelves, Elizabeth drew out a fat leather-bound family album. Baby pictures. It seemed appropriate given Laurel's news and Lily's pregnancy. One day, not too far away by the sounds of it, Brooke and Matt would join them, too.

Then she crossed to sit on the elegantly carved sofa beside

Cutter. Placing the album on her knees, she gave Cutter a secret little smile. Then she said, "Before Pamela serves dinner, gather around—I want to show you all how beautiful Kincaid babies are."

No one needed second urging, and within minutes she was surrounded by the family she loved.

* * * * *

Turn the page for an exclusive short story

*By USA TODAY bestselling author
Day Leclaire.*

THE KINCAIDS: JACK AND NIKKI, PART 5
Day Leclaire

"So, tell me, Nikki...how did you and Jack meet?"

They were gathered around Angela Sinclair's dinner table, enjoying a Saturday evening supper. Apparently, they'd reached the point in their three-month affair for Jack to take Nikki to Greenville and introduce her to his mother and half brother, Alan. And though she suspected Angela knew full well how the two of them had met, Nikki answered with a swift, reminiscent smile.

"I won him."

"Bid a thousand dollars for me at the Read and Write bachelor auction," Jack confirmed.

"Best purchase I ever made." Nikki's smile grew, warmed. "One look and I knew I had to have him. Best of all, my money went to assist literacy in everyone from nine to ninety-five. You can't beat that combination, can you?"

"No, I guess not." Angela cleared her throat and continued to regard Nikki with a friendly expression, though for some reason a hint of wariness rippled beneath the surface. "And what is it, exactly, you do for a living? I don't recall Jack mentioning it."

Nikki hesitated at the abrupt change in subject and returned her fork to her plate while she considered how best to respond.

Her glance touched on Jack before switching to Angela, who'd asked the question. "I'm a corporate investigator."

Angela's pale eyebrows shot upward and she studied Nikki with appealing hazel eyes that were identical to those of Alan, her younger son. "How interesting. Who do you work for?"

To Nikki's intense relief, Jack intervened, reaching across the table to rest his hand over his mother's. "She's not at liberty to talk about her investigations," he explained, his voice containing a rare gentleness. He'd treated Angela with that same hint of protectiveness and loving concern throughout the meal, as though his mother were a fragile piece of spun glass. Nikki couldn't help wondering if it related to Angela's vulnerability now that her role as Reginald Kincaid's mistress had come to light, or if some other cause were at the heart of the matter. "Her investigations are confidential."

"Oh, of course." Angela gave a light laugh. "I should know better considering I'm a nurse. We also have to maintain client confidentiality."

"Perhaps you can tell us about some of your cases," Alan suggested, his smile a warm reflection of his mother's, as were his golden-blond hair and innocuous, pretty-boy good looks. "Changing the names to protect the guilty, of course."

Alan had come as quite a surprise, perhaps because he and Jack were polar opposites. While Jack reminded her of his Kincaid half-siblings, Alan possessed none of the ruthless intensity that characterized his half brother, perhaps because his father had been so different from Reginald Kincaid, the man who had fathered Jack.

"To be honest," Nikki said, "they're not all that interesting. Most of my job involves straight background research." Of course, since she worked for the Kincaids—something she'd neglected to mention to Jack and which she was certain would come back to bite her badly in the near future—she didn't dare discuss any of her investigations. Particularly since the main case on her desk right now was investigating Jack Sinclair. Of course, she'd been asked to investigate him well after they'd started dating. And sleeping together. The situation made for a very precarious line she was forced to walk. Perhaps this would be a good time to deflect the attention. "So, what do you do, Alan?"

Almost as soon as she spoke, she realized she'd asked the wrong question. Angela pretended an intense interest in her dinner, while Jack watched his brother with sardonic amusement. "Yes, Alan. Tell us what you do."

For just an instant, Nikki caught a flash of something glittering in Alan's eyes, something that suggested the two brothers weren't as close as she'd assumed. Then the brief moment of animosity vanished and Alan offered another charming smile. "I'm between jobs right now," he confessed with self-deprecatory humor. "But TKG has offered me a position. It was one of Reginald Kincaid's dying wishes."

Nikki froze. Oh, no. Oh, please let her ears have deceived her. "TKG? The Kincaid Group?" she repeated faintly, sparing Jack a swift look.

He totally misread her shock, assuming it was because of his ongoing feud with the Kincaids versus the tiny detail she'd neglected to mention to him—that she was TKG's corporate investigator. What the hell was she going to do when Alan started working there? Eventually they were bound to run into one another. And when they did...

Jack would learn the truth about her.

"My father wanted to help my brother since he so often finds himself between jobs," Jack explained, intense irony rippling through his voice.

The comment struck a nerve, and for a moment anger flashed across Alan's expression before it collapsed into lines of grief. "Reginald was like a father to me, something I badly needed after my own father's untimely demise."

"Your father was Richard Sinclair?"

"That's right. He and Mother married shortly before Jack was born, though as I'm sure you're aware, Reginald Kincaid is Jack's biological father despite his use of my family name."

Nikki spared Jack another glance. *Okay, ouch.* Considering Richard Sinclair had been the only father Jack had known during the first nine years of his life, his brother's attitude must hurt. Not that Jack betrayed that hurt with so much as a flicker of an eyelash.

"After Dad was gone," Alan continued, "Reginald came back into Mother's life. Of course, he treated me with the same loving kindness he did his own son. We were quite close."

"I see," she murmured, although she had more than a sneaking suspicion she didn't see at all. Heaven protect her from Jack's family dynamics. Between his conflicted relationship with his Kincaid half brothers and sisters and his equally conflicted relationship with Alan, did he ever feel as though he fit in or possessed the sort of roots Southerners took such pride in?

"Closer even than Dad and me, isn't that what you've always claimed?" Jack added.

"Boys." From the exasperation in Angela's voice the exchange reflected an old rivalry, one that wouldn't be resolved anytime soon.

Nikki spared Jack's mother another glance. Though Angela held her head high, Nikki suspected she didn't appreciate having her illicit relationship with Reginald discussed over casual dinnertime conversation. If Nikki had learned nothing else at her mother's knee, it was how to deflect the conversation into less turbulent waters and do so with subtle deftness. Even so, she couldn't help but wonder how a clearly intelligent, loving mother of two, a woman dedicated to her nursing profession, had been content to spend a good portion of her life hidden away as the mistress of one of the scions of Charleston society.

Hours later, Jack addressed her unspoken question during their drive from his mother's estate to the home he kept in Greenville for the rare times he wasn't in Charleston. "I don't understand it, either," he announced, his comment coming out of the blue.

"Don't understand what?" she asked, though she suspected she knew.

"Why my mother made the choices she did. Both my parents claimed they loved each other and didn't care what society thought. Not that society thought anything until after Dad died. He went out of his way to keep our existence a deep, dark secret."

"I'm sorry," Nikki murmured.

"Nothing for you to be sorry about."

"Your parents...obviously they knew each other before Reginald ever married Elizabeth."

He slanted her a swift, amused look. "Obviously, since I'm proof of that 'knowing.'"

"Why didn't he marry Angela? Did he ever say?"

"They were both very young when it happened and Dad's parents were strongly opposed to the relationship. They were new money and determined to break into the old money bastions of Charleston's high society." He shrugged. "In order to do that, Dad needed to contract a fiscally and socially advantageous marriage."

"Which wasn't with your mother."

"No."

"Did Reginald just cave to pressure? That doesn't sound like the man I knew."

"You're right, he didn't. In an act of rebellion, Dad enlisted in the Army and ended up part of a secret operative unit. They were engaged in covert operations in hotspots throughout the world, so none of my mother's letters notifying him of her pregnancy reached him. At her parents' insistence, she married Richard Sinclair shortly before I was born in order to provide me with the pretense of legitimacy. Dad never knew, not until a full decade later when he was visiting his father in the same hospital where my mother worked."

"I assume Richard had died by then?"

"Yes." Jack shrugged. "But she once told me that she never loved him, not the way she loved Dad. She made a decent enough life with Richard, including giving him a son."

"Alan resents you." The comment spilled free before she could think better of it.

"I know." His hands tightened on the steering wheel. "Nothing much I can do about that, either, despite the fact that we got along well enough when we were kids."

Nikki swiveled in her seat so she could look at him. "What changed?" she asked, genuinely curious.

"Richard died. I suppose that's the root of our problems. Until then, Alan was part of this perfect little triangle, whether he was old enough to realize it or not. He was 'theirs' while I was just 'hers,' the odd man out."

"Then Reginald showed up and Alan became odd man out."

"Don't be ridiculous," Jack gently chided. "You heard my brother. Dad loved him as much as he did his own son."

"Got it."

It struck Nikki as intensely sad that Jack had never had a tight relationship with his various family members—that they had all kept him on the outside, nose figuratively pressed to the window. First there'd been the cozy triangle Alan had formed with his parents while excluding Jack, then the relationship he'd formed with Reginald, one that had to be kept quiet, which no doubt meant infrequent visits and never being allowed to have a father who fully participated in Jack's life. He'd have also had to deal with whatever comments and slurs were cast by other children, and later by his contemporaries. It couldn't have been easy. No wonder he'd been driven to succeed, had decided to actively compete against the Kincaids, possibly in a subconscious effort to prove himself their equals on a business footing, if nowhere else.

Tears pricked Nikki's eyes, making her grateful for the darkness enclosing the interior of the car. Jack was a strong, competent, tough man who would no doubt find her tears bewildering. While he went out of his way to protect his mother—the evidence of which she'd witnessed tonight—it never would have occurred to him to expect that same protection from his father. Instead, he'd been left to fend for himself.

No wonder he had a grudge against the Kincaids.

Jack Sinclair smiled in satisfaction as he opened the door to his home and ushered Nikki in ahead of him. He'd been right. She suited his plantation home, a home that epitomized gracious Southern living.

"This is…" She turned slowly to take in the foyer, the sweeping staircase, the mile-high ceiling and eighteenth century molding. "Okay, this is amazing. Absolutely gorgeous."

"I don't know why you're acting so surprised. You described this place to me on our first date."

It had been on their drive to his beach house for dinner. She'd shocked him by guessing what his mansion would look like, sight unseen, basing her deduction on what she knew of his personality. It was a game she and her father—a cop who'd gone down in the line of duty—had played during her youth. She informed him that his place would be an ideal blend of past and present, beautifully restored, the interior mating antiques with classic contemporary. Even more intriguing, she'd predicted that he'd put his own mark on the place in some way. Probably a way that had his interior decorator up in arms.

He'd be interested to see her reaction when she found that mark.

She laughed. "I'm not sure it's quite the way I described. It's more, far more." She tilted her head to one side. "And yet…it suits you."

"I'll save the grand tour until tomorrow."

"Really?" Nikki frowned in disappointment. "Why? I'd love to see it now."

He shook his head. "It shows best in morning light."

She gave a quick, agreeable shrug—another thing he appreciated about her, her easy-going nature. "Fair enough." She glanced over her shoulder at him. "What would you like to do instead?"

"Something a lot more entertaining than touring the house."

Awareness drifted into her sapphire blue eyes and a slow, sultry smile touched her mouth. "I can't imagine what that might be."

"Take a wild guess." He didn't give her time to guess, but simply swung her into his arms and started toward the staircase. "I've always wanted to do this with a woman. The house positively shouts out for it."

She wrapped her arms around his neck. "You're crazy, you know that? I'm no lightweight."

"You're perfect."

The instant they hit the top of the stairs, he headed down the wide hallway to the master suite. Nudging open the door, he carried her straight through to his bed and lowered her to the mattress. She smiled up at him and in that moment he knew that if he wasn't very careful he'd fall in love with her. He was already halfway there, maybe more. Just one teetering step away from the real deal. If he were brutally honest with himself, he'd admit he'd been falling bit by bit over the past four months and was about to go down for the count.

"You really are perfect, you know," he murmured.

She simply stared at him and shook her head. To his concern, tears glistened in her eyes. "I'm not, you know," she informed him in a low, distressed voice. "There's a lot I haven't told you about myself."

He came down beside her, easing her against the lightweight spread, the royal-blue silk an almost exact match for her eyes. "We all have secrets, private places we keep hidden from the world. I don't expect you to share those parts of yourself until you're ready."

"You don't understand."

He took her mouth in a soothing kiss, slow and light and gently teasing. She moaned softly, opened to him, gifting herself with unconscious generosity. She'd been that way from the start, totally giving in the way she responded to him, never holding back or playing coy. He'd never known a woman so lacking in artifice or feminine wiles, who put her cards on the table without fear or hesitation. Okay, so she had a couple wild cards she kept face down. Reasonable. But she couldn't hide who she was, not at her core.

"I don't need to understand everything," he reassured. "Not until you're ready."

He didn't wait for a response, but kissed her again, deeper this time, edging them toward the passion that exploded between them whenever they touched. This occasion proved no different. With a soft moan she slid her fingers in his hair, anchoring him. And that's when the world tilted and time stopped, just as it always did when they came together.

He thumbed open the buttons of her blouse, one by one, and spread apart the edges of the crisp violet cotton. She wore a bra beneath, the scrap of silk and lace several shades paler than her blouse. It cupped her creamy breasts, offering up their bounty and tempting him beyond measure.

"You have no idea how long I've wanted you here."

A wariness slipped across her expression. "Here in your bed? Or here in your home?"

"Yes." He hesitated, understanding the unspoken question. "Bringing you to Greenville and introducing you to my family isn't a step I take lightly."

She hesitated, nodded. "It's not one I take lightly, either."

Jack traced the line of her bra, watching Nikki's eyes go dark and a flush of want creep into her cheeks. "So I should expect you to return the favor?" To his surprise she fell silent. One of those deep, dark secrets? "You've gone quiet," he prompted.

She glanced at him with a wry smile. "Sorry. I was just thinking about how nerve-racking it is when you first meet the parents. I was scared to death to meet your mother. I'm sure you'll go just as quiet when we visit my mother and Grandmother Beaulyn. Guaranteed if you don't before we get there, you will the minute you meet them."

He lifted an eyebrow in open reproof. "Is there some reason you find it necessary to threaten me with your relatives?"

To his satisfaction, his comment caused her to relax and smile. "Seems only fair, given the minefield you forced me to negotiate at dinner tonight," she said lightly.

"The minefield you successfully negotiated." Quite finished with the topic, he flicked open her bra, watching with intense interest as the cups parted and the pale lilac scrap of silk fell away, revealing the most perfect breasts he'd ever seen.

She inhaled sharply. "Jack…"

"Right here, sweetheart. And more than ready to stop talking about family and discuss something far more interesting."

She laughed, tugging his shirt over his head. "That doesn't require any discussion. Just action."

He didn't need any further prompting. He kissed her again, taking his time in order to be very, very thorough. Bit by bit their clothing slipped away until there was nothing between them but the sigh of evening air slipping through the window, softly caressing their intertwined bodies. The light breeze carried in the music of the night, the raspy croak of tree frogs, and from a pond in the distance the deeper bass of their bullfrog cousins. Insects added their high-pitched chirps to the springtime song, underscored by the soft, distinctive whinny from a tree where screech owls often nested and would soon be fledging their young. And not far from the window he caught the faint crackle of leaves under hoof that spoke of deer wandering across his property.

For some reason nature's chorus only added to the perfection of their time together. Nikki must have felt the same, for she released a sigh of intense pleasure, relaxing within his embrace and smiling with such sweetness Jack wished he could somehow capture this moment and engrave it on his memory for all time.

"Nikki…" Her name escaped, the pure masculine need underscoring that single word adding an unmistakable note of passion to the music surrounding them.

She brushed a series of slow kisses across his chest, her hands sliding over his hip. Her fingers lingered on an old scar carved across his right hip toward his buttock. "How did you get this? The last time I asked we got distracted and you never said."

He'd distracted her deliberately, not wanting to dwell on a memory that had caused him so much pain. "I was hit by a car when I was twelve."

Her breath caught. "Oh, God, Jack. What happened?"

"Alan wandered out into the street. I got there in the nick of time to knock him clear." He offered a quick, humorless laugh. "Unfortunately, I wasn't in time to get clear myself. I ended up in the hospital."

"Your mother must have been frantic."

"She was."

"And your father?"

Naturally, she keyed in on the one element he least wanted to discuss. He answered her question with a slow, lingering kiss. And then another. As he hoped, the question faded away, unanswered. Inexorably, he eased them back to where they'd been before she'd found the scar, chased away the pain of the discussion with the pleasure of her mouth. Her honeyed skin. Her tantalizing caresses.

"I don't think I've ever wanted a woman as badly as I want you," he confessed.

"What are you waiting for?" Her arms circled his neck and she tugged him down. "Take me, Jack."

For some reason he wanted this time to be special, the most special they'd experienced to date. He couldn't say whether it was because they were in his Greenville home, a place he'd never shared with another woman, or because he'd found such perfection in this moment. The reason didn't matter, only that he act on it.

He started with a kiss, a kiss like the one that had started their affair. A kiss of introduction that had also marked them in some indelible way. She opened to him, just as she always did, but he caught something new in her kiss, both a vulnerability and a release, as though he'd breached an expected barricade, one he'd never realized existed. There was a newness to their kiss that spoke of a nakedness of the spirit as much as of their bodies, and he couldn't seem to get enough of it.

Slowly the passion built, warming the air and adding to the sweet fragrance. Jack ran a hand over Nikki's hip and cupped her bottom. She was beautifully shaped—long and lean, with ripe and rounded curves. She would never be a fragile Southern belle, but rather possessed the strength and fortitude of a steel magnolia, her stem planted strong and deep while her petals were soft and fragrant and alluring. She used those fragrant petals to wrap him up in velvet, clung to him as he joined his body to hers, matched him in an endless give and take.

The shattering came, more intense than ever before, stealing breath and intellect in its glorious aftermath. "It just gets better," he managed to say. "How is that possible?"

"I don't know." She buried her face against his chest and to his dismay he felt her tears. "I don't understand it, either."

"Sweetheart, what's wrong?"

She gave a watery laugh. "Nothing's wrong. It's all…perfect. I guess that scares me." She stared up at him, her eyes a flash of blue within the darkness of the room. "I just want it to go on and on. And I'm afraid it won't. That it can't."

"It can and it will."

He almost told her of the love building in his heart, of the ring buried in his dresser drawer. But not yet. When he took her for his wife he wanted to put a final period to the past and be in a position to move decisively into the future as head of both Carolina Shipping and The Kincaid Group. But that wouldn't happen until after the annual meeting at the end of June. Gently, Jack kissed Nikki, giving into desire instead of following his heart.

He let the moment go, only seeing the crossroad long after he'd chosen a path and allowed his heart's desire to slip away.

The next morning, Jack took Nikki on a tour of his plantation home, as promised.

"This is incredible," she informed him, marveling over the beautiful melding of past and present. She gestured toward the crown molding. "Is all of the wood trim original to the house?"

He leaned against a doorjamb and smiled at her enthusiasm and pleasure. "In the oldest section, every last piece. In the two newer wings, it's an exact replica. It's even the same type of wood."

They'd explored almost every inch, but she had a sneaking suspicion he'd saved one part for last—no doubt the room where he'd left his own distinctive mark, a mark she'd predicted had his interior decorator up in arms. He led her to a final door and shot her a quick grin, which told her they'd finally arrived at that statement. Opening the door with a flourish, he stepped back and allowed her to enter first.

She did and instantly burst out laughing. "It's a tiki bar," she marveled.

"Somehow, it's just not a plantation without a tiki bar," Jack informed her gravely.

She wandered through the room, pausing to stroke the sweeping surface of the bar. "This is wild."

And it was. From the bamboo flooring to the decorations, to the thatched bar featuring a wooden menu listing umbrella drinks in colorful chalk, to the electronic games and big-screen TV, the room had it all. Not a single detail had been overlooked.

"The windows along the wall by the pool are removable so it can be opened to the outside or left screened in."

"You know, I wouldn't have thought this suited you if I'd come across it anywhere else." She tilted her head to one side. "But now that I think about it, in an odd way, it does."

He wrapped his arms around her waist. "And why is that?"

She settled in close, absorbing his warmth and strength. "Because it's unconventional."

"Surely you're not accusing me of being unconventional."

He'd made the comment in a neutral voice, which had her pausing to consider. "For the most part, no. And yet, there's this rebellious streak that flows through you," she explained slowly. "It's almost like you're saying, 'You may think you have me pegged, but you don't. I'm not my father or my mother or any of my siblings. I'm my own person. And damn it all, if I want a tiki bar in my plantation mansion, that's what I'll have.'"

He fell silent for so long she wondered if she'd offended him. She tilted her head to glance up at him, moved beyond words when she caught sight of his odd defenselessness. Finally, he spoke. "You know, there are times when you can be uncomfortably astute."

"You're not alone, Jack," she whispered. "Not anymore. You've made a home here. You've made a place for yourself in the world, a place where you belong."

Without a word, he yanked her closer, wrapping her up in a tight hug. She gazed out over the beautiful home he'd created, realizing he was close to achieving everything he ever wanted…

so very close. If he could just let down his defenses a little more, he could have it all. And he deserved it all, just like this plantation deserved to fulfill its promise. To be imbued with the sort of love and happiness Jack could bring it.

If she listened carefully enough, she could practically hear the future. Could hear the plantation ringing with youthful footsteps racing across the wooden floorboards, the sound of children's voices echoing off walls that had known generations of love and laughter and stood poised to hear still more, to have their sons and daughters gamboling across the endless sweep of lawn like newborn fawns.

"Jack..." She turned to him, wrapped her arms around his neck and lifted her face to his, too overcome with emotion to say anything further.

She almost told him of the love building in her heart and of the secrets she kept from him. But not quite yet. When the time was right, she'd confess all. Maybe before the annual meeting that would determine who would become president and CEO of The Kincaid Group. But that wouldn't happen until the end of June. Gently, Nikki kissed Jack, giving in to desire instead of following her heart.

She let the moment go, only seeing the crossroads long after she'd chosen a path and allowed her heart's desire to slip away.

* * * * *

A VERY
PRIVATE MERGER

DAY LECLAIRE

Dear Reader,

What a fun project this has been! I can't begin to tell you how much I've enjoyed writing the mini-stories that have appeared at the end of each of the books leading to this one. It allowed me to give you a peek into the evolving relationship between Jack and Nikki, something I've never had the opportunity to write before. If you haven't read the other books, I urge you to pick them up. Not only are they fabulous stories, but you have the extra treat of reading the building love affair that leads to the start of *A Very Private Merger*.

As many of you know from the books I write, I love creating large families and then exploring each of their stories. This series fits right in. Not only does it explore the dynamics of the Kincaid family, it also allowed me to write a book about a man who's spent his life on the outside, longing to be part of a family he's been excluded from since birth. How many of us have reached out, hoping against hope that someone will take our hand? How many of us have been too afraid to make the attempt? Watch, as Jack decides whether to risk it all…with the help of a very special woman.

Welcome to *A Very Private Merger*, a story of redemption, of learning to trust and of creating that special bond with family. Oh, yes… And of course I couldn't resist adding my usual touch of humour. Enjoy!

Warmly,

Day Leclaire

To my readers, who have followed me through the years.
My thanks. My gratitude. And my love.

One

Son of a bitch!

Jack Sinclair stood on the sidewalk outside The Kincaid Group building and watched Nikki Thomas, his soon-to-be-former lover, give Elizabeth Kincaid a hug before heading into the Kincaid complex. As far as he was concerned, it was the ultimate betrayal.

Puzzle pieces he didn't even realize he was missing dropped into place in that instant. She worked for TKG, there was no other explanation. All this time—three amazing months together, an affair unlike any he'd experienced before, one that teetered on the brink of becoming something solid and permanent—and she'd been using him. Setting him up. Working for the enemy. He took a deep breath and reached for the cool, calm poise he'd spent a lifetime cultivating. He found it... but just barely.

There could be some other explanation for that hug,

his few remaining shreds of rational thought insisted. Since Nikki had purchased him at the Read and Write bachelor auction, an affair held at Lily Kincaid's home and attended by half of Charleston's elite, she could have met Elizabeth there. Or through a woman's club they had in common. Maybe Elizabeth and Nikki's mother were friends. They were all part of Charleston high society. No doubt they'd met at some event or another.

It could be just that simple.

Not only that, but Jack had asked Nikki in her role as corporate investigator to find out who owned stock in The Kincaid Group, specifically who owned the key ten percent not controlled by him or the Kincaids. Perhaps she was here on a fact-finding trip. All perfectly innocuous.

Well, there was an easy way to find out. He pulled out his cell phone and touched the screen to access TKG's main phone number. The receptionist answered on the second ring. "The Kincaid Group. How may I direct your call?"

"Connect me with Nikki Thomas, please."

The woman hesitated. "Nikki? Nikki Thomas?"

"She's your corporate investigator. She said I could reach her through this number."

"Oh. Certainly. One moment, please."

He disconnected the call and swore long and hard, his momentary hope for an innocuous explanation sweeping away like the wish for summer in the face of a frigid Arctic nor'easter. He'd known from the start that she was a corporate investigator, but her claim of confidentiality had kept him from asking key questions. Now she'd answer every last one of them.

He headed for the TKG building, driven by something so deep and primal and basic he couldn't put a name to it. He just knew it led to Nikki. To a confrontation with the woman who'd pushed through doors of intimacy he'd spent years barring and locking.

The woman who'd soon regret ever screwing him over.

Jack didn't waste any further time. He crossed the street, oblivious to the busy traffic. His entire focus remained on the four-story building in front of him and the woman who worked there. He'd been inside TKG several times over the past five months for meetings with his father's sons and daughters—the "Legitimates," as he referred to them. No doubt they referred to him as the "Bastard," a nickname he'd earned on more than one front.

He approached the reception desk. The woman seated behind the wide sweep of finely crafted wood took one look at him and snatched up the phone. He reached over the counter and disconnected the call without the least compunction. No doubt she had standing orders to alert one of the Kincaids whenever he appeared. He'd have done the same in their place.

"You know who I am?" he asked, his voice deadly soft.

She nodded mutely.

"Excellent. Then you also know I own a sizable portion of this company." He gestured for her to return the receiver to the cradle. "Nikki Thomas. Where?"

She'd picked up on his anger and intense concern flickered across her face. "What's your business with Ms. Thomas?"

"That's none of your concern. Where is her office? I won't ask again. Nor will I forget your lack of cooperation."

The receptionist's concern grew, along with an almost protective expression. Leave it to Nikki to instill such loyalty in her fellow employees. For a moment, Jack didn't think she'd answer. Then she caved. "Second floor...210," the woman murmured unhappily.

"You will not alert her to my presence, is that quite clear?"

"Yes, sir."

Jack circled the reception desk, debating briefly on whether to take the elevator or stairs. Stairs. Less risk of running into a Kincaid. Considering his current mood he didn't trust himself not to knock the unlucky person flat on their ass. It didn't take long to find Nikki's office. Her door was ajar and though she stood at a large window overlooking the harbor, he doubted she took in the stunning view, not with her head bent and what appeared to be the weight of the world resting on her fine-boned shoulders. In all the four months he'd known her, he'd never seen her look so defeated.

She wore her hair up, exposing the vulnerable paleness of her neck. Brilliant golden sunlight streamed in the window, losing itself in the ebony darkness of her hair while highlighting her potent feminine figure, showcased in a form-fitting royal blue suit. He'd watched her don that outfit just this morning, knew intimately what scraps of silk and lace hid beneath, their color a perfect match to her suit. He also knew— intimately—what she looked like in the panties and bra, how that shade of blue turned her magnolia-white skin luminescent, and how tempted he'd been to strip them away before returning her to their bed.

He clamped down on the surge of desire with a ruthlessness his competitors had come to fear...and respect. She'd betrayed him, something he doubted he could ever forgive. Now he'd find out just how deep that betrayal ran. And he'd know why. He closed the door. The metallic click sounded like the cocking of a trigger, the sound of the lock being thrown as explosive as a gun blast.

Nikki's head jerked up and she spun around, her expression confirming his worst suspicions. He must have still entertained a lingering hope that she'd offer a reasonable explanation for her presence at The Kincaid Group. Otherwise, he'd never have experienced such an overwhelming and devastating sense of loss.

"Jack." His name escaped on a sigh of guilt and dismay.

"I believe there's something you neglected to tell me, Nikki. Vital information that's four months overdue." He didn't dare approach. Not until he'd regained full control of his temper. "Care to rectify that omission?"

"I can explain."

He couldn't help it. He laughed. "How often has a woman said that to a man? Of course, there's usually another man in her bed at the time she uses that expression."

"It's probably as many times as a man's said it to a woman when she comes home unexpectedly to find him making love to someone else," Nikki retorted. Then her flash of anger faded, sliding into something that hovered between sorrow and regret. "I'm sorry, Jack. Saying I can explain is a rather ridiculous comment given the circumstances."

He leaned back against the door and folded his arms across his chest. "I wondered why you were willing to pay so much for me at the Read and Write bachelor auction. You claimed you bid for me because no one else would. But now I suspect it was all a setup. The

Kincaids came up with the clever scheme so you'd be in a position to spy on me, didn't they? It all makes sense now."

She held up a hand and her eyes flashed a swift warning. "Hold it right there. If you think for one minute that I bid on you at the Kincaids' request—"

"You bid a thousand dollars when no one else would." The anger he worked so hard to control escaped his iron grip for a split second. "You set me up right from the start."

She shook her head, the vehement motion causing silky strands of her hair to escape and caress her arching cheekbones, as well as the long sweep of her neck. God, he remembered burying his face in that sweet-scented hair only hours before. Remembered kissing a pathway along the pale, velvety line of her neck. How long would it take before the memories faded and he'd know peace again?

"I didn't set you up. Not then and not now."

She took a single step in his direction, but something in his expression drove her back, a stumbling retreat that brought out the predator in him. She must have sensed it because her breath quickened and her eyes—those damnable sapphire-blue eyes—darkened with pain and regret. She wrapped her arms around her narrow waist which only drew his attention to the fullness of her breasts straining against her suit jacket.

He forced his gaze away, forced himself to focus on her elegant, duplicitous features. They were beyond lovely, no doubt inherited from her mother, the aristocratic side of her family tree. He should have known that someone who'd been born and bred within Charleston's social elite couldn't be trusted. Hadn't his mother discovered that when Reginald Kincaid had made her his mistress?

Angela Sinclair had come from the wrong side of the tracks, which made her eligible for a bed partner, but she'd never been good enough to marry, any more than the son they'd borne together had been good enough to claim. Jack's mouth twisted. At least, he hadn't been claimed until dear ol' Dad had been dead and gone, leaving others to clean up the shattered mess the man had left behind.

All his life, Jack had stood on the outside of those fancy manors, while the Southern gentility had stuck rigidly to their social rules and order. Society had made him an outcast because of his bastard status, while welcoming the man who'd set the double standard, the man who'd proudly embraced the Legitimates, the children he'd fathered with Elizabeth Kincaid. All the while he'd kept Angela and his firstborn son a deep, dark secret. Now for the final piece of irony.

The one woman he'd grown to trust, to respect, whom he believed he could love for the rest of his life and had planned to offer the ring currently tucked away in his dresser drawer, was working for the Kincaids. No doubt their entire relationship had been built on a bed of lies. And hadn't he just enjoyed the hell out of that bed…until now.

Nikki held out a hand. "Please, Jack. You have to believe me. When I attended that bachelor auction and bid on you, I had no idea who you were. I didn't understand why no one else would make an offer. I mean, it was for charity. It didn't make sense."

"You really expect me to believe the Kincaids didn't put you up to it?" He shook his head. "Sorry, sweetheart. Considering you work for them and have kept very quiet about that fact makes it impossible for me to believe anything you have to say."

"I didn't find out until after that first kiss we shared at the auction," she insisted doggedly. "Lily found us by the carriage house, remember? You left and she told me who you were."

Oh, he remembered that first kiss, remembered every second of the overpowering desire that had swept them both away, a desire that made them blind and deaf to everything going on around them. He'd never experienced anything like it before. He rarely lost control, prided himself on keeping his emotions and reactions reined in at all times, safely walled away. But that night... That night he'd lost it, had been ripped in two by an imperative to possess, to mark the woman in his arms in some fundamental, primal way. To make her his in every sense of the word.

Is that what his parents had felt for each other, why they'd flouted society's rules and strictures? He shied away from the thought, unwilling to explore the possibility that allowed any gray into his black-and-white world. Of course, he hadn't made love to Nikki that night. But he had the next time they'd met, when she'd collected on the dinner she'd won at the auction.

Jack stared at her, watching, analyzing, weighing. "Even if I believed you... The Kincaids were all there when you bid on me. They knew you'd won a date with me. Are you trying to tell me now they didn't use that information? You're their corporate investigator, aren't you?"

"Yes, I'm their corporate investigator. Yes, Matt and RJ Kincaid knew about our dinner date. And yes, Matt asked me—"

Before she could finish her statement, the handle of

her office door jiggled. Discovering it locked, whoever had come—no doubt rushing to Nikki's aid—began pounding on the door. Jack frowned in annoyance. Apparently, he needed to work a bit harder on his intimidation skills since clearly the receptionist had called for reinforcements. Although to be fair, he'd only warned her not to alert Nikki of his arrival. He hadn't thought to include the rest of the Kincaids in his demand. The pounding reverberated against the wood, echoing straight through the hollowness filling his chest.

"Your rescue party, I believe." He tilted his head to one side. "Must have been the receptionist. Apparently, her concern for you outweighed my threats."

Nikki's mouth dropped open and a hint of outrage glistened in her eyes. "You threatened Dee?"

"Of course I threatened Dee. It's who I am, remember? I threaten. I act. And then I win."

She shook her head. "That's not true, Jack. That's not the man I've spent the last three months falling—"

Another burst of pounding interrupted her words, words he'd have given half his fortune to have heard her utter. "Sinclair, we know you're in there." His half brother, RJ's voice, Jack decided. Uncannily similar to his own, which only served to add to his anger. Irrational, but true. "Unlock this door right now or we're calling the police."

Jack lifted an eyebrow. "Well? Should I let them in?"

Nikki sighed. "That's probably best if you don't want to be arrested."

"Arrested for what? I own forty-five percent of TKG."

"Jack, please."

He shrugged and did as she requested. Might as well get this over with. He stepped aside, grateful he'd done so when the door banged open. RJ and Matt Kincaid piled into the office. While Matt aligned himself in front of Nikki, RJ confronted Jack.

"Are you all right, Nikki?" RJ asked, his sharp gaze fixed on Jack.

The resemblance between them went beyond the superficial. Both topped six feet by an inch or two and were more solidly built than Matt's lean, swimmer's body. They'd also inherited a substantial portion of their father's aristocratic good looks, including his dark brown hair and the general shape and expression of the eyes, even though the shade of blue differed dramatically. And as loath as Jack was to admit it, they also shared an uncanny knack for business, both excelling at it—which would make Jack's success when he gained control of The Kincaid Group all the sweeter.

Matt, on the other hand, had darker hair and his eyes were the image of his mother's, a sharp, currently infuriated bottle-green. Jack also sensed a strong protective instinct flowing through the younger of the two brothers, possibly due to his son's recent close call with a serious health issue. No doubt that combination of factors explained his current stance in front of Nikki.

"Nikki?" RJ prompted. "You're okay?"

"I'm fine. Jack and I were having a...discussion." She stepped out from behind Matt's broad shoulders. "Perhaps you can help."

"Sure. Get out, Sinclair."

Jack simply laughed. "That's not going to happen."

"Nor is it what I meant," Nikki interceded. "Maybe you could help by telling Jack what you asked me to do in regard to our investigation of him."

Beside her, Matt stiffened. "Are you kidding?"

"I'm dead serious," Nikki replied, her gaze pleading. "Matt, tell Jack at what point you asked me to investigate him and his business. Please," she added in a strained undertone.

Matt hesitated, but Jack could tell from his expression it wasn't in order to come up with a convenient lie, but because he was attempting to pinpoint the exact time frame. "You were on the phone with him, setting up your auction date," he finally said. "After you hung up, I asked you to see if you could uncover Sinclair's plans regarding TKG. Since he now owns forty-five-percent interest in the company we were hoping he'd indicate how he intended to use his shares."

"And," Nikki prompted. She smiled at his concerned expression. "It's okay, Matt. Just tell him."

He shot a resentful glare in Jack's direction. "I asked you to get a feel for the man. Is he someone you would want in charge of TKG?"

"So, you had Nikki investigate me and Carolina Shipping," Jack stated flatly. His gaze turned to Nikki and lingered there for a long, painful moment. Tears filled her eyes and he forced himself not to move, not to acknowledge the impact of them in any way. "I'll expect a copy of any and all reports you've generated about me on my desk by the end of today."

"You can't—" RJ began.

"I can," Jack retorted, cutting him without hesitation. "I'm majority shareholder of this company. I'm well within my rights to request that information. And if it's not on my desk by five, my lawyer will seek a court order forcing you to turn it over to me. Then we'll see just when and what you ordered Nikki to do."

Matt stepped in, frustration ripe in his voice. "You're our competitor, Sinclair. What the hell did you expect us to do? Sit idly by while you dismantle our livelihood?

There's no way you won't attempt to take over our family's business with that forty-five percent you keep waving in our face, just as there's no way you won't attempt to fold TKG into Carolina Shipping." He rested a supportive hand on Nikki's shoulder. It took every remaining ounce of Jack's self-control not to knock it off. The wave of sheer possessiveness that ripped through him felt as overpowering as a tidal wave. "FYI, I told Nikki that if I was wrong and you were on the up-and-up, fine. But you're not on the up-and-up, are you, Sinclair?"

"I am when it comes to business."

"Bull," RJ interjected. "You've been undercutting us from the start, using the murder rap the police attempted to pin on my mother to steal new business away from us."

"True." Jack shrugged. "So what? Business is business."

RJ's mouth tightened and his expression—one eerily similar to what Jack saw in the mirror each morning—sparked with impotent fury. "I won't allow you to take the business our father built and drop it in the crapper."

"Why would I do that?" Jack asked mildly. Oh, he was enjoying taking on the brothers who'd been put ahead of him his entire life. He'd hungered for this moment, just as he hungered for the moment when he'd step into his father's shoes as President and CEO of The Kincaid Goup. "TKG is a highly successful business, one I own considerable stock in. I have no interest in destroying it."

RJ hesitated, his gaze shifting to his brother where the two had a moment of silent communication. "Then what are your intentions regarding the annual meeting later this month?"

"I plan to attend."

Yeah, he was definitely getting too much of a kick out of this. Or he would if Nikki's eyes weren't fastened on him, pleading for his understanding. Oh, he understood, all right. He understood that he should never have trusted someone who moved in the rarified ranks of Charleston's elite.

"We'll be electing a new president and CEO. Who do you plan to vote for?" RJ pressed.

"I could tell you to wait and see, but there's no point." He took a single step in RJ's direction, not the least surprised when his half brother held his ground. He had a strong suspicion they were a lot alike in that regard, too—maybe too much alike—cut in the same mold as the father they both shared. "I plan to take over TKG."

Matt swore. "I knew it."

Jack simply smiled. "And I plan to do exactly what you thought I'd do. I plan to fold TKG into my own company." His gaze blistered first RJ, then Matt. "Welcome to Carolina Shipping. I suggest you don't get too comfortable. You won't be staying long."

And with that he turned on his heel and left the office. He didn't look back, though everything within him urged him to do just that. But he didn't dare. Because he knew that one look at Nikki's devastated expression would gut him.

At precisely five minutes to five Nikki Thomas pulled into Carolina Shipping's parking lot. Jack's distinctive ruby-red Aston Martin Volante sat in the prime spot closest to a door she suspected led directly to his office. She didn't attempt to confirm her guess. From this point forward, she'd need to play this very carefully, which meant entering the way everyone else did, through the front.

Opening a set of etched glass doors, she stepped into the foyer, taking a moment to absorb her surroundings. She'd never been here before, nor had she bothered to ask for a tour, in case Jack expected quid pro quo and felt he could or should ask about her job in return. She preferred not starting a conversation that might direct too much attention to her own work.

For some reason, the graciousness and Southern charm of the waiting area surprised her. It shouldn't. She'd seen his beach cottage—a misnomer if ever there were one since his Charleston home exuded wealth and contemporary luxury. And she'd also stayed at his home in Greenville, a sprawling plantation mansion that brilliantly blended the old South with the new.

At her entrance, the receptionist greeted her with a lovely smile. "Ms. Thomas?"

Nikki blinked in surprise. "That's right."

"Jack said to expect you. He bet me you'd show up right before closing." She laughed. "After all these years working for him, you'd think I'd know better than to bet against him. He has an uncanny knack for winning."

Nikki stifled a faint whiff of irritation. "So I've discovered," she said.

"Ah, clearly you know our Jack." *Our* Jack? "I'll show you to his office. He said you should go straight in."

She came around the reception desk and started down a wide hallway. Nikki pegged the woman to be in her mid-twenties, six or seven years younger than Nikki's own age. She wore a tidy pantsuit in a rich chocolate-brown that matched her eyes, her blond hair styled in a short, sassy cut that drew attention to her pretty features. She paused outside a set of double doors and gave a quick tap with her knuckle before swinging them open.

"Nikki Thomas to see you."

"Thanks, Lynn. You can shut down for the day."

"Okay. See you Monday." She offered Nikki another of her lovely smiles. "Nice meeting you, Ms. Thomas."

Jack glanced up from the file spread across his desk and gestured toward one of the chairs opposite him. The instant she sat, he crossed to the doors and closed them. For some reason the gesture struck her as ominous, adding to a vague dread that had been building all day.

Had it only been this morning when she'd woken to his mouth and body on hers? To the laughter and joy of their impromptu joining? To the delicious, mind-numbing aftermath? She closed her eyes at the memory, but couldn't seem to shut it down. Jack had carried her from their bed into the shower when the clock warned they'd be late for work if they didn't get up. Their shower together had prompted more laughter when they'd bumped and brushed their way clean.

And then had been the saucy moments when she'd dressed in the royal blue panties and bra set she was currently wearing. He'd joked about stripping away the bits and pieces she busily slipped on and suggested something that had brought a flush to her cheeks, while tempting her beyond bearing. Now she wished she'd taken him up on the offer since she doubted that opportunity would ever come again.

Without a word, Jack resumed his seat behind his desk—a captain at the helm of his ship. She shot him a swift, searching glance, but his expression remained closed to her. More than anything she wanted to break through the wall of ice separating them. But he was a master at closing his emotions behind thick barriers, no doubt a result of his unconventional upbringing. She knew from personal experience just how rarely he allowed others in, and just how badly he'd taken her betrayal.

In an attempt to distract herself, Nikki studied her surroundings. Like the waiting area, his office also reflected a graciousness overlaid with subtle hints of wealth and prosperity. No doubt it went a long way toward selling the various services Carolina Shipping offered its clients. It struck her as vastly different from TKG, where the rooms were appealing, but more functional in appearance, underscored with the strong masculine accent Reginald Kincaid had preferred.

The minutes ticked by and still neither of them spoke. Or perhaps the tension thickening the room spoke for them, whispering of pain and loss, secrets and deception. Unable to stand the building storm another instant, Nikki broke the silence, no doubt what Jack had intended all along.

"I'm sorry, Jack. I should have told you that I worked for the Kincaids right from the start." He didn't answer, just studied her with those unnerving pale blue eyes of his, the sheer lack of emotion ripping through her. She set the file folder she'd brought for him on the edge of his desk and nudged it in his direction. "I brought my reports, as requested."

His gaze flicked toward the folder then he stood again. This time he crossed to a wet bar and poured himself a drink. He glanced over his shoulder in her direction, lifting a dark eyebrow in clear question.

"No, thanks." Impatient with the continued silence, she said, "Are you going to say anything at all?"

"Hoping to get it over with quick and painless? Sorry, sweetheart. You're not getting off that easy."

She flinched at his sarcasm. Exhaustion dragged at her. It had been an endless day which would no doubt morph into an equally endless night. Thank God it was Friday and she'd have the entire weekend to come to terms with all that had happened today. "Jack, I made a mistake," she said in a low voice. "Are you really going to throw away what we have over a single omission?"

"What we have?" He took a long swallow of his drink. For the first time she caught a glimpse of his rage, the sheer depth and power of it leaving her shaken. "We *have* nothing. We *had*... Well, that's a different story."

Nikki blinked hard to hold back tears. "Please, Jack..."

"Don't." He slammed his drink against the wet bar, the cut glass tumbler singing in protest. "Just...don't."

"The Kincaids didn't know how serious our relationship had become. Nor did they ask me to do anything illegal or unethical."

Jack eyed her grimly. "You mean other than try to prove that I killed my father?"

Nikki shot to her feet. "Damn it, Jack. I know you didn't kill Reginald. I doubt the Kincaids even believe it of you. You could never do such a thing. You and your father might have had your differences, but I know what sort of man you are."

"And what sort of woman are you?"

"You know what sort."

His eyes chilled, growing colder than she'd ever seen them. "I do now."

Anger filled her, sweeping aside the tears. "I've never lied to you, Jack. Not about who I am or what's in my heart. Do you really believe I could have faked my reaction to your touch? To your kiss?" She dared to approach, part of her hoping to push through his self-control while the other part of her dreaded what might happen if she succeeded. "That I was pretending when you made love to me?"

Something fired in his eyes, flickering to life and melting through the chill that encased him. She stood within touching distance, a vulnerable spot to be in considering the depth of his sense of betrayal. Even prepared, his sudden lunge caught her by surprise. With a growl that hovered somewhere between fury and demand, he snatched her into his arms. And then he kissed her.

Where before he'd been winter-cold, now he exploded with blistering heat, taking without hesitation, claiming all she was and all she had. His mouth moved across hers in a passion laced with unmistakable pain. Her heart went out to him because she knew she'd caused that pain and would have given everything she possessed to ease it. She gave him free rein, offering herself to him unconditionally and without hesitation.

He didn't hold back, but she no longer cared. It had been like this from the start. From the first moment their eyes had met on a chilly winter evening while he'd been auctioned off before a crowd whose silence judged and ostracized him, there had been an irresistible spark. And later that evening when they'd talked, that spark had flickered into a flame, one that had leaped out of control the first time they touched. The first time they kissed—a kiss not that different from this one.

And when they'd gone on that initial date, her fate had been sealed. She could no more resist his pull than a wave could resist its tumbling journey to the shore. Even then she'd given him everything, despite the complications, knowing full well he was a man intent on destroying the Kincaids while Nikki was the one woman capable of stopping him.

Secrets. So many secrets.

Jack swept her into his arms and carried her to the sitting area of his office. There he lowered her to a plush sofa and followed her down. He kissed her again, slower this time, deeper, the passion thick and full and rich. She felt the slight tug and give of her suit jacket, followed by the cool wash of air across her skin before the heat of his hands replaced it, cupping her breasts through her bra.

"Show me that you want me," he said. "Prove to me that it wasn't an act."

Two

Nikki closed her eyes, the overwhelming desire of seconds before fading beneath Jack's clipped demand. "I have nothing to prove." She pushed at his shoulders, not certain whether she was relieved or disappointed when he pulled back. "Either you believe me or you don't. Either you believe in what we've felt for each other over the past four months or you don't. It's that simple."

"It's not that simple. You betrayed my trust." He sat up, allowing her room to swing her legs onto the floor. "But I still want you. God knows why."

"Gee, thanks."

"You spied on me, Nikki. I can't forgive that."

"And yet, you had no compunction asking me to spy on the Kincaids. Or is that somehow different?" She fumbled with her buttons, appalled to discover that her fingers trembled making the task nearly impossible.

"Here...let me." Sweeping her hands aside, he buttoned her jacket, realigning the buttons she'd shoved into the wrong holes. "First, I didn't ask you to spy on them. I asked you to investigate, which is quite different."

"How?" she asked. "Seriously, I'd love to know how you make that distinction."

"We were sleeping together while you were investigating me on the Kincaids' behalf. You aren't sleeping with the people I asked you to investigate." His eyes fixed on her. Narrowed. "Are you?"

She shot off the couch and spun to face him. Fury flowed through her and she didn't make any attempt to conceal the fact. "That's a filthy thing to suggest. You know Matt and RJ are both in committed relationships, on the verge of marriage. And just to be clear, I've never, ever had any sort of personal or intimate relationship with any of the Kincaids. Ever. I work for them. Period."

Something in her tone and ferocity must have gotten through to him. He inclined his head. "Okay, fine."

"No," she insisted. "It's not fine. You owe me an apology."

He stared at her with such an expression of disbelief it would have been amusing if the circumstances had been different. "Let me get this straight. *I* owe *you* an apology?"

She folded her arms across her chest. "You may recall that the first thing I did when I came here was apologize to you. I was in the wrong. I knew it and I said I was sorry. So, yes. You now owe me an apology for accusing me of sleeping with RJ and/or Matt."

"And/or?"

"Exactly. And, just for the record, I never slept with

your father, either. I think that covers all the Kincaid males, other than you."

"I never thought—" He broke off, his blue eyes turning even more stormy. "I'm not a Kincaid male."

She lifted her shoulder in a shrug. "Potato, pah-tah-toe. Apologize right this minute or I'm leaving."

"You're not leaving until we've had a chance to go over these reports of yours."

She simply lifted an eyebrow and waited.

"Son of a—" He scrubbed his hands over his face. "Okay, fine. I apologize. I shouldn't have accused you of sleeping with the Kincaids. But you were in bed with them, figuratively, if nothing else."

"I was working that entire time trying to prove your innocence." She closed her eyes and accepted the painful truth. "Except you're not innocent, are you?"

Jack slowly stood, anger rippling across his face. "What the hell does that mean? You just said you didn't believe I killed my father."

She waved that aside. "Of course you didn't."

"Then explain what you meant?"

"I mean that you plan to destroy everything your father spent his lifetime building." Unless someone stopped him. So many secrets. So many schemes. They wore her out, even though many of those secrets and schemes were resting in the palm of her own hand. She released her breath in an exhausted sigh. "Becoming involved with you was a mistake."

"News flash. I already figured that out."

She had to find a way to get through to him—other than this heartbreaking argument over her employers. They'd never see eye to eye on the subject. Nor did it get to the true heart of the problem—Jack's illogical vendetta against the Kincaids.

She dared take a step closer to him, seeing the wariness leap into his gaze, as well as a flash of something he struggled hard to conceal. Want. An irrepressible need that echoed the one sweeping through her. She moistened her lips and tried a new tack. "Jack, did you ever read the letter your father left you?"

She'd caught him off guard and his wariness grew. "No."

"He left one for each of his children. For your mother, too, from what I've heard. There must have been a reason for that. Something he wanted to say. Aren't you the least curious?"

"My relationship with my father was…complicated."

"Mine wasn't," she said simply.

"That's a bit cryptic. Care to explain?"

She hesitated. It wasn't a subject she liked talking about. It had caused a great deal of distress and pain in her life. But perhaps if he understood why she'd gone to work for TKG, he'd also understood why her loyalties were so torn. She forced herself to give it to him straight. "If it weren't for your father, I wouldn't have a career."

Jack shrugged. "Okay, so he gave you your start in the business."

"No, he didn't. I didn't even know him when I first started working."

"Then—"

"He helped me salvage my reputation after my previous employer ripped it to shreds." There. She'd said it. "He helped me out of a very tight corner."

A frown formed between Jack's dark brows. "What the hell happened?"

She hated discussing that time. Hated that she could have been so naive and foolish, especially considering her father had been a policeman and had drummed both caution and integrity into her practically from birth. But she hadn't been cautious. And the man she'd fallen in love with had lacked integrity, something that had ultimately rebounded on her.

She wished she'd accepted that drink when Jack first offered it, her mouth so bone-dry she felt as though she had to drag the words out from where they'd bottled in her throat. "It was my first real job after college, with newly minted degrees in police science and business administration."

"No one can accuse you of being an underachiever."

She smiled for the first time in what felt like days. "Did I mention my minor in criminal justice?"

"You did tell me you were considering going into law enforcement."

Her smile faded. "But I couldn't do that to my family, not when Dad went down in the line of duty. Instead, I made the classic mistake so many women do when they first start working."

It only took him a minute to make the leap. His uncanny knack for connecting the dots was one of the qualities she'd always appreciated about him. "You fell in love with your boss."

She couldn't help flinching. Hearing it stated so baldly made her aware of just how painfully young she'd been. How hopelessly inexperienced. "Yes. Even worse, he convinced me to keep our affair secret. He even proposed, promising that once we married, we could admit to the relationship. If my father had still been alive, I doubt it ever would have happened."

A hint of sympathy darkened Jack's gaze. "You did tell me he was an excellent judge of character."

"I thought I was, too." She paced the width of Jack's

office as though in an attempt to put distance between herself and those long-ago events. "I don't know. Maybe believing I was my father's daughter made me cocky."

Jack crossed to the wet bar, freshened his drink and poured her one, as well. "Here. I think you need this even more than I do."

She accepted the double malt scotch with a swift smile of gratitude and sipped, the rawness of the liquor catching in her throat and burning a warming path straight to her bones. Slowly she relaxed. "The details aren't really important. Let's just say Craig used my name for a land development scam he had going. When it all fell apart, he was long gone and I was left looking very, very guilty."

"How did my father end up involved?"

"Reginald was a close personal friend of my grandfather Beaulyn. Obviously, my mother's dad," she added.

Something swept across Jack's face, as though her grandfather's name rang a distant bell, and she froze, wondering if she'd made a terrible mistake mentioning his name. Then the moment passed. "But your father was a cop. I'm surprised the Beaulyns would have encouraged the match."

Nikki shrugged. "My parents met at college. It didn't matter that they came from different social backgrounds. Mom always claimed it was love at first sight. When I had my issues with Craig, your father felt he owed my grandfather and stepped in to help me."

"Explain that."

As much as she wished she could tell Jack the whole truth, the time had come to tiptoe. "Grandpa was a very savvy businessman who made an impressive amount of money in real estate. He was also old money, part of the upper echelons of Charleston's social elite."

Jack's eyes narrowed. "Which would have attracted Dad. One of the reasons he married Elizabeth was to penetrate Charleston's old-money bastions. Apparently new money didn't smell as good to them as old."

She suspected he spoke from current, personal experience and couldn't help remembering the charity auction where he'd been so soundly snubbed—right up until she'd bid for him. "I'm not in a position to argue the point. The bottom line is, Reginald caught wind of it, possibly through my mother. He stepped in and salvaged my reputation. Then he hired me to work for The Kincaid Group."

"So you feel you owe him."

"I do owe him, Jack," Nikki replied steadily. "Your father had his flaws, I won't pretend otherwise. But he also had quite a few strengths, most of which you've inherited. And there's no doubt in my mind that he loved his children—all of them."

"I assume that brings us back to the letter he left me."

She nodded. "Aren't you curious about why your father left you such a large percentage of TKG? Why he divided the other forty-five percent between RJ, Matt, Laurel, Lily and Kara?"

"No."

Okay, so that utter black-and-white quality was one of the characteristics she wished he hadn't inherited from Reginald. "All that matters is that he's given you the means to gain control of The Kincaid Group?" she demanded. "Offered you the opportunity to take revenge on your brothers and sisters?"

"They're not my brothers and sisters." Emotion ripped apart his words.

"Of course they are. And they've done nothing to

you, Jack. They didn't even know you existed until shortly after your father's death."

His mouth tightened. "They didn't exactly welcome us with open arms."

Oh, for... "Would you have in their place?" she asked in exasperation.

Jack made an impatient gesture. "Why are we even discussing this? You were supposed to come here in order to discuss your reports. Instead, we've done everything but."

"I hoped I could get you to see what a difficult position I'm in. What a difficult position we're all in because of Reginald's actions. The Kincaids want me to investigate you. You want me to investigate them...."

"Actually, I asked you to uncover the identity of the person or persons who own the remaining ten percent of TKG stock. Have you even bothered looking?" He broke off, the muscles along his jaw tightening. "Son of a bitch..."

Uh-oh. "Jack—"

His eyes narrowed and anger flickered to life in his eyes again. "You are looking, aren't you? Only it's for them. RJ's already asked you to find the missing shareholder because whoever controls them, wins control of the company. That's why you've been stringing me along all this time, so RJ can get to this person ahead of me and have them squarely in his corner before the annual board meeting."

Nikki allowed Jack's words to hang in the air, hoping against hope that he'd take them back. When it became clear that he wouldn't, she crossed to the doors of his office. She paused for a brief moment then turned. "You know, as much as I loved and admired your father, there was one quality about him I could never come to terms with. For such a caring, generous person, he was one of the most ruthless men I've ever met, especially when it came to achieving his own ends. It's a shame you've decided to emulate him in that regard."

And with that, she exited his office. She hadn't thought she could feel any worse than when she'd first arrived. But she did.

What was she going to do now? A battle was brewing between the Kincaids and Jack, one growing progressively more dangerous and messy. It only required a single spark for open warfare to erupt. Unfortunately, she was that spark.

Because as soon as either side discovered she owned those final ten percent shares of Kincaid stock, they would all come gunning for her.

How the hell had she done it?

Swearing beneath his breath, Jack snatched up the file Nikki had left on his desk. How had she managed to turn the tables on him so completely? *He'd* been wronged—by *her*. All this time she'd been working for the enemy, gathering God knows what information for his brothers and sisters—*not* his brothers and sisters, he swiftly corrected himself, but those damn Legitimates. And why? To use against him, that's why. And then she had the unmitigated gall to stare at him with those big sapphire-blue eyes all full of hurt and reproach as though *he* were the one at fault.

Well, he refused to buy into it. She should have told him the truth right from the start.

And if she had? What would he have done?

He swore again and dropped into his chair. Would he have attempted to turn her against her employers? Would he have bribed her? Used their relationship to have her go against her ethics, an ethical code instilled by the father she so adored? He didn't want to think he'd sink so low, but then, how rational was his need for revenge against the Kincaids?

Worse, she'd been appallingly right. He was every bit as ruthless as Reginald Kincaid; his entire life was dedicated to the pursuit of eclipsing the company his father had spent a lifetime building. Jack forced himself to stare unflinchingly at his motivations for creating Carolina Shipping and winced. It wasn't a pretty picture. He'd been his father's firstborn and had been denied that birthright thanks to circumstances beyond his control. As a result, he'd been determined to prove himself better and more capable than any of his father's other sons—for once in his life to be first and receive acknowledgment of that fact.

With his father gone, that would never happen.

Jack tipped his head back against the leather headrest and sighed. Great. Just great. Score one for Nikki. All these years he'd managed to remain delightfully oblivious to the underlying cause for his drive to succeed. Even more, he'd have been quite content to remain oblivious until the day he'd succeeded in taking over TKG. Now, even that was denied him, and all thanks to Nikki Thomas, the one woman in all creation he'd come within an inch of falling in love with.

And then there was the story she'd told him about her first job. About Craig. She'd been used once before and badly burned. Had she kept her silence about her job out of concern he'd use her the way Craig had? Granted, different circumstances, but still... Jack straightened in his chair and faced another unpalatable truth—score two for Nikki.

If he'd discovered she worked for the Kincaids,

chances were excellent he'd have used their relationship to try and turn her. The knowledge left a bitter taste in his mouth. Even worse, he'd been one short step away from attempting to put pressure on her tonight in order to find that missing shareholder. To somehow force her to give him the identity before turning the information over to RJ. What the hell had happened to him? And how the hell could he fix the situation?

When no easy answer presented itself, he flipped open the file and read through every word Nikki had written. He couldn't fault it. The report was concise, accurate and utterly unbiased, even the part that reported that his Aston Martin had been parked in a lot near TKG the night of his father's murder. God only knew how that was possible, since he'd left it in the parking lot of Carolina Shipping when he'd arrived at work and it was still there when he left.

The one detail which caught him off guard he found in a short addendum advising RJ Kincaid that her father, Peter Thomas, had been partners with the lead detective assigned to the murder case. That would be Charles McDonough. Jack grimaced. He'd met the man and might have liked him if the circumstances surrounding their meeting had been different. But being interviewed by the detective was not conducive to a budding friendship.

Jack returned his attention to the file. He didn't find any information that Nikki could have learned only as a result of their affair, and nowhere else. All of her facts were documented and annotated, with referenced sources. She'd have made an excellent cop, despite the fact that her family had put pressure on her to choose a different career after her father had gone down in the line of duty. Jack wished he could have known Peter

Thomas since he suspected the apple hadn't fallen far from that particular tree.

Then he had another, even more uncomfortable thought. What would Thomas have thought of him? Would he have lumped Jack in with Craig and warned his daughter to end their relationship? Quite likely. Jack shoved aside the file with a sigh. And didn't that just bite.

What was it about Nikki that forced him to take such a long, hard look at his own character—and find it lacking? He was honest, hardworking, generous. Okay, ruthless, hardheaded, driven. But for the past four months they'd been perfect for each other. Right up until those damn Kincaids got in the way again. Jack shoved back his chair. Well, he knew what he had to do and the sooner he got it over with the better.

It didn't take long to drive to Rainbow Row where Nikki owned one of the historic homes, an inheritance from her grandfather she'd once told him. And though she'd told him the night of the auction that she came from Charleston's elite on her mother's side, she'd neglected to mention it was the illustrious Beaulyn family. No doubt she was concerned that such a stellar connection would cause friction between them considering his general animosity toward high society. Still, the name rang a distant bell, and for more than its social significance.

Jack approached Nikki's door and debated knocking, then decided against it since he found it highly doubtful she'd let him in. Instead, he used the key she'd given him. He paused in the foyer, his gaze inevitably going to the stretch of wall where they'd collided while in the throes of their second kiss—an innocent embrace that had unexpectedly burst into a storm of desperate need.

It had been a continuation of the first kiss they'd shared on the night of the charity auction. From that incendiary start, the affair had swiftly taken off, flaming higher and higher over the past three months.

Right until it had crashed and burned this morning.

"Nikki?" he called out.

He heard swift footsteps coming from the general direction of the kitchen. A second later Nikki appeared. She'd changed from her business suit into some sort of light, filmy cover-up. He remembered it from one of the occasions when she'd spent the night at his beach house. It had been no more than a brief glimpse all those weeks ago, just the amount of time it took to see the tantalizing way it clung to her lush figure and the additional few seconds it took to strip it off her.

She paused a dozen feet away from him and stared for an endless moment, her eyes black in the dusky light. His expression must have given her some clue as to why he was there. With a small exclamation, she flew into his arms.

He held her tight, catching himself inhaling her unique fragrance, as though stamping it onto some primal memory that told him that this was his mate, the only woman who would ever be his mate. "I'm sorry," he murmured. She simply shook her head, burrowing against him. It took him a split second to realize she was crying. "Oh, God, don't, Nikki. I'm so sorry."

When she still didn't answer, he swept her into his arms and carried her upstairs to her bedroom. After toeing off his shoes, he climbed into bed with her and simply held her against his chest until she finished weeping.

"You okay now?" he asked gently, brushing back her fringe of bangs and kissing her forehead.

She ducked her head. "Don't look at me. I'm not

one of those sweet Southern belles who cries without smudging their makeup. I'm one of those whose nose turns red and runny and whose face gets all blotchy. Mother blames my Thomas blood since apparently a Beaulyn wouldn't dare do the ugly cry."

His mouth twitched in amusement. "So noted. I'm now too terrified to look."

To his relief a small hiccupped laugh escaped. "Okay, now I have to know." A hint of tension rippled through body. "Why are you here, Jack?"

"Do I really have to say it?"

He despised postmortems after an argument. How many of them had he been privy to whenever his parents fought and reconciled? Too many to count, their passion loud and messy, spilling over onto those too close to escape. No wonder he and Alan were so screwed up, though in totally opposite ways. His Sinclair half brother had always been appalled by the excess of emotion—emotion their mother, Angela, had never shared with Alan's father, Richard Sinclair.

Had Alan resented that fact? Jack had never considered the possibility before. Considering how protective Alan was toward their mother, the likelihood existed, despite the loving relationship he claimed to share with Jack's father, Reginald Kincaid. While Alan clung tighter to his parental relationships, Jack had closed himself off from others, building a protective wall around his emotions. Refusing to allow others to stir the sort of intemperate passion his parents shared, a passion that had destroyed so many lives.

Nikki released a long sigh, interrupting his musings. "Did you expect to waltz in here after everything that happened today and just pick up where we left off?"

He winced at the stinging note in her voice. "Expect? No. Hope? You're damn right I did."

"Jack."

"Okay, you want to hear it again? I'm sorry."

She peeked up at him through damp, spiky lashes. "Why are you sorry?" she asked suspiciously.

"I'm afraid—seriously afraid—that I might be like Craig," he confessed.

Nikki must not have anticipated that particular answer. She pulled back another couple of inches, confirming that she'd been dead serious about her crying jags. She wasn't a pretty crier. For some reason, it endeared her to him all the more. "Craig?" she asked in confusion. "You're nothing like Craig."

"I'm not sure your father would agree." He brooded over it for another moment. "I suspect if you told me you worked for TKG, I'd have used our relationship to convince you to spy on the Kincaids."

Her eyes narrowed a trifle, a steely gleam glittering through her tears. "FYI, you wouldn't have succeeded."

"Don't be so sure." He deliberately feathered his hand along her cheek and down the length of her neck, eliciting a helpless shiver. "I can be pretty persuasive when I choose."

She gave herself a little shake and pulled back farther still as though a few more inches of distance would improve her chances of resisting him. He'd have laughed if not for the hint of shrewdness in her gaze. "Just out of curiosity, what information would you have had me turn over to you?"

The question caught him totally off guard. Okay, so maybe his powers of persuasion were on the fritz. They certainly seemed to be tonight. "I don't know. Information I could use to gain control of The Kincaid Group."

"Jack, the only way you can gain control of TKG is if you also control the majority of the shares. The same goes for RJ. And since you asked me to find out who the missing shareholder is when you didn't know I worked for the Kincaids, and that's the same information you'd have wanted if you *did* know I worked for the Kincaids, I don't see how you could have used me."

It took him a moment to work through her reply. "Convoluted, but true," he conceded. "But what if I'd asked you to give me any defamatory information about RJ or Matt or one of their sisters? Information I could have used against them at the annual meeting?"

"I'd have said no," she retorted with a hint of exasperation. "Besides, there is no defamatory information. Jack, your brothers and sisters are nice people. If you'd only give them a chance you'd discover that for yourself."

His jaw set. "I have no intention of discovering that for myself."

"Oh, Jack." It was her turn to shift closer, to stroke a gentle hand along his raspy cheek. For some reason her powers of persuasion were working much better than his, damn it. "They're as innocent in all this as you are."

"That doesn't change their attitude toward me."

"Their father had just been murdered, a man they'd loved and respected all their lives," she shot right back. "A man they thought they knew as well as they knew themselves. Instead of being able to mourn him, they're faced with the news that he's been keeping a second family hidden away. That the pillar of Charleston society has feet of clay. It takes time to come to terms with that."

"They've had five months," he insisted stubbornly.

"Jack, they're no more responsible for the family dynamics than you are. Your life and how you were forced to spend it was your mother and father's responsibility. They're the ones who should be held accountable, not your brothers and sisters."

He was being unreasonable and knew it. That didn't change the fact that he'd lived his entire life in the shadows, had never known the acceptance his Kincaid kin had experienced from the moment they'd entered the world, all because he'd had the misfortune to be born a bastard. For years he'd competed head-to-head with The Kincaid Group, fighting and clawing for each and every sale, while his brothers had been handed their positions on a silver platter. Soon all that would change. Soon they'd be forced to answer to him. That moment couldn't come any too soon. Nor would it be any too sweet.

Nikki sighed, breaking the silence growing between them. "All I'm saying is that you might consider giving them a chance."

"Fine." He dismissed his relatives without the least hesitation. "Next problem."

"The missing shares," she said unhappily.

She keyed in on the remaining issue standing between them with unerring accuracy. He'd always admired her focus and logic, even if it was all too often coated with an unfortunate sentimentality.

He nodded. "Eventually you're going to find out who owns them, Nikki. How will you handle the information when you do?"

"To be honest, I don't know," she confessed.

"At the very least I hope you'll give both RJ and me the information at the same time so neither of us has an unfair advantage."

She wiggled against him, confirming how uncomfortable the subject made her. She'd always been that way about it, even before he'd discovered she worked for the Kincaids. Invariably, she'd change the topic whenever it came up in casual conversation. He'd always assumed it wasn't something that interested her. Now he realized it struck too close to home.

"I'll think about it," she finally conceded.

He'd have to be satisfied with that. "I have one more request."

"I'm almost afraid to ask...."

He caught the wary tone in her voice and suspected he'd pushed her about as far as she'd be pushed. Still, this was important. More than important. "I read through the reports you brought to my office. They were excellent, by the way. Very fair and accurate."

"Thanks. I try."

He winced at the chill that iced her words. "I noticed that Charles McDonough was your father's former partner."

She confirmed it with a quick nod. "Our families have maintained a close friendship. What's this about, Jack? What do you want?"

Time for dead honesty. "I need to clear my name," he stated tersely. "And I need you to help me do it."

Three

Nikki's expression softened. "Jack, I know you didn't kill your father. I wouldn't be in bed with you if I had the least doubt."

"You're the only one who doesn't have the least doubt." He yanked at his tie to loosen the knot. For some reason it threatened to choke him. "The police are looking my way. McDonough has already interviewed me a couple of times. I have a feeling I'm his most likely suspect."

"Looking is a long way from arresting you for the crime and even further from convicting you." But she sounded uneasy.

"I understand all that. Right now the evidence is barely circumstantial. My car parked near TKG the night of the murder is hardly persuasive evidence. That doesn't change the fact that someone killed my father. I want you to help me find out who. Or if we can't find out the actual identity of the murderer, at least help me prove it wasn't me."

She shook her head. "I can't and won't interfere with an ongoing police investigation. Charles may be a close family friend, but he won't tolerate that, not even from me," she warned.

"I'm not asking you to interfere. Nikki...your reports were brilliant." When she started to deny it, he stopped her. "No, truly. They were logical, careful, thorough. You have a very analytical mind and a knack for sifting through large amounts of data and extracting key nuggets of information. I need that sort of help."

She gave a helpless shrug. "I don't know what you think I can uncover that the police can't."

"I don't know if it's that they can't or if they simply choose not to, at least not when they have a convenient suspect at hand."

"Oh, no, Jack." She rolled onto her hip to face him and cupped his face. "Charles isn't like that, not at all."

He planted a kiss in the palm of her hand, the gesture taking on a symbolic feel. "The Kincaids would be delighted to have the police pin my dad's murder on me," he said. "In fact, I wouldn't be surprised if they weren't nudging McDonough in my direction. Not only would it take care of the problems I'm causing at TKG, it also sweeps the bastard son out of sight so the Kincaids can pretend I never existed."

"First, Charles can't be nudged. If he could, he'd never have arrested Reginald's wife for the murder. It wasn't until Elizabeth allowed Cutter Reynolds to step forward and admit that she was with him that night at the time of the murder—that they'd been having an affair for three years—that she was released."

Jack reluctantly nodded. "Fair enough. That doesn't

change the fact that over the past five months the suspect pool has gotten smaller and smaller. Hell, right now it's barely a puddle and I'm the only one left splashing around in it. I flat-out refuse to sit around and wait for them to find some trumped-up piece of evidence with which to hang me. Even if you refuse to help, I plan to look into this on my own."

Nikki frowned. "You're not giving me much choice, Jack."

"It's the Craig coming out in me."

To his relief, her frown eased then evaporated like morning fog hovering over the Cooper River. "You will never be like Craig," she informed him.

She spoke with such tenderness that it left him speechless...though not motionless. Gently, he pulled her into his arms and kissed her. His mouth drifted across hers, slow and easy. He nibbled at her bottom lip, running his tongue along the seam before dipping inward for a leisurely taste.

"Have I ever told you that you have the most perfect lips of any woman I've ever kissed?"

Her smile melded with the kiss. "Do I?"

"Mmm. They're just the right size and shape. Plump without suffocating a man. Wide without swallowing a man whole."

Her laughter rang out. "Heaven forbid."

"And best of all they're clever. Very, very clever, just like the woman who possesses them."

"Well, allow me to return the compliment. I just happen to think that not only are your lips perfect, but so is the way you use them." She ran a finger along his mouth, giving his bottom lip a little pinch similar to the nibbling bite he'd given hers. "Unlike some men who are long forgotten, you don't just dive in and attack my mouth."

For some reason his voice deepened, turning rough and gravelly. "I seem to remember attacking it a time or two."

"Only when the occasion called for it," she assured him. "The rest of the time you start slow and teasing, and oh, so tempting. Like this…" She gave him a vivid demonstration, one that had his mind clouding over and blood pooling in an area of his body nowhere near his mouth. "And then you slip in, like the sun slipping from the ocean and turning everything golden. You steal my breath, Jack. I don't understand how or why, but you do. And then you give me yours so I can breathe again."

He closed his eyes, more moved than he could ever remember. "Nikki…"

"Make love to me, Jack. Steal my breath and turn my world golden again."

Jack didn't need any further prompting. Rearing back, he knelt above Nikki and stripped away his suit coat and tie. The buttons of his shirt proved beyond his ability to manipulate and he dealt with them in the easiest possible way. He ripped his shirt open and tossed it aside, while she tackled his trousers, her hands as clumsy as his own in her haste to deal with his belt buckle and zipper. Though it seemed endless, it couldn't have been longer than a minute before all he wore was skin. And then he turned his attention to Nikki.

Her cover-up was a pale gleam, the color indeterminate, in the dimness of the bedroom. Beneath it she wore the royal blue bra and panties he'd had the pleasure of watching her slip on just that morning. Now he'd have the greater pleasure of removing them. He caught the hem of the semitransparent scrap of silk in his hands and drew it up and off.

She emerged, a bit more rumpled, but infinitely more beautiful. She'd let her hair down after she left his office and it flowed to her shoulders in an ebony curtain, the ends curving inward to cup her shoulders. The darkness of the color made a delicious contrast to her pearlescent skin, giving a richness to the sepia overtones. She fell back against the pillows and offered her siren's smile, a silent promise of pleasures to come.

For a split second, time froze, tilted. From the moment he'd first seen Nikki at the Read and Write auction, striding across the grounds of the Colonel Samuel Beauchamp House, her lean, shapely figure encased in form-fitting black wool, he'd wanted her. And when she'd paused to stare up at where he stood on a balcony overlooking the impeccably landscaped backyard and patio, he'd desired her with a ferocity he'd never experienced with any other woman.

She'd stood so fearlessly beneath him, gazing up with those stunning sapphire eyes and then she'd shocked him by bidding, offering a thousand dollars for the pleasure of his company for one night of dinner and dancing, when all those around her had refused to make a single offer, despite the fact that the event was for charity. Even more fascinating, she'd demanded an additional incentive—a single wish to be collected at a time of her choosing. She never collected on that wish, though he didn't doubt she would at some point. But he'd collected their very first kiss that same night, tracking her down and pulling her into his arms, driven to put his stamp of possession on her.

Instead, she'd put hers on him.

Ever since that first kiss he'd been connected to her

in a way he didn't understand and couldn't begin to explain. The depths of his feelings bothered him, perhaps because they were too close an echo of what he suspected his father felt for his mother. Worse, it disturbed the even tenor of his life, upset the clear-cut goals he'd set for himself. Disrupted the urges that had driven him for most of his life. She made him question himself, to look far too closely at his motivations. And he didn't like it. Not that his displeasure changed a thing. He still wanted her with a desperation he couldn't deny or sate.

"What's wrong?" Nikki asked, her voice soft and gentle, filled with a perceptiveness that arrowed straight through to the core of who and what he was.

"You have a knack for knocking me off balance and keeping me there." The words were dragged from him with an unwillingness he couldn't disguise.

"Should I apologize?" she asked gravely.

"Yes."

"A shame since I quite like having you off balance."

As though to prove her point, she took his hand in hers and gave it a yank, catching him by surprise. He fell forward, supporting his weight with hands he braced on either side of her head. "You're trouble," he informed her. "I knew it when you bid for me."

"You're mine. I made sure of it when I won you." She tugged at his shoulders, pulling him downward so skin pressed intimately to skin. She hesitated, her expression turning unusually serious. "I would never betray you, Jack. I want you to know that."

"Your reports proved that," he replied just as seriously. "There were a few details you could have included that you didn't."

"What sort of details?"

"Over the past three months I've mentioned various

new business contracts up for grabs. You could have reported those to the Kincaids."

Her brows drew together. "How do you know I didn't? I could have told them in person. After all, it would have been foolish to leave a paper trail."

"Even so, you didn't, otherwise I wouldn't have won the contracts."

"That doesn't prove—"

"I would have lost a few of them, probably more than a few, if you'd told the Kincaids about it. Not only that, but on at least two occasions you had access to my bid sheets, if you'd been so inclined to pass on the information."

"I wasn't so inclined," she replied, a tart edge sliding through her words.

"I'm well aware of that." He touched her hair in a reconciliatory manner. "Why are we arguing about this when there are so many more interesting things we could be doing?"

She shook her head. "I don't know. Okay, yes, I do." She caught his face between her hands and lifted upward to kiss him, a slow, soothing kiss that promised they'd soon be getting to every last one of those "interesting things."

"I just want to make it clear that no matter what happens in the future, I would never betray you."

The words held an ominous undertone, one he refused to dwell on. Not when he held a naked woman in his arms. "I appreciate the reassurance."

Before she could say anything else, he cupped her breast and took a loving bite from the apple. Her breath exploded from her lungs and she moaned in pleasure. "Again. Do that again."

Instead, he turned his attention to her other breast,

teasing the nipple with his tongue, allowing the warmth of his exhale to fan the dampness. She shuddered at the teasing sensation, moving restlessly beneath him, the friction adding to the tension building between them. He never tired of reacquainting himself with all that made her so deliciously female, her curves generous where they should be generous and delicate where they should be delicate. He waited until he felt the slight give to her muscles signaling her relaxation and then used his teeth to tug at her nipple again.

With an incoherent cry, she arched beneath him, her hands sliding into his hair and holding him close to her breast. Unable to resist, his hands skated downward, tripping across the toned ripple of her abdomen to the joining between her thighs. She opened to him and he cupped her warmth, reveling in skin so soft it defied comparison. And still, he teased, finding the moist seam that hid the feminine core of her at the same instant as his tongue penetrated the moist seam of her mouth.

She went under, dragging him with her, surging upward with her hips while she rolled with him until she lay on top. She was incandescent in her want, beautiful and determined, more giving than any woman he'd known. Her hands swept down his chest and she broke the kiss to follow the path of her hands, mimicking all he'd done to her earlier. Her breath came hot against his skin, her mouth and teeth avid against his own nipples.

And all the while her hands were busy, busy, busy, finding the source of his own desire and stoking it to the level of a raging inferno. Just when he didn't think he could take it another instant, she eased down onto him, enclosing him in searing heat. She paused for an eternity like some sort of pagan goddess, her head thrown back, her rich, dark hair cascading down her back. Then she moved, setting in motion the first steps to a dance she'd come close to perfecting in the three months they'd been together.

He grasped her hips, moving with her, leading then following until there were no leaders. No followers. Just two people melded together so completely, their movements and desires so in tune with one another, that for a moment he thought they were one. One body. One need. One thought. One emotion.

The dance swirled faster and faster until it could go no further. With a hoarse cry, Jack thrust upward, reaching for Nikki, pulling her close. He felt her shatter a split second before he followed her over, the tumble endless and endlessly satisfying. Gasping for breath, she collapsed against him, a boneless melting that would have had him laughing if only he had sufficient air.

He wrapped his arms around her and held her close, her name the only word he was capable of uttering. She pressed a kiss to his damp chest, delicious little shudders sweeping through her in the aftermath of their lovemaking. "I keep thinking it can't get any better," she murmured. "And you keep proving me wrong."

"I do my best," he said humbly.

He felt her smile against his chest. "Now be quiet and go to sleep."

"I thought that was supposed to be my line."

Her soft laugh rumbled straight through him. "Since I was on top this time, my line."

Jack was asleep before the smile faded from his face.

Nikki woke to the deepness of night, disoriented by the hard masculine body beneath her own. She shifted, realizing to her amusement that Jack slept soundly on his stomach while she lay draped across his back like a human blanket, his firm male buttocks cushioning her hips. Her soft chuckle caused him to stir beneath her.

"What the hell…?"

"Apparently, I've turned kinky in my sleep," she commented.

"I'd agree with you, except there's not much either of us can do in this position."

She gave his rump an appreciative pat. "Speak for yourself." Rolling off him, she sat up and blinked sleepily at the digital clock. The soft blue glow informed her it was almost two and the dinner she'd been in the middle of preparing when Jack arrived had gone uneaten. "Man, I'm starving. What about you?"

"I could choke down a steak if you forced me." He levered upward. "Along with the rest of the cow, right down to the hide, hooves and tail."

She wrinkled her nose. "Not so sure about the hide and hooves, not to mention the tail, but I do have a nice big steak with your name on it. It won't take a minute to grill."

"Lead the way."

Nikki retrieved her cover-up on the way out of the room, ignoring Jack's sleepy protest. "I'm not cooking naked. There are too many parts I might burn."

"That silky thing isn't much protection," he informed her, pulling on his trousers.

"Not from you, maybe, but it's protection enough from any cooking spatter."

Fortunately, she managed to avoid the spatter. She didn't even attempt to avoid Jack's occasional caress. Why would she, when they were so delicious? It didn't take long to pull together a quick meal, especially with Jack's help. His willingness to lend a hand in the kitchen—or anywhere else she needed it—was one of the things that had impressed her right from the start.

He exuded a tough, masculine competence, going about his chores with a calm ease and economy of motion that spoke of a man comfortable in his own skin. And despite the ruthlessness she'd accused him of inheriting from his father, he also possessed unlimited generosity toward others, as well as a deep-seated tenderness that came out at the most unexpected times. Of equal importance to her, he possessed an innate honesty that tempered that ruthless streak. It reminded her of her father and it saddened her that the two men would never know each other since she suspected they'd have been firm friends.

Though Nikki had turned on a few lights, the denseness of night invaded the house, adding an air of intimacy to the process. As soon as the meal was prepared, she carried it to an alcove off the kitchen where a small café table and chairs were placed for more informal meals. Aside from the overhead spots, darkness enclosed them like a cozy blanket.

Silence prevailed while they made inroads into their meal. After several moments, Jack shot her a direct look, regarding her with a calmness she often associated with his business face. "It occurs to me that you never answered my question earlier."

"What question is that?"

As he so often did, he answered with absolute directness. "Will you help me look into the murder of my father?"

She hesitated, recalling his warning that he intended to pursue it regardless of whether or not she chose to help. She didn't doubt his sincerity for a single moment. Nor did she doubt that his single-minded drive might lead him to places better avoided. Maybe if she were there to temper his actions, they'd both manage to circumvent trouble.

"I'm willing to help...with a few conditions."

He tackled his steak once again, a small smile tugging at his mouth. "Why doesn't that surprise me?"

"First, I won't do anything that harms the Kincaids or interferes with my job there."

Jack shook his head. "I can't promise that, Nikki. What if one of them killed Dad?"

"Obviously, that's a different story."

"If that's the case, then you'll have to be willing to look long and hard at them, to give serious consideration to the possibility that someone you like, someone you care about, could be the murderer."

"It's not them," she replied steadily. "Just as I know it's not you, I know that none of your brothers and sisters would kill their own father, any more than you would."

He leveled her with a hard look. "Stop referring to them that way. They're not my brothers and sisters."

"Alan's also a half brother and yet I've heard you call him your brother."

"Only when forced to," Jack replied unenthusiastically.

She couldn't help laughing. Not that she blamed him. Alan was...odd. Though charming and easy on the eyes, he seemed to dislike the sort of hard work that the Kincaids thrived on. And that included Jack, who she considered a Kincaid by blood, if not by name.

In looks, Alan took after his and Jack's mother, Angela. They both shared the same golden-blond hair and lively hazel eyes. But while Angela possessed an underlying grit and determination, despite a distinctive air of vulnerability, Alan simply conveyed weakness and the general attitude that the world owed him a living. Even when offered that living, as Reginald had in his will—requesting a position be made available for Alan at The Kincaid Group—not once in the past five months had Alan followed through.

"To get back to the point of the conversation, I have another condition which is that we can't interfere in the police investigation in any way," Nikki continued. "I won't put Charles in an awkward position or do anything to compromise his case."

"Agreed. Anything else?"

"I don't think so."

The words had scarcely left her lips before Jack leaned forward and gave her a swift kiss. "That seals our deal."

"Knowing you, I'd better reserve the right to add the occasional addendum to our agreement."

He shook his head. "Too late. You're welcome to try to add something else but I can't promise I'll agree to it."

"You're a tough man to bargain with."

"Hey, I was cutting you some slack."

"If that's cutting me slack, I'd hate to see when you're negotiating in earnest."

For a split second his expression altered, allowing her to catch a glimpse of the business predator he rarely revealed to her. A chill shot down her spine. Heaven help her, but she hoped she'd never have cause to face him across the negotiating table. Jack was a man who played for keeps and she'd do well to remember that. She hadn't realized it at the time, but he'd let her off the hook over today's fiasco with relative ease. It would have been far different if he'd been just a hair more ruthless, more unforgiving or hadn't given a damn about maintaining their relationship.

Then another thought struck, one she forced herself to dismiss, but suspected would linger in the far recesses of her mind for some time to come. What if he had another purpose for reconciling with her tonight? What if it had only been because he still needed her...versus he cared about their relationship more than his vendetta against the Kincaids or his desire to clear his name?

Jack paused in the process of clearing their plates from the table. "What's wrong?" he asked. "You look upset."

Nikki shook her head, avoiding his gaze. "It's nothing."

She forced out a smile and pitched in to help with the dishes. She was wrong. She had to be. Jack wouldn't use her like that. She spared him a swift glance.

Would he?

The two slept in Saturday morning, curled together so completely Nikki couldn't tell where she left off and where Jack began.

"So, what's our first move?" he asked after they'd polished off a light brunch.

She hesitated. "You're handing me the lead?"

"Sure, why not?" A quick smile came and went. "I'm not such a control freak that I don't know how and when to delegate. You can't build a top-notch company without that ability. I also know how to choose the best person for any given job. And for this job, you're it."

"Okay. I can handle it." Maybe. She gave it a moment's thought and realized the first step was fairly obvious. "We should visit Elizabeth."

Jack frowned and she could guess why. While the

Kincaids would consider Angela Sinclair "the other woman," for most of Jack's life Elizabeth held that position in the Sinclair household. Considering how protective he was of his mother, she didn't doubt he resented Elizabeth and her claim to the Kincaid name.

"Why do we have to see her?" he asked reluctantly.

"We don't if it'll be too difficult for you." She shifted closer, offering her warmth and comfort. "She's the most stressful of the Kincaids for you to deal with, isn't she?"

He hesitated, on the verge of denying it, before inclining his head. "She possessed what my mother spent most of her life craving. His name. Recognition. Acceptance. When I was younger, I would have given anything and everything to provide Mom with that. But it wasn't in my power."

"Nor was it Elizabeth's fault," Nikki said gently.

"Logically, I know that. But emotionally…" He shook his head.

"So, you hate her."

"Actually, I don't," he surprised Nikki by admitting. "It took most of my teenage years to get to the point where I could see what my parents were doing to her was wrong, dead wrong, not the other way around. She was the injured party, not either of my parents." He gave a quick shrug. "That doesn't change the protectiveness I feel toward my mother."

Nikki hugged him close, relieved when he returned the hug. She could practically see another barrier between them fading into nonexistence. "Of course it doesn't change how you feel about your mother. And it shouldn't."

"So, why do we have to meet with Elizabeth?"

"Other than the killer, she was the last person to see

your father alive. I think it's worth talking to her about what happened that night."

He took a split second to consider then nodded. "That's logical. Why don't you phone her. Somehow I think she'll be more willing to agree to a meet if the request comes from you."

She placed the call, not the least surprised when it took several minutes to convince Elizabeth to speak with them about Reginald's death. Nikki could understand her reluctance and desire to put that night behind her. But finally they agreed to meet at Maybelle's, a coffeehouse not far from Rainbow Row. She and Jack arrived first and arranged for a table toward the back, well away from the general flow of traffic. They didn't have long to wait before the widow put in an appearance. To their surprise, her fiancé, Cutter Reynolds, was with her.

She swept up to the table, aggression sparking in her distinctive green eyes and communicating itself in the tense way she held her elegant body. Though Nikki knew for a fact that Elizabeth Kincaid celebrated her sixtieth birthday this year, she remained a stunning woman, looking a full decade younger than her chronological age. She wore her auburn hair cut in a short, trendy style and had kept her figure trim, her athletic build showcased by an off-white pair of slacks and bronze silk blouse. Discreet bits of gold flashed at her ears, wrists and neck.

"I don't know what you want from me, but I doubt there's anything I can say to help you," she announced, lobbing the first volley.

Jack stood and regarded her for a long moment, then held out his hand. "Even so, I appreciate your joining us, Mrs. Kincaid, especially considering I must represent a living insult to you and your marriage."

She stared at his hand for a long moment. Behind her, Cutter murmured her name and just like that her anger slipped away. With a soft sigh, she took Jack's hand and gave it a firm shake. "Oh, for heaven's sake, call me Elizabeth. As if all this wasn't awkward enough." To Nikki's surprise she gave a short huff of exasperation. "And fool that I am, here I have us meeting in public where everyone can see and gossip about it."

Jack nodded in perfect understanding. "Since they're going to gossip, anyway, I suggest we say to hell with it and give them something juicy to gnaw on."

Her chin shot up. "And what would that be, Mr. Sinclair?"

"Well, instead of setting off fireworks the way they expect, we could pretend to be friendly. One of us could even laugh."

His comment caused Elizabeth to do just that. Cutter pulled out a chair and she settled into it. Then she fixed her cool gaze on Nikki, who waited to be cut to shreds in typical sweet-as-honey Southern fashion. Instead, Elizabeth inclined her head. "It's always good to see you, Nikki. Your mother and I had lunch just Wednesday past. I swear she looks younger every time I see her, which leaves me fit to be tied."

"She'll be thrilled to hear it."

"Don't you dare tell her I said that. There'll be no living with her."

The waitress stopped by, her avid gaze passing over the group, no doubt committing any comments she might have caught to memory, as well as everyone's demeanor. "Herbal tea, please, Jo," Elizabeth requested, obviously familiar with their waitress. "And are the blueberries local?"

"Yes, ma'am. We received a delivery just yesterday."

"In that case, bring me one of Maybelle's Bluebelles, otherwise I'll never hear the end of it," she ordered, referring to the pastry that was a house special. "In fact, bring some for the entire table, my treat."

"Yes, Miz Kincaid." Jo's fascinated gaze landed on Jack and clung, before reluctantly switching to Nikki. "And you, ma'am?"

"Coffee, black."

Jack nodded. "The same."

Cutter spoke up for the first time, offering the waitress an easygoing smile. "Make that three." He waited until she'd drifted out of hearing range before adding, "I hope you don't mind that I tagged along. Considering the topic of conversation, I knew this would be difficult for Elizabeth."

"I'm glad you're here," Jack surprised them all by saying before meeting Elizabeth's gaze. "And I apologize for causing you any more stress. I'm sure you're aware that the police investigation has shifted recently and I'm now under suspicion for Reginald's murder."

"I'm aware," she said shortly, "though I'm not sure how that has anything to do with me."

"It doesn't, but I'm hoping if I can gather as many facts about Dad—Reginald's death as possible, I'll be able to clear my name."

His slight stumble over his reference to his father didn't go unnoticed. For an instant, Elizabeth stiffened then she shocked him by offering a quick glance of sympathy. "He was your father, Jack. You won't upset or offend me by calling him that. You have as much claim on the word as any of my children."

For an instant, Jack closed his eyes. He hadn't expected such graciousness from a woman he'd come to realize was the most wronged of any of them. Nor had he expected the wave of shame and contrition that flowed through him. As much as he loved and admired his mother, this was one area and one subject where they differed dramatically.

And maybe it would help to say as much, to show the same graciousness that had been extended to him. "They both wronged you, Elizabeth. For what it's worth, I'm sorry. He should have asked for a divorce before he ever approached my mother again. It's what an honorable man would have done."

Elizabeth's mouth trembled for a brief moment before she steadied it. "You're quite right," she whispered. "It would have been more honorable. Just as it would have been more honorable for me to have asked for that divorce three years ago when I found his will and discovered your existence." Her mouth tightened. "And your mother's. I suppose Reginald and I were both foolishly attempting to protect our children, when in truth they didn't need our protection at all."

Cutter closed his hand over hers and squeezed. "That's all water under the bridge now, Lizzie. Something that can't be changed."

"Still, it hurt to learn he loved another woman more than he ever loved me. Just as it hurt when he left her a letter without offering me so much as a word of explanation."

Jack's eyes narrowed, sharpened. "I must have missed that at the reading of the will. You didn't receive a letter from Dad?"

Four

Pride came to Elizabeth's rescue and her chin shot upward while her green eyes turned vivid with anger. "I did not," she stated crisply. "Even worse were the final words spoken between us. While all of you were left with words of love, I'm left with words of anger. Words neither of us can take back."

"That was the night he was murdered, when you brought his dinner to the office?"

"It was."

The waitress arrived just then, looking distinctly put out when they all fell silent. She unloaded her tray onto their table. After checking to make certain they had everything they needed, she reluctantly departed again.

"Mrs. Kincaid—Elizabeth," Jack corrected himself. "Tell me what happened that night. What did you see? What did Dad say to you?"

She reached for a Bluebelle and broke off a fragment,

though she didn't eat it. Instead, she crumbled the flaky pastry between her fingers. "I've thought about it and thought about it until my head's ready to explode. I exited the elevator and walked to his office. I knocked, waited a bit for him to tell me to come in and then I—"

"Why did you have to wait?" Jack interrupted a recital he could tell had become rote.

Elizabeth hesitated as though no one had ever asked that question before. She brushed a hand through her auburn hair and gave an impatient shrug. "Goodness, Jack. After all these years I know better than to interrupt him when he's on the phone. At least that was my impression." Her brow wrinkled as she sifted through her memories of the event. "Now that I think about it, there was more of a delay than I'd have expected. Then he said to come on in."

"Was he still on the phone?"

"No, he'd already hung up." She gave an elegant wave, dismissing the subject. "Who knows, maybe he was talking to your momma. Anyway, I had his dinner in a large bag—his favorite, roast beef and potatoes. We'd had an argument the night before about how moody he'd been lately."

"Did he explain why he'd been so moody?" Jack interrupted.

Elizabeth shook her head, quite definite. "No, he just said it had to do with a recent problem that had cropped up and that he was afraid he'd delayed too long resolving it."

"What happened when you walked into his office?"

"I asked Reginald something innocuous like how long he thought he'd be, or how business was going. He snapped at me, told me he didn't have time for my fool questions and to get on home." Tears sparkled in

Elizabeth's lovely eyes. "He didn't even want the dinner I'd brought. I ended up throwing it away."

"I'm sure he didn't mean it," Nikki murmured. "He always spoke about you with the utmost respect. Despite everything, I know he cared deeply for you."

She dabbed at her eyes with her napkin. "Thank you, dear. I'd like to believe that, but the evidence suggests otherwise."

"Did he often snap at you like that?" Jack asked.

"Never. Even when we fought, he was never cruel or cutting the way he was this time. I guess that's why I was so hurt. I told him he had no call to speak to me that way and stormed out. I got back on the elevator. It stopped once on its return to the lobby and Brooke joined me. We exchanged a few words, though I was too upset at the time to remember what they were. Then I left the building and drove straight to Cutter's."

"Thank you," Jack said, and meant it.

"You know…" Nikki offered slowly, "I don't remember Charles saying anything about a phone call."

Elizabeth shook her head in confusion. "I'm sorry. Charles…?"

"Charles McDonough, the lead detective in the case."

"Oh, yes, of course." She gave a delicate shiver. "He made my life rather difficult for several months."

Jack could sympathize. Charles had given him some uncomfortable moments, as well. "Elizabeth, did you mention that phone call to Charles?"

She hesitated, taking a moment to consider. "I don't believe I did. To be honest I forgot about it until just now when you asked the question."

"Thank you. You've been quite helpful."

She lifted a shoulder in a dismissive shrug. "If you

say so. I'm not sure I said anything terribly earthshaking."

Jack returned his napkin to the table. They should go now. He should walk away this minute before he said something he'd regret. After all, she was a Kincaid. Though he sympathized with her, that didn't change his overall feelings toward her family or his plans for the annual meeting later this month.

But he found he couldn't just walk away. Maybe it was having Nikki there, her emotions so palpable he could practically touch them. Maybe it was seeing Elizabeth's untempered vulnerability, her pain and grief. Or maybe it was her generous acceptance of him that caused the breach in defenses he's spent a lifetime building. Regardless of the cause, he felt compelled to speak.

"Dad talked to me about you one time," he informed her in a low voice. He forced himself to continue, despite the difficulty of the memory or his reluctance to share it. "I was a teenager, grappling with my confusion over my parents' relationship and not understanding why my father refused to acknowledge me as his son. I called you a rather vile name." He offered a contrite smile. "One you clearly didn't deserve."

"I'm surprised Reginald didn't agree with you," Elizabeth retorted with a hint of acid.

Jack's smile grew. "He knocked me on my ass and dragged me outside for a man-to-man talk."

Elizabeth blinked in surprise. "He did? How...unexpected."

"I think that's what I'm trying to say, Elizabeth," Jack said gently. "It shouldn't be unexpected. That day he told me that he'd been very fortunate to love two of the finest women he'd ever known. He said he married you for money and status, but stayed with you out of love and respect. He described the life you'd carved out together and for the five children you shared. And I could tell you all meant the world to him."

Elizabeth's brows drew together and her eyes darkened in reluctant sympathy. "That must have been very difficult for you to hear."

Beside him, Nikki reached beneath the table and took his hand in hers. He spared her a brief glance, one that told her how much he appreciated her support. God, how he'd wanted to be part of the life his father had described. Had craved it with a yearning so intense it threatened to eat him alive. He wanted to belong the way his father's other children belonged, to have brothers and sisters who loved him and squabbled with him, but who in the end accepted him as one of their own.

That day with his father, he realized it would never happen. That for the rest of his life he'd be an outsider, never acknowledged. Never accepted. Never a Kincaid. It had been one of the worst days of his entire life and no doubt ignited the fire that raged within him to compete. To win. To prove he deserved a place in their lives, even if he had to bully his way in and seize it through sheer force.

But that wasn't the message he wished to convey. Elizabeth needed something far different from him and for some odd reason, he felt compelled to give it to her. "Dad told me that you were one of the most generous women he'd ever met. Just so you know, you share that quality with my mother. But he said you also possessed a sweetness that most women from your world lack. He said I could condemn him all I wanted, that he more than deserved it. But I was never to disrespect my mother or you, for you both acted solely out of love and always put others ahead of your own needs, some-thing he'd never learned to do. I'd have to agree with him, since otherwise, none of us would be in our cur-rent situation. And then he said of all those he'd hurt, you were the most innocent and the most wronged. I also have to agree with him about that."

For an instant, Elizabeth stared blindly. Then tears flooded her eyes and she turned into Cutter's waiting embrace. It took her several minutes to recover her com-posure, but when she did, she revealed the profound sweetness that Reginald had referred to, along with an intense gratitude. "I can't thank you enough, Jack. What you just said... I think that's better than any let-ter could possibly have been."

He frowned. "I will say it doesn't make sense that he didn't leave you a letter, Elizabeth. Maybe he intended to do it and died before he could complete the task. I'm sure yours would have been the most difficult letter he had to write."

Elizabeth shook her head. "I don't think so. I think yours would have been the most difficult because he knew he'd deprived you of so much. Would you mind my asking what he did say to you?"

Jack hesitated. "I haven't opened it," he admitted. "I've actually been tempted to burn it."

"But you haven't," she observed shrewdly. "I think you just need time and distance before you read it. I suspect you'll know when that moment finally arrives. Until then, don't do anything you may regret. Promise me you won't."

He inclined his head. "Fair enough. Since it's you asking, I can't refuse."

She hesitated. "I assume you received your invitation to Matthew and Susannah's wedding next weekend."

"I did."

"I truly hope you plan to attend." She spared Nikki a quick smile. "Please bring Nikki, if you'd like."

With no other choice but to accept the invitation, he inclined his head. "I'd like that."

The four stood and Jack collected the bill, waving off Cutter's offer to pay. When he held out his hand to Elizabeth, she brushed it aside and gave him a quick, fierce hug instead. He didn't know who she'd surprised more by the impromptu gesture, him or the rest of the coffeehouse patrons. Then she turned and walked away, her head held high, her back ramrod straight. But he couldn't help noticing a spring in her step that had been lacking when she arrived.

He stared after her, broodingly. Damn it, why did she have to hug him? Despite having shared that long-ago memory with her, he'd still managed to hold a piece of himself in reserve. To stay safely behind the walls he'd built and limit the damage their interaction had caused. But that hug had yanked him out into the open. Bared him. Left him more vulnerable than he could ever recall being. And he didn't like it. Not one tiny bit.

The instant they hit the sidewalk, he drew Nikki to one side and retrieved his cell phone. Punching in a number, he waited until the call connected.

"Harold Parsons."

"Harold, Jack Sinclair here."

"You do realize this is Saturday, don't you, boy?" The question escaped in a gruff voice, a perfect match for what Jack recalled of the lawyer's beetled brows, gray tufts of hair and shrewd gaze. "My offices are closed. Call back Monday."

"If you're closed, why did you answer the phone?"

A long, irritated sigh came across the airwaves. "What do you want?"

"My father left letters for everyone as part of his final bequest. But Elizabeth never received one. Why is that?"

"How should I know?" Harold snapped. "It wasn't in the file, therefore there wasn't one."

"Dad wouldn't have slighted her that way," Jack insisted. "When did he write the letters?"

"The last time he updated his will. He always updated the letters at the same time."

"Has there always been one for Elizabeth in the past?"

Harold paused. "Yes..." He drew out the word, his irritation fading as he realized where Jack was going with his line of questioning. "Until this time. Of course, there'd also been one for Alan in the past and there wasn't this time."

"I'm still not buying it, Harold. Alan, okay. He wasn't Reginald's son. But he wouldn't slight Elizabeth that way, nor embarrass her in front of the family. I want you to go through your offices with a fine-tooth comb. He wrote that letter, I'd bet my business on it. If it's gone missing, I want to know when and why. Otherwise, I want it found."

"I'll look into it."

As soon as Jack disconnected the call, Nikki gripped his arm. "What's going on?"

"I think Dad wrote Elizabeth a letter." He shook his head, correcting himself. "I don't think. I know, straight down to my bones, he wrote her one."

"What do you think happened to it?"

"Either the lawyer's office misplaced it. Or it's somewhere in Dad's office."

"If that's the case, maybe we should ask RJ to search Reginald's office."

Jack's mouth twisted in open irony. "Yeah, I'll call him up and suggest he do that. Considering how tight we are after yesterday's confrontation, I'm sure he'll get right on it."

She held his gaze with an uncomfortable steadiness. "If it's for his mother's benefit, he will."

Aw, hell. She was serious. "You really want me to call, don't you?"

"Yes."

"You're not going to let up until I do, are you?"

"Not a chance."

He glared at her, not bothering to disguise his frustration. "You know, today is turning out to be a real pain in the ass. First Elizabeth and now RJ. You do understand that I despise my Kincaid relatives on a good day. When I have to deal with them on one of my few days off, my level of despise increases exponentially."

She patted his arm. "So I gather."

He gave it to her straight. "I'm also trying to destroy them, take over their business and make a misery of their life as they currently know and enjoy it. You get that, don't you?"

"You may have mentioned it a time or two," she conceded with a meekness he didn't buy into for one little minute.

"FYI, helping them out is wreaking havoc on my plans to A) destroy, B) take over, and it sure as hell isn't doing much to C) make a misery of their life as they currently know and enjoy it."

His bitter complaint elicited a sympathetic smile. He didn't buy into that, any more than he bought into her meekness. "Let's help out today. Tomorrow you can get back to putting A through C into motion. You can even add D and E if it makes you feel better."

"Done." He stabbed a finger in her direction. "And just so we're clear, I'm holding you to that. In fact, I might just make you help."

She smiled blandly. "What do you think I've been doing?"

"If that's your idea of help, I'm in serious trouble."

"Nothing." RJ's voice sounded ripe with irritation, an attitude mirrored in his taut, withdrawn stance.

Clearly, he blamed Jack for getting his hopes up, Nikki realized uneasily. Not what she'd anticipated from this latest gathering of brothers.

"Nothing here, either," Matt agreed, also scowling. He shot Jack a look that blistered him for their wasted time and effort. "Not that I expected there to be."

RJ addressed Nikki in a testy voice. "I certainly hope you didn't get Mom's expectations up about this business with the letter."

She offered a reassuring smile. "Your mother has no idea we even suspect there's a letter. It was Jack who figured it out."

"Sinclair?" Both brothers spoke in unison, their gazes swiveling to stare—okay, glare—at Jack.

"What the hell are you up to?" RJ demanded.

"I already explained that to you. Try to keep up, Kincaid," Jack retorted.

To Nikki's concern he sounded tired, even his sarcasm bordering on exhausted. Of course, it had been a rough two days for him and the Kincaids weren't making it easy to drop decades' worth of barriers and give them the opportunity to know the man behind the ruthless facade. How odd that it had never occurred to Jack that instead of always standing on the outside, looking in, all he had to do was open the door to his own life and he'd no longer be on the outside. He wouldn't be alone anymore. He'd have created his own family, his own circle of friends, his own home, full of warmth and love.

This morning had provided an excellent start, thanks to Elizabeth's innate kindness. She had slipped under Jack's guard the easiest, but then, that was her nature. At heart she was a sweet, generous woman who went out of her way to help others. Her sons would be far harder to coax inside. Nikki's chin set into a stubborn line. But she would find a way. While Jack worked his way from A to E, she intended to work her way from one to six, straight through the Kincaid lineup— including Elizabeth—in order to win them all over to Jack's cause. One big, happy family. Or they would be until the annual meeting.

"This has been a colossal waste of time. I'm out of here," RJ announced. He lobbed a final warning shot in Jack's direction on his way out of the door. "Stay out of Kincaid business, Sinclair. You do anything to hurt our mother and I'll bury you so deep they'll need a backhoe to dig out all the broken pieces."

Matt started for the door after his brother then hesitated before leaving the room. "Why do you want that letter, Sinclair?"

"The hell if I know."

Matt turned and faced him, eyeing him closely. "I'm serious. Why?"

Jack was going to lie; Nikki could see it in his expression. She crossed to his side and looked up at him. She could practically feel the waves of pain and resistance pouring off him. Gently, she slid a hand around his waist and pressed close in open support. For a long, tense moment she waited for him to make a decision. Open up or close down. No doubt his instinct screamed for him to lie. To reject the opportunity to reveal the heart of the man lurking behind the merciless business facade. She knew an instant before he spoke that she'd won this round.

"You know our father." Each word escaped as though forced from him. "And you know how he felt about your mother. He'd never have insulted her that way. There's a letter for her somewhere."

Matt's eyebrows shot up in open skepticism. "And you're going to find it?"

"If I can."

"Just because it's the right thing to do?"

"Something like that."

He was closing down again, Nikki could feel it. Maybe he would have if Matt hadn't asked a question that caught Jack completely off guard. "Why did you visit my son in the hospital?"

Matt had faced a parent's worst nightmare when his three-year-old son, Flynn, had developed aplastic anemia following a strong viral infection. Fortunately, the medication the boy received worked its magic. Otherwise, his biological mother, Susannah, would have donated her bone marrow in an attempt to save their son's life. Her advent into their lives had led to a romance between her and Matt, one that promised another Kincaid wedding next week.

"Why did I visit Flynn?" Jack's mouth curved in a sardonic smile. "I don't know, Matt. Because it was the right thing to do?"

"Well, and because he wanted to see if he was a bone marrow match," Nikki added irrepressibly.

Her words couldn't have had a more dramatic impact

if she'd stripped naked and performed a hula dance on Reginald's desktop. Matt's mouth dropped open and he stared in patent disbelief. Slowly he shook his head. "No way."

Jack's smile turned cynical and he shot Nikki a glare that promised future retribution. Well, she could handle it if it meant Matt saw his brother in a slightly different light than he'd been portrayed to date.

"Right," Jack said, his voice desert-dry. "No way I'm capable of something like that."

"You offered to donate bone marrow?" Matt repeated.

"It was an easy offer to make since I doubt I'd have been a match."

Matt's expression grew more intent. "And if you had been?"

Jack shrugged, remaining mute.

Nikki rolled her eyes in exasperation. "Give your brother a little credit, Matt. You don't get tested if you don't intend to go through with the procedure if there's a match."

"He's not my brother," the two brothers said in unison.

A strained silence fell between them for an instant, one Matt finally broke. "When you visited Flynn in the hospital... You said you'd once been hospitalized as a kid. What happened, exactly?" A tautness dropped over his features. "You didn't need a bone marrow transplant, did you?"

Jack shook his head. "Nothing so dramatic."

Nikki shrugged. "If you consider getting hit by a car nothing dramatic. Personally, I find it terrifying."

He turned on her. "Would you cut it out! Stop telling them personal information. It's none of their business."

"Of course it's their business. They're family."

"When...when did that happen?" Matt stumbled over the question. "Were you all right? I mean, obviously you're all right. Hell."

"Awkward, isn't it?" Jack murmured.

Matt shook his head and then started to laugh. "Damn awkward. It shouldn't be. It should all be straightforward. I hate you. You hate me. Everyone's happy." His green eyes showed a hint of the same warmth as his mother's. "So, what happened, Sinclair? Were you so busy trying to take over the world even then that you weren't paying attention to where you were walking?"

To Nikki's profound relief she saw an answering amusement glittering in Jack's blue eyes. "My brother, Alan, was the one not paying attention. My mistake was knocking him out of the way and taking the hit for him. Not that the little brat ever thanked me. Denied he was even there."

"How old were you?"

Jack's smile faded. "Twelve. It was the Fourth of July."

"Oh, my birthday." Matt ran a quick calculation. "I'd have been all of one."

"Yeah, I know."

Matt stiffened, his gaze sharpening. "How hurt were you?"

"I'm still here, aren't I?"

But Matt wasn't buying it. "It was touch-and-go, wasn't it? And I'm willing to bet your mother called our father. Did he show up?"

"Eventually."

"Meaning, no. He didn't come, despite the fact that you might have died. And all because it was my first birthday and my mother would have suspected something if he'd taken off. So, you were on your own."

"Not at all. My mother was there." Jack shrugged. "She's a nurse. Probably saved my life that day since she knew what to do to stop the bleeding."

Matt nodded, a grimness cloaking him. "That's why you visited Flynn. Why you brought a toy. Because you didn't have any aunts or uncles or brothers or sisters to visit you when you were in the hospital."

"I had my mother." Jack repeated then attempted to deflect attention from himself. "Does it matter why, Matt? Whether you like it or not, Flynn's my nephew. He's an innocent and deserved my help regardless of how I might feel about his father."

"Of course, if you hurt Flynn's father, you also hurt Flynn," Nikki inserted smoothly. Based on Jack's reaction, that detail had never occurred to him. Typical. He was so focused on his own goals, he didn't always look at the big picture. Deciding that she'd helped heal as much of the breach between them as she could, she deliberately changed the subject. "Matt, do you know whether the police checked The Kincaid Group phone records the night of your father's murder?"

Instantly, his wariness returned. "Why?"

"Your mother said something about Reginald being on the phone when she arrived with his dinner. I was just curious to know who he might have spoken to."

"Huh." Matt's brows pulled together. "I think you'd have to ask Detective McDonough about that. I'm pretty sure the police obtained a court order requesting them. Since no one mentioned anything more about it, I assume either Dad didn't make or receive any phone calls that night, or they weren't significant to the case."

"Would you be willing to contact Charles and ask for a copy of those phone records?"

His wariness turned to open suspicion. "Why would I do that? And even more importantly, why would Mc-Donough agree?"

She answered his second question first. "He might agree if you explained that you wanted to see if anything jumped out at you. You'd know better than anyone who your father would normally speak to in the course of doing business. Considering the case isn't moving forward very fast, Charles might just agree." She used every ounce of persuasive ability she possessed. "Besides, how can showing us the records hurt anything? Maybe, just maybe it could help."

Matt stewed about it for a moment before reluctantly nodding. "I'll ask, but I make no promises."

The two men stared at each other for a long moment then with a sigh of profound irritation, Jack stuck out his hand. "Thanks."

Matt hesitated, just as his mother had when first offered Jack's hand. Then he took it in a firm grip. "Don't mention it. Apparently, family does this sort of thing. Like bring toys to their nephew in the hospital and have their bone marrow tested."

Jack nodded. "Apparently they do."

"They also attend family weddings. You'll be there next Saturday?"

"Wouldn't miss it for the world."

Jack turned on Nikki the instant they left The Kincaid Group building. "Don't do that again."

She smiled up at him, the very picture of innocence. "Do what?" she asked.

"Nuh-uh. I'm not buying it, sweetcakes. Not the

smile. Not the wide-eyed 'why whatever do you mean, butter wouldn't melt in my mouth' look. None of it."

"Why whatever do you mean?"

He pulled to a halt in the middle of the sidewalk. Sun rained down on them, the air dripping with humidity, while a fresh breeze from off the harbor tumbled her dark hair around a face bright with laughter. The afternoon light caught in her blue eyes so they glittered more brilliantly than the gemstones they resembled. The annoyed words he'd been about to utter died unspoken. All he could do was stare.

He reached for her, lifted her onto her tiptoes and took her mouth in a kiss he meant to be hard and passionate, but ended up landing with a soft, persuasiveness that had her moaning in delight. Her arms encircled his neck and she leaned into him, her feminine curves locking against him, fitting in place so perfectly he couldn't doubt they'd been two parts designed to one day become a whole. If they'd been anywhere other than standing on a sidewalk on Charleston's busy East Battery, he'd have made love to her right then and there.

Instead, a modicum of sanity prevailed and he gave her mouth a final nibbling taste before pulling back. "You have to stop interfering, Nikki. I'm dead serious. Now I'm stuck—correction—*we're* stuck attending another one of their weddings. If I'd wanted a relationship with the Kincaids, I'd have formed one long ago."

To his annoyance, she shook her head, her arms still linked around his neck. "No, you wouldn't have," she argued. "Even though all of you are grown and more than capable of forming your own decisions, you continued to respect your father's wishes by keeping your distance from the Legitimates, as you call them."

"Has it occurred to you I kept my distance because I had no interest in knowing them?"

Her expression grew even more tender. "You may have told yourself that, but it isn't true."

If she weren't still holding him in place, he'd have ended the conversation by simply walking away. And though he could have pulled loose, for some reason he didn't. "You're calling me a liar?" he asked.

"No. I just think when it comes to the Kincaids you've been very careful not to look at your own motivations too closely."

"Nikki, this is a pointless discussion. Now let go of me. I'm tired and I'd like to head home and enjoy just a few minutes of what's left of the day."

But she didn't let go of him. Nor did she stop pushing, pushing, pushing. "Jack, for once in your life, stop. Think. Consider why you've made the choices you have."

His mouth took on a hard, stubborn slant. "If you mean why I'm intent on taking down the Kincaids—"

"No, that's not what I mean. I mean, why did you decide to start up a competing company? Of all the possible businesses and professions you could have gone into, why in the world would you choose the very one where—guaranteed—you were bound to run into your brothers and sisters at some point? Why, Jack?"

This time he did grab her hands and yank them from around his neck. He took a deliberate step backward. Then another, rejecting every aspect of the question. Without a word, he turned and walked away. But no matter how long or how far he walked, he couldn't escape Nikki's question. Nor could he escape the painful knowledge that pierced him like a dagger. On some level Nikki was right. He'd wanted to run into the

Kincaids when he started up Carolina Shipping. He'd wanted them to know he existed. He wanted them to know the truth.

He was their brother.

Five

Nikki finally located Jack two hours later, sitting near the General William Moultrie statue on the outskirts of White Point Gardens, overlooking Charleston Harbor. She thought it appropriate that she found him beside the man responsible for the protection and defense of Charleston during the Revolutionary War since Jack so often assumed that role within his own family.

He didn't look at her when she took a seat on the cement wall beside him. After a few minutes passed, he broke the uneasy silence. "How is it that you see things the way you do?"

"I don't know. I guess it's a gift." She stared out across the water and shrugged. "Or maybe you'd consider it a curse. I just know it's a talent my father had, one he passed onto me. I think it's part of what made him such a great cop. He could talk to someone for a bit and get under their skin. Figure out what motivated them and why. He once told me that figuring out the motivation often helped him solve the case."

"You've gotten under my skin." Now he did look at her, his gaze dark with pain. "And I'm not sure I like it. I'm not sure I want you there."

She bowed her head and nodded. "I understand." She tried not to show the hurt, though she felt it. Dear God, how she felt it. "Maybe that's why so many cops prefer to associate with other cops." Her hand fluttered in a swift, helpless gesture. "Not only do they understand the demands and pressures of the job, but they don't end up feeling what the average person feels—like they're living under a microscope."

"That's not what I meant." He reached for her, tugged her close. "You've never made me feel like I'm living under a microscope. You just…" He released a sigh of sheer frustration. "You see far too much. And for some reason your vision is much clearer than my own."

She snuggled in, her throat constricting, making it difficult to speak. "You're just too close to the problem, that's all. I can see it because I have emotional distance."

Only she didn't. Not when it came to Jack. At some point in the past four months he'd become her world. And she couldn't imagine her life without him in it. She shut her eyes, praying she wouldn't start crying at the bittersweet awareness filling her. Before too much longer, she might not only have to imagine life without him, but live it without him, as well. His hand shifted and he caught her chin, turning her so she was forced to look at him.

"You need to stop now," he told her gently. "You need to understand that I don't have the sort of connection to the Kincaids you're hoping for and I never will. All of your attempts to create that connection are pointless because my plans for them haven't changed and they won't."

"Jack—"

He cut her off without hesitation. "Stop, Nikki. This isn't open for debate or discussion. I'm telling you how it's going to be. You can either continue to be with me… or we end this now. But this desire you seem to have of uniting the two families won't work. Ever. There's too much bad history between us for that to happen."

"There's *no* history between you," Nikki objected heatedly. "There was history between you and your father, and between your parents. But you only met your brothers and sisters five months ago. There's no reason you can't have some sort of positive relationship with them. Look at how well it went today with Elizabeth and Matt." Enthusiasm swept through her words. "Don't you get it? It's entirely up to you. If you'd just drop this vendetta you have going and consider working with them, instead of against them—"

He stopped her using the most effective means at his disposal. He kissed her. Whereas before his kiss had been gently persuasive, this one took command. This one led, giving her the option of following…or withdrawing. But she couldn't withdraw. It was far too late for that. Instead, she surrendered, utterly.

Her head tipped back against his shoulder and she opened to him, accepting his possession, shivering beneath the skillful way he aroused and teased. They were so perfectly mated in all the ways that counted. Their intellect. The love that burgeoned between them, bit by delicious bit. Their sense of humor. Their work ethic. Their generosity and protectiveness toward others. Even the way they viewed the world and those in it—with the single unfortunate exception of the Kincaids. Why couldn't Jack see that?

But he didn't and one look at the hard determination cutting across his face warned that he'd set his plans in stone. Any hope she had of swaying him would not just meet with disappointment, but with disaster.

"I will not tolerate any further interference on your part," he told her, his voice underscoring the hint of mercilessness she'd caught in his expression. "Are we clear on that point, Nikki?"

She pulled back from his embrace. "We're clear. But I don't have to like it." She folded her arms across her chest. "And in case *I* haven't been clear on that point. I don't."

"I believe you've been crystal clear," he said with a slight smile that did nothing to improve her temper. "Are you going home or would you like to spend the night at my place?"

She gave herself permission to stew for a full thirty seconds before lifting her shoulder in a quick, impatient shrug. "Your place."

"Excellent. We can break in the hot tub together."

Her eyes widened. "Hot tub? You have a hot tub? When did you get a hot tub?"

He tucked a lock of hair behind her ear. "It was meant to be a surprise for this weekend. I had it installed yesterday. You have no idea how hard I've worked to resist christening it without you. It's been sitting there calling to me all day."

"Funny." She slanted him a swift look. "I hear it calling to me, too. In fact, I think my name's written all over it with a giant arrow that says, 'plant backside here.'"

"I might have noticed your name." He held up two

fingers pinched together. "In teeny-tiny print and a warning label. Something to do with combustible materials."

She allowed her irritation to fade and amusement to take its place. "Combustible only when combined."

"Oh, I do plan on combining. And shaking. Maybe lighting a fuse or two."

Her mouth curled into a reluctant smile. As much as she wanted to stay angry at him, it wouldn't serve any useful purpose. "I think you already lit a fuse or two." She caught his hand in hers and tugged. "Come on. Let's go watch the fireworks."

"To hell with watching." He scooped her close. "I plan to set them off. Personally."

Nikki stretched out on one of the extra wide lounging platforms of Jack's hot tub and leaned her head back against his shoulder. With the simple push of a button pulsating jets exploded to life, sending warm water bubbling around them. A soft moan escaped her and she followed Jack's example of closing her eyes and allowing the swirling water to sweep away her cares—particularly those about the Kincaids and how she'd execute her plan to unite Jack with his brothers and sisters now that he was on to her.

"I think I just tripped and fell into paradise," she told him.

"Thank you."

Nikki gave a snort of laughter. "Falling onto you is heaven. Falling onto you while in a hot tub is paradise."

"I believe you've overlooked a step."

"What step is that?"

"The one where you're naked when you tripped and fell on me while in a hot tub." He opened a single eye and lifted a questioning eyebrow. "Explain again why you made us wear swimsuits?"

"Oh, I don't know..." A hint of sarcasm competed with laughter. "Maybe the small matter of our sitting on your deck out in the open."

"That's what the privacy screens are for. Besides, there aren't any homes nearby. I bought the property all around this place to ensure my privacy."

"And if someone wanders down the beach?"

"We're too far away for them to see anything... Much." His nimble fingers skated along her spine and an instant later the top of her swimsuit floated away. "There. That's a huge improvement. At least, we're halfway there."

Water frothed around her breasts like a teasing caress. She'd never realized how arousing pulsating water could be. "Would it help move us closer to paradise if I mention that the bottoms tie on?" Nikki tilted her head to glance at him. "No knots, either."

Jack's slow smile had heat gathering low in her belly, sliding like silk into her veins where it throbbed and pulsated in rhythm with the water jets. "So all I have to do is give them a little tug?" His hand brushed the curve of her hip. "Like this?"

A moment later her swimsuit bottoms bobbed to the surface, followed by a pair of male trunks. Nikki rolled onto her side to face Jack, supported by the churning water. Since their return to his beach house he'd relaxed. Well, as much as he ever relaxed. She'd pushed too hard, too soon. She realized that now.

Maybe if the annual shareholders meeting wasn't taking place so soon, a meeting in which a new president and CEO would be voted in to replace the late Reginald Kincaid, she wouldn't have had to escalate her plan to unite Jack with the Kincaids. Clearly, reconciling with two Kincaids in one day had been more than Jack could handle. That, combined with her assessment of the career he'd pursued and his motivation for choosing that career, had thrown him into full emotional retreat.

She slid her fingertips along his stubbled jawline then followed the contours of his mouth, gathering his smile in the palm of her hand, as well as a lingering kiss. "What are you in the mood to eat for dinner tonight?" she asked.

"You. Just you."

She laughed, delighted they'd gotten back onto more familiar footing. "No doubt you'd find that tasty, but not very filling."

"We can place an order at Indigo's if seafood appeals. I know how much you like that place."

"They deliver?" she asked in surprise.

His smile turned smug. "They will for me." His hand cupped her bottom and he urged her closer. "But later. Much later."

Jack's body slid across Nikki's and she shuddered beneath the abrasive combination of the foaming water and the light pelt of hair covering his chest and legs. Her nipples tightened, peeking above the surface like a pair of dusky pearls. He lowered his head and caught first one then the next between his teeth and she groaned, sliding her fingers into his hair and anchoring him at her breast.

And all the while his nimble fingers played beneath the surface, as tantalizing as the churning jets at stoking the heat gathering there. Her legs parted and her hips tilted upward, offering herself to him. Instead of mating their two bodies, he continued to tease, easing a finger into her warmth, sending her desire skyrocketing to an even higher level.

"I think I see fireworks," she said with a helpless groan.

"I haven't heard them go off, yet."

She couldn't stand another minute and she reached for him, fisting his hard length in her hands and fitting him to her. He sank inward and she shuddered. It took a few tries before they found their rhythm, the water throwing them off. And then the fire caught: a screaming flash that burned an unstoppable path from one to the other. His name escaped in a powerful rush, bursting into the air. Jack surged into her and Nikki arced helplessly upward, exploding into the grand finale.

They lingered there, the brilliance dazzling in its aftermath. Then bit by bit they drifted back to earth, sinking into the comforting embrace of the warm water, dissolving against each other in a tangle of arms and legs, lingering kisses and soothing strokes. Nikki closed her eyes and burrowed close, more vulnerable than she could ever remember feeling.

When would it fade? When would this desperate need for him ease into something more manageable, something that didn't threaten to break her heart? Maybe it never would. Their relationship hung by a thread, dangling above a bottomless chasm. The instant Jack discovered she owned the controlling ten percent shares of Kincaid stock—that she could throw control of The Kincaid Group into either his lap or RJ's, that thread would snap. Because she knew Reginald had intended the position of president and CEO to fall to RJ, had been told so by the late patriarch, himself. And no matter how much she loved Jack, she couldn't—and wouldn't—go against her conscience.

A conscience that demanded she vote for RJ to succeed his father.

Monday came all too soon as far as Jack was concerned. Reluctantly, he and Nikki prepared for work. Over the course of the past several months her business suits had joined his in the closet at his beach house. It never failed to amuse him how she would hang them so they marched boy/girl, boy/girl across the wooden support bar.

By the time he reached the kitchen, Nikki already had the coffee brewing. Though he'd told her repeatedly she didn't need to fix him breakfast, she'd shrugged him off, seeming to enjoy throwing their meal together most mornings. He decided it was a woman thing and let her have her head.

"Veggie omelets?" she offered.

"Sounds great."

It was his usual response since he saw no point in being particular in the face of Nikki's generosity. Then again, maybe tomorrow he'd tease her by saying no just to see what she'd do. A moment's reflection changed his mind. Or maybe he wouldn't. Considering the tension between them over the Kincaid situation, they sure didn't need him adding more conflict to the mix, not over his weak attempt at a joke.

Despite the fact he considered Nikki in the wrong for her interference, he knew she meant well. It was that soft heart of hers getting in the way. Fortunately, he'd put an end to it without too much trouble. And even if he'd been forced to reveal far more personal information to Elizabeth and Matt Kincaid than he would have under normal circumstances, he could live with it, so long as he didn't have to reveal anything further.

Jack pulled the ingredients needed for the omelets from the refrigerator and made short work of chopping the onions and mushrooms, and shredding the spinach. All the while, morning sunshine spilled across the kitchen and landed on Nikki, spotlighting her. It proved a constant distraction. He doubted he'd ever tire of watching her. There was something so vital about her, her movements clean and smooth, yet energetic. Her expression intent, yet easy, with a constant smile half formed on her mouth.

He thought again of the ring he'd bought last month and currently kept tucked away in his dresser drawer. He'd been on the verge of proposing at least a dozen times in the past few weeks. If it hadn't been for his recent discovery that she worked for the Kincaids, he might have already asked. But something held him back. Unfortunately, he knew what it was.

Nikki was keeping another secret.

The realization had come to him over the course of the weekend, beginning with her blatant attempts to resolve the conflict between him and his Kincaid relatives. Her determination had been underscored by something that felt almost like desperation, as though some crucial factor teetered on the outcome of her efforts. His suspicions had solidified during the night when he'd waken to find her standing on the deck, encased in moonlight, her head bent, her shoulders rounded. It was as though she carried an impossible weight. What he hadn't quite figured out yet, was whether or not it had anything to do with the Kincaids, or with her latest campaign of trying to form a connection between him and the Legitimates.

Well, hell. Why not just ask her?

Before he could the doorbell rang. Nikki glanced over her shoulder at him. "Who in the world would visit at this hour?" she asked, her eyebrows drawing together.

"Only one way to find out."

"If it's someone we know, invite them back for omelets," she called to Jack as he left the kitchen. "It won't take me a second to throw together an extra."

He opened the door, unpleasantly surprised to discover the detective assigned to his father's murder investigation standing on his doorstep. Though a couple of inches shorter and a decade or so older than Jack, Charles McDonough was a powerful, impeccably dressed black man with a shaved head that gleamed in the morning light, and dark, patient eyes reflecting a calm intelligence, coupled with an unswerving determination. He'd demonstrated that determination and intelligence the few times he'd interviewed Jack.

Charles inclined his head in greeting. "Good morning, Mr. Sinclair. I'm glad I was able to catch you before you left for the office." He glanced around. "Nice place you have here."

"Thanks." Jack fell back a step. "Come on in."

The detective stepped across the threshold, his deceptively casual gaze taking in every detail of the airy foyer and the magnificent great room that swept toward the back of the house where a wall of sparkling windows overlooked the restless ocean.

"*Very* nice," Charles amended his earlier comment. "If I owned a place like this I'd have every relative in the family tree crawling out for a visit. How about you?"

"I don't have much in the way of family. Just my

brother, Alan, and my mother. But they do stay here whenever they come to Charleston."

The detective gave a brief laugh. "Bet that's more often than you'd like."

"There are times…" Like when Alan arrived on his doorstep unannounced and lingered far longer than the "fish" rule that warned that after three days fish and guests began to smell—and should both be tossed out. Jack gestured toward the hallway to the right. "We're just having breakfast. I've been told to invite you to join us."

"Us?" McDonough's stride checked ever so slightly. "Sorry. It didn't occur to me you'd have company."

"That's all right. I believe you and Nikki are old friends."

"Nikki? Nikki *Thomas?*"

The detective stepped into the kitchen and his face tightened when he caught sight of her. A hint of anger sparked in his dark eyes at the familiar way she moved around the kitchen, her comfortable attitude telling the detective—or maybe screaming at him—she'd been here often enough to make herself at home. Combine that with the early-morning hour and it wasn't hard for a man whose profession made him particularly astute at putting two and two together to do some quick math and come up with a very awkward four…that Jack and Nikki were sleeping together.

Considering Charles and Peter Thomas, Nikki's late father, had once been partners, Jack suspected the detective possessed strong paternal feelings toward her. Paternal feelings that did not bode well for the man who was the "two" having sex with the other "two" in his equation.

Jack sighed. He was so screwed.

Nikki threw a sunny smile over her shoulder. "Morning, Charles."

"What the hell are you doing here, girl?"

"Having breakfast," she replied easily. "When I heard your voice I threw an extra omelet on for you."

"I don't want an omelet."

"Too bad. It's already cooking. I know you, Charles. If you're out and about this early you left before Raye even climbed out of bed. That means you grabbed a cup of coffee and a piece of toast, if that." She waved a hand toward the kitchen table. "Go on and sit. Jack, pour Charles a cup of coffee. He likes it with cream and extra sugar. Raye doesn't let him have the extra sugar, but we'll keep it our little secret."

"Darn it, Nikki," Charles snapped. "You haven't answered my question."

But Jack noticed he took a seat, anyway. Unfortunately the look the detective shot in his direction was just shy of murderous. Better to give him the information up-front and be done with it. "We met shortly after my father's death. We've been dating more than three months. It's serious. You can try to warn her off, but it won't work. She's intent on proving my innocence. Two teaspoons of sugar or three?"

The detective's jaw worked for an endless minute. "Four."

Jack's brows shot upward. "Ouch."

"Yeah, that's what Raye says. Dump it in there, hand it over and keep your comments to your own damn self."

Jack complied before taking a seat across from the detective. Nikki dropped plates in front of the two men and, gazes locked and loaded, they dug in. Charles paused long enough to groan. "God, Nikki, when did you learn to cook this good? You've been taking lessons from your grandma Thomas, haven't you?"

"She might have taught me a couple tricks."

He worked his way through the omelet, scraped his plate clean enough to remove the pattern then shoved it aside. "Knowing you have your nose stuck in this is a royal pain in the ass, Nikki, but it sure explains a thing or two." He eased back in his seat, turning his coffee mug in a slow circle that Jack suspected was his typical thinking mode. "Like why Jack here asked Matt Kincaid to get his hands on The Kincaid Group phone records."

Jack saw red. "Son of a—"

Charles waved him silent. "Kincaid can't lie worth a damn. As soon as I asked him why he wanted a copy he started squirming like a six year-old with both hands and a foot caught in the cookie jar. Didn't take much pushing to find out you were behind it." His gaze switched to Nikki and cooled. "Or rather, Nikki. Her mind works just like her daddy's did."

Nikki's eyes grew misty. "That's the sweetest thing you ever said to me, Charles."

"Why do you want the phone records, girl?"

"Actually, it was Jack's stroke of brilliance."

"Oh, yeah?" The detective's attention returned to Jack and cooled further still. "Exactly what stroke of brilliance might that be?"

Jack debated how much to say, well aware if he didn't explain it to the detective, Nikki would. Since that didn't leave him much choice, he went ahead and laid out his thought process. "The night Dad was killed, when Elizabeth Kincaid brought him his dinner, did she happen to mention to you that she thought she heard Reginald on the phone when she arrived?"

Charles shook his head. "She did not," he stated crisply, clearly displeased he lacked information Jack possessed. "Maybe because he wasn't on the phone. I checked the company phone logs, personally, as well as his cell phone records. One call, outgoing, well before Mrs. Kincaid arrived on the scene. It was to a golfing buddy, confirming a tee-off time."

"Then who was he speaking to?" Nikki asked.

Charles shrugged. "Himself? I've been known to do that when trying to puzzle through a snag in a case. Your daddy used to do it, too," he informed her.

A sudden idea hit Jack, one that explained a lot. "What if..." He spared a quick look in Nikki's direction, who gave him an encouraging nod in return. "What if the killer was in Dad's office when Elizabeth arrived?"

Nikki stared at him in open admiration. "Jack, that's brilliant. That never would have occurred to me, but it sure explains a few things that don't add up."

The detective blinked in surprise. "How did you come up with that idea?"

He didn't use the words "cockamamie idea" but Jack caught the silent inference, nonetheless. He shoved back his chair and stood, pacing toward the bow window overlooking the water, then back again while he gathered his thoughts. "Elizabeth told us that Dad was unusually curt with her. She used the word cruel."

"Yes, she used that word with me, too. Your point?"

"That's not typical of my father. And it sure isn't the way he taught me to treat women. Despite the fact he was involved with my mother, he loved his wife and had the utmost respect for her. When I asked Elizabeth if he'd ever spoken to her like that before, she said he hadn't."

"No, that's what his family and staffed claimed, as

well. It was one of the reasons I doubted her story," Charles agreed. "Go on."

"Why would he act so out of character that night? It doesn't make sense, unless…" He could only hope his idea didn't sound crazy to a trained detective. "Unless the killer was in the room at the time and Dad was trying to protect Elizabeth by getting her out of there in the most efficient and expedient way possible."

"That sounds exactly like something Reginald would do," Nikki murmured. She crossed to Jack's side and gave his hand a swift squeeze. She looked at him, her lovely blue eyes filled with sympathetic understanding. "It would explain so much, wouldn't it? And yet, how sad that one of his last acts was to treat his wife with such cruelty in order to protect her. It probably saved her life, but still… Reginald would have hated having those the final words ever spoken between them."

"Assuming that's what happened," Charles cut in. He tilted his head to one side and closed his eyes as though rolling the thought around, looking for flaws or other possibilities. "That's certainly one plausible explanation. Unfortunately, it's just as plausible that he found out about her affair with Cutter Reynolds and was struggling to come to terms with it. Maybe she arrived before he could regain control of his temper."

"How would he have found out?" Nikki asked. "If he'd hired a private investigator, you would have uncovered that information by now. I mean, none of his children knew. I assume, based on your interviews of friends and business associates, no one else did, either, or they'd have mentioned it."

"And if a friend or business associate knew, I guarantee the rest of Charleston would have heard about it within hours," Jack added a trifle sourly. "Maybe within minutes considering how fast the news spread about Dad's affair with my mother and the fact that I was a product of that affair."

Charles shook his head. "No one mentioned Elizabeth's involvement with Cutter. No one even hinted at the possibility. In fact, after she admitted to the affair, I took another run at those who'd most likely have known. She managed to keep her liaison with Cutter Reynolds well off the radar," he confirmed.

"Then how would Reginald have known?" Nikki asked.

"Okay, let's say that Jack's right and the killer was in the room at the time. So what? What more does that give us than we already know? If we look at what I've learned since Kincaid's murder, certain facts aren't in dispute." He ticked off on his fingers. "Point one. The murderer gained entry to the building through the front door when he walked in with Brooke Nichols shortly before TKG closed for the day. Point two. The killer had to be someone familiar with the building, as well as the location of your father's office, since he didn't ask for directions, but acted as though he knew where he was going. Even more, that he belonged there since it didn't occur to Brooke to question him when he bypassed the check-in desk. Point three. His familiarity with the building and the location of Reginald's office suggests to me that in all likelihood Reginald knew the identity of his murderer. That's why I've been focused on family and close friends. There's only one big stumbling block."

"Everyone has alibis," Nikki said.

"Yes."

Her expression turned uneasy. "Then point four

would be to look at whoever gains the most from Reginald's murder. In other words, motivation."

Charles nodded. "Exactly. So far, the only ones who benefit are the immediate family." The detective's gaze landed long and hard on Jack. "And of all the family you, Sinclair, with your forty-five percent share in TKG stock, stand to gain the most."

Jack forced himself to remain cool and calm, though McDonough ought to have his tough, gotcha look patented. It was that effective. "That doesn't change the fact that I didn't kill my own father. I wouldn't. Damn it, Detective, I couldn't."

"Then why was your car at a parking lot near TKG during the time of the murder?"

"I wish I knew." Since McDonough was being reasonably forthcoming, Jack risked a question. "How is it possible that you have photos or video of my car, but not of me?"

The detective rocked his chair back onto two legs. "That's just it, Sinclair. We do. We have a lovely piece of video featuring you climbing out of your expensive ruby-red Aston Martin and heading off in the direction of TKG."

Six

The words shocked the hell out of Jack and he sank into his chair. *"What?"* He stared at the detective in utter disbelief. He struggled to marshal his thoughts, to make sense out of something so beyond the realm of possibility. "How can you have a video of me when I was never there? It has to be a forgery. I don't know how or why someone would go to such extremes, but I'm telling you, I was working that night. I never left my office until well after the time of Dad's death."

Nikki chimed in, leaping to his defense. "And if it's true, why hasn't he been arrested and thrown in jail?"

Charles ignored her, keeping his gaze fixed on Jack for what seemed like an endless time. Then he closed his eyes and shook his head, swearing under his breath. "You really don't know, do you? Either that, or you're a damn fine actor."

The hot ball of tension forming at the pit of Jack's

stomach eased a fraction. Had the detective been lying in order to gauge his reaction? "All I know is that there's no way you have a video of me at that time and place because I wasn't there," he stated simply.

To his surprise, the detective opened up. "It was raining that night. Pouring. The person who got out of your car is about your size and height and wore a felt hat. You know, like one of those Indiana Jones knockoffs?"

"Right. We had a name for the idiots who wore those."

"Yeah, we did, too." McDonough's gaze flashed with humor and the men had a moment of perfect accord. "Not a word I choose to repeat in front of Nikki," he added.

"So, you never saw his face?" Jack asked.

"No. And what little we could see he disguised with a beard and thick glasses. He also wore a heavy raincoat, which made it even more difficult to get a good feel for his overall build."

Jack mulled over the description. "Any chance it was a woman?"

McDonough shrugged. "Doubtful. According to Brooke Nichols he was tall, nearly RJ's height."

"Another point against me."

"Put together, it makes for some serious circumstantial evidence against you." An uncomfortable silence descended, one McDonough eventually broke. "What did you and your father discuss when you spoke to him the day he died?"

"We spoke the day before, not the day of," Jack said absently.

The detective's gaze sharpened. "Wrong, son. When Matt asked about the phone records, I took another look.

There was a call from Carolina Shipping to your father's private line about an hour before closing."

It took Jack a second to absorb the information. "From Carolina Shipping? The main number or my own private line?"

Charles reeled off the number from memory.

"That's the main line. I always call him from my cell phone or my office, which is a different number from the main line."

"This time you didn't."

Jack's back teeth clamped together. "Why are you so determined to hang me for my father's murder?"

McDonough shrugged. "Why does every new piece of information lead right back to you, Sinclair? It stirs my curiosity, son. It truly does."

"Take another look at those phone records," Jack demanded. "You'll see that every call I ever placed to my father was either from my cell or my personal business line to either his cell or his private office number."

"Then if you didn't call him, who did?"

Jack's expression fell into grim lines. "Good question, one I intend to look into as soon as I get to the office."

"Uh-huh. Well, while you're at it see if you can't come up with an explanation for your car being at the parking lot near TKG. A better one than 'I didn't do it.'"

Jack struggled to contain his frustration. "I have a suggestion. Why don't you show me the video you have?"

Suspicion leaped into the detective's face. "Why?"

"I want to see proof that it's my car."

"They're your tags, son." Even so, McDonough weighed the idea then shrugged. "Set up an appointment and I'll see if I can get it approved." He shoved back his chair and stood. "Nikki, I'd like to warn you off this guy, but I doubt you'll listen."

She offered Charles a gentle smile. "Sorry. I'm in it for the long haul."

He sighed. "I was afraid you'd say that." He nailed Jack with an arctic look. "Walk me out." It wasn't a request.

McDonough didn't speak until they reached the front door. Once there, he turned on Jack, his expression vicious with intent, his voice a dark whisper. "Her daddy and I go way back, Sinclair. He took a bullet meant for me and there's not a day that goes by that I don't live with those consequences."

"She doesn't blame you." It was all Jack could think to say.

"God knows why. That doesn't change the fact that there's not a man on the force who won't stand for her. You understand what I'm saying?" The detective didn't wait for a response. He simply leaned in to hammer home his point. "You hurt her and you won't be able to cross the street without getting arrested for jaywalking. That's assuming you still have a pair of legs capable of walking once we're done with you."

And with that, he spun on his heel and left.

"How bad was the threat?" Nikki asked sympathetically.

Jack spared her a brief glance before returning his gaze to the road. "Nothing I can't handle."

"He didn't mean it."

"Right." A humorless smile cut across his face. "I think you have a tendency to underestimate how protective Charles is of you...and the extent to which he and his cop buddies will go, if our relationship causes you any grief."

"Here's a thought...." she offered brightly. "Don't cause me any grief."

"An excellent plan." His irritation faded, replaced by a sincerity that caused her heart to lurch. "Trust me, the last thing I ever want to do is cause you grief."

"Oh, Jack," she murmured. "There are times you say the most unexpected—and delightful—things."

"I mean them."

"I know you do." She touched his thigh, feeling the muscle clench beneath her gentle caress. "That's what makes them all the more special."

They turned onto East Battery, the traffic thickening. "Your place or mine tonight?" he asked.

"Your place is fine. I want to give that hot tub another spin."

"I'm all over that suggestion." He flashed her a quick grin. "And I hope, all over you."

"Count on it." Reluctantly, she switched her attention to the business of the day. "I assume you're going to look into who might have called your father from Carolina Shipping?"

"It's the first item on my agenda."

"And then?"

"If they made the call from Carolina Shipping, chances are I know the person. So, then I plan to have a long talk with the individual before turning them in to the police. It might be interesting to know their movements the night of my father's murder...including whether there's any chance they had access to my car."

"Huh. Your day sounds a lot more interesting than mine," Nikki complained. "I don't suppose you'd let me tag along for a little while? Two eyes and ears are always better than one."

"What about work?"

"I am working. I'm spying on you, remember?"

To her profound relief, he laughed. "Right, right. Can't imagine how I forgot." Jack passed the access road leading to The Kincaid Group, and continued on. "You can hang with me until lunch. I have meetings this afternoon that I'd rather not postpone."

She started to ask about them, but realizing it might be a conflict of interest, fell silent. They entered the parking lot for Carolina Shipping. Jack pulled into his usual spot beside a hedge of English boxwood, the fragrant scent filling the air. They exited the car and he unlocked the door leading directly from the parking lot into his office, confirming her suspicions about the private entrance. No wonder Charles still considered Jack a viable suspect.

"Too many people were in and out of my office," he said, clearly reading her mind. "Slipping out would have been a foolish chance to take. Anyone could have discovered me gone, and later told the police."

Nikki followed him inside and considered the timeline. "I agree. That's why none of this makes sense."

"So, why am I still a suspect?"

"I don't know, Jack. The killer needed a lot of time, time you didn't have. Not only did he have to wait for the building to clear out to confront Reginald in private, he also had to wait outside TKG so he could walk in with an employee in order to avoid signing the logbook at the front desk."

"That doesn't make sense. If he didn't sign in, why take the log sheet?" Jack asked.

"I wondered about that, too." Nikki worked through

the possibilities. "Maybe in case security made a note of his arrival?"

"Better safe than sorry?"

"It could be just that simple."

He mulled it over and nodded in agreement. "Sounds reasonable." He waved her toward a chair and picked up the phone on his desk and pushed a button. "I'm here, Gail," he informed his assistant. "Would you please have Lynn come to my office when she gets a chance? Thanks." He returned to the timeline. "So, once he's in he'd head for Reginald's office. No point in wasting time, right?"

"Not if he was worried about getting your car back to you before anyone realized it was missing."

"Next problem… How would he know my father would be there, and more importantly, be alone?"

"It was closing time," Nikki said slowly. "Your father often worked late. Let's assume the killer confirmed Reginald was still at the office by calling him from Carolina Shipping. Maybe the killer assumed Reginald would be alone."

"Hmm. Working late seems to run in the family." Jack approached, his gaze warming. "Not as much as it used to. At least, not for the past three months. You've had a seriously negative impact on my workaholic tendencies."

She grinned. "So my diabolical plan is working."

"All too well." He slid his arms around her and nuzzled the sensitive area just beneath her ear, driving every coherent thought from her head. "When I weigh the pleasure of work versus the pleasure of spending those hours with you, work can't compare."

"Oh, Jack," she whispered.

Unable to resist, she kissed him, putting her heart

and soul into the melding of lips and bodies. She'd never known a man capable of arousing her to such extremes, with no more than a lingering glance, a glancing touch, a touching comment. He loosened the buttons of her jacket and slipped his hands beneath, caressing her through the silk shell she wore.

Time drifted away, and she submerged herself in a desire more profound than anything she'd experienced before. Over the past three months she'd done more than fall in love with Jack Sinclair. She'd committed to him, allowed herself to bond with him, to open her emotions so completely that she couldn't imagine being with another man. Ever.

"Nikki, there's something I've been meaning to ask—"

A light tapping on the door interrupted them and the two reluctantly pulled apart. While Nikki buttoned her jacket, Jack made a visible effort to switch gears. Was it wrong she experienced a quick feminine satisfaction that it took several long seconds for him to pull it off?

"Come in," he called out as soon as they were presentable again.

Lynn stepped into the office. "You asked to see me, Jack?" Her gaze landed on Nikki and she smiled with the sort of sweetness Nikki was beginning to associate with her overall personality. "How lovely to see you again, Ms. Thomas. I hope you had a good weekend."

"Excellent, thank you. And please, call me Nikki."

Jack waited through the social chitchat with barely concealed impatience before smoothly switching to the matter at hand. "Lynn, I need to find out who placed a call to my father's office the day of his murder. It would have been from the main company line versus from my office. Around four, I believe. Could you check around?"

A swift frown replaced her sunny smile. "I'll get right on it," she said.

The instant she left, Jack glanced at Nikki. She could see him debating whether to pick up where they'd left off and take her in his arms. With a smile of regret, he stood and wandered over to the coffeemaker he kept by his wet bar. Gail had already brewed the first pot and he poured two cups, handing one to Nikki. He eased his hip onto the corner of his desk and took a slow, appreciative sip. She joined him, sitting in the chair closest to where he lounged and crossed her legs, balancing the cup and saucer on her knee with practiced ease.

"You know, the facts seem fairly straightforward and highly time consuming," Jack said after a moment's thought. "The killer parked in the lot where he was caught on tape. He then proceeded to TKG where he waited outside until he could enter with Brooke. He bypassed the security desk, no doubt taking the stairs to the fourth floor in order to hide until my father was alone, then confronted him."

"He couldn't anticipate Elizabeth arriving with dinner."

Pain touched Jack's face as they moved closer to the point where Reginald had been murdered. "Assuming my father knew his killer—or even if he didn't—there was undoubtedly some discussion both before Elizabeth's arrival and after her departure." His voice deepened. Roughened. "The killer would have had to wait until he was certain Elizabeth was gone and wouldn't hear the gunshot."

Nikki stood and set her coffee aside before doing the same with his. Then she wrapped her arms around him. "Don't. Don't go there," she whispered. "There's no point and your father wouldn't have wanted you to imagine those final moments, but to remember your actual relationship."

He leaned into her, his breathing deep and labored. "God, Nikki. I can't help thinking about how he must have felt during those last seconds of life. Was there something he could have said to prevent it from happening? Something he could have done? Something any of us could have said or done if only we'd known?"

"We may never know." A hint of steel slipped into her voice. "But we can and will figure out who did this. We'll have to be satisfied with that."

He straightened, steel filtering through his own voice, as well. "You're absolutely right. He then shoots my dad and returns to the lobby." The words sounded calm and objective, but she felt the waves of fury and grief rippling beneath.

She clung to her focus, forcing herself to remain logical, aware it was the best way she could help Jack regain his balance and some shred of objectivity. "Okay, but it's after closing and most everyone's gone. I was in the meeting when Tony Ramos, the investigator RJ hired to look into your father's murder, ran through the timeline from that point forward. Jimmy was the security guard on duty that night. He only leaves his station to use the bathroom, and he always locks the front door when the desk is unattended. That means the killer had to wait for Jimmy to take a bathroom break before stealing the page out of the logbook and escaping out the front."

"Did the investigator indicate when that happened?"

Nikki struggled to recall details from a meeting that had taken place over two months earlier. "Jimmy left his post shortly after Brooke and Elizabeth exited the building. He locked the door beforehand, which is his protocol. But when he returned to his station a few minutes later, he found the front door unlocked."

Jack shook his head. "None of this makes sense. I could have discovered my car was missing at any point and notified the cops. Or Reginald's body could have been found and the cops called. That's an endless amount of time. Far too long for me to be a serious suspect."

"Unless they believe you were working in concert with the actual murderer," Nikki suggested reluctantly.

To her surprise, Jack nodded in agreement, taking her comment in stride. "I've begun to suspect the same thing. If you look at the murder from a cop's perspective, it would explain how and why the killer used my car. And why Charles still considers me a suspect." His mouth settled into grim lines. "Whoever took my car was setting me up."

While she'd been avoiding going there, Jack cut straight through to the heart of the matter. "The killer wanted the police to discover the video from the parking lot showing your car—a ruby-red Aston Martin that everyone in Charleston knows you drive," Nikki commented. "Though if you were in cahoots with him it would have been damn stupid of you to have him use such a distinctive vehicle, one that would ultimately lead right back to you."

"And I'm not damn stupid."

"No, you're not." She retrieved her coffee and took a sip, turning various possibilities over in her head. "You know… Maybe we're looking at this backward, Jack. And maybe the police are, too."

He slowly nodded, quick to catch on. "Instead of asking who had a grudge against Reginald and killed him because of it, we should be asking who has a grudge against me and murdered my father, leaving me to take the fall. Unfortunately, there are more than a couple of names on that list, most of which are Kincaids."

A shiver of dread raced through Nikki and her coffee cup chattered against the saucer. "Oh, Jack. What if the police decide you're innocent? I don't think that's going to make the actual murderer very happy. He might decide to come after you, directly. You could be in real danger."

"Don't worry, Nikki. I can look after myself."

He didn't realize it, but his calm reply only increased her fear. How many times had her father said that to her? How many times had he smiled reassuringly— just like Jack was—and told her he'd be fine. That he was a cop, more than capable of looking after himself. It hadn't saved him from a bullet, any more than Reginald had been able to save himself.

Any more than Jack could.

"You can't look after yourself," she retorted sharply, setting her coffee aside. "Not if someone's intent on taking you out. There are too many possible ways to do it. It's too easy to accomplish—just look at what happened to your father."

"And your father?" he asked gently.

Despite the fact that she'd been thinking just that, she shocked them both by bursting into tears. Instantly, he stood and swept her into his arms, holding her close. "Easy, sweetheart, easy. We're going to get this figured out and then we're going to turn the whole problem over to Charles. Whoever killed Dad can't get at me if he's behind bars."

"And if we don't figure out who it is? Or if there's

no proof and the police can't lock him up? Or worse…"
She caught her bottom lip between her teeth. "What if
the killer implicates you and the police believe him?"

"We deal with one problem at a time. First, we need
to figure out who killed Dad. Then we figure out how
to prove his guilt while establishing my innocence."

Before she could argue the matter any further, a
knock sounded on the door again. Deliberately, Nikki
eased from Jack's embrace and pretended to busy herself refilling their coffee cups while she surreptitiously
dabbed the tears from her cheeks. Lynn entered the
room a moment later. From the corner of her eyes,
Nikki saw the receptionist twist her hands together,
her agitation palpable.

"Mr. Sinclair?" Her formal address warned her the
news wasn't good.

"What did you discover, Lynn?"

"I'm so sorry," she said quickly. "It's all my fault. I
let him use the phone. I didn't realize it was the wrong
thing to do. If you want my resignation, I'll understand."

"Slow down," Jack said, keeping his voice low and
soothing. He took the receptionist's arm and guided
her to the couch. "Come and sit. Let's start over. You
checked with the other employees about who might
have called over to TKG, and…?"

She sank into the thick cushion and regarded him
with nervous dread. "And no one had. Then I remembered your brother, Alan, dropped by. He asked to see
you, but you'd made it clear you didn't want any inter-
ruptions. I explained that to him. He smiled the way
he does. He's such a sweetie, you know? Always so
accommodating."

"Yeah, that's Alan. Accommodating."

"And he asked if I'd mind if he used the phone. Of course I didn't. I offered mine, but he needed privacy, so I showed him into the conference room. He was only in there about five or ten minutes, though at one point I thought I heard his voice raised. I kind of shrugged it off since maybe he was just joking around with someone. Then he returned. I said goodbye, but he must not have heard me. He just went directly out. Only..."

"It's okay, Lynn. Nothing you say about Alan will upset me."

"He seemed a little angry," she said reluctantly. "Usually he's so easygoing, you know? But I had the feeling that something about that phone call didn't go well and I remember thinking that maybe he hadn't been joking around, after all. Maybe he'd been mad at the person."

"That's great, Lynn, exactly what I needed to know."

"Really?" Her gaze clung to him. "You're not just saying that? I didn't do anything wrong?"

"Really. You didn't do a thing wrong. You can go back to work now."

She beamed, her brown eyes sunny with relief. "Thanks, Jack."

The door closed behind her and Jack looked at Nikki, his eyes glacial.

"Alan?" she asked. "Is it possible?"

"I find it hard to believe my brother would kill Dad." He stood and she didn't think she'd ever seen him appear more intimidating and ruthless. "Even so, I think it's time we paid my little brother a visit."

Seven

The drive to Greenville where Alan and Jack's mother, Angela, lived took just over three hours. Shortly after noon they pulled into the circular driveway of the large mountain estate his father had purchased for his mother. He, Alan and his mother had lived here from the time he'd been ten until he'd gone off to college.

Jack sat in the car and stared at the place he'd once called home. He'd moved out the day he'd graduated, his business degree clutched firmly in hand. He'd never returned, at least not to live. In part it had been to keep the peace with Alan, who'd made it clear Jack wasn't wanted. But mainly he'd been determined to strike out on his own, preferring to earn enough to buy his own home rather than living off the largesse of his father, just as he'd been determined to pay his own way through college. It had been a point of honor and pride.

"Mom broached the possibility of selling the place a

couple of months ago," he informed Nikki. "But Alan became so enraged, she dropped the idea."

"Are they home?" she asked.

"Mom will be at work unless today's a half shift. If that's the case, she'll be home soon. As for Alan..." His mouth curved into a sardonic smile. "Nothing has changed since you were last here. My brother is still between jobs, so he should be around."

"Got it."

Jack didn't bother knocking, but used his key. At the sound of the door opening, Alan appeared in the archway separating the spacious foyer from the living room. An inch or so shy of Jack's six-foot-one height, he had golden hair the same shade as their mother's. Although his pretty boy features were very much those of his father, Richard Sinclair, Alan's hazel eyes were identical to their mother's and contained a sharp, wary expression. He held a hardback book open in his hands and bent a corner to mark his place before closing it.

"Jack, this is a surprise." Alan's gaze switched to Nikki and he offered a congenial smile. "And Nikki. How lovely to see you again, if a trifle unexpected. You should have called to let me know you planned to visit, Jack."

"Should have. Didn't." He gestured toward the living room. "Let's talk."

"Would you care to join me for a drink?" Alan asked, starting toward the liquor cart.

"No, thanks. Have a quick question for you."

"And what would that be?"

"You stopped by Carolina Shipping around four the day Reginald was murdered. Mind telling me why?"

Alan gave a short laugh of disbelief. "You drove

all the way out here to ask me that? You should have phoned, Jack. It would have saved you a wasted trip."

But then he wouldn't have been able to see Alan's expression when they spoke. "You haven't answered my question."

"It's been so long, I'm not sure I even remember that day." Alan crossed to the couch and took a seat, placing one leg over the other in studied nonchalance. "Oh, of course. I recall now. I stopped by at some point that afternoon to invite you to dinner. But you were caught up in some big project and I didn't want to interrupt you."

"Dinner, Alan? That's a first. I don't remember you ever inviting me out before."

His brother picked up his glass and smiled over the rim, a hint of maliciousness peeking through. "If it helps reconcile you to the idea, I was going to make you pay."

"I don't doubt it." Jack continued to watch him, not disappointed to see his brother stir with the first signs of discomfort, nervously smoothing a wrinkle from the razor-sharp pleat of his trousers. "And while you were inviting me to dinner you just, what? Decided to call Dad from my building? Seems odd you didn't use your cell phone."

"I couldn't use my cell. The battery died."

"Why did you call Dad?"

Alan reached for his cigar, tapped away an expanse of ash and took a slow puff. "Since you weren't available for dinner I thought Reginald might join me. But as it turns out, he wasn't available." He shrugged. "I guess he had an appointment with a murderer."

Jack saw red. No doubt that was the intent. Swearing, he reached down, wrapped his fist in his brother's collar and jerked him to his feet. The cut glass tumbler crashed to the floor, along with the cigar, flinging ice chips, bourbon and a flurry of sparks in a wide semicircle.

Nikki returned the cigar to the ashtray then joined Jack, sliding her hand across his bicep in a soothing motion. "Let him go," she said quietly. "Hitting him isn't going to solve anything."

"It might not solve anything, but it sure as hell will make me feel better."

"All that will do is prove to Nikki what sort of man you are," Alan asserted. "How you loved lording it over me when Reginald forced his way back into Mother's life. Until then you were nothing more than an unwanted bastard. My father despised you. Mother told me so. Despised having you use the Sinclair name and being forced to claim you for his own. Despised having his legitimate son raised in association with filth. We were happy, the three of us. The perfect family, except for you trying to horn your way in. If Daddy hadn't died, none of this would have happened."

It revolted Jack to hear the full extent of the poison festering inside his brother, to have never suspected the scope and depth of his hatred. "You're right, Alan. Considering Richard was a man of modest means, you wouldn't have all this." He swept his hand in a wide arc to indicate their luxurious surroundings. "My father's money wouldn't have paid for that bourbon you guzzle, or that Cuban cigar you're puffing on. Or enabled you to spend nearly thirty years freeloading off his money. What happened, Alan? Did Dad threaten to cut you off? Did he insist you get a job? Demand you find your own place?"

"No! He loved me. Adored me." Alan's furious gaze

switched to Nikki. "You need to get away from him as soon as possible. He's not a safe man to be around."

"I know exactly what sort of man Jack is." Nikki tilted her head to one side. "What sort of man are you, Alan? Or maybe you've already answered that question."

He drew back a pace, surprised by her unexpected attack. "What the hell do you mean?"

"I mean… Where were you the night Reginald was murdered."

Alan's mouth dropped open. "I *beg* your pardon!"

"I'm just curious. You were in Charleston that night—"

"I most certainly was not," he denied indignantly. "I was right here. I left the city when it became clear Jack wasn't available for dinner."

"Or Reginald."

His mouth tightened. "Or Reginald. I decided to return home. When Reginald Kincaid met his unfortunate demise, I was right here with Mother. She held dinner for me. We watched TV for a time and then went to bed shortly before midnight. Not that I owe either of you any sort of explanation."

In the distance a key rattled in the lock and a moment later the door opened. "Alan?" Angela's voice came from the direction of the foyer. "I'm home."

"Your timing couldn't be better," Alan announced, glaring at Jack and Nikki. "Now you'll see how ridiculous your suspicions are."

Angela appeared in the doorway. Her surprised gaze landed on her two sons and then Nikki. She wore a set of light green surgical nursing scrubs, her hair twisted into a classic knot at her nape. She was a lovely woman with a figure more matronly than Elizabeth's, though it didn't detract from her overall classical beauty. She reminded Nikki a bit of Grace Kelly in her later years.

"Jack?" she asked uncertainly, stepping into the room. "What's going on?"

"Just having a discussion with my brother."

Angela released a tired sigh that crept into her eyes and dragged at her posture. "I wish you two would learn to get along."

"He thinks I killed Reginald," Alan claimed. He crossed the room to stand at his mother's side and wrapped an arm around her so they presented a unified wall. "Tell them what you told the police. That I was here with you at the time Reginald died."

Angela stiffened, her shocked gaze flashing to Jack. "You can't be serious. You can't honestly suspect—"

Jack stared at his mother, willing her to tell him the truth. "Was he here, Mom?"

She hesitated then shifted her footing, no doubt thrown off balance by Alan's overly possessive hold. She steadied herself with a hand to his chest. "Of course he was here. I told the police that, didn't I?"

"Actually, I didn't realize you had," Jack said quietly. "You never mentioned anything about it."

"Why would you think Alan might have killed Reginald?" Her eyes seemed to plead with him. "What in the world would make you think such a horrible thing?"

"He was in Charleston that afternoon."

"And?"

"And he called Dad on the phone from my office a couple of hours before the murder."

"As I said," Alan interrupted. "To invite him to dinner when you weren't available."

"That's it?" she asked, tears of relief welling into her

eyes. "You...you'd accuse your own brother of murder based on such flimsy evidence?"

Jack debated asking about the Indiana Jones style hat, but decided against it. There was no proof his brother owned one. And there was no point in tipping too much of his hand. In fact, he regretted coming here at all, for alerting Alan to his suspicions. But at the time Jack had made the decision, rational thought hadn't factored very strongly into the equation. Besides, he knew damn well what Alan would do if confronted by the police. He'd shift the blame.

Considering he'd gone out of his way to do precisely that by somehow stealing the Aston Martin and setting the scene to point in Jack's direction, more was needed than a nonexistent hat before going to the police. The phone call made from Carolina Shipping simply wasn't enough evidence, especially if Alan had their mother for an alibi. Time to stage a graceful retreat.

"I'm sorry, Mom. I didn't realize he was with you." He forced every ounce of sincerity he could muster into his voice. "I apologize, Alan. Seriously."

"And well you should," Alan said. Relief vied with righteous indignation.

"I guess I'm still more upset than I realized over Dad's death and it's making me a little crazy." Jack returned his glass to the liquor cart and glanced at Nikki. "We need to leave now."

She simply nodded.

He approached his mother and eased her from Alan's hold, kissing her cheek. "I'll call you in a few days."

"Yes. Yes, that would be fine."

He offered his brother an apologetic look. "Alan."

Alan smiled in triumph. "Jack."

Jack didn't speak again until they were in the car

and pulling out of the driveway. "It's not my imagination, is it? He killed Dad."

"Yes, Jack. He killed your father." Nikki stared out the front windshield, her mouth set in a grim line. "Now we just have to find a way to prove it."

"Here's a thought…"

Nikki rolled over in bed and rested her head on Jack's chest. When they'd first turned in, darkness held the room in a firm grip, but over the past hour, the moon peeked coyly above the horizon and cast its soft glow into the room, its silvery touch adding a brilliance to certain sections of the room while leaving the rest in mysterious shadow.

Five full days had gone by during which they'd endlessly examined various possibilities to explain Alan's alibi, as well as how he'd gotten his hands on Jack's car. They'd reluctantly concluded that Angela had lied to protect Alan. But they still couldn't figure out how to explain his use of Jack's car.

He ran a hand down Nikki's back in an absentminded caress. Unfortunately, there was nothing absentminded about her reaction to the stroking touch. "My main concern is that since Alan's my brother, it'll strengthen your detective buddy's suspicion that we're in on the murder together."

"But it would be downright stupid for you to give Alan your car while he's off committing a murder. Not when he could have rented something nondescript that the police couldn't connect to either of you. They might never have put his presence on that video together with the murder if Brooke hadn't remembered his overall appearance so clearly. He couldn't have anticipated that happening."

"Wait. Rewind."

"Where? What?"

"Alan could have rented something nondescript," Jack repeated slowly.

Nikki nodded. "Exactly. The only reason he didn't was in order to implicate you."

"Right, right. But... What if he didn't rent something nondescript? What if he rented a car identical to mine? What if he never took my car that night, just grabbed the license plates when he came to the office and stuck them on another car? What if it wasn't my car in that video, but a rental with my tags?"

"Oh, Jack. Is that possible?" She thought about it, the idea so out of left field it took her a minute to construct a reasonable counterargument. "That's a pretty distinctive car," she said slowly. "Not to mention pricey. What do those things run, anyway?"

"A couple hundred and up."

She stared, openmouthed. "Jack, that's obscene."

"Yes," he said with ripe male satisfaction.

"Would a rental company even carry that particular model and color? I'm not sure I'd want to let one of those off the lot."

He shrugged. "Shouldn't be too difficult to find out. There are companies who rent exotic cars. I'm not sure how many, though, or whether this particular make and model would be one of—" He broke off and shot up in bed. "Son of a bitch. Why didn't I think of this before?"

"What?" She sat up in alarm. "Think of what? What's wrong?"

"My car. Some idiot backed into the rear driver door two days before Dad's death. I forgot all about it."

"No doubt because you had a few other matters on your mind," she suggested gently.

He grimaced. "That's entirely possible. Still... I had the car repaired the next week. But, if we're lucky—and I mean very lucky—maybe that video will help prove that Aston Martin at the parking lot the night Dad was murdered isn't my car. I guess it didn't occur to me to ask Charles McDonough if the video showed the dent because I assumed it was my car." He turned to her, urgency sweeping through him. "We need to call him first thing tomorrow."

She shook her head. "Not tomorrow." At his blank look, she released her breath in exasperation. "It's your brother's wedding, remember?"

"Matt's not my brother," he instantly replied. But she couldn't help noticing it contained far less heat and conviction than in the past. His expression turned brooding and he settled back against the pillows. "Do you wake up Charles or should I?"

"I'll do it."

Nikki sat up and turned on the bedside lamp. A soft glow encompassed them, a circle of light holding the dense shadows at bay. She punched in the number, waiting for Charles McDonough's gravely bark at being awakened so late. Instead, the call went to voice mail. She gave a swift sketch of their theory and asked that he call at his earliest convenience.

"He's out of town until tomorrow afternoon," she informed Jack.

Jack frowned. "I guess a short delay won't hurt anything. I guarantee, Alan's not going anywhere, not when he can live in the lap of luxury at Mom's. Or rather, freeload in the lap of luxury. We'll go see Charles immediately after the wedding. With luck, he'll tie up his murder investigation before the annual shareholders' meeting."

Nikki froze. Praying Jack didn't pick up on her tension, she said, "That's the end of next week, isn't it?"

"Yes." He glanced at her, his blue eyes narrowing. "Have you tracked down our secretive stock owner, yet?"

She so did not want to take their conversation in this new direction. "I'll have the information before the meeting," she promised evasively.

"There aren't many days left. Just another week. And I'll need to have enough time to get them on my side." He sat up, frustration carved into his expression. "Unfortunately, I'm not certain whether I can pull that off. I mean, how am I supposed to convince someone that I'm the best choice to lead TKG when I'm under suspicion for murder? When my own brother is most likely responsible?"

"The Kincaids aren't going to blame you for Alan's actions. I'm sure this stockholder won't, either."

"No?" Jack ripped aside the bedcovers and paced across the room. Moonlight played over his magnificent physique, giving delicious definition to the endless ripple of muscles, painting them in streaks of silver and shadow. No question about it. Nudity became him. "I'm not so sure I'd be as accepting of the Kincaids' role in Dad's death if our situation were reversed."

"But none of you are to blame. There's no reason you can't reconcile with—"

"Don't."

That single word, spoken with such acute pain and explicitness, caused her to fall silent. Without a word, she left the bed and approached. "I'm just trying to help."

"We've already settled this issue, Nikki. Don't help

me. Not with the Kincaids. I don't want you interfering."

His words cut sharp and deep. In desperate need of fresh air, she opened the doors leading onto the deck and stepped outside, not caring that she didn't have a stitch on. She crossed to the railing and rested her hands on it, staring out at the ocean. The moon had escaped its watery bed, radiant in its fullness and shedding its light across the untamed landscape. Marsh grasses tilted beneath a gentle breeze, while wild sea oats stood sentry duty along the dunes, intent on their job of stabilizing the sand against the capricious winds that so often battered the coastline. Their laden heads bobbed against each other and she could just make out their dry, raspy whispers.

The landscape at night appeared so different from during the daytime, the sweet radiance of silver light softening sand, dunes and ocean. Nikki wanted to absorb the beauty before her, tuck it away somewhere safe to be taken out when her time with Jack was over. Tears pricked her eyes. They were down to mere days now. Seven. Seven days before she'd be forced to confess her role in The Kincaid Group's future. Seven days before he turned from her. Despised her. Cut himself off from her. She didn't know how she'd handle that moment when it came.

She sensed his presence a second before his hand cupped her shoulder. "You were made for moonlight," he told her, unwittingly echoing her earlier thoughts about him. "Almost as much as you were made for nudity. Every time I see you like this I think of the goddess Diana."

"The huntress. Goddess of the moon. Goddess of

childbirth." Nikki released a heartbreaking laugh. "She was committed to remaining a maiden, unlike me."

Jack's soft laugh rumbled against her back. "Thank God you weren't."

Her mouth twitched and she leaned against him. "She must not have met anyone like you or she wouldn't have remained a maiden for long."

Gently, inexorably, he turned her to face him. "Nikki, I know you want me to form a close relationship with my Kincaid relatives. But you need to know that's not going to happen. Ever."

"I do know."

He shook his head. "But you keep hoping."

She turned her back to the ocean and searched his face, his expression fully exposed by the moonlight, while hers remained in shadow. "Is that so wrong?"

"Not wrong. Pointless. Especially if—when—our relationship changes."

She froze, the breath stuttering in her lungs. Did he know? Had he guessed? "Changes?"

He must have caught some hint of her agitation because he smiled. Taking her left hand in his, he slipped a ring on her finger. Endless seconds ticked by before her brain absorbed what he'd done. He tilted her hand so it caught the moonlight, reflecting off a circle of glittering diamonds that surrounded a huge sapphire.

"Marry me, Nikki."

Her brain closed down. So did her capacity for speech. He must have taken her muteness for consent because he pulled her into his arms and covered her mouth with his. There beneath a benevolent moon, he kissed her with a passion that didn't allow room for thought. Unable to resist, she encircled his neck with her arms and gave herself up to rapture.

She barely felt her feet leave the deck, barely registered their transition from outdoors to in. Even when the softness of his mattress rose up to support her, she could only sigh against his mouth, opening to him more completely than she ever had before. How long had she loved him? How long had she hoped that a miracle would happen and he would fall in love with her, too? For reasons she couldn't quite summon to mind, the possibility of an engagement, of marriage, of creating a home with Jack and bearing his children had seemed an impossible dream. But in this moment out of time, she allowed herself to dream, to be swept off to a place where fantasies became reality. In the far distance darkness stole across the glorious horizon, a darkness she turned from.

Later. Later she'd deal with the darkness. But for now, she'd step into the light and grab hold of the gift that had fallen so delightfully and unexpectedly into her hands.

Threading her fingers through Jack's hair, Nikki pulled him downward so he fell into her mouth and onto her body. Oh, God, could anything be more delicious than that delectable joining of lips, of the abrasive, unmistakably male hardness moving against her softer, more giving curves? She opened to him, his tongue tangling with hers while his hands shaped her breasts and teased her nipples with quick, urgent little tugs.

He eased back from the kiss, drifted downward to replace his hands with his mouth. "You have the most beautiful breasts I've ever seen."

A strangled laugh escaped her. "I never know how to respond when you say something like that. Am I supposed to thank you? Say nothing? Deny it?"

"You can't deny the truth." He shifted lower, nipping at the flat planes of her belly. "And then there's your skin. Like cream. Not quite white, not tanned or leathery like some women who spend too much time in the sun."

She choked on a another laugh. "Heaven forbid."

"But a lovely, rich cream. And tasty." He inched lower. "I want another taste."

He slid his hands beneath her thighs and parted her. Then he did just as he'd promised and tasted. "Jack!" His name escaped in a breathless shriek.

She wanted to tell him to stop, that it was too intimate. But the gentle, insistent probing of his tongue and mouth drove every thought from her head and she could only feel. Feel that delicious roughness of whiskers and tongue, feel the hot tension build, feel the heat and desperate need pooling between her thighs. And then he found the small bud that was the source of all that need and tension. Found it. Caught it between his teeth. And tugged.

Nikki instantly splintered, coming apart in his hands. She arched upward, her fingers fisting in the sheets while her muscles drew bowstring taut. Air squeezed from her lungs and she shuddered as her climax slammed through her. It held her in its grip, refusing to let go, pulsating through her in an endless wave. Her nerve endings jittered to a dance unlike anything she'd ever experienced before and she felt like a swimmer who'd gone under for the count, her vision darkening while she struggled to breathe where no air existed.

She managed one long inhalation before Jack levered upward and in one swift thrust mated their bodies. Her body instantly tightened, started the swift build all over again. She wrapped him up in arms and legs and clung with all her might. She picked up the rhythm he set, meeting him thrust for thrust, desperately reaching for that pinnacle once again.

Jack's breathing deepened, quickened. So did their movements. Perspiration turned their bodies slick with need and heat, intensifying the abrasive slide of skin against skin. She heard him chanting "moremoremore-more" and found herself giving him more, as much as she had to give. She'd never been so open, so free, so desperate to meet demand with demand. And still they climbed and still the desire built until there was no place else for it to go. He surged inward a final time at the same moment she rose to meet him. They froze, held there like a pair of living statues captured at the perfect moment of climax, teetering on the brink of release. And then the tidal wave struck, washing over and through them, tumbling them onto the bed in a confusing heap of tangled limbs and pounding hearts and breath exploding in helpless gasps.

Jack groaned against her ear, the unexpected blast of heat causing her to shudder. She'd never been so hypersensitive before, not to the extent that even something as simple as his breath against her skin felt like the most delicious form of torture.

"What the hell happened?" he demanded. "I've never..."

"Never?"

"Not ever. You?"

"Not even close. Not within a million miles of what just happened."

He flopped onto his back. "I should have proposed sooner."

His words caused her to stiffen. All of a sudden the darkness invading her fantasy world crept closer. Much, much closer. "Jack..."

"Right here." The words were slurred and he rolled toward her and dropped a possessive arm across her waist. "I think you killed me."

"Jack, we need to talk."

In response he gave a soft snore. One glance warned he'd gone out like a light. The blanket of sleep must have been as king-size as the bed because she could feel it settling around her, too. She lifted her hand to look at the engagement ring. Over the past hour it had gained substantial weight since for some reason she could barely lift her arm. She stared at it, the promise it stood for mocking her with its brilliant flashes of diamond, silver and sapphire-blue.

She had no right to this ring. No right to wear it when she knew their marriage would never take place. Tears filled her eyes. She should have told him. She should have told him from the start that she owned those shares. And when he asked her to throw her shares in with his? Their affair would have ended because she'd have told him she couldn't. Wouldn't.

Her hand dropped to her side and her eyes fluttered closed. At least she had the past three months, something she wouldn't have experienced if she'd told him. And she had the rest of the night before she'd be forced to return the ring. The rest of the night to dwell within her fantasy world where Jack loved her and they were engaged. Where marriage hovered on the horizon instead of dark threat. Where the soft shades of their future children gamboled across the sweep of grass that surrounded his Greenville plantation. Where happiness dwelled, the only place it could dwell since it wouldn't survive outside of her fantasy.

Sleep claimed her. But just beforehand came the unsettling realization that not once in all the time she'd known Jack had he ever said he loved her. Thought almost woke her. The tear that escaped almost had her resurfacing.

Instead, she retreated into fantasy.

Eight

Something was wrong.

Jack couldn't quite put his finger on it, but at some point between the amazing passion they'd shared and the strident glare of morning light, Nikki had changed. She sat beside him, staring out of the front windshield of his Aston Martin, her hands wrapped tightly around a metallic sequined clutch, which hid her engagement ring from view. The electric-blue sequins matched those on her dress, a light smattering that started at her hip and dusted her silk dress like brilliant stars against a pale blue sky.

"What's wrong?" he asked quietly.

"What?" Startled from her reverie, she forced out a smile that didn't quite reach her eyes. "Oh, nothing. I guess I'm still half asleep."

He considered letting it go at that, then decided to press a little harder. "Seriously. What's wrong?"

The silence stretched for endless minutes. "This isn't a good time, Jack," she finally said in a low voice. "We're on our way to Matt's wedding. Why don't we talk afterward?"

"Talk. That means there is something wrong."

She released her breath in a long sigh. "Will Alan be at the wedding?"

More than anything he wanted to pull the car over and demand she tell him what the bloody hell was going on. He stewed for a full mile. "Yes, I'm sure Alan will be here, if only to reassure himself that we no longer suspect him. Considering your current attitude, we have every chance of success since he'll assume you've begun to suspect me of my father's death, instead of him." He paused. "Have you?"

"Don't be ridiculous." She spoke with such vehemence he had no choice but to believe her. "You could no more kill Reginald than I could."

"Okay. Good. Fine."

"What about Angela? Will she attend?"

It was a deliberate change of subject and Jack reluctantly went along with it. "Yes, just like she attended Kara and Eli's wedding, though I suspect it's the last place she wanted to be. It's not easy playing the 'other woman.'"

"No, I'm sure it isn't. It takes a lot of grit—a characteristic she passed onto her eldest son, if not her youngest."

Jack wanted to turn the conversation back to whatever had upset Nikki, but they'd arrived at the Colonel Samuel Beauchamp House, the use of Lily's home her gift to the bridal couple. The irony of the venue didn't escape him any more than it did Nikki. They'd met here. He'd stood on the balcony off the master bedroom salon when she'd entered the garden that night and bid a cool thousand for the pleasure of a dinner date with him… and the added bonus of a single wish. Then she'd disappeared into the darkness with him in pursuit. He'd caught up with her near the carriage house not far from where today's nuptials would take place. The instant they'd touched, they'd fallen headlong into passion. And when they'd exchanged their first kiss, there within the intimate embrace of a dark winter night, that passion had exploded out of control.

Nothing had changed since then. If anything, it had grown more intense, built to a level Jack knew he'd never share with another woman…had no interest in sharing with another woman.

"You never made your wish," he mentioned.

Nikki spared him a short, bleak look. "I'm saving it. I have a feeling I'm going to need it before much longer."

Seriously. What the *hell* was going on? He fought back a surge of impatience, battling against instincts that demanded he force the issue, regardless of time or place. He clung to his few remaining scraps of patience. "That sounds ominous," he limited himself to saying, downright impressed with his calm, easygoing tone.

"Not ominous, just true."

They exited the car and Jack reached for Nikki's hand. That's when he saw it—or rather, didn't see it. The ring finger of her left hand was bare. He froze and every last ounce of patience vanished in a surge of raw fury. Calm evaporated. As for easygoing… Screw easygoing. He'd never been easygoing in his life. Why start now?

"Where is it?" The words escaped low and harsh, far harsher than he'd intended.

She flinched. "I didn't think it wise to wear it today."

There was only one explanation for her newfound wisdom. She came from Charleston elite. He was a bastard, not to mention a murder suspect. "You're ashamed of our engagement." He threw the statement at her like a gauntlet.

"No! I...I'm just not sure there's going to be an engagement. At least, not yet. Not until we have a serious talk." She faced him, her eyes dark and shadowed with pain. "Jack, all this has caught me by surprise."

He held up her bare hand. "Yeah, all this has caught me by surprise, too." No matter what she claimed, she wouldn't be hedging over their engagement unless she distrusted him on some level. Was it the murder... or merely who and what he was? "What's going on, Nikki?"

She tugged free of his grasp. "Please not here. Not now."

He planted his size fourteens in the sweeping driveway and refused to budge. "Oh, hell, yes, sweetheart. Right here. Right now."

Her mouth set in a stubborn line. "Do you realize in the four months I've known you that you've never once said you love me?"

"Let me count the number of times you've said those words." He held up his hands as though to count. "Huh. Unless my addition's off, it's the same number of times I've told you."

She spared a swift look toward the house, taking in the stream of guests, some of whom had paused to watch their argument. Her breath escaped in a painful sigh. "Jack, I've been in love with you almost from the moment we met," she confessed in a low voice.

"Then why have you never said so?"

"Probably for the same reason you haven't. We've both been hurt. I told you about Craig. About how he used me. It makes it very difficult for me to say the words. I can also understand, based on your parents' affair, that you might have a rather unfortunate view of love, as well."

"Unfortunate view. An interesting way of putting it."

"But when you proposed... Why didn't you tell me you loved me then?"

"We got a little distracted."

A brief, reminiscent smile came and went. "That's true."

Jack dropped his hands to Nikki's shoulders. "Sweetheart, I love you. I wouldn't ask you to marry me if I didn't." His declaration provoked tears. He gently thumbed the moisture from her cheeks. "Don't. Not when I just told you I love you."

"I have a confession to make," she said in a low voice. "And when I make it you won't love me anymore."

He stiffened, uncertain how to respond to that. He'd been aware, ever since Charles McDonough came to his beach house, that she was keeping something from him. Now he'd find out what. "Nikki," he began in concern.

"Trouble in paradise?" Alan's question came as an unwelcome interruption. He approached, his expression settling into lines of deep concern. "I did warn you about my brother, Nikki." He managed to hit the perfect blend of sorrow and indignation. "Jack's not a safe man to be around. I can escort you out of here, if you'd like. He won't stop us with everyone watching."

"Not now, Alan," Jack bit out.

His brother ignored him and held out his hand to Nikki. "I'm here for you, my dear."

She took a swift, instinctive step backward. "Not a chance in hell," she told him.

Alan's hand dropped stiffly to his side and embarrassment reddened his cheeks at the slight. He glanced around, fury replacing his embarrassment when he realized how much attention they'd attracted. Without a word, he spun on his heel and walked away.

"Oh, God, I shouldn't have done that," she whispered. "We were trying to allay his suspicions and all I've done is make them worse. I just couldn't help it. When he reached for me all I could see was the hand of a murderer."

Jack sighed. "Don't worry about it. You weren't going anywhere with him. I wouldn't have let you. So even if you hadn't rejected him, I would have reacted, and more forcefully than you. I also doubt that anything we could have said or done today would have eased his suspicions. It was ridiculous of me to think we could. Just as nothing I did during our childhood was sufficient to create a fraternal bond between us."

"Not even saving his life?"

"That only made it worse, especially when I didn't cooperate and die."

Nikki flinched. "Don't say that."

"You do realize that if I hadn't saved him that day, Reginald would still be alive."

She turned on him, hands planted on her hips, eyes flashing like the sapphire in the engagement ring she wasn't wearing. "Except that the guilt of standing by and doing nothing would have eaten you alive. You wouldn't be the man you are today if you'd allowed your brother to die. That's not who you are, Jack."

Did she have any idea how much her vehement defense meant to him? She couldn't possibly realize how those three simple sentences of support cut straight through to his marrow, gutting him. So few people in his life had shown such keen understanding of who he was at the very core. In part it was because he kept himself aloof from others, distancing his emotions and barricading all vulnerabilities from possible attack or harm.

He'd learned the importance of that at school, when he'd been subjected to various slights and slurs once his illegitimacy came to light—and Alan made certain it came to light on a regular basis. Girls had been warned away from him, as though he carried something they might catch. Boys sneered at his bastard status. Like tended to gravitate to like and there were damn few kids like him. Though the taint had followed him to college, the facts surrounding his birth weren't as relevant, anymore, until gradually it hadn't mattered at all. At least, it wasn't relevant to what he'd accomplished with his life. But those early years had left an indelible mark.

"Nikki..." He wanted to explain it to her, explain how those experiences made him sensitive to slights—such as her refusing to wear his engagement ring in front of Charleston's elite. But the faint strains of music issuing from the back of the mansion warned they were out of time. Regret swept through him and he forced himself to set it aside. He cupped her elbow, urging her toward the spacious patio and garden. "Come on. Let's do our duty and then get the hell out of here."

He paused to give his mother a kiss before taking a seat behind her and Alan, who sat at attention, refusing to look at them. Not that Jack objected. He'd had more than enough of his brother for one day.

The ceremony was lovely, or so everyone claimed. Since he was no expert, he wasn't in a position to debate the issue. In his opinion his three Kincaid sisters, who acted as Susannah's attendants, looked beautiful in their halter top dresses. The bride was downright stunning, her slender figure showcased in a strapless gown. It molded to her hips before flowing outward in a long, sweeping train. Matt appeared poleaxed by her, a suitable expression for a man about to be married.

The opening chords of the processional drifted across the gathering and three-year-old Flynn walked his mother up the aisle. Someone had slicked his dark hair down but hadn't quite managed to keep the bow tie of his little tux from being knocked askew. But most moving of all was seeing him beam from ear to ear, his adoring gaze shifting from his father to his mother. And when the couple eventually exchanged their vows— ones they'd written themselves—the emotional words stirred tears in a good portion of those assembled.

The ceremony didn't take long, fortunate since the cooling breeze flagged just enough for a subtle wave of humidity to seep through. "I assume we have to stick around for a while?" Jack asked in an undertone, hoping against hope that Nikki would insist they leave right away.

She instantly dashed those hopes. "For at least an hour."

"Hell."

His mother joined them. Behind her, Jack caught a glimpse of Alan's retreating back. "Would you mind if I stay at the beach house tonight?" she asked, her face pale and drawn.

"Problem?"

She shrugged. "Alan's in one of his moods. We could probably both use a break from each other's company. I'm not due back to work until Monday, so I thought we could spend a little time together." She offered Nikki a smile, a genuine one, Jack was relieved to note. "The three of us, of course."

"I'd enjoy that," Nikki replied with an equally genuine smile.

"You're welcome to stay as long as you want, Mom," he assured her. "We're going to cut out in about an hour. I'll track you down when it's time."

"Thanks. I guess I better go be sociable." She spared a glance toward the cluster of Kincaids and sighed. "Even if it kills me."

Over the next hour, Jack kept a discreet eye on his watch, counting down the minutes until they could leave. He popped a small round puffball of some sort in his mouth before glancing at his watch yet again. Ten more minutes. Ten more minutes and they'd be out of here. He could handle another ten.

Maybe.

He also kept an eye on Alan, who'd shed his affable facade and revealed a hint of a more familiar petulance. It didn't bode well for the future since that petulance often led to his lashing out, without considering the consequences. Jack debated whether or not to talk to him in an attempt to smooth over troubled waters before they grew any more turbulent. Before he could, Nikki touched his arm.

"Jack, look."

She drew his attention to Elizabeth who sat at a table with Cutter, the two chatting with her three daughters. Harold Parsons, the family attorney, approached. He took his time greeting each in turn, no doubt showing the kindness and courtly charm he reserved for the Kincaids, versus the more irascible attitude Jack had experienced. After a few minutes of chitchat, he held out a familiar looking envelope, The Kincaid Group's distinctive logo decorating one corner. It was identical to the letter Jack had received at the reading of the will—the one his father had left to him and which he had yet to open. While Jack's sealed letter was heavily creased and careworn from frequent handling, a coffee ring stain marring its surface, Elizabeth's appeared pristine.

"He's apologizing," Nikki murmured.

"Son of a bitch, he had it all along."

Elizabeth said something that appeared to be a question, her head tilting to one side. In response, Harold gestured in Jack's direction. Almost as one, the four women swiveled to look at him, open shock on the faces of his three sisters, an expression of intense gratitude on Elizabeth's. She excused herself and disappeared in the direction of the carriage house, no doubt to read her letter in private.

Jack frowned. "I wonder what it says? I hope it's something nice. If Dad was as cruel to her in the letter as he was the night he died—"

"Reginald wouldn't do that," Nikki insisted.

Elizabeth reappeared a few minutes later. The girls fluttered around her in a flurry of questions and concern. She spoke at some length before excusing herself and heading in their direction, her eyes fixed on Jack.

"Oh, man." He waited, grim-faced, prepared to take whatever Elizabeth planned to dish out.

To his shock, she dished out a tight hug and a lingering kiss on his cheek. "Thank you," she told him, her voice choked with tears.

Over her shoulder Jack caught a glimpse of Alan who stared at the embrace in stunned disbelief—disbelief that rapidly transitioned to outrage. He'd been so pleased by his own welcome into the Kincaid fold, quick to rub his open-ended Sunday dinner invitation in Jack's face. Alan had been even more pleased by the Kincaids open dislike of Jack and took every opportunity to mention it. No doubt this mending of the familial breech both shook and infuriated him.

Elizabeth started speaking and he transferred his attention to her, sliding the problem of his half brother to the back burner. "You have no idea how much this means to me. The fact that you're the one who insisted there had to be a letter…" She shook her head. "Oh, Jack. I was so certain Reginald had deliberately slighted me. Instead, he accepted full responsibility for his actions. He said just what you told me, that he'd been fortunate enough to love two women in his life and that he'd never meant to hurt me the way he had."

"I'm glad I could help." It was the only thing he could think to say. Apparently, it was the right thing.

She smiled. "You're very much like him, you know. Only you have a sense of integrity and honor that he sometimes lacked." She caught his hand in hers and gave it a tug. "Come over and join us. Get to know your sisters."

"They're not… I'd rather—" He shot Nikki a glance that clearly said "get me the hell out of this." Instead of getting him the hell out, she threw him to the wolf in sheep's clothing.

"Go on, Jack," Nikki encouraged. "It's long overdue."

"Yes, I insist." A thread of wolfish steel underscored Elizabeth's words.

Left without any other choice, he followed in her wake. He snagged Nikki's arm when she hung back.

"If I'm going down, you're going down with me," he informed her in a bitter undertone.

Laurel, Kara and Lily stood in a row, oldest to youngest, and looked like lovely flowers in their bridesmaid dresses. Though they'd all met before, Elizabeth introduced each in turn. Laurel was the image of her mother, with auburn hair and flashing green eyes, her coloring enhanced by her buttercup-yellow dress. Kara, the shortest of the three, wore an emerald-green that brought out a hint of bronze in her brown hair and blended nicely with her eyes. Someone had mentioned that she ran Prestige Events and had organized Matt and Susannah's wedding as her gift to them. Finally he turned his attention to Lily, a more vivacious version of her oldest sister with golden-red hair that curled down her back. She was clearly the outgoing one of the group as well as being in the final stages of pregnancy. A children's book illustrator, he vaguely recalled. Her dress matched her blue eyes and cascaded over her baby bulge.

"Thank you, thank you, thank you," she said, swooping over to give him a quick, energetic hug that pressed that huge, rather scary baby bump tight against him. "You have no idea how upset we've all been over Dad neglecting to write Mom a letter. I can't believe it didn't occur to any of us that it might simply have gone missing. And I can't tell you enough how much we appreciate the fact that it did occur to you."

Laurel, TKG's long-distance PR Director now that she'd married her husband, Rakin Abdellah, fixed Jack with a shrewd gaze. "Nikki was right all along. You're one of the good guys. You have no idea how relieved we all are to discover that."

"I'm not one of the good guys," he instantly denied.

He turned on Nikki. "You have to stop telling people I am. Why would you lie to people about that?"

While his Kincaid sisters laughed as though he'd said something funny, Nikki smiled. "Because you are a good guy."

Before he could prove otherwise, Lily chimed in. "We've been so worried about your intentions toward The Kincaid Group. Thank goodness we can put that concern to rest." Her hand rubbed distressing little circles across her distended belly, her wedding rings flashing in the sunlight. With luck her soothing touch would keep the kid right where it was until well after the reception. Jack opened his mouth to explain in no uncertain terms just how wrong she was when she added, "That sort of stress isn't good for the baby."

He clamped his back teeth together and altered course slightly. "There's still the outstanding ten percent," he warned. "Nothing's decided until we determine which way the final shareholder plans to vote."

Laurel offered a smile that appeared uncomfortably genuine. "True. Of course, if you throw your vote to RJ, those shares become moot."

Crap! Five sets of feminine eyes stared at him with various degrees of warmth, from Elizabeth's sweetness, to Laurel's friendliness, to Kara and Lily's delight, to Nikki's open relief. Her eyes filled with a distressing combination of love and tears while the mouth he couldn't seem to get enough of quivered into a hopeful grin.

How the hell did she do it? How the hell did she keep arranging events so he ended up on the receiving end of Kincaid gratitude? Well, it wouldn't last long. Not when they found out he had no intention of throwing his forty-five percent in RJ's corner. Then all those lovely smiles would fade and they'd rip him to shreds. At least then their relationship would return to normal.

"Time to go," he announced, slipping his hand under Nikki's elbow.

Before he could escape, the Kincaids descended once again, giving him an endless stream of farewell hugs and well wishes. He'd almost reached the breaking point when they finally let go. Without another word, he spun on his heel and moved at a rapid clip across the patio. Nikki had to practically run to keep up.

"Slow down, will you. And don't forget we need to collect your mother."

He turned on her. "No, I will not slow down, not until we're out of earshot of all those damn Kincaids." He continued moving until they rounded a corner and were clear of viewing and hearing range. "I warned you about interfering, Nikki. I told you I have no interest in establishing any sort of familial relationship with them. But did you listen? No."

She jerked her arm free of his hold. "Wait just one minute, bubba. That lovefest back there had nothing to do with me. You were the one who suspected Reginald left a letter for Elizabeth. You were the one who called Harold Parsons. And you were the one who didn't correct your sisters when they assumed you'd vote for RJ at the annual meeting."

"For the last time, they are *not* my sisters."

"You know something, Jack? I've had it with your denials. Whether you like it or not, they *are* your sisters. And the reason you didn't correct their assumption is because you didn't want to hurt them. Now quit dumping your B.S. on me and try smelling what you're so busy shoveling for a change. Until you do, I'm going home." She jabbed a finger to his chest to emphasize her final words. "Alone."

Spinning around, she struck off down the driveway toward the street. He stood there a minute, too stunned to move. What did she mean "try smelling what you're so busy shoveling"? He'd never been anything but completely up-front about his feelings toward his brothers and sisters—*not* his brothers and sisters. He lowered his head and swore beneath his breath. When had he started referring to them as brothers and sisters? Because somehow, at some point, that's precisely how he'd begun to feel about them.

Okay, maybe not RJ. But the others...

He knew how dangerous it was to open himself up like that. He was a bastard and nothing would ever change that. If they considered him kin, it was on those terms and those terms alone. It wasn't because they liked or respected him. They were simply stuck with him.

And yet... He couldn't help but recall Matt's friendly smile, and the way he'd greeted Jack today with a slap on the back and a one-armed hug. Of course, his brand-new marriage made him so euphoric he'd probably have done the same to a pink-haired baboon with bad breath and a coat full of fleas. And then there had been Elizabeth's effusive greeting. Also understandable considering her emotional state after reading the letter his father had left for her. Same with his sisters. They were so excited about the letter he'd been briefly swept into their circle of love.

Still...it felt good. Too good.

Jack shot his hands through his hair and groaned. How had it happened? When? Somehow a door opened and he didn't have a clue how to slam it shut again. Of course, it would slam shut at the annual board meeting. Then he'd see how chummy his "family" remained. Which brought him to his next problem.

He stared in the direction Nikki had taken. He refused to let her leave. Not until they straightened out a few vital details, such as why she refused to wear his ring. He'd also demand she tell him what secret she continued to keep from him. Not to mention forcing her to explain once and for all why she was so determined to reconcile him with the Kincaids. Granted, he'd also apologize for acting like a prize jerk. But something was going on here and he wanted to know what.

He reached the street and didn't see her. But if she was busy walking off her mad, he could make an educated guess which way she'd gone in order to return to her Rainbow Row home. He set off in that direction, moving at a ground-eating pace. Rounding the next corner, he saw her a couple of dozen feet ahead of him. She approached an alley running along the back of the homes occupying that block—including the Colonel Samuel Beauchamp House. The narrow access road connected to the main boulevard and she spared a quick glance toward the alley before starting across.

Jack heard the screech of tires the exact second Nikki did, her head jerking toward the alley. He couldn't say what warned him of her imminent danger. He simply knew that—like with Alan all those years ago—she was about to be hit by a speeding car. He didn't think. He broke into a flat-out run. A few paces ahead of him, Nikki froze, everything about her communicating intense alarm. He reached her a split second before the car and snatched her backward with such force they both hit the pavement, and hit hard.

They rolled toward the street and dropped into the

gutter. He tried to cushion the impact, but had a feeling she'd collected more than her share of scrapes and bruises. The car skidded around the corner onto the main street, so close he could feel the heat from the exhaust and the stinging kick of dirt and gravel. The engine gunned and it took off without stopping.

"Nikki!" His hands swept over her. "Sweetheart, how bad are you hurt?"

She trembled against him. "I'm...I'm okay. I think." She struggled to stand. If they'd been anywhere else other than in a filthy street, he'd have made her lie still while he examined her for injuries.

"No, not yet," he insisted. "Don't get up until I check you out."

Gently, he eased her to a sitting position on the edge of the curb and ran through a curtailed version of the basic A through E primary examination his mother had taught him. Nothing broken. No indication of a head injury. Just some general scrapes and bruises.

"Okay, you pass," he said in relief.

"Oh, Jack!" She threw her arms around his neck and clung.

"Easy. Easy, honey." He could feel the dampness of tears against his dress shirt. "What happened, do you know?"

"He came at me. He almost hit me. If you hadn't gotten there in time..." She began to cry in earnest.

"Who, Nikki? Did you see the driver?"

She pulled back a couple inches. A painful scrape rode her cheekbone and along her chin where the metallic sequins from her purse had connected with her face. "Oh, Jack. It was Alan. Alan tried to kill me."

Nine

By the time Nikki and Jack returned from the police station, she barely had enough energy to pull herself from the car.

Between her various aches and pains from her tumble to the street, and her mental and emotional exhaustion from the endless rounds of questions Charles McDonough had asked, all she wanted was to crawl into bed and pull the covers over her head. One look at Jack warned he felt the same way.

"Will your mother be okay?" she asked.

"Should be. McDonough said they wouldn't charge Mom for lying to cover for Alan, not if she testifies against him."

Deep lines of pain carved a pathway across his face. More than anything Nikki wished she could ease that pain, but there was nothing she could say or do that would change the reality that Jack's brother had killed his father. Worse, his mother had lied to protect the son she sincerely believed innocent.

In fact, it hadn't been until Charles had shown the video from the parking lot the night of the murder that the pieces fell into place. There was no dent on the Aston Martin that drove onto the lot, proving it couldn't have been Jack's car. Between the accident pictures he pulled off his cell phone, and the receipt for the repair provided after a single phone call to the mechanic, it became clear that the car in the video wasn't Jack's.

Even more damning was the hat and coat Alan wore that night. One look and Angela burst into tears. She'd bought Alan both items and finally confessed she had no idea what time Alan returned home that night since she'd fallen asleep on the couch while reading. When she awoke he'd been sitting in a nearby chair, also reading, and claimed he'd been there for hours. She had no reason to question his statement until recently.

By the time they left the station a warrant had been issued for Alan's arrest. Nikki suspected that once they checked his bank records and credit card statements, they'd find the necessary evidence proving he'd rented the same make and model car that Jack drove. Knowing Charles and his bulldog tendencies, it wouldn't take him long to build all the circumstantial evidence into a strong case against Alan.

"I just wish Mom could have come home with us," Jack said.

"Don't you think she'll be safer in protective custody until Alan's been apprehended? I hate the thought that he might go after her now."

"Mom's safety is one of the few points McDonough and I agree on, otherwise I'd have insisted they release her." He nudged Nikki toward the flight of stairs leading to the bedroom. "Come on. Maybe it won't seem so bad if we drag each other up."

Together they climbed, tugging off clothes as they went. By the time they hit the bedroom, they were both naked. Nikki beelined toward the bed, brought up short by the hard, powerful arm Jack wrapped around her middle. He swung her off her feet and headed for the bathroom.

"Shower first. I want to make sure all those abrasions get cleaned out again." Jack reached into the stall—a huge tiled expanse with multiple jets—and turned on the water. "Plus, it'll help take the edge off our poor aching muscles."

Hot, steamy water blasting out and Nikki stepped into the middle of the pulsating jets and groaned in sheer delight. "Oh, God, I just died and went to heaven."

"Brace yourself against the wall," he instructed. "I'll take care of the rest."

She followed his directions. She didn't think she could love him more, but the next few minutes proved her wrong. He carefully soaped every inch of her body, beyond gentle when he found and cleaned each scrape and abrasion. His hands kneaded the various bands of muscles from ankle to neck, his thumbs digging in and soothing tendons she didn't even realize had become knotted into throbbing tangles. And then he finished his self-appointed task by drawing her up for the sweetest of kisses, causing more knots to develop, but ones from a far different cause.

She wrapped her arms around him and lost herself in the steam from the shower and the more intense steam from his kiss. He fumbled behind her and the spray of water subsided. Somehow he found towels and wrapped them up in a delicious cocoon of damp bodies and soft cotton. She couldn't begin to imagine where he found the energy when she barely had enough to find the bed. He even managed to dry her with swift, brisk strokes that left her skin tingling, before applying the towel to himself. Together they fell into bed and into each other's arms.

"Will they find Alan?" she asked.

"Eventually." He tucked her against his side, a sweet alignment of curves and angles that fit together as they had from the start...with utter perfection. "I doubt Alan went home to Greenville, not once he calmed down and considered the ramifications of attempting to run you over. Since he missed, he had to suspect we'd go to the cops and report him. He also can't access much money from his bank account since it's the weekend. I guarantee Charles will have his funds frozen first thing Monday morning."

"It's not your fault, you know," she said gently.

Her comment caused lines to bracket Jack's mouth, grief settling into the deep grooves. She'd found the source of his pain and cut straight through to the heart of it. "I'm not sure the Kincaids will see it the same way."

"Reginald's murder was your brother's fault and no one else's. Not Angela's. Not Reginald's. And not yours. There's something wrong with Alan at the core." She rolled onto her hip and cupped Jack's face. Whiskers rasped against her palm in a tantalizing abrasion, while tension built along his jawline. "Reginald had six children and not one of them turned out like Alan. Every last one of you has made something of your life. Alan received the exact same benefits the rest of you did— more even than you were willing to accept. And he wasted the opportunity. He has the attitude that the

world owes him a living instead of his owing the world
for his existence and giving back in some productive
way."

"Maybe if—"

Nikki shifted her hand so her fingertips covered his
mouth. "Don't. All the 'what ifs' and 'maybes' in the
world won't change anything and will only make it
worse. We can't know what might have happened if we
turned left instead of right. Gone backward instead of
forward. Jumped instead of ducked. We can only deal
with what is, not what might have been."

Jack's tension eased ever so slightly. "I would have
stopped him if I'd known how sick he was."

"None of you realized the extent of it because he hid
his true personality so well. Everyone thought Alan
was charming. People liked him. I know I did, at least
at first." She shrugged. "He has a talent for hiding the
darkness inside."

Jack grimaced. "I knew it was there."

"Did you ever worry that he'd harm your mother
or father?"

"No, of course—" His breath escaped in a long sigh
and he pulled her close, simply holding her while he accepted the same truth his mother had. He hadn't wanted
to believe Alan capable of such evil because he'd judged
his brother by his own standards of decency and mo-
rality, standards Alan had rejected long ago. "No, of
course not, or I'd never have left him alone in the house
with my mother."

She hugged him tight. "And you would have warned
your father."

Jack traced a finger along the curve of her cheek.
"How do you do it?" he asked in a rough voice. "How

do you manage to take something that's so dark and bleak and turn it around?"

She smiled. "I just show you the same problem from a slightly different angle. You do the rest."

"Like with my...my brothers and sisters?"

It was the first time she'd heard him use those terms of his own volition. She shut her eyes, tears pressing hard. She gave herself a few seconds to gather her control before replying. "That's right, Jack. I'd already met most of your family so I knew they were good people. It was only a matter of showing you that side of them."

"Well...most of them," he said with a sour edge. "The jury's still out on RJ."

Her laughter contained a hint of the tears she fought so hard to temper. Exhaustion. No doubt they came from exhaustion. "Then my job's almost done."

"It will be as soon as you uncover the missing shareholder."

She burrowed against him. She couldn't handle this. Not now. Not when she could barely keep her eyes open. A heavy bank of fatigue hit her with such force she couldn't even think straight. "Jack—"

Before she could say anything more, he kissed her, a kiss of passion tempered with tenderness. And though she shifted against him, eager for more, she could feel herself fading. The delicious taste of his kiss was the last thing she remembered before sleep claimed her, a lovely drifting into dreams where Jack held her safe and secure and all was well with their world.

She woke to another kiss, a kiss of tenderness edged with passion. Her instantaneous response hit before she fully surfaced, and she gave herself to Jack without hesitation. Her eyes flickered open at the same moment he mated their bodies and the air escaped her lungs in a soft gasp of delight. She couldn't imagine a better way to greet the morning and she moved with him, their rhythm one of sheer perfection.

Only a few more days. Just a handful. Just a handful left to change his mind about taking over The Kincaid Group. From taking revenge on brothers and sisters who'd never harmed him. How could she possibly get him to see this final problem from a different angle, to somehow turn it all around? Simple. She didn't. There wasn't an angle in the world that would convince him to hand the running of TKG over to RJ, any more than there was any possible angle which would make her ownership of those crucial TKG stock shares more palatable.

She pushed the worry aside and embraced the moment, her pain and fear lending a desperate urgency to her lovemaking. He must have picked up on it on some level because he caught fire, driving them higher, further, every stroke and caress burning with an incandescence they'd never experienced before. She literally felt as though he'd filled her with such brilliant passion she couldn't contain it all without bursting into flames. Recklessly, she threw herself into the fire and allowed it to consume her, all of her, building the pyre as high as it would go. And then she built it higher still.

It couldn't last. Together they hit the peak, teetered for the briefest of moments, before their climaxes ripped through them, a shattering so intense Nikki couldn't remember where she was or when…though the "who" in the equation remained crystal clear. Jack shuddered in her arms and collapsed on top of her.

"Fifty more years," he insisted.

She shook her head in confusion. "What?"

"I want fifty more years of that. Maybe sixty."

She laughed, even though her heart was breaking. "I'll see what I can do."

"Hot tub, shower or food? Since we have sixty more years, I can be generous and let you choose."

"Food. I'm starved. I can whip something together. Pancakes? Omelets? Grits?"

"Yes."

Nikki grinned. "Coming right up."

They ate out on the deck in their bathrobes, enjoying the warm breeze flowing off the ocean. She deliberately kept the conversation light and casual. They'd had so many dark issues to deal with the day before, she just wanted to kick back and relax. To pretend that their future held endless Sunday mornings like this one. Even as she wallowed in the pleasure of it she knew it wouldn't last.

And it didn't.

Jack took a long swallow of coffee, eyeing her through the steam rising from his drink. "Truth time, Nikki," he announced.

She paused with her cup halfway to her mouth. Carefully, she returned it to the saucer. Her heart rate kicked up. Did he know? Did he suspect? "What truth, Jack?"

"You didn't wear your engagement ring to Matt and Susannah's wedding yesterday. Why? Were you ashamed to admit to all your society friends that you'd agreed to marry me? Ashamed to admit it to the Kincaids?"

She immediately leaned forward and caught his hand in hers. "No!" she told him, filling that single word with absolute conviction. "That's not it at all. I've never cared about those things. It's not how I was raised."

"It would be understandable considering your mother's a Beaulyn," Jack suggested. "The crème de la crème of Charleston high society."

"Granted, my mother could have had her pick of any of the men within that sphere. But she loved my father—a cop—and that's who she married." More than anything Nikki wanted to reassure him on that point and a hint of urgency rippled through her response. "Do you really think she would have raised me to think any differently?"

"Then why didn't you wear my ring yesterday?"

She closed her eyes. The time had come. Selfishly, she thought she'd have a handful of days before admitting the truth. Now they slipped through her fingers like grains of windblown sand. Slowly, she released his hand. "Because I didn't want to agree to an engagement that's going to end almost as soon as it begins."

Jack shoved back his chair and stood, towering over her. "What the hell does that mean? What's going on, Nikki?"

She forced herself to give it to him straight. "I know who owns the final ten percent of TKG stock."

His eyes narrowed, anger flashing through the crystalline blue. "And you've already given the information to RJ?"

She shook her head. "He doesn't know."

That gave Jack pause. "Then why would you think I'd end our engagement over the missing shareholder, unless..." He stilled and she caught understanding dawning in his gaze. "Son of a bitch. It's you, isn't it?"

"Yes," she confessed. "I own the shares."

"All this time we've been involved—intimately involved—and you've kept this from me?"

She flinched at the outrage underscoring his question. "I think you can guess why."

"Oh, no guessing involved, sweetheart." Somehow he'd managed to turn the word "sweetheart" into a curse. "There can only be one reason. You don't trust me."

"It isn't a matter of trust," she instantly denied.

He cut her off with a sweep of his hand. "Bull! We met nearly five months ago. You had all the time in the world to tell me you were the shareholder in control of the final ten percent of TKG stock. I guarantee you would have been up-front about your ownership if you trusted me."

"It wasn't you I didn't trust, Jack." Time for utter honesty, no matter how miserable it made her. "It was what you would do with the information I couldn't trust."

He didn't pull his punches. "You mean what I might pressure you to do with those shares."

"Something like that," she admitted.

He paced to the railing, his long, impatient strides eating up the deck. "Let's start over." He turned and faced her. "How did you come into possession of the shares?"

"My grandfather, Todd Beaulyn, encouraged your father to expand into real estate. Reginald needed to borrow money in order to do so."

He thought it through. "I assume your grandfather provided the funds in exchange for ten percent stock in TKG?"

"Yes."

"And you then inherited the shares from Beaulyn, along with your Rainbow Row house?"

She nodded. "I was his only grandchild, and my mother wasn't interested in the house or the shares."

"That's quite an inheritance."

She kept her gaze steady on his. "It's also the other reason Reginald hired me when my career went south. Your father wanted me to understand the inner workings of TKG so I'd be able to make intelligent decisions about how to vote my shares when the time came. Of course, since he owned ninety percent to my ten percent, there wasn't much voting involved while he was alive."

"How is it possible that RJ doesn't know you own them?"

"Reginald didn't tell anyone he'd sold off a portion of the company in order to expand into the real estate market," she explained. "As part of the contract, my grandfather agreed to keep the sale confidential and buried ownership beneath several levels of holding companies. Granddad was a clever man. You'd have to know where to look to find it."

"No doubt Dad didn't want any flack from the family."

She shrugged. "Could be. When I inherited the shares, Reginald asked if I would also maintain the same confidentiality as my grandfather. I agreed."

"Of course, he had you over a barrel," Jack pointed out. "It's not like you would have refused considering he'd just saved your professional reputation by offering you a job."

"I would have remained silent, regardless," she insisted.

Jack leaned back against the railing and folded his arms across his chest, his eyes winter-cold. "Let's see if I have this straight. You worked for The Kincaid Group the entire time we've been together—without bothering to mention that fact to me. You've also owned the outstanding ten percent shares, also without bothering to mention it, and even knowing it was information I required in time for the board meeting. In other words, our entire relationship is founded on lies."

Exhaustion swept over her. "I didn't tell you about my connections to The Kincaid Group because I wanted to have a relationship with you. Once you found out the truth, our involvement would end. And you know why, Jack." Pain filled her at the undeniable fact that who she was would always come second to what she owned. That he would always want her more for those shares than for love. "The stock will always come between us because I hold the solution to your goal of destroying the Kincaids."

"If our relationship ends it's because you've kept secrets from a man you claim to love, not because of where you work or the stock you own."

Nikki shot to her feet. "I don't *claim* to love you. I do love you. What possible benefit is there for me in our relationship other than love? You made it clear from the start that you despised the Kincaids, that you intended to take them down and, no doubt, me with them. If I'd told you about the stock shares what would you have done?"

"Exactly what I intend to do now. Ask to buy your shares or have you give me your proxy, which is the same thing RJ will do."

"RJ wants them in order to preserve TKG. You want them so you can destroy the Kincaids," she shot back.

"I've already told you. I have no intention of destroying The Kincaid Group."

"Only the Kincaids."

She saw the split-second hesitation. The slightest crack in the fierce determination he'd shown up until now. She deliberately changed the subject in order to throw him off-kilter, hoping against hope she could get him to look at the situation from a fresh angle—one that might put an end to his ridiculous need for vengeance. "Why do you own this house, Jack? Why do you own the plantation in Greenville?"

He shook his head. "What the hell are you talking about?"

"How many bedrooms do you have, combined between the two places? A dozen? Two dozen? Three?"

"I never bothered to count."

"How many square feet?" She hammered him with the questions. "Ten thousand, twenty? More?"

Jack shot a hand through his hair, his irritation palpable. "What's your point, Nikki?"

"You bought homes, Jack. *Homes.*" She stressed the word, hoping against hope he'd pick up on the significance. "Homes which are meant for large families. And yet, there's just you. Well, and your mother and Alan," she felt obligated to add.

"They never lived with me."

She pounced on his statement. "Exactly. Your mother and Alan have—or rather, had—their own home. So, why didn't you buy some sort of ritzy two bedroom apartment overlooking the harbor? Why a home, Jack?"

"Stop using that word. They're not homes. They're houses. Investments."

She released her breath in a sigh. "I think some part of you knows differently. I think on an unconscious level you want to fill them with family, maybe because yours has always been so fractured. You could have that. You could have your family here."

"I don't want them."

"You're lying." She dared to step closer, urgency threading through her words and communicating itself in the tension of her body. "All these years you've believed you were on the outside, looking in. Instead, you've locked yourself away in homes crying out for a family and refused to open the door. Don't you get it, Jack? You're already inside. You just have to let others in here with you."

"Are you finished?" He'd closed down, ruthlessly cutting off access to any sort of emotional connection. "I'd like to settle our business issues."

"I'm not even close to finished. But since you want to discuss business, let's do that. Are you really going to take over the company your father spent all these years building, just so you can extract some sort of petty revenge by tossing your brothers into the street? By finding ways to destroy your sisters? Will that satisfy you?" she demanded.

"Yes!" The word escaped in a harsh whisper, ripped from the deepest part of him. "Yes, that would satisfy me."

"Because you'd win. Because then everyone would know that Reginald should have acknowledged you from the start because you're the best of all his sons, of all his daughters. Better than Matthew. Better than RJ. Better than Laurel and Kara and Lily. And once you've proven that, then what, Jack? What will you be left with?"

"The Kincaid Group."

"A shell. A shell without a heart and soul because you'd have carved the heart and soul out of it. A business is just a thing. Oh, don't you get that?" A heartbreaking urgency filled her voice. "It's the people who run it, who create it, who shape it...that's what makes it great."

"You're saying I can't provide the heart and soul?"

Didn't he see? "I'm saying that if you cut your family out of the business, you'll also cut part of yourself out, as well. You may not realize it at first because you'll be too busy celebrating what you perceive as a win. But eventually you'll discover how cold and sterile the business has become. How lonely and passionless. That it *is* just a business. That you've destroyed something that can't be replaced."

"The heart and soul?" he asked dryly.

She nodded. "At some point you'll realize what you've managed to win doesn't give you any satisfaction."

"I can live with that."

She stepped back. "But I can't."

He followed the path of her retreat. "What will it take to convince you to sign your proxy over to me?"

His question brought home how vast the chasm separating them was and made her want to cry. Instead, she lifted chin and faced him down. "Nothing. Nothing you can say will convince me to do that."

"So, you're going to give RJ your proxy?"

"It's what Reginald wanted, what he once told me he intended. I owe it to your father to respect his wishes."

She saw it then. The deep, unfathomable pain of having his father—once again—put his legitimate son ahead of his bastard. "Jack, it doesn't have to be like this."

"I think it does."

Desperation drove her to try anything she could to resolve the conflict between them. "I still have a wish from the bachelor auction. You owe it to me."

He simply shook his head. "That's not going to work, Nikki."

But maybe it would. Maybe there was one final person who could sway Jack, who could convince him to change his course and choose a new path, one that led to new beginnings instead of revenge. It was a risk. A hideous risk. And one that forced her to break her word to Reginald. Would he have understood? Would he have supported her decision? She closed her eyes, praying she was making the right choice. Because if she was wrong… As though in response to her prayer, a morning dove landed on the railing and cooed a soft benediction, one that felt like approval.

Taking a deep breath, Nikki opened her eyes. "I'll give you my proxy under one condition," she informed him.

That gave him pause. "Name it."

"You read your father's letter. You read your father's letter—and I mean out loud at the board meeting—and I'll give you my proxy." She could see the refusal building in his gaze, see him pulling back and shutting down.

"I'll read it, but not at the board meeting. Not out loud."

"It's my wish, Jack. You gave me a wish and I'm calling it due." She pushed and pushed hard. "Unless you're a man who doesn't honor his promises?"

He swore, long and virulently. "I can't believe you'd demand that of me. Whatever is in that letter is private and not something I intend to share with the Legitimates."

"I'm sorry, Jack." And she was. But she couldn't think of any other way to heal the breach between him and his Kincaid family. She could only trust that whatever Reginald wrote would help complete the reconciliation that had begun with Elizabeth and steadily worked its way through the rest of the family until only RJ remained. "Do you agree?"

He clamped his back teeth together. "I agree."

But everything about him, from his tense posture, to the blatant frustration and fury glittering in his eyes, to the growl that underscored his words, warned that he resented being forced to concede. No doubt she'd pay for that. Of course, she'd already figured that out, already allowed the hope of "happily ever after" to fade like the distant memory of an impossibly sweet dream.

He took a single step in her direction. "Shall we seal the deal like we did at the bachelor auction?"

He didn't give her time to react. He fisted his hands in the collar of her robe and pulled her up to meet his kiss, a hard, ruthless demand. It tasted of anger, laced with passion. It spoke of pain, underscored by hunger. It felt like a man pushed to the brink, lashing out. And yet, she sensed a hint of the tenderness that always flavored their lovemaking. She gave everything within her without hesitation, meeting his demand with her own. Showing her love in the only way she had left, knowing he'd reject the words, but couldn't quite turn from the desire that connected them. Bound them and made them one.

He tugged at the sash of her robe, loosening it. The silk parted, opening to him, just as she had always opened to him. He swept his hands over her. Memorizing her... Branding her... Saying goodbye. Tears filled her eyes and she wrapped her arms around him and savored these final moments together. When he released her and stepped back, she knew it was over. Could feel the deliberate withdrawal, the icing over of emotion and intent.

"I suggest we discuss where we go from here," he informed her.

He turned his back on her and crossed to the railing. He planted his hands on the salt-treated wood and stared out at the ocean. It was calm today, an ironic dichotomy to his turbulent relationship with Nikki. Although he'd suggested they discuss their next step, he had no idea what it might be.

He'd trusted her. Opened himself to her in ways he never had with any other woman. He'd let her in and she'd betrayed him. He didn't know how to deal with it. Did he end the affair? Consider himself fortunate that she hadn't really accepted the engagement ring he'd offered? Everything within him rejected the mere thought. He didn't want to end things between them.

Okay, fine. So they'd renegotiate their agreement. They'd start over and this time he'd set very clear parameters. First, all cards on the table. No lies. No secrets. And they'd go slow. Maybe that had been part of the initial problem. From the moment they met, from the moment they'd first touched, passion had exploded between them. Neither of them had been able to think straight, mainly because they couldn't keep their hands off each other. So, this time around he'd put rational thought ahead of sexual need. They would approach their relationship with calm, cool deliberation. He'd treat it the exact same way he did business, with logical steps that led to an ultimate end goal.

"Here's what I've decided," he announced. He gripped the railing and hoped like hell he could convince her to go along with the plan. "We'll continue seeing each other. But there will be ground rules. If you can't agree to them, better we call it off now."

He waited for her to protest, to tell him in no uncertain terms where to get off. It had always been one of the characteristics he most appreciated about Nikki.

They just needed to open negotiations so he'd know they still had a chance. She didn't respond and he turned, her name on his lips…only to discover her gone.

Ten

The next five days were the longest Nikki could remember.

One by one they crept by while the day of the board meeting marched ever closer. Everything seemed to hang by a frayed thread over a bottomless precipice. Alan continued to elude the police. Jack didn't call. And Nikki constantly worried about the bargain she'd made with him—whether it had been a smart decision or the stupidest of her life. She also worried about whether Reginald's letter would help, or make matters worse—assuming they could get any worse than they already were.

And all the while she grieved Jack's absence. Better get used to it, she warned herself, since that wasn't likely to change, even after the board meeting. Not only did Jack despise her, but once she signed over her proxy, the Kincaids would despise her, too.

She closed her eyes, fighting tears. Without Jack, her bed had become a cold and lonely place. Guilt kept her up most nights, adding to her exhaustion. Worst of all, she missed him with an intensity that physically hurt. Missed talking to him. Missed their laughter. Missed curling up on the couch with him while they read or watched TV. Missed how those quiet times so often turned to an equally quiet passion where books dropped to the floor or the TV was turned off and they slipped into each other's arms...and into each other.

There were so many little things she'd taken for granted. Like the way he'd pull her into his arms and spoon her tight against him during the night. How she'd wake to his kiss, to his lovemaking. The casual breakfasts they enjoyed on the deck or at the kitchen table, while they shared a cup of coffee and revealed their innermost thoughts and feelings. She longed for a return of those quick phone calls during the day that were a more effective jolt than any amount of caffeine. Not to mention the end of her workday and that sweet, breathless moment when she first saw him again. The anticipation of the coming embrace, after which they'd talk and nuzzle, mating scent and touch and bodies. Nikki closed her eyes and gave in to tears that came with increasing regularity—no doubt in part hormonal.

She'd lost Jack and had no idea how she'd ever fill the emptiness that loss created.

He'd lost Nikki and had no idea how he'd ever fill the emptiness that loss created.

Somehow she'd become an integral part of his life, filling up all the holes with her laughter and generosity. With her boundless love. Right from the start, she'd accepted him when no one else would, proving it by bidding an outrageous sum for a simple dinner. Well, and a wish, one he would give a substantial portion of his bank balance to take back.

That didn't change the fact that she possessed a unique capacity for forcing him to see what he'd rather avoid, to look at his life from a fresh perspective. More often than not he didn't care for the view, perhaps because it caused him to alter a course he'd set in stone a very long time ago. Too long ago.

It wasn't simply the passion they shared, though that went far beyond anything he'd ever believed possible. No, what drew him to her was something far more basic. He'd fallen in love with who she was at the core. Not only did she treat him with innate kindness and acceptance, she treated everyone that way, without artifice or pretense, but with a genuine spontaneity intrinsic to her character.

He crossed to his dresser and removed the sapphire and diamond engagement ring Nikki had left there, along with his father's letter that he'd resisted opening for the past five plus months, perhaps because he instinctively knew the contents contained a terrible emotional burden. A dark coffee ring stained the creamy-white envelope from when he'd anchored the letter to his deck railing with his coffee cup. At the time, he'd considered the mark appropriate, a dark smudge that reflected his birthright...or birth wrong. A ring that connected all the Kincaids within its unfortunate darkness.

He tossed the envelope onto his bed and frowned. Somehow that darkness had faded over the past few weeks, easing and lightening the more he'd gotten to know his Kincaid family. He suspected Nikki bore responsibility for that, as well, the way she'd affected so many areas of his life. She'd pushed and prodded him out of the darkness and into the strong, unwavering light, relentless in forcing him to see the truth. Her truth. His frown deepened. Or was it hers?

All these years he'd stood on the outside, his vision obscured by the tightly shut doors and thick, plated windows he believed separated him from his father and the Legitimates. Perhaps those windows and doors had screwed with his perception. Maybe by opening them—as Nikki had done—he could finally see clearly. Or maybe Nikki had been right when she'd said that he wasn't the one on the outside, that he'd barricaded himself within his home, refusing to lower his defenses so others could join him. Was it possible?

He scrubbed his face, the shadow of a beard rasping against his hands. Hell. He could feel the grain of truth running through her observation, despite his resistance to the idea. Well, he'd promised to read his father's letter at the board meeting in the morning and he'd honor his promise. But he hadn't said he wouldn't read the damn thing beforehand. Decision made, he snatched up the letter and broke the seal.

And what he read ripped apart his tidy little world.

He was late.

Nikki sat at the conference room table and nervously checked her watch. The Kincaids had already gathered. Laurel sat next to Matt and occasionally murmured a comment in his ear. Lily and Kara were quietly chatting, while RJ stared at Nikki. She could feel his building suspicion regarding her presence there. A single folder sat squarely positioned in front of her, the only contents her proxy which she'd already signed over to Jack. Just as RJ opened his mouth to speak, Jack entered.

He appeared every inch the executive businessman in a suit and dress shirt in unrelenting black, along with a gray, black and maroon striped tie. Discreet bits of gold flashed at his wrists from both his Rolex and a pair of knotted cuff links. RJ rose and Jack waved him back into his seat then held out a preemptory hand to Nikki. Her throat went instantly dry. Praying her fingers wouldn't tremble, she passed him her folder.

He continued to stand, taking instant charge of the meeting. "This proxy gives me the fifty-five percent controlling interest in The Kincaid Group necessary to take over as President and CEO. We can go through the motions of a vote, but it wouldn't change the fact that I'm now in charge."

"What the hell…!" RJ shot to his feet again. "Who owns those ten percent shares? How did you get the proxy?"

Nikki steeled herself to meet RJ's furious gaze. "I own them. I inherited them from my grandfather, Todd Beaulyn, who was given them by Reginald when he expanded into the real estate market. I signed over my proxy to Jack this morning."

Voices exploded around the table, the Kincaids all talking at once. Jack waited them out. "Object all you want. It's a done deal. Next order of business…" He removed a sheaf of papers from his breast coat pocket, his gaze drifting to meet Nikki's. "This is the letter my—*our*—father left me, which I will read."

"What the hell do we care what Dad had to say to you?" RJ demanded.

"Maybe it's important." Matt caught his brother's arm and drew him back into his chair. "Besides, I want to hear what Dad wrote."

Swearing beneath his breath, RJ subsided and gave a reluctant jerk of his head to indicate his consent.

Jack smoothed out the pages and began to read, "'Dear Jack, in some ways this is the most difficult letter of all those I've written today. Although I owe each of you an apology for the selfish decisions I made during my lifetime, you were the one most injured by those choices.'"

He broke off, his gaze arrowing in on his brothers and sisters. "Just so you know, that's not true. Elizabeth was the one most injured. When I was conceived your parents hadn't met. I was an accident of birth. But afterward, when he found us again..." Jack shook his head. "He should have divorced your mother before he ever started an affair with mine."

Nikki watched the Kincaid siblings exchange quick, surprised glances. Laurel nodded in agreement. "Thanks, Jack. I didn't expect you to feel that way. As it happens, we agree with you on that point."

He inclined his head. "To continue... 'You lived your life in the shadows, never acknowledged, never enjoying the benefits that your brothers and sisters received their entire lives. I know how you longed for that legitimacy. To be part of the family we shared. To have a father attend all your sporting events and celebrate your school accolades. To be there in the evenings after work. To simply be available for something as basic as a game of catch. I wasn't even there for most of your birthdays. Nor was I there the day you needed me most, the day you almost died.'"

From across the room, Nikki caught the hitch in Kara's breath, knew how much the words affected her. Dampness gathered in her soft green eyes, along with sympathy. "Oh, Jack. Matt told us about that. I'm so sorry."

Nikki could tell Kara's sympathy caught him by surprise. He hesitated, as though not quite certain how to respond. Even Matt and RJ exchanged looks that clearly acknowledged that Jack had received the short end of the "father" stick.

"It's okay. I survived," Jack finally said. He fumbled with the pages, looking for his place before continuing. "He goes on to say, 'I wasn't there for you, Jack, not the way I was for the others. And for that I apologize. I apologize for my weakness in trying to have the best of both worlds—the society my family held in too high esteem and the two women I loved too well...and not well enough. I have always loved you and been proud of the son I never claimed. And I apologize for my weakness in attempting to take too much from life without giving enough in return. I ask your forgiveness—'"

His voice faltered, broke off, and in that instant, Nikki realized he couldn't go on. She shot to her feet. This was her fault. Entirely her fault. She'd put him in this position without considering how intensely personal Reginald's letter might be, or how difficult he'd find it to read to his brothers and sisters. She'd merely hoped that his father had explained his decision in never acknowledging Jack and thereby help to heal the breach between the two families. She crossed to his side and slipped the creased pages from his hands.

"Don't," she murmured. "I'm sorry. I should never have asked you to read it aloud." She turned her attention to the Kincaids. "This is all my fault. I agreed to sign over my proxy if Jack promised to read his letter here today. I should never have put him through that."

"No." Jack's jaw set. "I going to finish it. I want to finish it."

"We get the idea," Matt said gently. "It's not necessary to read more. We understand why you have it in for us and for The Kincaid Group. I suspect I'd feel the same in your place." His sisters nodded in agreement while RJ stared at the table, his jaw set in a mirror image of Jack's.

"I said I'd finish it and I will." He took the letter from Nikki and snapped it open. Clearing his throat, he continued, though a desperate roughness filtered through his voice. "'I ask your forgiveness, not only for myself, but for your brothers and sisters. You should have been a brother to them from the beginning. I suspect you would have benefitted from that contact, just as their lives would have been far richer having you part of theirs. Believe it or not, you and RJ are very much alike, both with many of the same strengths... and weaknesses. I hope you won't allow the weaknesses you share to prevent you from having the relationship I denied you all these years. I'm opening a door, son, a door that I kept closed.'"

Jack paused. He looked up then and quoted the rest of the words from memory. "'I've left you forty-five percent interest in The Kincaid Group to help make up for all I neglected to give you, all I neglected to be for you. But I've also given you the shares so you would have a choice. To walk through the door I've now opened and be the man I know in my heart you are. Or you can close and lock that door...and have your vengeance. It's your choice, Jack.'"

He folded the letter and returned it to his coat pocket. Silence gripped the room, a silence so profound Nikki swore she could hear every breath taken, the beat of each heart. Slowly, RJ stood and looked at Jack. For the first time regret instead of antagonism colored his expression. "I wish Dad had raised us together. And I for one am sorry for what he did, how you were made to feel an outsider. I think for the first time I understand why you would choose vengeance and I really can't blame you. I wish you'd make a different choice, but I probably would make the same one if I were standing in your shoes."

Matt climbed to his feet, as did the women. One by one, they came to him. Embraced him. RJ was the last to approach. He held out his hand and waited. Jack didn't hesitate. He took it in a firm shake.

"If you'll all sit down again, we'll finish this," Jack said. "Before we continue, there is one personal detail I'd like to resolve." He turned to Nikki and took her hand in his. "A week ago you agreed to marry me. I'd like to know if you intend to honor our engagement."

For a split second Nikki couldn't move, couldn't think. Didn't dare hope. His steady gaze remained on her, open and unguarded. Intuition warned that she could shatter him with the least wrong word. "You still want to marry me?" she asked cautiously.

"Yes. The question is...do *you* want to marry *me?* You know who I am. What I am. What I intend to do. Do you stand with me or against me?"

"Oh, Jack." Tears overflowed her eyes and she

swiped at them with a trembling hand. "Don't you know by now? I've always stood with you."

For a long moment Jack couldn't move, couldn't think, the rush of relief was so profound. He closed his eyes for a brief moment and a muscle clenched in his jaw before easing. Thank God. He didn't know what he'd have done if she'd rejected him. He retrieved the engagement ring from his pocket, the sapphire a perfect match for her eyes, the diamonds a perfect match for her tears, and slipped it onto her finger. Then he gathered her close and kissed her. "I love you," he whispered against her mouth. "Trust me. That's all I've ever wanted—for you to love and trust me."

"I do trust you." Passion gleamed in her eyes, along with unmistakable faith. "And I love you with all my heart."

"Then let's get this over with." She returned to her seat and Jack's gaze swept his brothers and sisters, all of whom eyed him with an understandable wariness. This next part would be almost as difficult as reading his father's letter and he suspected it would end any possibility of a relationship with the Kincaids. "At this point you should know that a few hours ago the police arrested my brother, Alan Sinclair, for the murder of our father."

His words fell like a bombshell.

"Nikki and I had begun to suspect him a few weeks ago and have been working hard to gather the evidence to prove his guilt. Alan has confessed, claiming he killed Dad in order to prevent him from cutting off future financial assistance. Apparently, Alan believed our mother would inherit a generous amount, enough to keep him in the lap of luxury for the rest of his pathetic life. I had no idea or I'd have done everything within my power to stop him. I know nothing I can say will make up for what he's done. But I'm more sorry than I can express that I'm in any way related to that sorry son of a bitch."

Matt shot Jack a grim look. "I second that motion and vote in favor of his rotting in prison for the rest of his miserable life."

"Seconded," Laurel said.

"I believe that's one motion we can all agree on," Lily stated, her eyes flashing with anger. She turned a hint of her anger on Jack. "But if you think we blame you for his actions, you're crazy."

"Once again, I second the motion," Matt said.

He elbowed RJ, who nodded in reluctant agreement. "I hold you accountable for plenty, Sinclair, but not that."

Jack gave a brisk nod. "I appreciate it. If you have any other questions about the situation, Detective McDonough is available to fill you in. At this point, I intend to move onto new business."

"Give it to us straight," RJ insisted. "We're now Carolina Shipping and anyone with the last name Kincaid is out of a job, right?"

Jack smiled. "Not quite. My next motion is to bring Carolina Shipping under The Kincaid Group umbrella."

"Wait." Laurel leaned forward, frowning. "You're going to fold your company into ours? Not the other way around?"

"Not the other way around," Jack confirmed. He crossed to the conference room door and opened it. "Harold, if you'd come in now."

Harold Parsons, the Kincaid lawyer entered the

room, clutching a packet of papers. He nodded to the group at large. "I'd like to state for the record that I don't appreciate being dragged out of bed at the crack of dawn to take care of matters which should have—and could have—been addressed weeks ago."

"Understood," Jack replied. "I'm sure your appreciation, or lack thereof, will be reflected in my bill."

"Count on it," the lawyer snapped.

"What's going on?" RJ demanded.

"Harold is about to pass out documents that reapportion the shares of TKG."

RJ shot to his feet. "You can't do that."

"Yes, I can. And yes, I have." Jack lifted an eyebrow. "Unless you don't want a fifteen percent share in the business to replace the nine percent you currently own?"

RJ started to reply, then broke off with a look of utter confusion. "Come again?"

"As I started to say, I'm reapportioning the shares of TKG so each of us owns an equal amount, which comes to fifteen percent apiece. Nikki, of course, will continue to control the ten percent share left to her by her grandfather. Once you sign, we'll vote on my next motion which is for RJ to take over as CEO and President, while I head up the shipping end of the organization, which includes Carolina Shipping. I will remain in full control of this particular TKG asset. I assume Matt will continue as Director of New Business. And I'm hoping that Nikki will stay on as our corporate investigator." He paused. "Any objections? No, I didn't think so. In that case, the motion passes. Next order of business..."

Before any of his brothers or sisters had time to recover from their shock, he swung his bride-to-be into his arms. "Nikki and I are leaving for the rest of the day. Don't bother calling. Neither of us will be answering our cell phones." And with that, he left the room.

Behind him, voices exploded in excitement. He simply smiled. *Okay, Dad, I opened the door. Let's see who decides to walk through.*

As it turned out, the entire Kincaid family walked through the door Jack opened. At Elizabeth's insistence, they broke with tradition and every last one of them showed up on his doorstep midday Sunday, loaded down with an endless stream of hot dishes. Fragrant scents wafted from the various containers. And every last one of his guests greeted him with a hug and kiss, or a manly handshake and a slap on the back. He didn't know quite what to make of it all.

They all oohed and aahed over the house…and then made themselves right at home, filling it to overflowing with family.

Nikki spotted Jack's confusion and laughed. "Just go with it," she advised. "You opened the door and here they all are."

"Well, hell. I was thinking one at a time, not everyone at once."

"Deal with it." She wrapped her arms around his waist. "All or nothing is often how it works with family, Jack. It's one of the fun parts."

"I'll take your word for it." He snatched a quick kiss then sank in for another deeper one. "I'm hungry."

"Good thing there's lots of food."

Jack shook his head. "I'm not hungry for food."

She grinned, wagging her finger at him. "That's all

you're getting until we're alone again. Come on." She caught his hand in hers and tugged him toward the dining room. "Let's go join your family."

Angela showed up in the middle of the mass confusion surrounding the organization of dinner. Startled to find the Kincaids there, she started to make her excuses. Elizabeth stopped her, drawing her off to one side. Jack stiffened, seeing the unmistakable lines of tension that invaded the two women. This had all the makings of two trains on the same track, headed for a collision. He hesitated, not certain whether he should let them talk through their differences or if he should intercede. He wasn't the only one watching with bated breath. So were Elizabeth's daughters.

"Trust my mom," RJ advised, coming up behind Jack and clapping him on the shoulder. "She knows Angela is in a bad place and that in order to have you as part of our family, it means finding a way to work out her differences with your mother. I promise, she won't make the situation any worse. And maybe, just maybe, getting to know each other will help them come to terms with old history, not to mention their grief over Dad's death."

Even as Jack watched, he saw the two women shed tears, then embrace. "Your mother is an unusual lady," he said slowly. "Not many women would show such kindness and generosity toward their husband's mistress."

"She's one of a kind." Pride filled RJ's voice.

Once Angela had been welcomed into the fold, the organization of the meal was like watching a coordinated assault. Plates and silver appeared on his dining room table, followed by food and drinks. Someone found his stereo system and turned on background music. Then they all took their seats, somehow forming a pattern of brothers and sisters, in-laws and parents, until they'd jumbled together in a companionable mix.

Jack had expected some awkwardness over their first meal together. Instead, he found it—well, maybe not one-hundred-percent comfortable—but certainly lighthearted and fun. "Comfortable" would occur over time, he suspected. The thought brought with it a rush of unexpected pleasure. He had that time now, had the opportunity to build a relationship with these people, to create what he'd never truly had...a family.

He also learned a lot about the Kincaids that he'd never known before. He discovered that the baby Lily and Daniel were expecting any day now was a son, and since they'd married quietly at the courthouse so they wouldn't steal Kara's thunder by having a wedding right before hers, the soon-to-be parents intended to renew their vows in a huge celebration in October. He also learned that Kara's husband, Eli, had first been engaged to Laurel. Of course, Jack could tell just by looking at Eli and Laurel that they didn't share any sort of chemistry. Fortunately, nature had taken its course and the appropriate sister had discovered her perfect partner. Laurel glowed with unmistakable love and her husband, Rakin, announced that the Kincaids could expect an influx of new business thanks to his Middle Eastern business connections.

Most intriguing of all was when RJ and Brooke admitted they were also expecting a baby, the mother-to-be blushing prettily. The instant the news came out, Elizabeth returned her fork to her plate and eyed her children one by one. "Clearly, I didn't explain how this is supposed to work," she informed them in true matriarch fashion. "So, listen up. First we marry *then* we get pregnant. Are we clear on the order from this point forward?"

Lily and Brooke exchanged quick grins. "Yes, Mom," they said in unison.

"Just practicing," Brooke added, "for when we're married and I get to call you Mom for real."

Tears welled up in Elizabeth's eyes and she cleared her throat before speaking. "No need for you to wait. It's lovely having another daughter to call me Mom, as well as having another grandchild on the way." Elizabeth picked up her fork again. "I will add there are the occasional exceptions to premarital pregnancies which serve to prove the rule." She glanced at Jack and smiled with sincere warmth. "And for which I, personally, am very grateful."

"I propose a toast," RJ said, holding up his glass. "Here's to all of us."

"To new beginnings," Lily called out.

"To creating a home," Nikki added.

Matt shot Jack a shrewd look. "To unlocking doors and opening windows."

Jack was the last to lift his glass. He could feel the final protective barriers give way and reached for Nikki's hand, gripping it hard. It felt good to be free of those barriers, better than he could have believed possible. He allowed the last of his resistance to be swept away, allowed himself to embrace and accept what he'd secretly longed for ever since he was a teenager who'd been told he'd never be accepted by his father.

His gaze swept the table before settling on Nikki. "Most of all…here's to family," he said.

* * *

Much later that evening, Jack and Nikki wandered onto the deck, and wrapped each other in a warm embrace. "It all turned out well, didn't it?" he asked.

She leaned her head against his shoulder and released a sigh of blatant satisfaction. "It did, yes."

He kissed her, a slow, lingering kiss. "Thank you, Nikki."

"For what?"

"For giving me a family."

She smiled, a secretive little curve of lips that tempted him to kiss her again. "A family that's about to grow larger."

He chuckled at the memory of Elizabeth's motherly reprimand. "Thanks to Lily and Daniel, and Brooke and RJ. And despite Elizabeth's disapproval."

"Mmm. I'm afraid she has even more reason to disapprove."

He stilled. "What do you mean?"

"Exactly what you suspect I mean." She snuggled in close. "I think you'll make a wonderful father. Don't you?"

He struggled to reply, the words catching in his throat. "I'm going to be a father?"

A hint of concern slid into Nikki's sapphire gaze. "Will that be a problem for you?"

"No," he said slowly. "In fact, I think I'm going to be a great father."

Nikki smiled in satisfaction. "So do I."

Jack gazed out over the ocean waves toward the horizon, realizing he'd finally achieved everything he'd ever wanted. By letting down his defenses, he'd won his heart's desire—a home and family, filled with the sort of love and happiness he and Nikki would bring to it. And a child. Their child. A product of enduring love and the first step toward their future together.

If he listened carefully enough, he could practically hear that future. Could hear his home ring with youthful footsteps, the sound of their voices echoing off walls that would eventually know generations of love and laughter. To be a father to them, there day after day, participating in each and every phase of their lives. To grow old with the woman he loved, with the relatives he'd so recently claimed and the children they were busily creating. Oh, he could hear that future, all right.

Hear it filling his home to overflowing.

Hear it filling his life with love.

Hear it gifting him with the most precious of all commodities...

A family.

* * * * *

The World of Mills & Boon®

There's a Mills & Boon® series that's perfect for you. We publish ten series and, with new titles every month, you never have to wait long for your favourite to come along.

Blaze®

Scorching hot, sexy reads
4 new stories every month

By Request

Relive the romance with the best of the best
9 new stories every month

Cherish™

Romance to melt the heart every time
12 new stories every month

Desire™

Passionate and dramatic love stories
8 new stories every month